Acclaim for *Savage Art*

"The tension is real, the intensity almost unbearable at times. Danielle Girard knows how to rivet your attention and keep you reading all night long. A terrific debut!"

—*New York Times* bestselling
author Michael Prescott

"A suspenseful debut, *Savage Art* explores one of the dark places: the soft underbelly of vulnerability. But [it] isn't just about jeopardy, it's also about hope and resourcefulness and perseverance in the face of terror."

—*New York Times* bestselling
author Stephen White

"A gripping first novel. . . . Vivid characters and a very scary villain."

—*New York Times* bestselling
author Phillip Margolin

"A terrific read, guaranteed to . . . make you sleep with the lights on."

—*New York Times* bestselling
author Lisa Gardner

continued . . .

"Girard plunges her readers into a horrifying journey through a cunning, diabolical mind. *Savage Art* definitely deserves the label 'page-turner,' but should not be read at home at night alone."
—*The Piedmont Post*

"A tautly written thriller that will be difficult to put down . . . frightening." —*The Mystery Reader*

"[An] extremely intense and frightening novel. Definitely an author to watch." —*Romantic Times*

"Tense and fast-paced . . . likable characters, lots of action, and solid deductive reasoning. . . . *Savage Art* is a thriller that looks deep into madness and still entertains—no mean feat."
—*The Mystery Review*

"*Hannibal* watchers have to read this great serial killer book. . . . The heroine is fascinating. . . . So good fans will want sequels."
—*Midwest Book Review*

RUTHLESS GAME

Danielle Girard

AN ONYX BOOK

ONYX
Published by New American Library, a division of
Penguin Putnam Inc., 375 Hudson Street,
New York, New York 10014, U.S.A.
Penguin Books Ltd, 27 Wrights Lane,
London W8 5TZ, England
Penguin Books Australia Ltd, Ringwood,
Victoria, Australia
Penguin Books Canada Ltd, 10 Alcorn Avenue,
Toronto, Ontario, Canada M4V 3B2
Penguin Books (N.Z.) Ltd, 182–190 Wairau Road,
Auckland 10, New Zealand

Penguin Books Ltd, Registered Offices:
Harmondsworth, Middlesex, England

First published by Onyx, an imprint of New American Library,
a division of Penguin Putnam Inc.

First Printing, June 2001
10 9 8 7 6 5 4 3 2 1

REGISTERED TRADEMARK—MARCA REGISTRADA

Printed in the United States of America

PUBLISHER'S NOTE
This is a work of fiction. Names, characters, places, and incidents either
are the product of the author's imagination or are used fictitiously,
and any resemblance to actual persons, living or dead, business
establishments, events, or locales is entirely coincidental.

For Chris,
who makes every day a dream come true

Mom and Dad, thanks for "perseverance of purpose;" it must be in the genes. Nicole, Tom, Steve, and Blake, thanks for putting up with all the hoopla of the last year with grace and humor. Claire, for having your daddy's patience and your mama's rhythm. Bob, Donna, and Sue, for taking me in and pretending all my quirks are normal. To the friends who stuck by, supported, reassured, and put up with a nutty schedule, and especially to Marcie. And to Danell, for making balance a possibility.

As always, this book is a culmination of a lot of great help. It wouldn't be what it is without the following very talented writers: Joanne Barnes, Taylor Chase, Diana Dempsey, Lisa Hughey, Monica McLean, Malia Martin, and Sonia Rossney. In addition, thank you to Dr. Jack Simon, for sharing his psychiatric expertise (for the book, not me, although I may be next). To Inspector Edwin Skeels, for introducing me to the Berkeley Police Department, and to the many officers who answered my bizarre questions, even over the phone. Any errors are mine alone.

Finally, thank you to Helen, who knows how to think big and still focus on the details. And to Genny, for those both torturous and magnificent fifteen-page letters. And to both of you for friendships that continue to amaze me.

Prologue

March 17, 1971

The wet fabric started to slip and she held her bound hands to her face and tried not to watch. It was too terrible, too terrible. She just wanted her mommy. Where was her mommy? Where were all their mommies?

"Fourteen is just too many," he growled as he lifted the body of Jimmy Rodriguez and set it next to the others.

There were eleven. She had counted. Eleven times she'd heard them scream, eleven times she'd heard them stop. She was last in line, but he was getting closer. Only Billy and Marcus were before her. He'd be to her soon. She shifted against the cold cement floor, the puddle she'd made like wet ice cream against her skin.

She heard Billy sobbing and she started again, too. She couldn't help it. She kept waiting for someone to come and save them, but no one did. He had killed Mrs. Cooney and Mr. Choy. He walked onto the school bus and shot them. And then he forced each of them to drink a cup of punch. He put something in it. She saw him. And she shook her head when he told her to drink it. But he hit her hard and she knew she had to or he'd shoot her like he did Mrs. Cooney.

He looked at her now and licked his lips. She started to cry harder, pushing herself away from him. "No," she whispered. "No, no, no."

"Can't I save some for later?" he called.

She stopped crying and looked around, peering out

of the small gap in her blindfold. Why was he asking them that?

She nodded. Save some for later.

"Tomorrow, I'd be fresh and ready again."

She nodded. "Tomorrow," she whispered. "Tomorrow."

It was quiet for a moment and she moved her head to look out of the corner of her blindfold. She heard feet moving toward her. Was it him? Looking down, she saw white sneakers like Brittany's.

"What do you think you're doing?" he screamed.

She jumped, feeling someone behind her. But his voice was far away. Someone touched her hands and she could feel the rope on her wrists loosening. "Billy?" she whispered, but no one answered.

Then, her hands were free. She rubbed them together. She wanted to pull at her blindfold but she was afraid he would see her so she didn't move.

"I said what do you think you're doing?" he repeated.

She held her hands together as though they were still tied. He was yelling at her. But he wasn't getting closer. Just stay still, she told herself.

"You can't shoot me, for God's sake," he screamed.

Suddenly, someone was behind her again. She heard a loud clacking sound and then it was silent. She whipped her head around but couldn't see. She started to shake.

There was something hard and cold in her hands. It was heavy. She remained silent, feeling her hands shake as she held the heavy thing. She looked out of the corner of her blindfold and saw all white. White with wings, she thought. Wings.

She didn't feel scared, though.

Someone moved her finger and she heard a loud pop. Then another. She dropped the heavy thing and pressed her hands to her ears.

And then it was over.

Chapter One

Twenty-nine years later

The harsh blare of a car horn pulled Alex Kincaid from sleep, an uncomfortable ache burning in her lower back. Shifting positions, she felt the rough edge of a chair. She must have fallen asleep in the den. It had been years since she'd done that, awakened with an empty bowl of popcorn in her lap and an old rerun of *Taxi* on TV. Her mind meandered through the evening before, but she didn't recall if she had been reading or watching television before bed. She settled back in to sleep a few more minutes.

A car rushed by and she shifted again, wondering when her street had become so noisy. Usually no more than one car passed every twenty minutes. But this morning it sounded as though there were a parade going by. No wonder she never slept in the den.

No, that wasn't right. The den was in the back of the house. The cars couldn't be heard from there.

Forcing her eyes open, she stared out her windshield. Her windshield? Confused, she looked at the car around her. Sitting upright, she clutched the steering wheel. What the hell was going on? Above her, the yellow leaves of the fall oak trees sheltered the morning sun, creating patterns of light across her dash.

A cover of dew beaded across her windows. The cool California morning made her shiver. A row of Victorian and Tudor homes stared down at her from the hillside like thick-necked soldiers preparing for attack. What was she doing in her car?

She glanced down at the familiar navy sweat pants and gray Cal T-shirt, trying to remember going to bed the night before.

She'd taken something one of a handful of doctors had given her to help her sleep—Restoril. The endless insomnia had finally driven her to be so exhausted, so totally beat, that she'd regressed to trying the meds again. She'd slept. She'd actually slept. But when had she gotten up? And left her house and driven to—she looked around at the houses—big houses, larger than anything in her neighborhood, all built high off the street, their large windowed fronts staring down at her questioningly.

And where the hell was she?

Leaning forward, she ran her hand over her lopsided ponytail and looked around. There has to be a good explanation for this. Her eyes closed, she rubbed at the pain in her temples. Someone must have called her. Her brain kicked into gear as she tried to picture her phone, tried to remember it ringing. Her mind sputtered and stalled like a dying car. She didn't remember talking to anyone.

Hoping one of the houses would nudge into her memory, she stared back at the imposing facades. The block didn't look remotely familiar.

Cars raced down the street, their drivers dressed in ties and suits. Work! Her fingers searched her wrist for her watch. It wasn't there. But she always wore her watch. Turning the key in the ignition, she glanced at the clock on the dashboard. It was nearly seven A.M. "Damn it." She was going to be late for work.

She started the car and glanced at a street sign. Yolo Avenue. She'd never heard of that street.

She'd been sleepwalking; that had to be it. She'd never done that before. It had been so long since she'd even slept through the night. And this was worse than sleepwalking—she had sleep-dressed then sleep-driven and who knew what else.

Fighting off the battling anger at not remembering, she steered the car down Yolo until she saw a familiar street sign. Henry. She was in Berkeley, actually only a half dozen blocks from the station. Yolo was on her beat, but she had never come across it before. Ingrained in her subconscious, somewhere, was this street. That was why she'd ended up there. She shook her head and sped across Shattuck to Ashby. That was the last time she was going to take sleeping pills.

Wishing she had a siren, she blared her horn at the slowpoke drivers around her and sped for home. She parked the car in front of the small home on Pine Lane that had once belonged to her mother. The front grass needed cutting. The hedges had grown up and begun to block the front windows, giving them the appearance of shaded limousine windows, only in green. The Spanish-style house needed painting, too. Its pinkish salmon color always looked as if it had been bought on sale. She wanted the house to be white. But until now, she hadn't realized how much she'd let the house go—suddenly, the house was a disaster.

As she locked the car door, she felt both strangely rested and also unnerved. Neither was a sensation with which she was familiar. She brushed the nervousness off. She didn't have patience for catastrophe now. Rushing up the steps, she shivered, her T-shirt much too thin for the cool morning air.

As she moved, she reminded herself of the positives. At least she had awakened in her own car. What if she had found herself in a stranger's house? What if she had done something crazy—like driven into a pole or a dog or a child? What if she had robbed a bank?

What if nothing. Nothing had happened. She opened the door to her house and looked around. Everything was normal here.

The drug had a strange effect on her sleep patterns or something. Alex's sleep patterns, or lack of them, had been a popular subject in her household growing up. Maybe she would have a chance to stop by James's office and ask if he remembered anything like that.

She was a very logical person—calm, cool, collected. She didn't drink heavily, exercised religiously and kept her distance from suspicious people. She walked in the crosswalk and flossed her teeth, for God's sake. Things like waking up on a strange street did *not* happen to her.

A man's face suddenly popped into her mind. He had been in the bagel store yesterday. He had approached her as she was getting bagels and coffee for herself and her partner. He'd used her name and then Greg had come in and she'd turned away. When she looked back, he was gone. She'd never seen him before or since. And why was she thinking about him now?

Pushing it aside, she just hoped she still had time to shower and dress to be at the station before eight. The patrol captain had little tolerance for tardy officers.

Rushing around, she cursed herself for not programming the coffeemaker the night before. The thought of going without a caffeine fix was torture, but there wasn't time. She glanced at her wrist for the third time in ten minutes. Where the hell was her watch?

Thankfully her job didn't require much primping, and she preferred it that way. She had never worn much makeup. The last thing she wanted to do was look more dainty and feminine. At only five foot three, it was difficult enough to be taken seriously. As she passed the mirror on her way out the door, she caught her reflection.

She cringed at the way her normally curly auburn hair hung limply on her shoulders. Dark circles stood out beneath her eyes, which were so bloodshot it was impossible to tell they were green.

Back in the car, she considered trying to remedy her appearance but decided against it. The one day she had actually put on lip gloss, her partner had teased her that she looked more like she belonged in front of a group of kindergartners than in a police uniform. And while she knew Greg had probably been joking, she was sure there were others who would readily agree with him without so much as a hint of humor. She didn't want to be singled out, just left alone. She was proving herself as a rookie—top of her class, best record so far. No sense screwing it up by reminding them that she was a girl. She could swear that every once in a while, when things were going really well, they forgot. And in those moments, she loved being on the force more than anything.

At ten to eight, she pulled into the parking lot next to the familiar gray building that housed the police department. The yellowed windows on the lower level still bore the bars installed after the station had been bombed back in the sixties. Though she had been on the force only a short time, she'd learned to enjoy the history and idiosyncrasies of the building. It would be strange when the new building was finished.

Alex straightened her back and got out of the car, thinking about what tests today would bring. As one of the few females on the force, Alex was at the receiving end of more than her share of jokes. She was used to it. Facing the teasing of the other officers was fine most days. Bra and panty jokes, she could suffer through.

Issues of her strength, her tolerance, her endurance for the job, those she wouldn't. She'd been a physical trainer for eight years before the rundown with a mugger made her realize she wanted more.

And she'd been tired of women whose idea of getting in shape was leg lifts while having their bikini line waxed. Alex was faster than all of the women and some of the men on the force. She'd proven it at the academy and she'd do it again if anyone questioned it. But mental strength and stability were not so easily measured and she refused to let anyone question hers.

And if anyone found out about last night, that would be the first thing to come into question.

She just prayed no one ever found out.

Chapter Two

Alex locked her car and ran in the front door and up the closest of the two half-circle staircases on either side of the lobby. The stairways always reminded her of an elegant hotel lobby from some old black-and-white movie, and they seemed out of place in the middle of the dilapidated station entrance.

At the top of the stairs, she ran into one of the consulting psychologists, carrying a tall stack of files. As they bumped, the files dropped to the floor.

"Sorry," Alex said, leaning down to scoop them up.

"Don't worry." Dr. Richards straightened the files in her arms. "It's a zoo in there today."

Alex nodded, handing her a stack of papers. "Always is." That was what she loved about police work. Every day was a new adventure.

Alex edged her way through the crowd of people waiting at the desk.

"I'm telling you, he said he wanted to buy the cycle," one man yelled. A black leather jacket covered his white dress shirt and the jacket of a gray suit, a helmet tucked under his arm. "Brand-new BMW bike. Fuck," he muttered under his breath.

Alex moved past another man who rolled up his sleeve and showed his tattoo to the administrative officer. "Does that look like an eagle to you? It's a goddamn Tweety Bird. I paid a hundred bucks for an eagle and the asshole won't give me my money back."

Alex looked at the tattoo. It was definitely not an

eagle. She thought even Tweety looked tougher than the wimpy bird on his shoulder. Rotten luck.

"That's really not a police issue. You should contact the consumer bureau to file a report," the officer behind the counter explained.

"A report? I ain't going to file no damn report. I want my fucking money back."

Alex wished she had time to stay and watch the man get himself thrown in jail for assaulting an officer. Through a large solid oak door, she entered the administrative division where they housed the fingerprint and mug-shot files. The department planned to scan them all so they would be accessible by computer at any station in California and eventually the nation. Great intentions but the process was unbelievably slow. She'd had to "thumb" through the records more than a few times in her months on the force, and it wasn't an enviable job.

"Morning, Alex," Detective Sam Portreo called. A brown tie curved over his round belly as though it had been starched against a bowling ball. This particular tie was his favorite because it hid the coffee stains.

"Hey, Sam. How's it going?"

His coffee cup raised, he gave a half smile. "I could complain, but what good would it do?"

"Exactly. Nice tie, by the way."

"Never been cleaned," he said proudly.

"I'm impressed."

"Knew you would be."

On the way down the hall, she leaned into her brother's office.

"Hey," James called, waving her over.

She leaned over his desk and pointed to her empty wrist. "I'm late, but I wanted to ask: Do you remember if any of us walked in our sleep as kids?"

James raised an eyebrow. "Sleepwalking now?"

She shook her head, realizing the question sounded strange coming from someone already late for work, especially to James. James was Internal Affairs and his intense stares made an average cop's suspicious nature seem like child's play. "I just thought I remembered something from when were kids."

"Not that I know of." Then, turning back to his work, he added, "You'd better get to work. And no sleepwalking walking on the job."

Feeling better, she almost smiled at the remark. It was the closest James would come to humor on the job. He took his work very seriously. It was something she respected about her brother despite the fact that it occasionally made him difficult to be around.

In the locker room, she dressed as quickly as she could. It was normally a ten-minute process with the lace-up ankle boots, the twenty-five-pound equipment belt, and a bulletproof vest. This morning, she finished in five. The first few steps with all the extra weight always made her feel as though she were walking through water. Today, rushing around, it felt more like she was running through water.

As she reached the second-floor squad room—a square, windowless area—she scanned for her partner. They were due in the briefing in three minutes.

Four patrol officers, one with a ball tucked under his arm, headed in after their morning two-on-two basketball game.

"You should join us some time, Alex."

She smiled and waved off the comment. "I'd hate to embarrass you guys."

"I think they need bigger help than you can offer," another joked.

"And I thought guys always swore size doesn't matter," she sparred back.

The first one laughed and the two exchanged high-fives. One of the others mumbled something about kicking their butts tomorrow. Alex turned back to search for Greg.

Other officers waved from tables, but Greg was no-where in sight.

"I wondered when you'd show up. Late date last night?"

Alex turned to see Brenda behind her, her long, lean frame easily six inches taller than Alex's.

Alex covered her mouth, remembering. "I was sup-posed to pick you up this morning! I'm so sorry."

Brenda laughed, her flawless black skin creasing into tiny lines around her eyes as she smiled. "No biggie." She waved her finger at Alex. "I did call your house, though. No answer. Who's the latest? Because when you cut him loose, I've got someone to get you up with."

Some people seemed to find it weird that Alex was thirty-five and happily unmarried. Alex had relation-ships—some short, some longer. But none had worked out. In the end, it was always for the best. Some peo-ple were good at relationships, some weren't. Alex put herself in the "suck" category. If she met someone special, she'd worry about it. For now, it was one less thing to concern herself with.

Brenda's huge almond-shaped hazel eyes widened as she waited for an answer. "So, is it still Tom?"

Alex smiled. "Not last night."

Since going through Los Medanos Police Academy in Contra Costa County with Brenda, Alex had found herself sharing more with her than with anyone else. But confiding wasn't something she did much of. Her former fiancé and her best friend in L.A., both cops, had often said she kept more secrets from them than they did from each other. Nobody knew her better than those two.

And they knew each other very well, too, she real-ized when she found them in bed together two months before the wedding. Still together, from what Alex heard from friends in L.A.

Strangely, after a brief pissed-off period, the whole

incident had rolled off her like water off wax. She was further from being concerned about marriage than ever.

"I totally overslept," she lied, thinking it wasn't so far from the truth.

Brenda frowned. "Overslept? You all right?"

"I know, the one time I can actually fall sleep, I can't wake up."

"You don't look rested. You sure you slept at home?"

Alex looked up at Brenda, catching the jest in her gaze. "Positive."

Someone yelled Alex's name and she turned to face her partner, Greg Roback. Thankful for the distraction from Brenda's questions, she took a step toward him. Greg was easily six foot five and so skinny he looked like he might break in two like a pencil under pressure. Only slightly meatier, Alex knew why they were often called the bean team.

"Are we late?"

He shook his head. "But we're about to be."

The shift briefing meeting was held in a cramped windowless room in the center of the building. The walls were littered with everything from wanted posters and APBs to furniture sales and baby announcements.

People milled about as Alex sank into a hard plastic seat and the captain started the meeting. He was in a sour mood, so the normal repertoire of jokes was kept to a minimum. He went over a couple of internal memos and let them know they had an armed robber on the loose driving a white Honda Civic.

"Great. That'll be easy to spot," Officer Nancy Yim joked from up front.

There was a round of laughter and the captain cracked a crooked smile.

He read off the car assignments and tossed his clipboard on the table. "That's it. Get out there."

Alex stood and headed for the door. "What's up with the captain?" she asked when they were out of earshot.

Greg shrugged. "Political bullshit, probably."

She followed Greg out the door toward their squad car, stifling a yawn. She almost always drove the first shift, preferring to drive in the morning when she was most awake and alert. Usually that meant right after the first cup of coffee of the day. Today, without her caffeine and a good night's sleep, Alex thought she'd fall asleep before they were out of the station's parking lot.

"You know what Al Capone's business card said?" Greg asked, throwing out the first trivia of the day.

"Used furniture dealer."

"Damn. How'd you know that?"

"Saw *The Godfather* six times," she said.

Greg shook his head. "You're the weirdest chick I know."

"Thanks. What's up with Lori?"

"Over," he answered flatly.

"Why?"

"She threw a fit when I wanted to watch the game." He shrugged then looked over. "I missed breakfast. Want to run by Noah's?"

"I'm dying for a cup of coffee," she agreed.

His seat belt clicked into place as she started the car. "Miss your morning fix?"

She nodded.

"Coffee machine broken?"

"Something like that."

"I heard you missed a pickup, too."

"I overslept, Roback. Drop it, okay?"

"Sure. You overslept. From the woman who never sleeps. I'll buy it."

Alex didn't answer him, but she was thinking he was right. She'd never even slept through the garbage pickup. How had she slept through driving somewhere in her car?

Greg pulled something off the seat. "Alex, this is gross."

She looked over at one of her chewed-up pens and snatched it from his hand. "Deal with it. At least it doesn't stink up the car like that monstrosity you eat for breakfast."

"It's getting worse. Everywhere I look, I find some slobbery pen. You know, there are easier ways to get out that aggression. Joe in Narc's always looking at you. I bet he'd go for some one-on-one."

"No way." She backed the car out of their spot and pulled through the parking lot.

"This must be the no cops rule. You ever going to explain that to me? What did a cop ever do to you? I mean, besides that jackass fiancé. Is that what this is about?"

"I get enough of cops at work, thank you."

"Speaking of which, when are we going to do that report for the captain?"

More at ease, she gave him a smug look. "Finished it yesterday after you went home."

"You didn't."

She grinned.

"I knew there was a reason I loved having you as a partner."

"We both know there are a thousand reasons. But don't think I'm giving you any credit for this one, Roback."

He grinned. "You wouldn't leave me out."

"I'm actually looking forward to it," she said.

"Yeah, right."

She winked. "What about this one: All the clocks in *Pulp Fiction* were set on one time."

Greg smiled. "Four-twenty."

"You've heard that one before."

"It's one to one." He looked over at her. "See the game last night?"

"Knicks won?"

"You missed the game?"

She shrugged. "I was busy."

"Busy last night, overslept this morning. You going to tell me about him? He's got to be something if he's getting you to fall asleep. He wear you out, or what?"

"Quit probing," she teased. "What are you—jealous?"

"You're dreaming," he snapped back. After an awkward beat, he said, "Did you know the giant squid has the largest eyes in the world?"

Alex laughed. "Did you know an ostrich's eye is bigger than its brain?"

"They use Murphy's Oil Soap to clean elephants."

She looked over. "What the hell's Murphy's Oil Soap?"

Greg smiled. "How the hell would I know? I'm a bachelor, for Christ's sake."

She laughed again. "Did you know cats have over one hundred vocal sounds and dogs only have about ten?"

"Dogs are still cooler," Greg responded.

"Definitely."

They drove the rest of the way to Noah's in silence. Another police car sat at the curb in front. Alex smiled at the way Noah's bagel shop had replaced Dunkin' Donuts as a cop hangout. At least it was healthier.

For them, stopping at Noah's had become a ritual, always ordering the same thing. For him, it was an onion bagel with garlic cream cheese. The smell in the car got so bad even the people who had to ride in the back complained about it.

"Hey, I'm addicted," he would say with an exaggerated shrug of his shoulders. She had taken to keeping a pack of breath mints for him in the glove compartment.

"The usual?" her partner asked.

Nodding, she leaned back against the interior of the front seat and closed her eyes. She heard him close his door and walk around the car.

"Maybe I should get you a decaf."

Prying her eyes open, she looked at Greg, his long, skinny frame bent down in the door. She smiled and closed her eyes again. "You trying to kill me?"

He laughed. "That obvious, eh?"

Squinting against the sun's morning glare, she opened her eyes. "If I don't have coffee in my stomach in three minutes, I'm going to get violent."

Greg raised his arms in surrender. "Sheesh, I can take a hint."

She blinked hard, taking in the familiar sights of downtown Berkeley. Across the street was Barnes & Noble. It was where she came on her days off—her favorite brewpub, Jupiter, was two blocks in the opposite direction. In the last decade, this area of Berkeley had really cleaned up. That change made it very easy to patrol and she was thrilled that it was part of her beat.

Of course, bagels and coffee on the way to work in the morning didn't hurt, either. And nothing made her happier than a cup or three of black coffee first thing.

Motion caught her eye and she glanced down the side street, her internal alarms sounding. An older female lay on the sidewalk, and she spied a young Caucasian male running up the street.

Alex glanced toward the bagel shop, but Greg was nowhere in sight. The woman started to get up, so Alex revved the engine and sped after the suspect. Sirens screeching, she lunged through traffic. A car leapt in front of her. She swerved to miss it. "Shit!"

The running man made no move to stop.

Almost on his tail, she halted. The bumper of the

squad car came within feet of the perp. Moving quickly, he ducked down a narrow alley. Her hand was on the door before the car was completely stopped. The emergency brake on, she threw open the door and bolted after him.

Alex drove her feet against the pavement, determined to catch him even if it meant a marathon around the damn city. She pressed her shoulder radio. "Officer Kincaid here." Her eyes nailed to her suspect, she sucked in a quick breath.

"Go ahead," came the voice of dispatch.

"Female down on Dwight at Shattuck. Suspect proceeding down alley at Shattuck and Channing," she panted. "I'm on foot pursuit. White male juvenile, seventeen or eighteen years, six foot, plus or minus. Dress is jeans, red T-shirt, black baseball cap."

"We read," came the response.

Alex knew backup would be on its way immediately, but there was no time to waste. If she stopped, she was guaranteed to lose him.

The suspect shot a quick glance over his shoulder.

"Stop, police," she yelled.

The kid leapt onto the fence at the end of the alley and climbed like a monkey scaling a tree. She had no doubt he had done this before. But so had she. On the other side, he jumped to the ground and continued running. He had a good head start.

"You can't outrun me," she muttered. She pulled herself up the fence. The sharp wire cut her hands, but she didn't ease up. She swung her legs over the top and dropped to the ground on the other side. Concrete jolted her ankles as she landed.

The perp disappeared and she forced her legs faster, keeping her breath at an even pace. She hoped the suspect wasn't a damned marathoner.

At the other end of the alley, she bolted onto the street, glancing in both directions. He was gone. "Damn."

Spinning around, she caught a glimpse of the suspect just as he came down on top of her. She hit the ground with a thud, her head knocked sideways against the hard pavement. The perp was above her, holding her arms.

Trapped, her breath came faster. She struggled against his strength, fighting off the wave of nausea that always came with being confined.

His grip tightened.

Focused, she contained her breathing until she felt a slight loosening of his tension. Then, in a lash of anger, she freed one leg and rammed her shin into his groin.

With a groan, he rolled off her onto his back. She was on him before he could recover.

Shaking off the pain in her head, she pulled her cuffs from her belt. His right hand in her grasp, she bent it back and rolled him over with a forceful tug. Her heel digging into his back, she cuffed his right hand. "Didn't your mother teach you any manners?"

"Fuck off."

She wrenched his left arm behind him and cuffed it. "I don't think so."

With a hard yank, she dragged him to his feet and shoved him toward the street.

Just then, Greg pulled around the corner and jumped out of the car. "Saw the car down the street and knew something had happened. You okay?"

She nodded, pushing the perp toward the car and letting Greg handle him. As Greg put the suspect in the back, she touched the area just above her ear and felt a warm spot of blood. She moaned.

In the car, she leaned back as Greg drove toward Shattuck. "Arbor's bringing the woman down to the station to identify him," Greg said. He motioned to the perp. "We just have to drop him off. Arbor should meet us out front. He'll do the paperwork."

"Yeah, yeah, fine, but where's my coffee?"

"I didn't have time to get it. We've got to run back after we drop the thug off."

A moan fell from her lips as she closed her eyes.

In front of the station, Greg stopped and pulled the suspect out of the car, handing him over to Arbor.

Alex waved to Arbor as Greg drove off again.

"Let's get some coffee before you attack your next victim," Greg joked.

"I'm serious. I don't think I could do it again without some caffeine."

He parked in front of Noah's. "This one's on me, Wonder Woman."

She smiled. "It's the least you could do, Robin."

"I don't even get to be Batman?"

"Not the way you drive."

In less than a minute, he was back. When he opened the door to hand her the coffee, he touched her head.

Wincing, she pulled away.

"Jesus Christ, Kincaid. You're bleeding."

"No shit, Sherlock."

"You need a doctor."

"It's barely a scrape. Come on."

As Alex took a long sip of French roast and started to relax, a call came through.

"Adam Nine, code four-fifty-nine at the corner of Henry and Yolo. Please report."

Alex nearly choked at the address. *Yolo Avenue.*

Chapter Three

"You okay?" Greg asked.

Alex nodded, forcing herself to swallow.

"You leave your thick skin at home this morning?" he asked, smiling and watching her closely.

She scowled. "Hell, no. Watch it or I'll spill my coffee in your lap."

"You'd never waste precious caffeine."

She pointed at him, trying to seem playful. "Not on your sorry ass."

When he stopped looking at her, she turned toward the window and wondered about the fact that until this morning, she'd never even heard of Yolo Avenue and now it had shown up twice in less than two hours. She'd never been a believer in coincidences, but she would've liked to think it could be that. Either way, she was about to find out. "Henry and Yolo. Let's go, Tonto."

"I thought it was my day to be the Lone Ranger." He winked and picked up the radio. "Nine, code four-fifty-nine, go ahead," he responded.

"Housekeeper on site reporting homeowner unconscious inside. Sending medical assistance."

"Copy," he said, replacing the radio and flipping on his siren.

Alex set her coffee in the drink holder. The caffeine could wait. It didn't feel like she'd need it to be wired this morning after all.

"You know where Yolo is?" Greg asked.

She nodded, directing him to follow Henry Street. Cursing, he sped up, swerving around a car that refused to yield to the sirens. When the streets cleared, Greg sped through the signal and turned onto the small street.

At 1112 Yolo, he pulled to the curb and parked. Alex looked up the street to the corner where she'd awakened only two and a half hours earlier. It was fewer than fifty yards away. She balled her fists and forced herself out of the car.

A stout older woman stood on the sidewalk, wringing her hands together. Her graying hair was pulled back into a low bun, wire-like pieces sticking out in a prickly halo around her head. Wearing a black dress with a white apron and sneakers with hose, the woman had the face of a hound, with large droopy eyes and a thick nose.

Nothing about her appearance suggested she had been involved in a struggle. It wouldn't be the first time Alex had seen a grandmother look innocent as day, only to find out she'd killed someone. The first suspect was always the person who had reported the crime. No such thing as a Good Samaritan in a cop's world. Truth was, suspicion simply ran through a cop's veins like blood. It made cops miserable to live with, but it helped on the job. Since Alex didn't live with anyone, she considered her suspicious nature pure benefit.

Alex wondered when the housekeeper had arrived. And for that matter, who had seen Alex parked there this morning? Someone must have. People didn't often sleep in their cars in this neighborhood. It was bound to have drawn attention.

Greg approached the woman first and Alex followed without allowing herself to be distracted.

"You have to hurry. I can see him through the window," the woman said, waving her arms frantically.

Greg pulled a notebook from his pocket. "What's your name, ma'am?"

She leaned over his notebook. "Ramona Quay. That's Q-U-A-Y. I keep the house."

"Do you have a key?"

She shook her head. "I get here before he's gone to work and he lets me in."

"What about when he's not home?"

"Then, we make other plans. Sometimes he leaves a key out for me." Her head continued to shake in a firm, continuous motion as though she were emphatically denying something. "But that's only happened once or twice."

"What's the gentleman's name?"

"Mr. Loeffler. William Loeffler. He's an attorney downtown."

Alex nodded, feeling relieved. The name wasn't familiar. And looking at the large, half-timbered Tudor house, she knew she had never seen it before. The fact that Alex woke up down the street from there that morning was definitely a strange coincidence, but that's all it was. Her first coincidence. Maybe she'd be a believer yet.

"Mr. Loeffler lives alone?" she asked.

The woman nodded, still rubbing her hands together in nervous agitation. "Used to be him and his wife here." Mrs. Quay glanced at her feet and clenched her teeth as though cursing herself for saying too much. "They been separated about six months."

Warning bells sounded at the word "separated," but Alex kept her thoughts to herself. The wife would need to be questioned. Greg and Alex hurried up the stone steps, Ramona close behind. The house was painted white with thick beams such a dark brown they were almost black. It appeared to have been recently repainted and the yard was carefully kept.

When they reached the porch, Alex checked the door. It was locked. Her hands cupped around her face, she stared through the window. A man lay sprawled on the floor, his feet closest to them. Dressed in jeans, running shoes, and a plaid flannel shirt, the man wasn't at all what Alex had pictured. And dressed like that he wasn't on his way to work—not at any of the law firms she'd seen. When the call had come through, she'd pictured an older man, fallen dead from a heart attack.

The man she saw appeared thin, fit, and about her age. Alex could make out his dark hair, but she couldn't see his face. Maybe he had fallen and hit his head somehow. They rang the bell twice to avoid entering and alarming anyone. Cops got shot that way more than anyone liked to think about. But no one came to the door.

"Mrs. Quay, I'm going to have to ask you to stay here," Alex directed.

The woman continued to clasp and unclasp her hands as she nodded.

Greg and Alex circled the house, Alex leading. She waded through the knee-deep ivy toward a small clearing beside the house. Her ears honed for activity from any side, she climbed over a small gate that wouldn't open and stopped at a side door. The sight of glass shards on the wet ground made her halt.

Greg followed her gaze. "What is it?"

Her hand motioned down as she surveyed the house and spotted a small broken window on a door that led to what looked like the dining room. She patted her pockets in search of the stash of tissue she usually kept. "Do you have something I can use to open this door?"

Greg pulled a handkerchief from his pocket and handed it to her. "I'm going to status EMT backup." He pressed the speaker on his shoulder and said, "This is Officer Roback at 1112 Yolo. I've got a four-fifty-nine and a possible two-forty-five," he reported, letting the dispatcher know they were dealing with a break-in and a possible assault with a deadly weapon. "Victim appears to be unconscious. We're going in. Over."

"We read," came the response. "EMT's en route."

Using the handkerchief on the very tip to avoid ruinning potential prints, Alex turned the pointed door handle and entered the dining room. With the handkerchief tucked in her pocket, she gripped her gun between her hands and prepared to shoot if necessary. Halfway into the dining room, she halted at the smell. It had the rich spiciness of cologne, but was almost too rich. Flowers maybe? Perfume? Sucking in another breath, she tried to place it.

Suddenly, the room swayed beneath her, and she moved to hold on to a chair, catching herself before she did. When Greg shut the door behind them, a breeze crossed her face and she was fine again. The smell disappeared. She looked in both directions for the source, but there was nothing. Balanced, she ignored the rapid pulse in her throat, and continued across the hallway toward the body.

The library was cool and damp, the hardwood creaking beneath her feet. Lessons from the academy drummed through her mind as she waited for signs that she and Greg weren't alone.

She crossed a large burgundy area rug and halted over the body. The crimson wave that had spilled onto the carpet had dried like thick tomato sauce. The man lay with his face only partially showing, the one visible eye bulging and bloodshot. His neck was slit open, the purple veins exposed, the skin pasty and yellowed where the blood hadn't dried. Blood saturated the collar of his maroon plaid shirt, making it look crusty and darker at the top. Pieces of tissue and blood had sprayed in a two- or three-foot diameter around the body.

Swallowing hard, Alex was glad Mrs. Quay hadn't seen that from the window. She started to circle and realized that one hand was missing at the wrist. "Jesus," she whispered.

"Let's check the perimeter," Greg said.

Alex stood up, and together they moved slowly from room to room, starting upstairs and working their way down. Guns drawn, they moved around each corner, listening intently.

As they searched the last room, she shook her head. "It's empty."

"Unpeopled," Greg corrected as they returned to the corpse.

"Right, unpeopled," she agreed, her eyes fixed on the body. Unable to draw her gaze off the man, she found she'd unconsciously pressed her hand to her own throat and pulled it away. Her knees felt sloppy beneath her, but she bent slightly and resisted the desire to sit. She remembered her trips to the morgue. The first few minutes of dead body were the worst. After that, like anything, you got used to it.

She shut her eyes and could still envision the room. When she opened them again, it was as though she had seen the crime scene from the other side of the room.

"I think we can skip checking for a pulse," Greg said.

Alex was still picturing the room as though she were standing on the other side. She tried to move but couldn't. It was as though someone had taken the remote control for her body away from her and had paused her reflexes.

"You're looking a little pale. You okay?"

She kicked herself back on and nodded, not trusting herself to speak.

"This is your first corpse. It's not supposed to be easy. You want to get a breath of air?"

She forced herself to shake her head, letting her eyes move past the body. "I'm fine."

Greg grinned. "Tough guy." He pressed his radio. "This is Adam Nine. Come in."

"Nine, go ahead," the dispatcher responded.

"We've got a DBF. Cancel EMT. Call the ME's office instead. And notify the detectives on duty."

"Copy."

Alex looked down at their DBF, "dead body found," and wondered what the man had done to deserve such a death.

Beside her, Greg put his hands on his hips and shook his head, following her thoughts. "Wonder who this guy pissed off."

With her gun tucked back in its holster, she knelt and studied the side of the man's head. His dark hair was graying by his ears and thinning in a small circle at the back of his scalp. Except for one eye and the side of his nose, she couldn't see his face.

"You doing okay down there?"

She looked up, feeling more steadied the more clinical she became. "Fine, why?"

He shook his head. "Couldn't pay me to get that close."

"You're a cop, Greg."

With a wave of his arm, he dismissed her comment. "Medical examiner gets these guys. I work for the living."

"Smell's not bad yet." At the morgue, she'd encountered corpses that had been discovered by their smells days and even weeks after death. It wasn't a pleasant experience.

Careful not to disrupt anything, she poked the dead man's muscles through his sleeve. The muscles were taut with rigor mortis, but she knew that wouldn't indicate exactly when he had died. Rigor mortis tended to start between two and six hours after death, then disappeared in about the same time frame. Alex had paid extra attention to the basics because she hoped to end up in the detective division. Which also meant getting used to death.

Inhaling deeply, she returned her gaze to the victim's neck and then followed the trail of blood that looked like finger paint along his chin and neck. She circled the body with her gaze, searching for blood splatter and the evidence that the technicians would use to determine how and when the man was killed. Except for the pool of blood and a little tissue, the area surrounding the body was relatively clean. Alex guessed the victim might already have been lying down when he was shot.

Feeling solid, she studied the stump where his hand had been, scanning the remnants for defense wounds and finding none. No pooled blood there. She guessed the hand had been removed post-mortem. Forcing a detached, clinical mode, she surveyed the area around the body. Every few minutes, she glanced back at the body to test that she was still in control, that she could do it.

"What's this?" Greg asked.

She turned to see Greg lean over and pick something off the floor with a tissue.

In the white cloth, he cupped a small gold loop earring.

Alex's eyes widened as she touched her ears. It was one of hers.

"It's yours?"

Fire lit in her cheeks.

"Alex?"

She showed him her empty left earlobe. "It must have just fallen off."

He handed it back to her. "Rookie, we call that contaminating the crime scene."

She saluted, trying to make a joke of it.

He handed her the earring. "Lombardi would have your head on a platter." With a sardonic smile, he stopped and motioned to the body. "Guess that wouldn't be too funny to this guy."

Alex forced a smile and put the earring back on as Greg pulled his notebook from his pocket.

"Must've fallen out of your pocket," he said.

"My pocket?"

She looked up at him and started to shake her head when he said, "You didn't have it on in the car either."

She blinked hard and forced the earring into her ear before turning her back to Greg. "Damn thing is always falling off," she lied. She knew the earring hadn't been in her pocket. She'd never put it there. She never even took the earrings off. She slept in them, ran, showered, everything. She must've knocked it off in the struggle with the perp, and it had just gotten stuck in her clothes or her hair. She was amazed that she hadn't lost it.

Someone knocked on the door and Alex turned to see Ramona Quay peering in through the glass.

"I'll handle it," Alex said, heading for the door.

The housekeeper's eyes were wide, her hands now red from wringing them together. "Is he going to be all right?"

She shook her head. "I'm sorry, Mrs. Quay."

The woman dropped her hands to her sides and began sobbing. Thankful to have someone else to worry about, Alex led the woman down to the car.

With the patrol car door open, she seated Mrs. Quay on the passenger side. She found a package of tissues next to Greg's breath mints in the glove compartment and gave her a handful of them.

Alex took out her notebook and pen. "I need to get some information from you."

"How . . . how did it happen?" the woman asked, her large nose bending almost in half as she wiped it with a tissue. Her eyes seemed suddenly droopier as tears ran down her cheeks, creating little pink lines in her dry skin.

Putting the notebook down, Alex squatted on the curb in front of her. "We're not sure yet."

"What do you mean, not sure?"

"We'll have to do some checking before we know what killed him." The fact that a close-range shot appeared to have almost detached his head from his body was a likely explanation for his death, but Alex kept that to herself. The police had good reasons for not disclosing the cause of death. Even if not a suspect, Mrs. Quay could become a material witness. She may have seen something or known someone who wanted Loeffler dead. And for that reason, they needed to talk to her before she found out anything about the crime scene. Plus, who knew how the woman would take it, and Alex didn't need anyone having a coronary on her.

"He had a very good heart," she said. "He was in very good shape. Always ran downtown and stopped for a bagel and ran home—every morning."

Alex nodded. "I don't think it was his heart, Mrs. Quay. I believe someone wanted him dead. Can you think of who might want to hurt him?"

She shook her head quickly. "I can't believe. Mr. Loeffler."

Alex listened while Mrs. Quay expressed disbelief at the demise of her employer. But the woman couldn't offer any clue as to who might have wanted to kill him. "No, he was a good man. No one would do this to him."

As Alex turned, an olive green Chevrolet as old as she was pulled to the curb. It was Detective Lombardi's. "It's a one of a kind," he always bragged.

When Lombardi stopped by the patrol car, Alex excused herself from Mrs. Quay. As he surveyed the area, his eyes looked small and beady like an animal's. Instead of walking, Lombardi lumbered, moving the way an elephant grazed, heavy and slow.

A black trench coat that looked as though it had

been through a gang war hung over his broad shoulders. It had a bullet hole in the right shoulder where he'd been shot once, and another midway down the right side where he had shot at someone from his pocket. Like a medal of honor, he wore the coat day in and day out, no matter what the weather. He once came to the station with a pair of swim shorts beneath it.

At the academy, she had heard cop stories like this one. Lombardi considered the coat his protective shield, and wearing it, he felt invincible.

"Up here?" Lombardi asked, motioning toward the stairs.

She nodded. The crime scene van pulled behind her squad car, and a team of three investigators, carrying large black plastic cases, emerged from the van.

Lombardi moved past her and waved for the crime scene investigative team to follow. "Come on, girls," he said, although there were two men and only one woman.

As always, Lombardi smelled like dirty ashtrays. The smell reminded Alex of her own days of smoking. As she always did when he passed, she inhaled, longing for just one more cigarette.

The female investigator rolled her eyes. Alex nodded her pity. Lombardi was old school. He didn't see a place for women on the force, except maybe as secretaries, and, of course, to clean up after him.

Returning to Mrs. Quay, Alex sat down on the curb. "Do you think you're up to giving me some information?"

The woman sniffled and gave a weak nod.

As she pulled her chewed-up pen from her pocket, Alex noticed Mrs. Quay glance at it. Alex really did need to get a pen she couldn't chew on—maybe a steel one.

Returning her attention to her notebook, Alex wrote down Mrs. Quay's name, address, phone num-

ber, and the standard questions about the housekeeper's arrival this morning. "Did you see any strange
cars on the street?" As soon as the question was out,
Alex cursed herself for asking. A good cop would
have let someone else ask that question. She poised
her pen for the response, promising herself she'd put
it in her report, no matter what it was.

Mrs. Quay stared out at the street in silence. When
she looked back, she shook her head. "I don't think
so. I don't really know. I never notice. It's such a busy
street in the morning."

Dismissing her own selfish relief, Alex put her hand
on Mrs. Quay's arm. "Don't blame yourself. You
might remember something later."

The woman nodded, staring at the ground.

"Are you going to be okay here for a minute?"

She gave a stiff smile. "I'll be fine."

"I'll be back down and we'll get someone to take
you home."

Mrs. Quay looked up, her eyes wide again. "I'd prefer to go to my daughter's."

"Of course. We'll get you to your daughter's, then.
I'll be right back." Excusing herself, she followed
Lombardi's group up the stairs.

Inside, a photographer snapped pictures of the body
while the other investigators collected data. One man
moved along the carpet on plastic kneepads, a pair of
tweezers in one hand and a plastic bag in the other,
collecting hair and fiber samples. After he finished,
they would vacuum the rest of the area for anything
he missed.

Another held a flashlight to the table beside the
body. With a grunting noise, he pulled a fluffy brush
out of his coat pocket and dipped it into powder,
brushing it across the table. Then, like a proud child
with a new toy, he blew the excess powder off. In the
black dust, Alex saw a fingerprint.

Lombardi knelt beside the victim, snapped on some

gloves, and handed a pair to Greg. Lombardi's eyes met Alex's and he dangled a pair of gloves. "You, too, Sugar."

Alex glared. "Sure thing, Pops."

Greg laughed while Lombardi pretended he hadn't heard her.

An adolescent-looking man with bad skin arrived from the medical examiner's office. On his knees, he laid a thick black plastic bag beside the body while another man, much older, brought in the gurney.

Alex put the gloves on and waited for instructions. She stood silent, knowing Lombardi and Greg were waiting for her to react. They were going to move the body. This would be her first contact with a dead body, and she swore she wasn't going to miss a beat. She'd heard stories of the process, things that dripped or fell from the corpse. In one case she'd heard about, the head had fallen off. If Alex wanted the detective division, she needed to maintain her cool. And Lombardi would be goading her wherever possible.

"I'm finished," the photographer announced.

"You ready for it?" Lombardi asked the medical examiner's assistant.

He nodded without speaking.

"Then we can move it," Lombardi declared with unnerving enthusiasm as though this was the most exciting part of finding a corpse. "Watch the blood from that arm—don't get it all over yourself."

Alex smiled broadly at Lombardi despite the wake that bounced in her gut.

"Over here, Kincaid."

She inhaled deeply and approached the body.

"Don't touch his skin. We don't want to lose any prints."

Though she'd heard the advice, she couldn't help but feel an odd sense of awe at the image of finger-prints left on the dead man's skin, a final testament to the agony he had endured. A niggling voice whis-

pered in her ear: *Will yours be among them?* She
shook it off. She'd followed regulations and hadn't
touched a thing. She thought of her earring and
touched both ears quickly. Greg caught her eye and
raised an eyebrow but she only smiled in response.

"You take the shoulders, Kincaid. Roback and I'll
get the body. You make sure it all ends up in the
bag," he called to the guy from the ME's office. "Just
onto his back, okay? On three. One. Two. Move."

Alex rotated the man's shoulders. His neck wobbled
as the remaining shards of muscle and ligaments struggled to hold the weight of his head. She'd been right.
He'd been shot in the back of the neck and the bullet
had exploded on the other end, leaving very little of
the front of his neck remaining.

At the sight of the exposed veins in his neck, she
swallowed the bitter taste of bile that rose in her
throat. She would not be sick. A wave of the metallic
smell of blood and burnt skin hit her nose and she
blinked hard. She would not be sick, she repeated to
herself.

Greg was groaning on his end. "Jesus, he stinks."

"What are you—a girl?" Lombardi chided.

"No, but I've got a good nose and this asshole
stinks."

Alex remained silent.

The victim's head knocked back against the ground,
the thin tissue ripping, and she looked straight at his
face for the first time. Gasping, she jumped back.

Lombardi looked puzzled. "What the fuck?"

An image flashed through her head. A man's face—
this man. But how did she know him? A cold sweat
breaking across her body, she backed up slowly, her
heart racing.

"Kincaid, what's wrong?" Greg stepped into her
line of vision, but she could still see the man.

Her knees wobbly beneath her, she began to shake.
Fighting it off did no good. Small white dots formed

before her eyes. Damn this. Damn it all. She shook
her head, trying to push the image of his face from
her mind. Why did she know this man's face? The
image in her mind shuttered and she saw the front of
Noah's Bagels. He'd tried to talk to her. He'd used
her name. Pointing, she tried to speak.

Greg centered her shoulders to him, forcing her
gaze off the man. "What?"

"What the fuck's wrong with her?" Lombardi bellowed.

She looked at Greg but pointed to the man. "Him—"

He gave her a light shake. "What about him?"

"He—" The white dots grew, filling her field of vision. She blinked hard, but it only got worse. The
room started to spin as she fought a wave of dizziness.

"He was at Noah's yesterday," she gasped. He'd
used her name. What had he tried to say? "He asked
me a question." She turned away from Greg, feeling
dizzy. "Did you see him?"

Greg looked at the victim and shook his head. "No,
what did he say?"

"You knew him?" Lombardi demanded.

She shook her head, the room spinning. "He spoke
to me in Noah's yesterday—he used my name."

Greg shook his head. "Your name's on your uniform, Kincaid. What's the big deal?"

She looked around the room, feeling it circle beneath her. She reached out to grab something but all
she caught was air. She pictured her uniform and
shook her head.

It was a big deal, she thought. Her legs collapsed,
and she slammed to the floor with a thud. Then, everything went black.

Chapter Four

Alex strained against the net of tight cobwebs that circled her brain. She was hung over and exhausted and everything hurt. And yet she couldn't remember drinking. It had been a while since she'd had anything to drink. Her insomnia kept her away from alcohol. The nights she drank were always the roughest in terms of sleep. She lifted her hand to her head and felt a plastic bracelet scratch her cheek. She opened her eyes and stared down at it. A hospital I.D. band. She blinked hard, then, remembering the street and the body, she jolted upright.

James pulled away from a chair nearby. "Glad to see you're up."

She ignored her brother, trying to remember the pieces before he told her. A tight knot formed in the bowel of her gut. She'd blacked out. The knot grew until it seemed to fill her belly. She'd blacked out on the job. "Damn," she whispered, wishing it had been a dream. She didn't dream. She hadn't dreamt—or remembered a dream—ever.

"You really had Lombardi scared."

She watched James watch her. Captain of Internal Affairs, assessing other cops was his job. At that moment, she wished he were just a regular brother. Someone to come and make sure she was okay and to invite her to dinner. James was anything but. Every question, no matter how innocent-sounding, was a cross-examination about her guilt, her intent, her ability on the job. She thought about waking up in her car. He didn't know about that. He didn't need to know. Fainting was hardly grounds for an internal investigation.

She often thought it had been a mistake to come and work for the same police department where James was. But this was home. The only one she'd ever known. Her time in L.A. had been fun, but it had never felt permanent or even real. Los Angeles was, truly, la-la land. And six years there had been five too long.

Only being mugged had given her the impetus to leave. She'd been coming home late one night and been attacked just one hundred yards from her front door. He'd wanted money, he told her. But he'd come with a knife, and after she surrendered her handbag, he'd still held her. She remembered his hot breath in her ear, the feeling of him pressed against her. It no longer gave her chills or made her palms sweat. Now it just pissed her off. Thankfully, he hadn't gotten the chance to get any closer.

She'd known that she'd fight him to the death if he tried to rape her. The knife against her neck, she'd waited until a moment when his grip slackened before breaking free from his hold and landing her knee in his groin. He'd dropped his knife but not before slicing the edge of her jaw.

The small scar was physically all that remained of that night. Mentally, it had been the cause of a lot of change. She'd left her job, her friends, L.A. All three had been superficially appealing, but not deep enough to sustain her interest. The threat of death had made that instantly clear.

"You want to tell me what happened," James said, pacing along the side of her bed as though he were in front of a jury box.

She crossed her arms. "Not particularly."

"Why don't you anyway?"

"You here in an official capacity, James? Or did you think you'd put the job aside and see if your sister is okay?"

James halted and turned back. "You want sympathy? How can I give you that when I don't even know what the hell it would be for? What the hell happened? You knew that guy?"

Just then, the door opened and James's twin walked in. Brittany was the opposite of her brother, and in many ways, of Alex, too. Though she and Alex looked alike—lean figures with reddish auburn hair and light eyes, Brittany was calm and somewhat reserved. The observer, some would say. She was a child psychologist and a damn good one. Brittany stood between James and Alex. "Glad to hear you're respecting the fact that she's recovering from trauma," she scolded James. Her tone was strong and firm, the voice of someone who knew she was right and didn't need to prove it.

James stepped to the edge of the room and leaned against the windowsill. "I was just trying to figure out what happened."

Brittany nodded and turned to Alex. "Of course. A cop," she said, motioning to James. To Alex, she said, "How do you feel?"

"Fine."

"Did you feel any symptoms before you blacked out? Light-headedness? Anything like that?"

Alex remembered feeling off balance as she'd walked into the dining room. "A little, I guess."

"I'm sure it was a delayed concussion from the fall your partner told us about," she said. Then, her back to James, she mouthed, "If you need to talk, you can call me."

Alex nodded.

As though sensing he'd missed something, James returned to the bedside, eyeing his twin, who ignored him, before speaking again. "The department wants you to talk to a counselor."

Alex frowned.

"It's a matter of course," Brittany added, taking the edge off James's request. "Anytime something traumatic happens on the job, they send the officer to a counselor. James always makes everything sound so dire."

He did, at that. "Who do I call?" she asked, still talking to Brittany.

"There's Margaret Schroeder," James answered.

Alex groaned. "Mad Dog Schroeder?" The woman was infamous at the station for her mood swings. She'd be gentle as a kitten one minute and a pit bull the next. "No thanks."

"There's Ross Berman or Jane Reed," James continued. "Gillian McArthur. She's new, but I've heard good things."

"What about Judith Richards?" Brittany asked.

Alex remembered the name. "The one who used to work with Mom? I just saw her at the station yesterday morning."

"Yeah, I think she still does some work there," James agreed. "I can ask."

Brittany nodded. "Call her. She'll remember you. You used to talk to her about your nightmares when you were a kid."

"Nightmares? When was this?"

"You were little—" She turned to James, who shrugged. "First and second grade, maybe. Something like that. Anyway, Judy's great. She's the one who helped me get into the graduate program at Cal. She's dealt with some incredible cases. She's done a lot of work with ex-cons—she even had two patients who shot each other. She managed to talk one of the shooters out of killing her. She's also written some fascinating articles on criminal psych." She turned back to James. "Call and see if she's available for Al to talk to."

He nodded but didn't respond. Then, he stepped closer to the bed with an ominous look. "I do have some questions to ask in an official capacity."

"I'm sure they can wait," Brittany said.

James let his mouth fall shut.

"I can answer them," Alex offered, knowing he'd corner her sooner or later.

James nodded and smiled satisfactorily at Brittany. "Did you know the deceased?" he asked Alex.

Alex straightened her back and crossed her hands in front of her. "No. I think he came up to me in Noah's Bagels the day before yesterday. At least, I think it was him."

"What did he say in Noah's?"

"Nothing. He never had a chance."

James frowned and made a note in a small spiral notebook he always carried. Alex had even seen him pull it out at a family dinner.

"We got a call," Alex continued. "Roback came in and called me, and I left."

"So, the dead guy—Loeffler—he never said anything to you?"

"He called my name—that was it."

"He said 'Kincaid'? That's it?"

A nurse came through the door as Alex considered James's question. But he hadn't called her Kincaid. "I need blood," the nurse exclaimed as though they might each have a bag of it in their pockets.

"Hers, I hope," Brittany joked, stepping back with her hands up.

"Oh, sure, sacrifice me," Alex complained. "Haven't I had a rough enough day already?"

The nurse chuckled, wrinkles forming exclamations around her eyes. "It's yours I'm after," she said, approaching the bed. Her gray hair was tucked up under what looked like a white shower cap, her white nurse's outfit snug over her full figure.

"Are you sure? I think she might have a better sample. We're all related, you know."

The woman ignored Alex, though her smile remained. She took Alex's arm and tied a tourniquet around her biceps.

Alex watched the nurse draw blood, her mind on Loeffler. He hadn't called her Kincaid. That would've been the name he'd seen on her badge. It would've made sense. And yet he'd called her Alexandra. No one had called her that since her mother had died.

"I've still got questions for you," James said.

Brittany waved him off. "Later, Spillane."

Alex nodded in the direction of James as the nurse began to check her vitals. How the hell had the dead guy known her first name?

Alex waited for the doctor to discharge her. Dr. Pletcher was a nice enough man. Tall, thin, with a small, steep nose and an easy disposition, he hummed lightly to himself as he worked, as if he were working on a car rather than a person.

"I think you're free to go," he announced, hanging the stethoscope over his neck. "No signs of concussion, not even a real bump."

"What caused me to black out?" Alex asked.

Dr. Pletcher pursed his lips and shook his head. "It's hard to say. Most likely it was the fall you took. The brain's a difficult organ to figure. We're not quite there yet." He made a note on her chart and tucked it under his arm, looking like he was ready to skip down the hall with Dorothy in her red slippers.

"Doctor?" She stopped him as he was heading out.

He turned back, his brow raised.

"I had a general question."

"Sure."

"What might cause someone to wake up somewhere strange and not remember how he got there?" As soon as the question was out, she regretted asking it.

It was like asking a parent about sex or drugs—even the mere mention of the topic led to the immediate suspicion of guilt.

Though he watched her intently for a moment, she kept her expression neutral, refusing to confirm that she was speaking of herself. Holding her chart to his side, he approached the bed and sat in the chair next to it, staring at the wall on the other side of her bed. "Delirium, epilepsy, and certain dissociative reactions like fugue states can cause memory disorders."

"What's a fugue state?"

"It's a personality disorder characterized by amnesia and usually involves flight from an area of stress or conflict."

"Uh, in layperson terms, please . . ." Just as she spoke, the door opened and Greg came into the room.

He saluted to the doctor and put his hand out. "Greg Roback. Nice to meet you."

"Harry Pletcher."

He winked at Alex. "Just came to see if my partner's going to be back in battle soon."

The doctor nodded. "A day or two and she'll be raring to go."

The doctor turned back to Alex and started to speak.

"Great," she interrupted, hoping to keep him from returning to the conversation they'd been having. "I'll be anxious to get back."

"I think you should take it easy for another twenty-four hours. As long as you don't experience the dizziness again, you should be okay to return to work." The doctor made another note and started out the door.

Alex exhaled and turned to Roback.

The doctor pulled the door open and then turned back, one finger raised like Einstein making a discovery. "I almost forgot to answer your question about fugue states," he said, stepping back into the room. "A fugue state happens when something triggers the mind to block out certain memories—sometimes the loss is associated with a specific person or object, so that someone won't remember anything that relates to that object or person. And sometimes people suffer a complete memory lapse for short spans of time after something traumatic has happened."

Alex nodded, feeling Greg's stare. "Interesting," she said, trying to cut Pletcher short.

He seemed oblivious to her discomfort. "A lot of people who were in the forces in Vietnam now suffer from post-traumatic stress disorder. Many don't remember chunks of the time they were there. Others are still reliving actual combat over and over."

"What else can cause a fugue state?" Greg asked, and Alex knew his mind was working.

Dr. Pletcher took another step back into the room and shrugged. "I was just telling Alex that we usually don't know exactly what triggers it—it can happen spontaneously for no reason at all." With a shake of his head, he added, "I have to admit, this isn't my area of expertise." He paused. "Sometimes drugs can have these sort of side-effects."

"Which drugs?" Greg asked and Alex cringed.

The doctor nodded, thinking, as he glanced at Alex again with one brow raised. "The same symptoms can be associated with certain benzodiazepine derivatives, for instance."

"What's a benzodiz—?"

Pletcher smiled and Alex shifted uncomfortably in the hospital bed. "Benzodiazepine is a drug derivative. Valium, for instance, is a benzodiazepine. Restoril is another."

Dr. Pletcher looked down at her chart and raised an eyebrow. "You took Restoril last night."

Both men stared at Alex. "Did you experience some sort of amnesia?" the doctor asked.

She shook her head. "I was just curious."

"The drug she took could cause that kind of reaction, though?" Greg asked. "This Restoril?"

Alex stared at Greg.

Dr. Pletcher shook his head. "Usually not. Certainly not retrograde amnesia—forgetting what happened before she took it—like in fugue states. In high doses, Valium could cause some loss of memory."

"But not Restoril?" Greg pressed.

He shook his head. "Most likely not."

Alex nodded. "We weren't talking about me, Roback," she said, knowing his mind was already working through why she'd asked the question in the first place.

Pletcher looked at her and nodded as though he knew she was lying. "People do react differently to drugs, so there's no way of telling exactly what the reaction might be."

Alex felt a small trickle of relief. "That's very helpful, Doctor."

The doctor looked from her to Greg. "Any other questions?"

"None," Alex said in a firm tone before Greg could speak.

"I'll leave your discharge paperwork with the nurse. She'll come by in a few minutes to get you out of here. You can get dressed in the meantime."

The doctor left the room and Alex avoided the heavy pull of Greg's gaze.

"I need to get dressed," she said, finally making eye contact.

He held her gaze, searching.

She crossed her arms and stared back. "You're not going to stay and watch me dress."

He grinned. "I wouldn't mind."

She pointed to the door. "Out."

He made no move for the door. "Kind of an interesting conversation you were having with the doctor. You want to tell me what the hell that was about?"

"Fine. Stay." Alex threw the covers off her bare legs and stood from the bed to get dressed.

"Why were you asking about memory loss?"

She crossed to the long thin closet where her clothes had been hung and pulled down her black uniform pants. "It wasn't anything."

"The drug you took causes some sort of amnesia. You were asking about it. That's a coincidence?"

Alex tucked the hospital gown under her chin as she fastened her pants. "You missed the beginning of the conversation. I asked about the blackout, if it could've been anything other than the hit on my head. He mentioned that these benzo—things sometimes cause blackouts or fugue states. I asked what it was. I was curious, Roback. I'm a cop, it's my nature. Don't make such a fucking big deal about it. You sound like James."

He stood silent for a minute. "I know you, Kincaid, and there's something going on. You don't have to tell me now, but I'll figure it out eventually."

"The only thing going on is that I'm trying to get dressed and you're not going away."

"Right," he said, still eyeing her. She refused to blink. "See you later, then."

"Later," she said as he walked out the door.

As the door closed slowly, she thought again about what the doctor had said. She hadn't gone through anything traumatic, except seeing the body. But that had happened after she had woken up in the car.

Maybe she had *pre*-traumatic stress disorder. She shook her head. It wasn't funny.

But who knew how she'd ended up on Yolo. It had to be an odd reaction to the Restoril. Pletcher said people had different reactions to drugs.

A drug reaction. If a perp had told her that, she'd have read him the riot act.

Chapter Five

The drive home was quick, but even the small effort wore Alex out. Inside her house, she ignored the blinking answering machine light that indicated she had three messages and dropped her jacket on the couch alongside a sweater and a pair of pants that had been there easily three weeks. She wondered briefly if one of the messages would explain where she'd been the night before. A strange chill rippled across her back and she shook it off. She was tired—no, she was unusually tired. Insomnia kept her at the same level of sleep deprivation as someone with a brand-new infant. What she felt now wasn't tiredness, it was exhaustion.

She also knew better than to let herself get right into bed. It was only four in the afternoon, and if she went to bed now, she'd be awake at nine and up all night. Instead, she changed into shorts and a sports bra and went into the dusty basement, which she had converted into a workout room with some old carpet and free weights. There, she practiced tae bo moves until her stomach ached and her legs and arms burned.

Then, she gathered the laundry from across the floors and furniture and started a load of whites, adding bleach. She thought about what a mess the rest of the house was but refused to clean it now. It had waited this long, it could wait another week or so. More likely it would be a month before she'd finally break down and call the woman who used to clean for her mother and offer her seventy-five hard-earned dollars to come and make it livable again. Anything not to deal with it herself.

Finding the bottle of Restoril in the kitchen cabinet, Alex flushed the remaining pills and tossed the empty container in the trash, thankful to be rid of them. Enjoying the silence of her house, she sat down on a stool while the water heated for her tea. She had always loved having her own space. These days she couldn't imagine sharing a place with a roommate, let alone a husband and children. Visiting her siblings' houses proved that to her often enough.

With three boys running around, James's house was a zoo. She couldn't believe his wife Sheila could stand all the noise. And though Brittany's house was quieter, it was ten times as organized. She was a neat freak. Everything in her house had its specific spot. Dishes had to be stacked just so, tall glasses to the left, short ones to the right. Alex shook her head at the thought.

Even when Alex made the effort to help out at Brittany's, she never got it right. All the mixing bowls had to be stacked biggest to smallest; the damn Tupperware was separated by size. And Brittany's daughters were too neat to be considered normal children by her standards. They made their beds daily, Saturday and Sunday included.

No, she liked living alone. Even engaged, she and Michael had kept separate residences. Ironically, it was just weeks before they were due to move in together that she discovered her best friend, Trisha, in bed with her fiancé. Living with someone no longer held any appeal at all.

She poured herself tea and took a sip, heading for the bath. Upstairs, she took off her clothes and put on her heavy terry-cloth robe. It had been a gift from her nieces, obviously picked out by Brittany. Pink-and-white striped, the robe always made her feel silly, but it was the most comfortable thing she owned and she relished the feel of it now, the tiny terry-cloth loops soft against her skin. She took a deep breath and forced the band wrapped around her chest to loosen. A bath would be just the right medicine.

In the bathroom, she plugged the drain and started the water. She loved her bathroom. Its low slanted walls left just enough space for a full-height shower on the tall end and her bath tucked along the low side. A tiny old Asian table sat beside the tub, covered with bubble baths and soaps. The only sign of Alex's femininity was here. The only time she pampered herself was in this room. Any guests were banished to the functional guest bath. This room was hers alone.

She set the tea down and let the robe fall off her shoulders. Reaching to take off her watch, she stared at her empty wrist. Her watch still hadn't turned up. Where the hell had she left it?

Dismissing it, she pick up her tea and stepped into the bath. The steam warmed her face as she leaned back to let the hot water rise against her skin.

The smell of raspberry bubble bath mixed with orange spice tea. She closed her eyes, breathing the aroma as she settled deeper into the hot water. This was exactly what she needed—a little unwind time.

Setting her tea on the table, she submerged her arms, goose bumps rising like tiny grains of soft sand on her skin. She leaned her head back against the rounded edge of the cool tub surface and closed her eyes. It amazed her that she didn't do this more often. The bathtub always made everything seem so much simpler.

As the muscles in her neck started to loosen, she realized she must have been stressed about the job. She'd been putting an enormous amount of pressure on herself to perform. Having James for a brother hadn't helped, either. She refused to let anyone even entertain the notion that she was on the force because of him. And it meant always working twice as hard to prove otherwise.

She reminded herself to call Tom and thank him for the flowers and to cancel their date tomorrow. She didn't think she'd be up for anything so soon. Plus, Tom was getting a little serious. Backing him up a bit would be a good step.

What she really wanted to do was get back on the case, help Lombardi if he would let her, if he'd even speak to her. That way, she could follow it through, sort out her own reaction. As she saw it, working the case was the best way to rid herself of her skittish reaction to the dead body.

The sound of the ringing phone pulled her from her thoughts. Groaning, she refused to get out of the water. The machine clicked on, her own voice announcing that she wasn't able to answer. Straining to hear, she waited for a voice to fill the air after the beep, but none did. She shrugged and started the hot water again, the heat tickling her toes.

As she sank back into the bubbles, the phone rang again. She sat up and frowned, listening to the machine. Again there was no message. Though she tried to sit back and relax, she couldn't stop thinking about who had called.

When the phone rang a third time, she cursed and lifted herself out of the bath. Dripping wet, she put her robe on, tying it as she hurried down the hall. In her bedroom, she lifted the receiver. "Hello?" She knew her voice sounded aggravated, but she was. If this were some salesperson, she was going to let him have it.

"Alexandra?" a strange-sounding male voice said.

She wrinkled her brow, thinking again of Loeffler's use of her Christian name. "Yes. Who's this?"

There was a short pause.

"Hello?" she repeated.

A hushed voice replied, but Alex couldn't make out the words.

"Who *is* this?" she asked.

"I saw you on Yolo last night," came the response. Her jaw dropped and Alex pulled the phone away from her ear, to stare at it. His words were like a blow. She thought about the murder. Maybe he had seen something. "What's your name?"

"What do you think you're doing? Do you remember?" His words were mechanical and awkward, like he was reading off a page.

"Who is this?" she repeated. "Tell me what you saw."

"What were you doing there?" he continued without addressing her question. "See if you can find the present I left for you and the one I took." The line clicked and went dead.

Alex frowned. "Hello?"

There was no answer.

She dialed *69 and heard a recorded voice say, "We're sorry. The call return feature cannot be used to return your last call."

Alex waited for the phone to ring again, but it didn't. Padding back to the bathroom with the cordless phone in her hand, she thought about who it could have been.

One of Loeffler's nosy neighbors? But why call her? He didn't sound like he had information for the police. Had someone really seen her on Yolo, maybe even followed her there? Was it someone holding a grudge against her? She couldn't think of anyone who would want to get to her. She hadn't made any recent arrests except the punk kid, and he couldn't have seen her on Yolo the night before.

Maybe the caller had something to do with Loeffler's death. As she had so many times in the past fourteen hours, she focused on waking up in her car. How could her presence on the street where a murder took place just be a coincidence?

Filled with an uncomfortable feeling of anxiety, Alex returned to the bath and leaned back in defeat, her head against the edge of the tub. Who the hell was that? And what did he mean about presents?

She thought about phoning the station to report the call. But she knew what she would ask if someone tried to report crank phone calls. A cop's first concern was what you could prove. And her answer was: Nothing. She couldn't prove a damn thing, which meant calling the police was a waste. Especially when she couldn't even answer the caller's question. What *had* she been doing there?

Chapter Six

She couldn't see. She blinked and opened her eyes again but still no images appeared. Only darkness, with an occasional spot of light like a star in the distance. It was as though someone had hurled her into outer space, leaving her surrounded by nothing but the dark sky. But she wasn't in the middle of space. She was on the ground. She could feel it, cool and moist like cement, uncomfortable beneath her. Dust stuck to her fingertips.

Her vision was gone. With her face tilted toward the sky, she expected something to appear before her eyes. Was she blindfolded? She couldn't tell. Instinctively, she tried to touch her face, but she couldn't move. Her arms were caught behind her back. Was she tied up? She wiggled her hands, but didn't feel anything holding them down. So why couldn't she get them to her face? Fighting against an invisible rope that bound her, she struggled again.

What was wrong with her? Her limbs wouldn't move. Nearby, someone was crying, the voice small and meek like a child's. But it seemed so close, right beside her. Who was it? Was she looking through a mirror at herself? Moisture cooled her eyes and face. Was it raining? She lifted her face toward the sky but felt no drops.

"What do you think you're doing?" a voice called out, its tone a hot flame against her skin, sharp and scalding.

Bolting up, Alex blinked hard and stared into the

darkness around her. Her heart thumping like a drum, the room slowly came into focus—her bedroom, her own bedroom. She sighed and lay back on the bed. She pictured a warehouse in her mind, and realized she'd been having a bad dream.

Her fingers moved across her face, pushing her hair from her eyes. She'd dreamt. She could picture the scene of her dream. When was the last time she'd done that? Her brow felt moist, and cool perspiration wet the back of her neck.

Rolling onto her stomach, she bunched one pillow under her right arm, pulling it to her chest. As she closed her eyes, she tried to think of soft rain or the crunch of gravel under her feet when she ran the Oakland fire trail. The gravel shifted and she inhaled deeply, pacing herself in her mind. Tomorrow, she would take a long run. She had almost managed to push herself back to sleep, when she heard a strange crunching sound.

Her eyes shot open. She heard the noise again. Not gravel. Someone walking on broken glass maybe. Someone in her house.

Alex tore the covers off and flung her bare feet onto the cool hardwood floor. Her gun was hanging on the holster in the downstairs closet. She used to keep it close, but then half the time she couldn't find it.

"Crap," she muttered, looking around. Her stretched T-shirt slipped off one shoulder and she quickly righted it. She lifted the baseball bat from the corner beside the bed and crept to the door.

With a deep breath, she pulled the door open slowly. Downstairs, she heard the sound of drawers opening. She halted. Someone *was* in her house. She looked back at the phone by the bed. She should call the police, but there wasn't time. She thought about the man who had called her. Had he been stalking her? Whoever he was, she wasn't letting him get away.

Hoisting the bat over her shoulder, she poised to strike and started down the hall.

She reached the top of the stairs and strained to hear below. It was silent now, although she hadn't heard the door. She moved slowly, creeping like a cat, but the wood on the stairs was old and it moaned beneath her feet. Her eyes adjusted to the blackness and she searched for shadows or movement. She paused three stairs from the bottom and waved the bat in a small circle like a player preparing to hit. Her arm muscles tightened and she kept the bat moving. It was all about having the momentum if she needed it.

Taking the last three steps, she glanced in each direction and then turned toward the den. She'd thought the noise had come from there. She took two steps and then spun around. She was sure she'd heard something, but couldn't see anyone.

Just as she started back, she felt his presence behind her. She whipped the bat around, but the man ducked and the bat hit the wall.

Before she could pull it back for another shot, he pushed her. She fell flat on her back, knocking the wind from her chest. In an effort to catch herself, she had dropped the bat.

Struggling for breath, Alex rolled and tried to regain her perch. She searched for the bat with her hands splayed on the cool floor. In one quick move, he landed on her back, pressing her down as she struggled to turn and free herself. "Get off me," she screamed.

She bucked at him, squirming to get loose. "I called the police—they're on their way."

"Don't threaten me," he snapped in the voice she'd heard on the phone. He cupped her head in one hand and slammed her face down.

Her forehead smacked the floor with a loud crack. She groaned and tried to fight, but her vision swam momentarily, leaving her dizzy. After a few seconds, she pushed herself up, steeling herself to be knocked down again. But when she looked around, the man was gone.

She stood quickly and, keeping her back to the wall, found the light switch. She blinked into the harsh glare as she searched the room for signs of the intruder.

One of the small windowpanes in her back door was broken, glass strewn across the floor. The door was now wide open. An engine gunned on the street. "Bastard," she screamed, grabbing the bat and running barefoot out of the house.

All she caught were the red taillights as he drove away. Dropping the bat, she sprinted after the car, hoping to get a look at the license plate when the car stopped at the corner.

Her feet pounded against the cement, jarring the bones in her ankles and sending pain through her shins. The spot where her head had hit the floor pounded in time with her stride. She pushed forward. The car reached the stop sign at the end of the block and she sprinted harder, faster. Every second counted.

But the car didn't stop. Instead, the driver barreled through full speed to the next corner and made a quick right, tires screeching as he disappeared from sight.

"Fucker," she cursed. She leaned over, pressing her hands into her knees as she caught her breath.

Suddenly, headlights shone toward her and she bolted behind the neighbor's Volvo for cover in case he had a gun. The car moved closer. Music blared from the radio.

A hand reached out of the car and Alex ducked. Something hit the street with a thump and she looked up. A newspaper. The newspaper delivery man. "Shit," she said, feeling foolish.

Running back into the street, she hailed down the vehicle. The driver of the red Ford truck was unshaven, with bushy eyebrows and small tired eyes, a cigarette hanging from his full lips.

"What?" he asked without removing his smoke.

Still breathless, she stopped at his window. "Did you see a car pass you on the next block?"

Only when his eyes took in her appearance like a starving man taking in the sight of a sirloin steak did she realize that she was wearing only a T-shirt and boxer shorts. Crossing her arms over her chest, she drew his gaze back to her face.

She stared hard, daring him to say anything inappropriate. Though she didn't smell alcohol, he smiled slowly and his eyes were dazed and unfocused, as if he had been drinking. She knew the look, and she recognized the other smell wafting from the truck. This was Berkeley, and normally she wouldn't bother with someone minding their own business, smoking some weed. But this guy was pissing her off.

"Uh, what were you saying?" he mumbled.

"A car—down that road, going the other way."

"I saw it. So what?"

"Did you get a good look at it?"

"I see cars every day on this road. I never pay attention." Without the view of her chest to enjoy, he seemed suddenly bored.

Annoyed, she sucked in a quick breath. "Any idea what kind of car it was?"

"What do I look like, a cop?"

She bit the inside of her cheek and forced herself not to reach in and pull him out through the window. "Listen, bud, I was just wondering if you got a look at the car."

After a moment of thought, he shook his head. "Nope." His chin cocked in the air, he looked back at her. "If you want, though, you can hop in and we can try to go catch him." One of his eyebrows snuck up his forehead and he gave her a crooked smile, his gaze traveling over her from head to toe.

She rolled her eyes. That was it. He had gone too far. She reached into the window and twisted his shirt in her fist. "What's your name, asshole?"

"Hey, hands off the digs, man. What's your deal?"

Alex didn't loosen her grip. "What's your name?"

He raised his hands dumbly. "Ray—the name's Ray, like sunshine."

"Ray what?"

"Denwood. Ray Dodson. You can call me Ray." He jacked up his eyebrows again.

Slowly, she let the smile curve on her lips. "Well, you can call me Officer. Officer Kincaid."

She watched his reaction, enjoying the quick disappearance of his dopey smile as adrenaline took over and his eyes darted around his truck for any incriminating evidence left in plain sight.

"And then you can tell me what exactly you have burning in there," she continued. "A controlled substance perhaps? From the smell of it, I've got enough to drag your ass out of the truck and search it."

"Uh—" His mouth remained open but nothing came out.

"I asked you for a little help. Did you see the goddamned car that passed you back there or not?"

His tongue hanging partially out of his mouth, he shook his head.

Letting go of his shirt, she wiped her hands together. Then, she walked slowly to the front of the truck, glanced down at his plate, and committed the sequence to memory. When she had it down, she walked back to the window and leaned in to Ray.

He sucked in a deep breath, as though he was going to try to hold it for the rest of the conversation.

"You know what I'm going to do, Ray?"

As he shook his head, a small whimpering noise escaped from his throat.

"I'm going to ask a favor."

He nodded quickly. "Sure, Officer. Anything."

"I want you to think long and hard about the car that passed you. If you remember the color, the make, anything, I want you to leave me a note as soon as possible. If I catch this guy and he saw you and you haven't contacted me, I'll find you."

"Absolutely, Officer. Anything I can do to help."

"And another thing. From now on, I want my paper right on the front porch every day, got it?"

Silent, he nodded again.

"Better yet, how about on the doormat? Is that going to be a problem, Ray?"

He shook his head.

"I didn't hear you."

"No problem, Officer."

"Get out of here."

Without listening for his response, she headed back to the house. She expected the truck to peel off but when she looked back, Ray appeared to be moving about six miles per hour.

Alex went inside and turned on every light she could find, stepping around the glass in the den. She searched the room for a sign as to what the intruder was looking for. She saw her Nikon camera staring at her from the top of her entertainment center. A stereo with CD player sat untouched behind the glass. Her wallet was still where she'd left it on the table by the door. And yet, in the kitchen, all the cabinets and drawers had been pulled open. What kind of burglar left a camera and a stereo but searched through drawers containing silverware?

The kitchen phone caught her eye and she ran a finger across it. Maybe she should call this in. She clenched her jaw and closed her eyes. She pictured the talk in the station when the word got out that she'd called in a crank call. But an intruder, that was serious. She looked around the room. Her gut said it all related to her waking up on Yolo. And she wasn't ready to tell anyone about that. She hoped she'd never have to.

She thought about keeping the break-in quiet. She wasn't hurt. Nothing was missing. Maybe there was something she could do on her own. Process the scene herself and avoid having to admit what had happened the other morning. She let her breath out. It was worth a try.

Taking the stairs by twos, Alex returned to her bedroom and pulled a small satchel off a shelf in her closet. Unzipping it, she looked inside. As a prank in the academy, she and few friends had gotten a hold of some black dusting powder and dusted the inside of a classmate's car. The black leather seats had hidden the dust and only after sitting down had he realized that he was covered in powder. The powder was notoriously difficult to get off, and he'd had to meet his in-laws for dinner with a black backside. Alex had kept the brush and powder in case the mood struck her again. Now she had better use for them.

In the kitchen, she found heavy plastic gloves in the cabinet under the sink and pulled them on. Using what looked like a big powder brush for makeup, she proceeded to dust the surface of the open cabinets, trailing black as she went. There were partial prints everywhere and it was difficult to tell which were newest. She continued across any cabinet or drawer she thought he might have touched, until she felt she had gotten them all.

Next, she brushed the broken glass from the window into a paper bag and stapled it shut. Using a roll of transparent packing tape, Alex lifted the prints she found off the cabinets and onto clean white sheets of writing paper she never used. When she was done, she had eight decent samples. The rest of the prints were piled on top of each other until they were completely illegible.

Sitting at her desk, she pulled out an ink pad that

had been her mother's and printed herself on a clean sheet. She was no expert, but she knew the basics of fingerprinting from the academy. There were four types of print classifications: the plain arch; the tented arch, where the arch was almost triangular in shape; the whirl, where it looked like the ridges created a spiral; and the loop, which looked like a tented arch that had circled back on itself. Some people had all four types of prints. After a fingerprint analyst determined the basic print style, he or she classified an additional ten to twelve points and entered that series of numbers into a computer search. Alex couldn't do that, but she should be able to at least determine if all the prints were hers.

Alex's prints were all whirls, the most common type. One by one, she walked through the prints she'd found, searching for one that wasn't hers. She matched her pointer finger twice, her thumb four times, and there were two prints of her index finger. There were no one else's prints. She thought about the statement that made about her life. She really didn't have people over. With the men in her life, she went mostly to their places, more comfortable not sharing her house. With friends, she met them out. Only Roback occasionally came over, and they spent very little time in the kitchen.

The lack of prints told her something far more important, though—that her intruder had been careful. Alex would have much rather seen prints all over the place. The fact that someone worried about the possible evidence trail meant he was thinking—and a thinking criminal was a dangerous one.

Alex caught her reflection in a silver bowl on the counter. Leaning down, her hands still smudged with ink, she ran her fingers across the bluish black formation on her forehead. She thought back to the struggle, to the moments before he pushed her head to the floor. She'd felt his thumb on the inside of her arm. He couldn't have been wearing gloves.

Taking the powder, brush, and tape into the small downstairs bathroom, Alex turned sideways in the mirror. She dipped the brush into the powder with her left hand and brushed it along the inside of her arm. The light was awkward, so she twisted her arm to try to see if the print showed on her skin. Unable to tell, she went and found a flashlight, shining the light on her skin. Nothing. Setting the light down, she proceeded to dip the brush in the powder and test another patch of skin, more to the right. Nothing. She tried again, imagining his finger on her skin. Where had he touched her? She thought about the kitchen gloves she had worn and wondered if they had rubbed the print off.

On the last try, she chose a spot farther up her arm. Studying the results in the light, she saw something. Twisting the flashlight to get a better angle, she caught the image of tiny ridges that formed what looked like a tented arch. It was almost a perfect thumbprint. "You screwed up, asshole."

Blowing off the excess dust, Alex cut a piece of tape and lay it across the print, making sure there were no air bubbles. Then, in a smooth motion, she pulled the tape off and put it on a clean piece of white paper. She compared the print to the others she'd found. It was definitely not hers. Prints only lasted on cool, dry human skin, and she was thankful he'd touched her arm rather than her neck, where the moisture would've ruined the image.

She looked down at the black print and wondered what she could do about finding a match. She'd need a fingerprint analyst, since she didn't have any suspects' prints to compare it to. If she called the police and reported the incident, finding the matching print might be a simple matter of sending it to the lab to do a computer search. But she didn't want to call it in. If she did and she didn't mention the incident on Yolo, then she would be lying. She didn't want to lie. She just didn't want to tell the truth yet either. And there was someone else who could help her with the print.

Elsa Thomas owed Alex a favor for getting her nephew out of trouble a few times. Her husband was a fingerprint analyst at the Contra Costa County Sheriff Department's Criminal Information Bureau. He could classify the print and have it run on the state's fingerprint system, CAL ID.

If they didn't find a match in California, he could run it in the FBI's AFIS system, too. Sending it to Elsa's husband, Byron, also meant it wouldn't go to the same lab she dealt with for Alameda County. Byron was definitely her best bet. She trusted Elsa to handle the matter with the same discretion that Alex had used when her nephew should have been arrested for stealing a neighbor's car.

Alex pulled her address book from the kitchen drawer and found Elsa's numbers. It was the middle of the night so Alex dialed Elsa's work number and left her an urgent message, asking Elsa to call as soon as she had a minute and could talk freely.

There was nothing to do now but try to get some sleep. She'd clean up tomorrow. Alex looked around at the black powder that dusted the counters and floor. She still had no idea what the man was after, why he'd come, or who he was. She thought about the caller. *See if you can find the present I left for you and one I took.* It seemed impossible to imagine that he and the intruder were two different people.

Having tucked the thumbprint and the swept-up glass into a cupboard, Alex opened cabinets and drawers in search of what "present" he'd meant. She found nothing. Nothing had been left or taken that she could see. She eyed the knife block that had been her mother's and counted six knives and four empty slots. Suddenly she wondered if one was missing. Had there been seven before? Eight? She never paid attention. Had he been in the kitchen looking for a weapon to kill her? He'd had a chance and he'd let her go. She didn't think he wanted her dead, but then what did he want?

A sense of dread poured over her like ice water. He was smart. He was strong. He knew things that could damage her, things from the night she couldn't remember. And now he wanted something.

Chapter Seven

Alex arrived at the station at ten after seven, determined to force things to move forward again. She had arranged, with James's reluctant help, to assist at the Loeffler crime scene for a couple of days. The doctor had written that he didn't want her back on the streets, and helping with the investigation was a good way to utilize her without disobeying doctor's orders. The department was just understaffed enough to get her captain to go for it. She'd spent an hour covering the bluish black bruise above her right eye. Between the makeup and the careful placement of her bangs, it was just barely hidden.

On her way to meet James, she stopped by the reference area and located the copy of the *Physicians' Desk Reference*. With a quick look over one shoulder, she found the listing for Restoril. Running her finger down the entry, she scanned the adverse reactions—drowsiness, headache, fatigue, nervousness, lethargy, anxiety, blurred vision, nightmares. No violence.

"What've you got there?"

Hearing Greg's voice, she started to close the book, but he put his hand in it before she could get it closed.

Throwing it back open, he scanned the page until he found what she'd been looking at. "Restoril, huh?"

"Just curious," she said.

He backed her to a file cabinet. "Bullshit."

She waved him off and started to leave. "Think what you want, Roback."

"Something's going on, Alex."

"Nothing's going on," she snapped back.

He reached up and pushed her bangs aside. "What happened to your head?"

She flinched and pulled back. "I was jumped by a mugger if you don't recall."

"I thought you hit the back of your head."

"Well, he got me in the forehead with his fist."

Watching her, he shook his head. Then, when she didn't respond, he said, "I heard you're working the scene." His tone was cool.

She nodded.

"I guess I'll see you around then." He turned and walked away before she could answer.

She put away the *PDR* and headed to James's office.

"You ready?" he asked when she arrived, handing her a cup of coffee.

She took it and thanked him. "Yep," she said, looking at the dark coffee. It would be her third cup since four this morning, and she wasn't sure it was a good idea. Her stomach already had the rattle of a baby's toy.

To keep herself from drinking any more, she set the coffee on the table.

"Lombardi's heading back over to the house this morning. Captain Lyke was going to call him, so he should know you're coming by now. Just go on back there and I'll see you later." James started to say good-bye.

"James."

He looked up.

She met his eyes. "I just wanted to say thanks."

"Don't thank me. Just don't do anything stupid."

She knew what he meant was don't do anything stupid *again*. She wouldn't. She was back in control.

In her gear, she headed for the detective division.

Elsa hadn't called back, but it was still early. She felt a little nervous as she walked down the corridor.

This was normal. Her first cadaver, she reminded herself. Her first death. But the body hadn't bothered her. It had been something else—recognizing him, perhaps. Forcing air into her lungs, she opened the door and stuck her head into the detective division.

Lombardi sat hunched in his chair. "Wondering when you'd arrive," he said without turning around.

She glanced at the clock on the wall. It was only seven-twenty.

"I like to start by seven."

"Right." Before her mouth had a chance to debate the issue, she bit her tongue.

"We're heading back to the house." He turned and looked at her for the first time. "So, if you've got everything together . . ."

She motioned to herself and nodded. "This is it."

Leaning back, he cocked an eyebrow. "Normally the detective division wears street clothes. It's hard to be undercover when you're dressed as a cop."

She stared down at her uniform and winced. "It's—"

"Yeah, yeah. Habit, I know," he interrupted, lumbering out of the chair and turning away from her.

"I'll remember tomorrow."

"I would hope so," he mumbled, just loud enough for her to hear. Pulling his lucky coat off a tall stand-alone coat rack that looked as though it belonged in an old Dick Tracy movie, he slung it over his shoulders. "One more thing," he added as they stepped into the hall.

"Sure."

"No more fainting. I can't take that shit."

Refusing to allow her mouth to open, she nodded and followed him out of the station. "We can take my car if you want," she suggested when they reached the police lot.

His eyebrows nearly firing off his forehead, he halted in the street. "And you drive?"

"Yes."

Without breaking a smile, he emitted a long, loud chortle. "No way. I don't ever go anywhere with a broad driving. I enjoy my life, thanks."

Suddenly, she couldn't hold herself back. "Speaking of bad drivers, did you hear what happened to the side of the station over there?" She motioned to the back of the lot, knowing it was Lombardi who had done the damage. "Someone reversed right into the wall."

"Shut up, smart ass," he growled.

She fastened her seat belt, though Lombardi made no move to do the same. "So what's the status with the case so far?" she asked to redirect the conversation.

Lombardi seemed to relax against the seat. "We finished the printing last night—while you were out cold, I figure."

Allowing him a return jab, she nodded. She deserved it.

"It's all at the lab now. Won't know for a couple days at least. The DNA takes a month, if they're quick. Fibers, more like two weeks."

"Who was he?"

One eyebrow lifted, he glanced over at her. "Here's where things get interesting." He said the word in three syllables—in-trest-ing. "He was a criminal prosecutor in the city. Did mostly kid stuff—abuse, the kid that was killed and found on the coast last year . . ."

She nodded.

"Well, it was that kind of shit."

"Sounds like the type to gather enemies."

"And fast. He's also recently separated."

Remembering Ramona Quay's slip, she asked, "Where's the wife?"

"Kensington." Kensington was the next town past

Berkeley, a small, mostly residential area. "I sent Kostopolis to talk to her this morning. Guess the wife's living with a new boyfriend, and his kids weren't crazy about Mr. Loeffler."

Alex looked over at him. "What do you mean they weren't crazy about him?"

Lombardi shrugged. "You need a map? Older kid says he hates Loeffler's guts. Still not sure why. Maybe because he blames him for his dad's new live-in girlfriend." He shook his head and then spit out the window. "Jesus, I'm glad I never let Martha convince me to have kids—crazy Menendez brothers and shit. Who needs that? I got people out here that want to kill me. I don't need to go home to it."

"How about your wife?"

For a moment, Alex saw the flicker of a smile, but he didn't let it through. "Really fucking funny, Kincaid. Jesus Christ, I got Jerry fucking Seinfeld now."

She smiled. "You think the kid could've killed Loeffler?"

"Possible."

She thought for a moment, unable to make sense of the theory. "Why would the new boyfriend's kid kill Loeffler? If he didn't like his dad's girlfriend, he'd kill her, not her soon-to-be ex-husband."

He shrugged. "Maybe. Got to look at it every way. I mean, why does any of this crap happen? I only got to solve it. I don't pretend to get it."

"Any idea why they cut off his hand?"

He shook his head casually. It was as though they were talking about the weather. "Nope. Probably meant something to the perp, though. Some guys think they're making a statement—you know, some guy's beating his kid or something and Loeffler's the prosecutor. Guy thinks he should be able to beat his own kid, right?"

Though she wasn't sure she followed, she nodded for him to continue. "So he gets thrown in jail and when he gets out, he kills Loeffler and cuts his hand off to show how no one stops him from fucking with his own kid."

"That's what you think happened?"

He glanced over at her and shrugged. "I got no idea. Just a thought. Whatever the reason, guy's fucked up."

"So what are we doing?"

"Going through the house for anything we can figure out."

As he turned onto Yolo, she tried not to think about the previous morning. He took a long look at her, as though waiting for her to crack. "We agreed, right?"

"Agreed?"

"No fainting," he said, pulling to the curb.

"Right."

He cursed again, and Alex looked out the window. The bottom of the stairs was roped off with crime scene tape, and a group of reporters crowded the area. News that one of the local D.A.'s was murdered had clearly gotten out. Lombardi was out of the car before Alex even had her seat belt off.

She got out and pushed past the reporters, reaching the house before Lombardi.

"Excuse me," one of them said, grabbing at her arm.

"No comment." She extracted herself and headed up the stairs. It wasn't her job to comment. Since she'd been on the force, she hadn't watched the news with the same eyes. Like wolves, reporters seemed to smell fresh blood and pounce.

"Detective, are there any suspects at this time?" one hollered.

"Is it true this was a mob hit?" another yelled.

"Is it true that the deceased was recently separated and the wife is now living with her new boyfriend?"

Lombardi stood three steps up and waved his arms to shut them up. "As soon as we know anything, we will make a statement to the press. In the meantime, I'm not at liberty to answer any questions."

As the pack of reporters started firing questions at him again, he turned and headed up the stairs.

"Bunch of vultures," he mumbled as he reached Alex at the top of the stairs.

He pulled two pairs of surgical gloves from the cardboard box tucked under his arm, handed her one, and then put his own on before touching the door. Inside, several people were at work already. They really did start early.

Lombardi motioned her to follow him and he led her toward the dark hallway. The staircase formed a straight-edged C in the middle of the entryway, a skylight shining down on the wood floors. A rich burgundy rug covered the middle of the stairwell like a long red tongue. Suddenly, there were a million details she hadn't noticed before.

As Lombardi opened a door and flipped on a light, she focused on the room. Painted maroon, it had mahogany bookshelves along an entire wall. Just like a lawyer, she thought. An elk head stared at her from the far wall, mounted above a spacious wooden desk.

"And I thought *I* was having a bad week," she mumbled. She hoped that thing was mounted well. This was not the day to have something fall on her head.

Loeffler's desk was strewn with papers in no apparent order. The fingerprint crew had long since come and gone. She wondered if they had made this mess. She thought about the intruder who had rifled through her kitchen, and she suppressed the angry shivers that ran along her arms.

"You think someone was in here?"

Lombardi looked around. "Not sure. That, or the guy was a slob. See if you can make some sense of this shit."

"Right."

He pointed to two large file cabinets along one wall. "Check all of it—every scrap of paper, every book. Pull anything remotely screwy."

She nodded.

"Don't doubt yourself. If it looks like it has a strange-colored ink, pull it. Any questions, I'll be around."

"Got it."

He started to leave and stopped. "It's not a one-day job, Kincaid. Someone else will go through it after you. I never leave anything to one person's opinion."

"Thank God," she muttered when he left. She started at the desk, reading each piece of paper, trying to soak in its content and figure its worth. Next, she separated the papers by subject and created piles on the floor. Organizing the life of a dead guy wasn't exactly how she had envisioned spending her days, but she knew as a detective it would be a large part of her job. She wondered who would organize her stuff when she died. As she started to look through things, she also couldn't help but wonder if she would find something to explain why she'd been on Loeffler's street that morning.

Pushing the thought aside, she picked up his Palm Pilot, searching for anything that looked interesting. It was just a cursory check since the contents would be downloaded to a computer and systematically searched back at the station. The conveniences of technology.

Sitting in Loeffler's big chair, Alex used the stylus pen and clicked through his calendar. He had notations all over the place, but few of them made any sense to her. An L followed by a person's name seemed to indicate a lunch date. D probably meant dinner. The names looked mostly like last names, so it was tough to tell if they were men or women. Three days ago he'd had an "L=Sam School." She assumed Sam must be one of his clients.

In between meals, he had names with shorthand notations that she thought probably referred to his cases. The day before he died, he had three meetings. One read "NT SEC @10, SQ." Maybe NT was a person or maybe it referred to a case. The only thing she could think of for SEC was the Securities and Exchange Commission, but Loeffler was in a different type of law. Alex made notes: NT? Name? Person? Case? SEC? SQ? Some questions? Was that a place? The next was "L=Mrs. @1." Alex guessed that was probably a lunch with his wife.

The last entry on that day was at six P.M. It read "Call: N, K, DR, and PAPD." Alex wrote the initials down. PAPD sounded like Palo Alto Police Department. It was the only one she could figure. She made a note to look for cases that involved the Palo Alto Police. She worked her way backwards in his calendar without much success. He seemed to have lunch with the missus two or three times a week. Perhaps they were trying to work things out. She made a note that someone should find out where they'd eaten and how it had gone.

Loeffler also had a standing breakfast on Wednesdays with someone named Keith. And he ate every Thursday night with Cam. She wrote the names down to cross-reference with the rest of his files, although she assumed they were friends. Also, there was a weekly notation for "Q" at 7:30 each Monday, which Alex thought was probably was Mrs. Quay's weekly cleaning date. She could confirm that one easily enough. Other than that, she couldn't make out a single thing in Loeffler's shorthand.

By noon, she was exhausted and famished. Brenda and her partner, Lou, a short, stout Italian with dark sideburns and a thick mustache, brought by sandwiches.

"I got you turkey, lettuce, tomato, pickles, yellow mustard, no mayonnaise," Brenda said, handing her the Subway bag.

"You're an angel."

"I know." She motioned to Alex's head. "That guy really smacked you, didn't he?"

Alex nodded.

"Hurt much?"

"Not so much anymore."

Brenda nodded. "Listen, I was hoping we could have dinner this week. Just to talk."

Alex looked at her friend and raised an eyebrow. "Roback talk to you?" she asked, wondering how much he'd told her.

Brenda raised her arms in a gesture of innocence. "Can't a girl ask a friend to dinner?"

Alex opened the sandwich and took a bite. "Right."

"He's a little worried. So?"

Alex swallowed, realizing how famished she was. "I'll come, but I'm fine." She glanced over her shoulder. "Just embarrassed as all hell," she lied. "So, if we go, just regular girl talk. Agreed?"

Brenda touched her shoulder and shook her head. "Can't stand to have anyone see you're human, can you?"

"Hell no. Anyway, we're not supposed to be human. We're cops."

"Right. Advice I think you take too seriously. Perhaps the reason you're still single and thirty— "

Alex put her hand up. "Enough."

Brenda shrugged in defeat. "All right. I'm done."

Alex looked at her friend with a skeptical eye. Brenda was never finished. "You'd better be. I'll get up and leave the restaurant if you bring up this nonsense at dinner. It upsets my appetite."

Brenda shook her head. "All the women I know your age are scrambling for a man. You, you're sending them away. Girl, you amaze me."

"I'm glad. I've got no one else to amaze."

"You know, Mark works with a very nice professor of—"

She glared at her friend. "Set me up, but not this week. Now, are we having dinner or not?"

Brenda surrendered. "Fine. When?"

"How about tomorrow? Pomodoro's on College at about eight."

"Perfect. Mark's teaching that night anyway."

"I'll be there. I've been craving Italian."

Brenda laughed. "Knowing you, you've been eating nothing but pasta for weeks."

Alex shrugged. "True, but I still crave it."

"Let me know if you change your mind about the professor. I think he's available Saturday."

"Saturday—that's four days away and he doesn't have plans? I'm worried already."

Brenda leaned forward and lowered her voice. "What happened to that guy Jed? You never talk about him anymore."

Alex shrugged.

"He was sweet, attractive, and real into you."

"He was nice enough, but he wanted to *talk* about every little thing."

Brenda laughed out loud. "You sound like one of Mark's baseball buddies. So it's Tom?"

Alex shrugged. "That's depends. Any cute baseball buddies? Maybe you should set me up with one of them."

Brenda laughed and excused herself, and Alex went outside to finish her sandwich. Engulf was a more accurate description. The sandwich disappeared in three minutes flat. Even Lombardi looked impressed.

Back in the den, she started in on the filing cabinets, opening each and peering at its contents. She wanted to do the most entertaining stuff first.

She tried to open the bottom drawer, but couldn't. She hadn't seen a key in the desk. Maybe he kept it with him. When she slammed the top drawer to go ask Lombardi, she heard the faint tink of metal against metal. Halting, she opened the drawer again. No sound. Slamming it, she heard the tink again. It came from behind the cabinet.

Reaching around the cabinet, she walked her fingers along the cool metal. Her hand hit a hook and she felt for the keys. "Bingo," she said.

Dangling the keys, she looked for the best match. Her first try opened the drawer. She sat on the ground and leaned over the drawer, picking up the first in a stack of videotapes. "Little Tammy's new trix," it read in black print. Who was Tammy? Putting it aside, she looked through the rest of the pile. From the titles, she guessed they were probably porn. It shouldn't have surprised her. Why else keep the videos under lock and key?

As she stacked the tapes on the floor, something at the bottom of the drawer caught her eye. She pulled out what looked like a class picture and studied it. "Mrs. Weiserman's Second Grade Class," the sign beneath the rows of children read. Frowning, she studied the faces.

Someone had drawn thick black Xs through the children's faces. She looked through the rows. All the faces were X'd out except two—a little blond boy in the first row and a taller dark-haired boy at the back. To one side, someone had also drawn in a stick figure with a red pen. It had long curly hair and its face remained X-less.

She remembered doing something similar to her fifth-grade class picture. With a thumbtack, she had poked over all the kids she didn't like. Her mother had been furious. Lots of kids probably marked all over their class pictures, but Loeffler didn't have any kids. She wondered if it was related to one of Loeffler's cases or to the porn.

Holding the picture in her left hand, she picked up the last tape again with her right hand and glanced at its title. "Pre-pubs," it read and she wondered what on earth that meant. She read the fine print—starring

Pretty Priscilla O., whoever that was. Not that she was up on the porn stars. She spotted the TV and crossed to it, then pushed the tape into the VCR and turned on the power.

As she waited for a picture to appear, she glanced at the school picture again. Something about the kids' clothes was strange. They looked old or something. The sign at the bottom of the picture caught her eye again. 1970 to 1971, it read. 1971? Chewing on her pen, Alex stared at the faces. Was this an old case Loeffler was working on?

A small voice caught her attention and she looked up at the TV to see a young, curly brown-haired girl no older than ten or eleven, completely naked, her hand around a grown man's penis.

"Holy shit," Alex said, running for Lombardi.

Chapter Eight

Lombardi followed Alex toward the den, a roast beef sandwich smothered in mayonnaise hanging from his lips. "Can't this wait a minute?" he mumbled past the bite he'd shoved into his mouth.

She stayed a step ahead of him, wanting to gauge his reaction when he saw the video. "I don't think so." Watching his face, she entered the den and halted.

Lombardi squinted and slowly moved closer to the television. His eyes grew wide, and she saw their whites for the first time. He dropped his sandwich, spitting the bite from his mouth into his hand and turning from the TV in disgust. "Holy shit."

She kept her eyes off the screen, refusing to look at the little girl's tiny mouth around the man. The tape had been upsetting once—she didn't need another go at it. "That's what I said."

Lombardi dropped his sandwich in the garbage. "Turn that shit off."

Averting her eyes, Alex flipped the television off.

Lombardi stared out the window for a moment and then faced her again. He shook his head. "Guy was a fucking prosecutor—worked for the city. The media's going to love this."

She nodded. "I know. Sick, isn't it?" Although she couldn't see the man's face, she knew it wasn't Loeffler—the build was wrong.

A deep frown turned Lombardi's mouth down.

"World's one crazy asshole after another. Are there any last names on the labels?"

She shook her head.

"Damn. I must've done something in my last life. Maybe I was Hitler or some shit because someone's punishing me for something. I always get the sick bastards. At least it's a lead."

Pausing, she made the calculation. "I think Hitler would've have died after you were—"

He glared at her. "Can it, Kincaid. Let's take the tapes with us. Find out where they're from. The tape looks homemade. Get a list of his cases. See if any were child pornography–related."

"Case-related. Maybe you're right."

"Maybe—maybe not. Lawyers are fucked up. Some poor sucker in the lab is going to have to look through those tapes for an adult face or try to track down the names of the kids. For all we know, Loeffler made them himself."

"That would give some parent a hell of a reason to knock him off."

Lombardi met her gaze. "Exactly. I'll send the tapes to the station. Jesus Christ." With a quick look back, he added, "Good job on that."

"Thanks."

His eyes narrowed. "Holding up okay?"

She stared at the floor, embarrassed. "Fine, thanks." Turning back to the drawer, she put the tapes in a plastic evidence bag.

People were packing up by quarter to six. Though Alex would have liked to work longer, Lombardi wouldn't let her stay at a crime scene on her own. Truth was, she wasn't all that anxious to go home. Home didn't hold that much appeal anymore, she thought as she stretched her legs. She had spent the majority of the day on her knees, sorting files into stacks that now littered the floor. Loeffler kept a lot of files at home.

From what she could tell, they were mostly photo-copies of the originals that were surely stored at his office. Maybe he kept duplicates for security or per-haps he preferred to work here with the elk.

She had read a few of his cases. One thing was for sure, William Loeffler prosecuted some real sick puppies. The worst she'd read was about a man who had killed his own two kids, locking them in the trunk of his old car and lighting it on fire because they hadn't behaved. He'd been convicted and sentenced to death. A small justice it seemed now, a tiny price to pay for murdering his children.

Alex shook her head and squeezed her eyes shut, hoping that somewhere in heaven or hell there existed a justice system that was truly just. She thought about the guy she'd taken down yesterday. At least she was making a difference. If nothing else, she could keep some of these fuckers off the streets.

On a legal pad, she had listed the names of the criminals Loeffler had prosecuted. She had twelve al-ready, and she had gotten through only one of his three file drawers. A child killer, two hit-and-runs, three pedophiles—one a day-care professional, one a teacher, one an uncle, all people with access to chil-dren. That's what they always said about pedophiles. She thought about her little nieces and nephews and wondered about their day-care professionals, their teachers.

Six parental abuse cases. What disgusted her most was the number of children who had to stand up in court against their own parents, children whose an-guish and pain had been brought to light by strange bruises caught in school or unusually frequent visits to the ER. And when the arrest was made, the child screamed for his or her Mommy or Daddy—screamed for the very same person who had broken their bones and blackened their eyes.

Don't get involved, Kincaid. She knew better. In

only six months, she had seen battered children, heard the lame excuses parents gave her for their children's horrible injuries—burns and belt marks, the marks of adult hands bruised into their tiny thighs. It was sick, demented, and it was her job to stop it. But it wasn't up to her to think about what the children would suffer after the abuses had ended. The family psychologists, people like Brittany and Judith Richards, had to pick up the pieces and reform the broken child.

She couldn't do that—wasn't trained to do it. Certainly not if she wanted to keep her objectivity, which was what made her a good police officer, would make her a strong witness in the courtroom. It was her job to gather the facts, not make judgments. Judges made those.

Still, somehow a crack had started to develop in the strong metal cover she thought she had secured around her emotions. She had to find the leak and seal it before it began to interfere with work.

Picking up the class picture again, she stared at it before setting it in its own pile. Nothing she had come across so far could explain either the child porn tapes or the strange photograph. Maybe she would have better luck tomorrow.

Lombardi appeared at the door, his lucky coat pulled to his chest as though he gained comfort from its proximity. Maybe she ought to get a lucky coat. Based on her week so far, she could use one.

She gathered her legal pad and notes and brushed her pants off, taking a last look around the room.

"It'll look just like this tomorrow," he said.

She smiled. "I know. I'd like to keep going—"

He shook his head. "Save your energy. I hope you can think of better things to do with yourself this evening."

Of course she could, couldn't she? As she headed out the door, she thought for a moment. Sad thing was, nothing came to mind. She had canceled her date with Tom. Her empty house flashed before her, and suddenly she wondered if Tom had made other plans. He would at least get her mind off work. She stared at her empty wrist. "Shit," she cursed. "What time is it?"

"Five to six. Late for a date?"

"No, a guy's coming to fix my window." As soon as the words had spilled from her mouth, she wished she could steal them back.

Lombardi's gaze fixed on hers, and blood rushed to her cheeks. "What happened to the window?"

"A kid hit a ball through it," she lied.

Lombardi stared at her a moment too long.

She stared back. It wasn't her style to flush. Her ancestry seemed to stop at her forehead. Though she had red Irish hair and occasionally the fiery Irish temper, she didn't have freckles or the naturally ruddy complexion that was typically Irish.

Thankfully, Lombardi didn't comment, turning abruptly and heading for the front door. "I'll drop you at the station, then."

Exhaling, she followed him and chastised herself for not watching her mouth.

Alex arrived at her house just as the glass truck pulled away. She honked for him to stop as she parked at the curb. The repairman had long graying frizzy hair, the thinning strands pulled into a low ponytail and bound by a rubber band. His wiry eyebrows came together when he frowned. Heavy jowls wobbled as he growled, "You're late."

She nodded apologetically. "I know, I'm sorry. I got caught at the station."

His frown lifted slightly as he lumbered out of his car and slammed the door. "You on the radio?"

Leading him toward the back door, she shook her head. "Police station. I'm a cop."

Though she didn't turn around to see his expression, she thought she could imagine it. It was probably the

same one she had seen at least two hundred times,
especially from men. But even the women eyed her
head to toe and said things like "A cop? But you're
so small," or "I thought cops had to be strong." She
stopped at the door and pointed to the broken pane.
"The window's right here."

Silently, he pulled a tape measure from his tool belt
and measured the sill.

After studying the window another minute, he said,
"Just need some tools from my truck."

While the repairman worked on the window, Alex
waited impatiently. She wanted him to be done so she
could put the incident out of her mind. She wanted
the window to be the end of it. Sitting herself on the
couch, she looked around the downstairs for something to do. She dialed Tom's number and waited for
an answer. When she heard the familiar greeting on
his answering machine, though, she hung up. Another
night in.

The click and clack of the repairman's tools finally
stopped.

"All done," he said.

With a deep breath, she looked at the window and
nodded. "Thanks."

"No problem."

It was over. She exhaled. Thank God.

"Just be easy on the door the next twenty-four
hours or so."

"Will do." Relieved that sixty dollars was enough
to erase the incident, she retrieved her checkbook and
paid him. She shut the door gently and locked the
bolt.

Tomorrow was another solid day of work and she
wanted to be sharp for it. The phone rang and she
stared at it through two rings, cursing herself for pausing. Gathering her courage, she snapped it up.

"Alex," the older female voice said.

"Yes," she said, after a moment's hesitation.

"It's Judith Richards."

Alex exhaled. "Thanks for calling me back."

"No problem. What can I do for you?"

"I wanted to talk to you about something that happened on the job."

"James called to tell me a little about it."

"Of course."

Judith hesitated. "It's department policy for a captain to call before the officer does. James was just doing his job."

"Normally you would have heard from my captain, then, instead of James. But I did want to set up a time to meet with you." She paused to shift the conversation away from James. "Brittany told me you used to come over for coffee and cookies after school and we'd talk about my dreams."

"You sound like you don't remember."

"I remember your visits, but not the dreams specifically."

"That's not unusual. It was a long time ago. You used to have nightmares. I think your mother was more worried than she needed to be. Most kids I talk to have nightmares. Plus, I've dealt with much, much worse than that."

"I heard something about your patients who shot each other."

"Now that was the strangest situation I've ever had. And the scariest. I do some work with people recently released from prison. Brittany probably told you about that." It was a statement, not a question. "She was always fascinated by that story. I sometimes wonder what kept her out of law enforcement while you and James became officers." Judith paused. "Anyway, as I said, your mother used to have me over, but that was ages ago."

"Were my nightmares more frequent than normal?"

Judith laughed. "I just think you had more lung

capacity than most kids. They heard you on the next block."

"Do you happen to remember when they stopped?" Alex asked, growing intrigued.

"Not exactly. Your mother said you just seemed to outgrow them. I'd guess you were about eight or nine."

"I'd be curious to hear more about them, if you remember."

"I'm sure I can dredge up some of it," Judith offered. "It's a little unorthodox, but why don't you come to the house on Friday for dinner and we'll chat. Mad Dog Schroeder is driving me a bit nuts with extra work, and I hadn't planned to go back to the station until next week if possible. Does that work for you?"

"Perfect."

"Great." Judith recited directions to her house in North Berkeley and Alex wrote them down along with the date and time. She wondered how much would change in three days.

Alex thanked her and hung up. Starving, she hunted for something to eat. She found a box of penne then checked the refrigerator for pasta sauce. Besides the milk, of which she polished off almost a gallon a week, there was little else in the refrigerator. She had tried to keep vegetables, but even carrots couldn't survive long enough for her to get around to eating them. Moving the milk aside, she pulled out a jar of Classico four cheese sauce.

She ate quickly, as she always did, leaning over the counter in her kitchen. She didn't find food relaxing, so she made meals the way she did everything else—efficiently and with purpose.

Ready for some much-needed sleep, she brushed her teeth and flossed, something she rarely remembered, then was headed for her bedroom when the phone rang. She glanced at her bedside clock, thinking this was about the same time the phone had rung last night.

It was him. She was ready. She let the machine click on and picked up the receiver as soon as it had started to record. "Hello?"

The line was dead.

She set the phone down and took two steps before it rang again. He wasn't going to wait for the machine. Impatient, she snatched the phone up.

"Kincaid," she answered, in an attempt to sound tough despite her pounding heart.

"Kincaid now, is it?" came the same spitting voice.

This time she was prepared, though, and her anger rushed up. She was not playing games.

The caller laughed in her ear, his voice cracking into high squeals of delight.

Her stomach tied in a knot of metal, Alex forced the fear from her veins. She had to be in control. "This will be your last call. I'm having this number disconnected after we hang up. So why don't you go ahead and say whatever it is you called to say? Then, you can crawl back into whatever hole you came out of."

"Oh, that's not nice, Kincaid."

"You have five seconds." She wanted to hang up, but curiosity at what he knew won out. "One."

"Well, if that's how you want it, we might as well cut to the chase."

Something sour rose in her throat and strangled the words as they escaped from her mouth. "Two," she continued.

"Having the glass replaced won't make me go away. I know what you're thinking. I could see it in your eyes when you paid the glass guy and sent him on his way. It's not that easy. You haven't even found the presents I left you."

"Presents?"

"Presents," he repeated. "One of them is kind of fun . . ."

"And the other?"

"Is just nasty. And whoever finds that one is going to want to put little Alex behind bars."

"You're full of shit," she snapped.

"Try another cup of tea, Alex. Maybe that will help jog your memory."

Alex thought about the tea she'd had in her bath. He'd been watching her back then. The thought gave her chills. She spun to the window. "Listen, you son of a—" But the line was dead.

Furious, she slammed the phone down and ran to the door. Throwing the door open, she stared in both directions down the dark street. He could have been anywhere—in a parked car or behind a bush or tree—watching her. The thought attacked her like a thousand pins, sending stabs of panic through her chest.

Back inside, she closed and locked the door and proceeded to shut the curtains. He would be smiling, she thought, but she didn't care. With the curtains shut, she dialed *69 and again heard the error recording.

"Damn," she croaked, slamming the phone down.

Marching to the center of her kitchen, she paused and then turned in a slow circle. "Tea," she said out loud. "Tea." She opened the cupboard where she kept the tea bags and searched through them one by one. Nothing appeared strange. Lifting one to the light, she stared through it, wondering what he could've replaced the tea with. But it just looked like tea. *Put little Alex behind bars,* he'd said. She looked for a tea bag she didn't recognize, thinking maybe he'd planted marijuana, but there was nothing.

Next, she rummaged through the drawers where she kept the tea strainer, opened the teakettle, emptied out the teapots that had been her mother's, sitting high on shelves. Nothing. Nothing. Nothing.

What the hell present was he talking about? She

pushed her bangs off her forehead and flinched at the bruise, still tender beneath her hand. Determined, she decided to make herself a cup of tea just like she had the other night before her bath.

She filled the kettle with water, scanning the area around the sink. Then, opening a canister where she kept some specialty teas, she searched through it and found one cranberry craze. Nothing appeared out of the ordinary. She opened the cupboard and pulled down a mug and set it on the counter. As she did, she frowned and looked back up at the shelf that housed her eclectic collection of mugs. Two back, she spotted one she didn't recognize.

Pulling up a chair, she took a dishcloth and reached for the unfamiliar mug. Touching it only along one edge to avoid destroying fingerprints, Alex lifted it off the shelf. She twisted it until she saw a photograph that had been scanned onto one side of the mug. She'd seen similar mugs being sold in souvenir shops. It was a casual snapshot of a man and a woman on a beach. She stared at the woman. She wasn't familiar. Turning her gaze to the man, she gasped. The teakettle whistle blew and Alex spun around, the mug leaping from her hand and making a loud popping sound as it broke on the floor.

Alex didn't move, listening to the screaming kettle as though it were her own voice. From a jagged piece of broken mug, William Loeffler stared up at her.

Chapter Nine

Alex closed the paper bag containing the pieces of the coffee mug and put it on the shelf next to the bags containing the caller's fingerprint and the fragments of her window. Then, taking a last look around her kitchen, she climbed the stairs toward bed. She thought about the first call and then the break-in. She'd been stupid not to report it. It was unprofessional.

A cop should always obey the law to the letter. She knew that's the way James would see it. And as soon as she'd realized someone was in her house, a smart cop would have called the police. Why hadn't she? She tried to get inside her own mind, remembering the morning before, waking up in her car, then seeing Loeffler. Because she didn't know what had happened that night. And someone else did. What if she'd done something bad—something terrible. Could she have killed Loeffler? No. It was impossible. She couldn't have killed anyone. She refused to believe it. But she wished she'd handled the situation differently.

There was nothing she could do about the past now. She could hardly call the police about a break-in that had happened over twenty-four hours ago. Better to just keep it to herself. If it got out now, it would look like she had something to hide. Plus, she needed to follow this through. It was personal now, and she'd be taken off the Loeffler investigation. Loeffler wasn't someone she knew. How had she suddenly been thrown into a dead man's life? With that thought echoing through her head, she lay down and tried to sleep.

Sleep had not been kind. Behind her eyelids, all she had pictured was Loeffler's face. The way it had looked on the mug, the way it had looked when he called her by her first name at Noah's, and the way it had looked in death flashing back and forth. When morning came, it was almost a relief. But even as she drove to Loeffler's house the next morning, she pictured his face on that mug. The woman beside him was dark-haired and round-faced and their expressions held the simple satisfaction that marriage seemed to give to some people.

Lying in bed last night, she'd gone through her affiliations: grade school, middle school and high school in Berkeley. It was hard to remember grade school, but Loeffler wasn't in her high school yearbook. She searched for his wife, too, under her maiden name, Sandy Bree. Alex had gone to Cal, Loeffler to Stanford. She'd walked through her sports, friends, the academy, L.A., the club where she'd worked, friends of friends, classes she'd taken down there. Nowhere could she come up with a William Loeffler. And she was good with names and faces. If she'd seen either Loeffler or his wife before, she would have remembered them.

Maybe the killer had seen her at the house, and had somehow found out she was a cop. Maybe he was just screwing with her. Why stick around to torment her? It seemed too risky. Unless her reaction was part of the game. Had he stumbled upon her sleeping and just followed her? She shook her head. It depended on too many variables, too much coincidence. She didn't buy coincidence. What had he taken from her house? And, more importantly, where was it going to end up? Today was a second chance to find out what possible connection there was between her and Loeffler. And since she still hadn't heard back from Elsa, this was all she could do. When Alex arrived at Loeffler's house, the yellow crime scene tape and a standard patrol car greeted her. Waving to the officer, she hurried up the stairs and found Lombardi in the den. Another detective, whom she recognized from the station, stood beside him, and she hesitated in the doorway until Lombardi waved her forward.

"Look more like a detective today," he said.

She looked down at her jeans and sweatshirt. "Yeah, no uniform."

"That, and the circles under your eyes are becoming a permanent feature. All you need is a lucky coat and a potbelly and you're set."

Refusing the urge to let her fingers touch the sunken skin beneath her eyes, she forced a smile. "I'll think about it." She thought about the taunting phone calls she'd received. Maybe Lombardi was getting them, too. No, she'd have heard.

"Alex Kincaid, Jimmy Norton. Jimmy, Alex."

She shook hands with a short balding man in an oversized UC Davis sweatshirt. His perfectly round face made his head look like a red beach ball, with a full nose and high, bulging ruddy cheeks to complete the image.

"Jimmy's going to deal with the tapes."

She nodded.

Jimmy's expression was unchanged and she wondered if he didn't know what was on the tapes or if he was just used to dealing with that sort of perversion.

"He'll be handling it at the station, creating photos from the video via a computer and trying to match the faces with names. Once he's done, he may ask you to help with the matching."

"No problem."

"In the meantime, you can continue to work in there. Once you've gotten through all that shit, we need to box anything relevant and get it to the station. Someone else will come through for a second round tomorrow. Think you can handle that today?"

She glanced around the room and forced herself to nod. It didn't seem possible to get through the rest of the room today, but she knew the answer Lombardi wanted. And she wanted to be the one to go through Loeffler's things first.

Before she could say another word, Lombardi led Jimmy out of the den and closed the door behind them. She looked around at the piles on the floor, pushing her hair off her face. There was a ton of work to do.

On her knees, she opened the second file cabinet drawer, continuing where she'd left off. What had seemed interesting to her yesterday now left her agitated and impatient. Loeffler kept voluminous records of his cases, but as in his Palm Pilot, his notes were in shorthand she didn't understand. She had started a list of his abbreviations yesterday and glanced at it again now, trying to match one she'd found to the list. She had hoped by seeing them more than once, they would start to make sense. So far she'd had no such luck.

She made it through every piece of paper in the room by noon, and still nothing. Looking around, she searched for anything she'd missed. Besides the books on the shelves and a few framed pictures, she'd turned the place upside down. She thought about the other rooms in the house. Was her name written down somewhere? Why had Loeffler's killer presumably taken a mug from this house and put it in *hers*?

Frustrated, she pulled the rubber band out of her hair. The band snapped against her hand. "Damn." A small red welt appeared beside her thumb. Rubbing it, she blew out her breath. "Move on, Kincaid," she told herself.

As she stooped to pick up the hair band, something

on the bookshelf caught her eye. She crossed the room and sat down on the carpet. A line of tall, thin books filled the bottom shelf of the case. But in between two of them was a manila folder. Pulling out one of the books to loosen them, she placed it beside her and pulled out the folder. The tab read "S.S."

Alex opened the file on her lap and found a picture and a pile of newspaper clippings. The picture was of a man with pumpkin-colored hair and an awkward smile. On the back were the initials B.A. She turned her attention to the heading on the first newspaper clipping: "Sesame Street Murder leaves Palo Alto City District Horrified." Alex read the story, dated March 18, 1971.

> *In what police officials are calling the most heinous crime in county history, Walter Androus kidnapped a class of fourteen second-grade students from Florence Hemingway School during a class outing to the Ghiradelli Chocolate Factory. It is believed that Androus intercepted the bus carrying the students on a small street behind the school by pretending to be a chaperone arriving late.*
>
> *He then hijacked the vehicle and killed the driver, a chaperone and two parent volunteers. Their bodies were found in an empty Dumpster near the abandoned warehouse where he forced the children to ingest low doses of Valium, then blindfolded all of them, raped at least three and killed eleven of the fourteen.*
>
> *Police responded to a phone call they believe was made by one of the children and arrived at the scene.*
>
> *Walter Androus was found . . .*

Alex flipped over the photocopy, but the back was blank. Where was the rest of the story? She looked at the date again. 1971. It was so long ago. From the diploma on the wall, she guessed Loeffler would have been six years old. She and Loeffler had graduated from college the same year. She would have been six, too.

Could he have been working on something related to this case? Was he prosecuting the killer after all these years? She focused on his diploma again. It could be Loeffler's class, she thought, glancing at the date on the article, or someone he knew. She searched for the class photo she'd seen the day before. It was from the same year as the murders.

Across the room, she found the picture and stared at it again, studying the two young boys whose faces remained X-less. One looked vaguely like Loeffler, but it was impossible to be sure.

She stared at the picture of the man with the red hair again. The initials were B.A. Was this man Walter Androus? The article mentioned Palo Alto. She'd seen Palo Alto somewhere else, too. Picking up the phone on Loeffler's desk, she called the station and asked one of the secretaries to call Palo Alto to get the old file on the murders. Maybe something would turn up there.

Turning back, she set down the class picture and clenched her hand to her chest, trying to steady its tremor. Why was she behaving so strangely? None of this had anything to do with her.

The door opened and Greg walked in. She put the newspaper article down on top of the class photo and turned to greet him. "What's going on?"

"I thought we could talk."

Alex didn't like the tone of his voice. He sounded like he had a surprise, and it didn't sound good. She couldn't take any more bad surprises. "I'm kind of busy. Can I take a rain check?"

"I don't think so."

Alex knelt down to one of her piles and began to sort it again. "Come on, Roback. I'll see you later."

He grabbed her arm and pulled her to her feet in an angry motion. "You've got some explaining to do."

"The hell I do," she said, jerking her arm free and stepping back. "Don't fucking touch me." She looked at the closed door, knowing there were a dozen cops within earshot. "You're not my damn keeper," she snapped in a harsh whisper. "I don't owe you shit."

"I'm not trying to keep you, Kincaid," he said, his face more angry than she'd ever seen. "I'm trying to fucking save you."

"What makes you think I need saving?"

"This." He pulled a photo out of his pocket and handed it to her. She recognized it as an evidence photo. Just that fact made her feel suddenly shaky. Without touching the picture, she stared at it. It was of something lying on carpet in what she recognized as Loeffler's living room. But she couldn't make out the item. "What the hell is it?"

"A watch."

Alex felt like she'd been punched in the gut. She'd known her watch was missing. Goddamn it. Why hadn't she realized. But what could she have done? It was just a Timex Indiglo. They were a dime a dozen. She shook her head. Not hers. Hers was different.

Unable to look up at Roback, she stared at the photo, wanting to know where it had been, where they'd found it. But seeing it in an evidence photo, she couldn't get herself to ask. Instead, she stepped back and leaned against Loeffler's file cabinet, defeated.

"You want to explain this?"

She shook her head.

"It was at the crime scene, Alex. Like your earring. The earring that you weren't wearing when we walked into Loeffler's house that morning. What was that earring doing on Loeffler's floor? And this watch—it was under the body—caught around his belt. I know this watch, Alex. It's yours."

She shook her head.

He rattled the picture in her face, his expression angry and also scared. He was scared for her. But not as scared as she was. She was terrified.

"See the tag on the photo? The watch is inscribed, Alex. It says 'SF Marathon, July 1997.' I remember when you got it from that dork Dwayne. I had come with James to cheer you on."

Alex looked up at Greg. She didn't know what to say. "You shouldn't have taken the picture. It's evidence. It should be in the file."

"Jesus Christ, Alex. Do you know how serious this is?" He turned around and looked at the empty room. Then dropping his voice, he said, "I almost told them it was yours. But then I thought about the earring and realized you couldn't have lost both there that morning. I was watching you. You never had your arm under his body."

He let out his breath and wiped his hand over his face. "I had to talk to you first." He shook his head. "I know you didn't do that to him—not the hand and everything. You couldn't. But you were there. Why the hell were you there?" He paused and touched her arm. "Let me help you. Tell me what's going on."

She shook her head without looking at him. "I can't."

Greg stared at her, their eyes locked as he studied her. "I'm going to have to tell them what I know."

She rubbed her face. "Can you give me until tonight? I'll call you. I'm being set up, Greg. I don't know who or why, but someone is screwing with me." She thought about the fingerprint from her arm and the mug. "I can prove it."

Just then, the door opened and Lombardi lumbered in. "Break it up, love birds. You can play kiss-face on your own time. We got work to do here."

Chapter Ten

Alex took her shoes off and put her feet up on the coffee table. Her head buried in the sofa cushion, she refused to move, hoping her insides might unwind from the events of the day. She was thankful that Brenda had to cancel their dinner plans. She wasn't up for facing anyone. Not after the news Greg had delivered today.

She ran her hand over the spot where she'd worn her watch. Her earring, her watch. Things she never took off and she'd lost both in one morning at a crime scene. She'd been there—at Loeffler's house—the night he was killed. There was no other explanation. That reality was so terrifying that she couldn't bring herself to move. She tried to think positively. There was no definite evidence that linked her to the murder. It wasn't as though she was headed straight to jail. Someone would need to prove that there was motive.

She thought about her caller, wondering what sort of motive he was dreaming up for her. She rubbed at her temples and tried to figure a way out. At least she had Greg. He'd kept quiet on the watch this far. And he swore to at least hear her out before turning her in. That was the most she could ask for. She just hoped she could convince him that she was being framed. She needed to call him. Eat first and then she'd call.

Dragging herself from the couch, she pushed all thoughts from her head as she padded to the kitchen.

She found the last bagel in the fridge, cut it in half and stuck it in the toaster. A bagel and peanut butter for dinner sounded as good as anything else she could come up with.

While it was toasting, she opened a notepad and wrote down the events so far to talk over with Greg. First, woke up on strange street, no memory. She stopped after that one. It was the worst of them. If the situation was reversed and Greg told her he'd awakened on a weird street with no memory of going there, she'd have told him to quit smoking crack. It was going to be hard for anyone logical to swallow that all she'd taken the night before was a mild sleep aid. And a cop was taught to be especially skeptical.

Opening the cabinet, she brought out the three makeshift evidence bags. She pulled the fingerprint out of its bag and examined it to be sure it was still clear. In the black dust, she could see the pattern of her skin beneath the print and she thought about the fact that this man's hands had been on her skin. Who else had he touched? Loeffler?

She chewed on the end of the pen and tried to think of things she'd missed. Her stomach growled. Dinner! She smelled the burning bagel before she saw the smoke. She bolted into the kitchen. "Damn, damn, damn."

She waved her hand through the smoke, ripping the toaster cord from the wall and trying to find something to pry the bagel from its smoking depths.

With a dull knife from the drawer, she wedged out the blackened bagel, cursing at its heat before dropping it on the counter.

The smoke detector at the top of the stairs made chirping sounds of alarm. "Oh, crap." She knew it would soon start to squeal like a trapped cat. Before too long, the entire fire department would probably show up. She lifted the toaster and set it on the stove, then turned the stove fan on and used her arms in an attempt to sweep the smoke into it.

The smoke detector's chirps grew steady and loud. She pulled a broom from the closet and lunged up the stairs, using it to wave smoke away from the alarm in broad, sweeping strokes. The alarm quieted down and she returned to the kitchen, panting as she dropped the broom on the floor.

Her stomach growled, testy. She grunted at it and picked up half of the destroyed bagel, starting to scrape at the charred remains. When she had finished scraping it, she had a bagel the thickness of a tortilla shell. She scrunched her nose and tossed it in the sink. The last bagel, what luck.

As she pulled the fridge door open to see what else she had to eat, someone pounded on the door. She froze and looked down the hall.

Leaving the refrigerator door open, she crept toward the front door. The shadow of a man's frame formed behind the curtain and she halted in her tracks.

"Alex!" a man's voice said.

She sighed in relief. It wasn't the caller's voice. This was a voice she knew.

"Greg?"

"Hey, partner. Let me in."

She pulled back the curtain and saw Greg's face. In one arm, he held a massive pizza box.

She was salivating as she opened the door. "You should call before you pound on a cop's door. I almost shot you. Pizza?" She grinned. "What the hell took you so long?"

"You were expecting me?" Halting abruptly, he sniffed. "Is something—"

"Yeah, yeah," she interrupted, passing him on the way to the kitchen. "I burned my dinner."

"What was it?"

"A bagel."

Greg laughed. "Healthy." He followed her to the kitchen and put the box and his wallet on the counter. "Maybe we should go eat in my car. I'm a little worried about secondhand smoke."

With a glare, she pulled two plates down from the cabinet. There was a strange awkwardness to their teasing and it added tension to Alex's already knotted gut. Unwillingly she found herself staring up at the coffee mugs, wondering if there had been any recent additions. But tonight they were all familiar.

Forcing her eyes off the shelf, she glanced at the box in Greg's hand. "What'd you get?"

"Half veggie, of course. Think I would come over here with the wrong order?"

She smiled and opened the box. "You're a good man."

"Wish other women realized that."

"Someone'll figure it out. I can't be the only smart woman you know."

He punched her playfully. "You might be." There was a heavy pause as his expression dropped.

She searched for something to say but came up empty.

"You okay?" he asked her.

"Been better."

He nodded. "Me, too. You've got me scared, Kincaid."

"I know." She set the plates out and they loaded pizza on to them. "I'll explain it. But it's not good." She met his gaze. "Someone's really trying to fuck with me." She looked around to see what they were missing. "Let's go sit. You want a beer?"

Greg hesitated and then nodded. "Only one, though. I'm headed in at eleven—working nights until you're back."

Alex opened the fridge and took out two beers and they walked into the small den and sat down to eat. "You're working nights?"

He nodded. "With Gamble."

Wayne Gamble was a know-it-all desk jockey who drove everyone at the station nuts. "Rotten luck."

"You have no idea. Guy's a nightmare. What bothers me most is that everybody's-best-friend, I-know-everything attitude of his. Walks through the station like we're at a goddamn party. And the neck-craning thing drives me nuts."

She tapped her beer against his. "I'll be back in no time." She spoke with considerably more confidence than she felt.

After a long drag on his beer, he met her gaze. "You'd better be. Today he took ten minutes to brief me on the proper procedure for a code three. I've been a beat cop for five years. He's been sitting behind a desk for ten and he thinks that gives him clout to tell me how things work on the streets.

"We brought in a d and d," Greg started, referring to a drunk and disorderly. "And Gamble went off about the smell of the man. No shit, Sherlock—guy's a bum—he reeks of alcohol." He shook his head and ate a bite of pizza before looking back at Alex. "Man, I'm surprised someone hasn't shot him yet."

Alex rolled her eyes and nodded. "Why'd they put him back out on patrol, anyway?"

"Guess he wanted another shot at it. But he can't even keep a partner."

"What about putting him on a bike or a cycle?"

Greg laughed. "He's too fat—guy's gotta weigh two fifty. You should hear what they call him in the locker room."

Alex scrunched her nose. "I'm not sure I want to—"

He grinned. "Inner tube. Big and fat with a tiny hose."

She grimaced. "Jesus Christ, I'm eating."

He grinned. "You love it when I talk dirty." Their eyes met and Greg's smile disappeared. He set his plate down. "You have to tell me what the hell's going on."

Alex set down her plate, too, took a long pull on her beer, then set it on the table. Folding her hands together, she searched for a way to start. "You already know that I took that sleeping pill the night before we found Loeffler."

"And you had some sort of reaction?"

She looked up at him and then down at her hands again. "I woke up in my car."

"That's why you didn't pick up Brenda in the morning like you were supposed to. And why you were late that morning."

She gave him a stiff smile. "You going to let me tell the story?"

He nodded and drank his beer until it was gone.

She didn't offer him another. She knew he'd want it and he had to go out. They both could have used a few more drinks for what she was about to tell him.

"You woke up in your car," he started for her.

"Right. I don't remember leaving the house or going out, or anything. I just woke up and there I was."

"For someone who usually can't sleep through anything, that's pretty amazing."

He was trying to joke, but they both knew how serious this was. Not just because of the link to the murder but also because she was a cop. She couldn't be waking up in strange places. The station couldn't take a risk like that on an employee. "It was freaky, Greg. I had no idea how I'd gotten there. At first, I didn't even know where I was."

"What does this have to do with Loeffler?"

"I woke up on his street."

The air hissed from Greg's lips as though he'd sprung a leak. He paused and fiddled with his empty beer bottle. "You were in his house."

Her shoulders dropping, Alex leaned her head into her hands. "I don't know. I have absolutely no memory."

"But it doesn't end there, does it?"

She shook her head. Standing, she retrieved the bags of evidence and told him about the phone calls, the break-in, the attack, the new bump on her head, and the fingerprint.

"You didn't kill him," he stated as though it were a fact.

She nodded. "I know I didn't."

"But it's scary as hell not remembering."

"It's fucking terrifying," she admitted. "I can't figure out why I would've been on that street or in his house. I don't know him. I *didn't* know him," she corrected.

"There's only one person who knows what the hell you were doing there."

She nodded. "His killer."

"All we have to do is get that guy and it'll be over."

"I sure as hell hope so."

"The question is, how do we get him?"

She told him she wanted to get the print run and the evidence processed without going through normal channels. He agreed that Elsa Thomas was their best bet on the print. "But she hasn't called me back," Alex added.

Greg squeezed her shoulder. "I heard her say she's off tomorrow. We can go visit her. I'm not working."

She didn't say no. Truth was, she wanted Greg's help. But she also knew he could lose his job for helping her even as much as he already had. "You shouldn't come. It's not your problem."

He shook his head. "It is, though. Drop it. You'd do the same for me."

She nodded, but she wasn't sure she would. People at the station had told her that Greg's feelings for her went deeper than a partnership, but she'd always ignored them. He was her friend, her partner, and that was it. Only she was beginning to believe he saw it differently. And at that moment, she was selfishly happy to have him care enough to risk so much.

"You should have the phone traced."

"I can't. Not without help from the department."

"It's not safe to do this without backup, Alex."

She shook her head. "Don't make me sorry I told you."

He nodded. "Okay. Leave it on. Maybe he'll call. Have you tried to record the conversation?"

"He never talks into the machine."

Greg rubbed his face. "Write down as much of the conversation as you can."

"I know the drill."

"Of course." He paused. "We'll make progress tomorrow. Right now, you need to get some sleep."

"Easier said than done."

"You want me to stay?"

She shook her head.

"I'd feel better. I can sleep right here on the couch."

"I'm fine."

He turned away from her and looked around the den.

"I really appreciate it, Roback."

He nodded without turning back. "Yeah, no problem." He stood and stretched. "Did you know a duck's quack doesn't echo?"

She smiled.

"No comeback?" he teased.

"A little slow tonight."

"A goldfish has a memory span of thirteen seconds."

"Male, huh?"

Greg smiled. "That's my girl."

"Porcupines float in water."

"Cats have thirty-two muscles in each ear."

"Dogs are cooler," Alex said.

Greg nodded. "Much."

"Thanks, Roback."

"No problem. Call me in the morning?"

"Definitely." Alex walked him out, after he checked the doors and windows and had assured her that the house was locked up. As she closed the door, she almost felt relaxed. They just needed to catch this guy and it would be over.

As soon as she stepped away from the door and thought about bed, the phone rang. She froze.

She hurried to the den, wiping her palms on her pants, hoping the gesture might calm her some. But it didn't. Her hand shaking, she waited for the machine to pick up before she answered. When she heard the beep sound, she lifted the receiver on another extension. The line was dead.

She hung up, turned her back, and the phone rang again. The answering machine was still rewinding the outgoing message, so Alex answered.

The cackling response made her stiffen. "Hello."

"What do you want?"

"Don't you think you should've told your little friend what's going on?"

"What do you mean?"

"I mean, you're a police officer, Alex. You were at the scene of the crime. You didn't tell anyone. That's not very professional of you, is it?"

She gripped the chair to quell her anger. He was watching them, but at least he hadn't heard their conversation. That was some consolation. He didn't know she had Greg on her side. "I didn't do anything."

The man laughed, a high-pitched hyena laugh.

Pulling the phone from her ear, she took a deep breath.

"Are you sure, Alex? You found the pants, didn't you? That looks like something to me."

Pants? Alex couldn't speak. What pants?

"Oh, what fun. Something new for you to find. I always loved treasure hunts." The line went dead.

Alex slammed the phone down. "Fuck. Fuck.

Fuck," she swore, kicking the wall beside the phone. Pain seared through her toe and she hobbled to a chair.

"Goddamn it." Holding her toe, she picked up the phone and hit *69 to redial the number, praying it would work this time.

"Hello?" a woman's voice answered.

"Yes, can you tell me what number I've reached?"

"I don't know the number. You've got a pay phone at Broadway and College across from the fine arts school."

Less than two blocks away.

"Hello?"

Panic tightened her throat as though the caller's hands pressed against her larynx.

"Hello?"

She coughed, holding her throat. "Yes. Did you see anyone using this phone about two minutes ago?"

"No, I just got off the bus. I haven't seen anyone."

"Thank you," she whispered, replacing the receiver. Her fist pressed to her chest, she sank down to the floor and pressed her back against the wall. The phone call had come from around the corner.

Gripping her toe, she said, "Pants. Pants." She thought about waking up that morning on Yolo. She'd been wearing her navy sweatpants. Of course he'd done something to her pants. She knew he'd been close enough to touch her. He'd taken her earring and her watch. She shuddered at the thought of his hands on her.

Limping to the laundry room, she dug through the pile of dirty laundry until she found her navy sweatpants and looked at them. They looked like they always did. She shifted them in the light, trying to figure out what clue he had tried to give her. She felt the thick cotton then dug through the pockets. They were empty.

She got down on her knees and burrowed into the

pile to see if something had fallen out—a note or a business card, something that would tell her exactly what she had been doing on Yolo.

"Nothing," she said out loud, standing up and tossing the sweatpants back on top of the pile. Her hand hit the light switch just as something caught her eye. Her heart in her throat, she switched the light back on, her eyes focused on a dark spot. She fell to her knees, ignoring the pain as her toe stabbed the floor.

She picked the pants off the pile and brought them close to her face, staring at the spot. It looked like a handprint. Her fingers ran across the stain—it was dry.

Taking the sweatpants to the kitchen, she set them on the counter and pulled a dull knife out of the drawer. Shuffling around, she ripped a paper towel off the roll she kept under her sink and laid it on the dry counter.

She scraped the stain with the knife. Tiny burgundy pieces fell onto the paper towel. Once she had a dime-sized pile, she stopped. Picking up one of the pieces, she put it in her palm and added a drop of water. The red turned brighter, more familiar.

She frowned. It couldn't be. With the red liquid close to her face, she smelled it. She couldn't be sure what it was. She dipped her finger in the liquid and brought it toward her lips. But before she tasted it, the iron smell rose to her nostrils. Yanking her finger from her face, she coughed at the smell. Blood. It was blood.

Incredulous, she stared at the pants again. The blood was on both legs, the handprint on one and a finer dust, too—like splatter. Her hands shaking, she swallowed hard. An image of Loeffler sprang to her mind.

How had she ended up with blood on her pants? And what if it wasn't hers?

Just then, she heard the front door open.

Chapter Eleven

Alex spun around as Greg walked back into the room. "You left the front door unlocked." He looked down at the paper towel and her pants and back up.

"What are you doing here?"

"I got halfway home and realized I forgot my wallet," he said, staring at the blood. "Is that what I think it is?"

She nodded slowly.

Greg looked around. "He here?"

She shook her head.

"He called."

She nodded, sinking onto a stool.

"Whose blood is it?"

She shook her head again.

"Christ, Alex. Talk to me."

"I don't know," she choked. "He called and told me to find my pants. These are the ones I was wearing when I woke up on Loeffler's street."

Greg came to her side of the counter and spread the pants out on the dry surface. "There's a handprint on one leg."

She nodded.

Greg put his own hand up to it.

Alex could see that the handprint was considerably smaller than Greg's. "Jesus, Kincaid. I think that's your hand."

Tears lined the edge of Alex's eyelids. She blinked hard, terrified.

"They have to go to the lab."

She nodded, unable to speak. Unlike fingerprints, blood was living matter. It had to be processed as soon as possible or it lost its usefulness. She thought it ironic that the blood she was rushing to get to the lab would probably serve to further incriminate her.

"You have a paper bag?"

Alex pulled a paper grocery bag from the pantry and handed it to Greg.

He folded the pants carefully and put them in the bag, loosely rolling the top. Blood always had to be transported in paper because plastic trapped the moisture and could ruin the sample. The rules of evidence tumbled around Alex's head as she tried to grasp that she was the suspect, her home the scene they were processing. "I can get these to the lab tonight," Greg said. "I'll give them to my friend Lou Buono. He owes me for the Zoretti case. I'll just ask him to process them and tell him I'll give him the details in a couple of days."

She nodded. What more would they know in a couple of days? Almost a week had passed, and each moment her chances of survival seemed to worsen.

"You have your pager?"

"I've got it," she said, her throat hoarse, like someone's who'd been screaming or crying or both.

"Lock your door this time. Turn off all the ringers and try to get some sleep. If something comes up, I'll page you." He put a hand on her shoulder. "Try to get some sleep."

Alex nodded as Greg started for the door, the bag in his hand. She lifted his wallet off the counter. "You forgot this again."

He reached out for it but she held on. "You're getting yourself in deep, Roback. Risking your job. It may not be smart to hang around."

Greg pulled his wallet from her hand. "I guess I

think you're a pretty safe bet." Then he turned and headed for the door.

"I hope you're right," she whispered after him.

Greg paged her at eight A.M. and was on her doorstep at nine-fifteen. She came outside in a heavy hand-knit sweater and jeans. The suspect's fingerprint was under her arm in a thick manila envelope. Looking up and down the street, she shivered. The dense fog filled the hills and rolled over the houses, leaving her feeling like she was wearing a damp blanket over her shoulders. She couldn't seem to get warm and she was out of coffee. She felt lousy—sick to her stomach and tight and achy all over.

She opened the door to Greg's Chrysler LeBaron and sat down.

"Sleep?"

She shook her head. She'd spent the majority of the night hunched over a notepad in bed, trying to force what she knew into some logical solution. She felt no closer to an answer now than she had been that morning on Yolo.

"I didn't think so. You look like shit."

"Thanks."

"This might help." He handed her a tall Starbucks cup.

"You get me some frilly drink?"

"Tall French roast. Black."

Alex took a sip, letting it burn her tongue and the back of her throat. It was heaven.

Greg pulled from the curb and Alex strapped herself in. He took a long drink of his own coffee and Alex knew he hadn't slept either. He would've gotten off at seven this morning. It didn't give him any time to sleep. "You know a cockroach can live nine days without its head before it starves to death."

Alex looked at Greg. "That's nasty, Roback."

He shrugged. "Just trying to make conversation."

"You talk to Elsa?"

He nodded. "We're meeting them at nine-thirty."

"What'd you tell her?"

"That you got the print of someone messing with you, but you wanted to know who it was before you decided how to deal with it."

Alex stared out the window as they entered the Caldecott Tunnel. She remembered as a kid, she and James and Brittany had always held their breath coming through the tunnel. If you could hold it the whole way, you got a wish. Alex thought it might have been worth a try if she weren't so exhausted. She could certainly use the wish.

On the east side of the tunnel, Alex looked out at the rolling green hills of Moraga and Orinda. A series of wealthy hill neighborhoods, the area always seemed so different from the concrete jungles of Berkeley and Oakland. Elsa had moved out there ten years earlier to get away from the lousy schools in Oakland. While the schools were improving, Elsa and her husband Byron seemed more than happy to stay where they were.

Greg exited the freeway and pulled into a small parking lot. "Lillie's Kitchen. Here we are." He turned the car off as Alex took the last swig of coffee. "Anything you want to talk about before we go in?"

She shook her head. "Let me do the talking when it comes to how and where I found the print."

"I couldn't imagine it any other way."

"Smart ass," she muttered, pulling herself out of the car. It felt a few degrees cooler this side of the tunnel because there wasn't as much fog. Alex crossed her arms and shivered. Waiting for Greg, she looked around before they started inside. Lately, she always seemed to have one eye over her shoulder.

Lillie's was an old ranch-style house that had been converted into a restaurant. The inside was a cluster of small rooms filled with plain tables covered in checkered tablecloths. It was refreshingly toasty and Alex could smell strong coffee, both of which warmed her to the place immediately.

Elsa and Byron weren't there yet, so Greg and Alex got a table for four and sat down to wait.

A young woman with a long blond ponytail approached the table. She wore jeans and a white shirt with the clunky slides everyone was wearing now. Other than a new pair of running shoes or an athletic bra, Alex hadn't been shopping for clothes in years, and she was still wearing worn-out tennis shoes for all occasions.

"Coffee?" the waitress offered.

Alex nodded.

"Two," Greg said.

"You want to wait for the others to order?"

"Yeah. Shouldn't be longer than a couple of minutes," Greg said.

Alex found herself watching the door. She had the uncomfortable sensation of feeling out of place in her own skin. It was the lack of sleep. Even sitting, she couldn't get comfortable. She was anxious and yet too tired to move. Her eyes felt heavy, but she knew she wouldn't sleep. This stage of insomnia was the beginning of a bad cycle of exhaustion, and she knew she needed to try to break the pattern before it got too bad. Exercise would sometimes do it. After this was done, she told herself, she'd go to the gym where the cops hung out. She'd work out with some of the guys. They always pushed her. And today, she needed to push and be pushed.

The door to Lillie's opened and Elsa came in, followed by Byron. They were a striking pair, but not in the traditional go-together sense. Elsa was tiny with high cheekbones and the kind of coffee-ice-cream skin tone that came from mixed parents. Her husband, Byron, was tall, thick, and blond. He had bright blue eyes like a husky's and white-blond hair. He looked

Northern European, a bit like a bleached Arnold Schwarzenegger. They came in holding hands, and the gesture looked as natural as if their hands had been in their pockets or dangling car keys.

Elsa caught their eye and led Byron to the table. They said hello and she re-introduced Byron to Alex and Greg. He'd met them both at various PD functions where he'd probably met fifty-plus cops in a single afternoon.

"Thanks for coming," Alex said.

"No problem," Elsa answered. "You know I appreciate what you've done for Jamie."

Alex nodded.

"He's not in trouble again, is he?" Byron asked.

Alex shook her head.

"I told you I already asked that," Elsa said to Byron. She looked back at Alex. "He's been roughing around again," she admitted.

"I haven't heard anything," Alex said. Typically, her nephew liked to hang out with his buddies on the edge of the Cal campus. Shattuck had a small population of punks and Jamie was usually among them. It was their beat, and Alex and Greg usually ran into him on Fridays after the gang had all been paid and could score some weed.

"I don't know where he's going. Seems like a new crowd." She shrugged. "My sister's got some new guy living there—a real creep."

Byron touched her arm. "Jamie'll be okay. He's coming out this afternoon to stay with us for a few days." He squeezed Elsa's hand. "I don't think they came to check on Jamie, babe."

Elsa shook her head. "Course not. Sorry. Listen to me." She stopped, put her hands in her lap and looked up. "What's going on?"

"We'll look out for Jamie, Elsa," Alex told her.

"We always do," Greg added.

"I know. Thanks." She smiled. "Now, what can we do for you all?"

Alex pulled the manila envelope off her lap and opened it. Handling the edge of the paper, she drew the print out and showed it to Byron. "I need you to run this print."

With a sideways glance at Elsa, he took it and studied it for a minute. "Clean thumbprint. It's a tented arch, pretty unusual characteristics. If it's in the system and coded correctly, should be easy to match." He looked back at Alex with one eyebrow raised. "Lifted off skin. Yours?"

The question threw Alex off for a moment. She could feel Elsa staring at her. Finally, she nodded.

"He hurt you?" Elsa asked, concerned.

She shook her head. "It's someone messing with me, but I didn't get a look at him."

Byron looked at the print and nodded. He reached for the manila envelope and Alex handed it to him.

"Why not take it to our guys?" Elsa asked. "Nate Glazier could analyze it as easy as Byron. Even Lombardi's pretty good."

Alex didn't answer

Byron put the fingerprint back in the envelope and looked up. "I think there are some things people want to handle without their colleagues knowing about them."

"That's exactly right," Greg said. "I hope you're comfortable with that, Elsa."

Elsa digested the situation slowly and nodded. "I certainly am. I know my Jamie has always appreciated the way you all have handled his issues."

Alex nodded. "Thank you, Elsa."

Byron tucked the envelope under the table just as the waitress returned to take their order. "I'll do it first thing in the morning. Now, let's eat. I'm positively starving."

They ordered huge breakfasts and Greg and Byron

started talking final four. "It's going to be Michigan State this year with Dreaves."

"No way," Greg said. "UNC's got Phillips and Ramsey."

"You're both wrong," Alex said, leaning across the table. "It's going to be Syracuse. With Robinson and Ewing, they can't lose."

"I'm with Alex," Elsa chimed in. "Syracuse is the bomb."

Alex sparred with the guys as they talked sports, and thought about Elsa's choice of words. The bomb. Whoever the print belonged to had done a hell of a job setting off explosives in Alex's life.

It was like she was walking in a field of land mines and she wondered when the next one would detonate.

Chapter Twelve

Alex spent the afternoon with Diego Ruiz. At Alex's same height, Diego was 99 percent muscle. He seemed to move at one hundred miles an hour at all times and didn't need sleep. He was a beat cop who worked the night shift and spent his days at the gym. He was also one of the few gay men on the force brave enough to come out of the closet. He'd confided in Alex a few times about the difficulty of being gay in his family. First generation from Mexico, the machismo ran very deep.

His four older brothers mostly avoided him, his father didn't speak to him, and his mother continued to ask if he'd met any nice girls lately. Only his two sisters tried to understand.

When he'd come out at the station, he'd worried about retribution from other officers. But Alex was confident he was safe—you'd have to be a moron to mess with Diego. He was quick as a fox and strong as an ox. Mostly, though, he was just a nice, smart guy and people liked him even if they didn't all appreciate his lifestyle.

Alex almost always found him at the gym. Today, he was in the boxing ring running circles around a rookie, Jim, from Alex's class at the academy.

"I quit," Jim finally said, pulling off his face guard and gloves.

"You're smarter than you look," Diego said.

"Hey, I know when I'm beat."

"You're getting quicker, Jim. I really had to move out there."

"Yeah, yeah. Don't bullshit me. You barely broke a sweat," Jim moaned, wiping his wet brow on the edge of his gray T-shirt. "You come to get worked?" he asked Alex.

She nodded.

"You look like you already been worked," Diego said, climbing out of the ring. He motioned to her head. "You run into a building?"

"It ran into me," she corrected.

Jim laughed and headed for the locker room.

"I can tell you got troubles, girl," Diego said when they were alone. "You want to talk?"

"I want to sweat."

He nodded. "I can do that." Dropping his gloves on the ground, he motioned her to the punching bags. "Let's start here."

Diego worked her on the heavy bag, then the speed bag, before they sparred in the ring. He forced her to box as well as kick, and she used roundhouse and side kicks to hold him off. He pushed her just enough to get her to work to her body's limit. There were rarely any women in the gym, and today was no exception. Alex found that there were always a few men standing around watching when she got in the ring. Diego was kind to her, always giving her a chance to breathe when she got too tired, and never pounding her when she was losing steam.

But he didn't let her wimp out either. He consistently made head and neck shots so she was forced to stay on her toes to avoid getting knocked down. And, occasionally, she landed on her butt. Usually to a round of applause from the audience that gathered to watch. But Alex appreciated Diego's method and he was effective in motivating her to completely exhaust herself. By the time Greg showed up after his nap, her legs were shaking beneath her from exhaustion and she was barely able to lift her arms to push the sweaty bangs off her forehead.

On her back, she pulled her legs up over her head to stretch out, but ended up collapsing spread-eagle without moving.

"I was thinking of taking a little jog," Greg said, leaning over her. "You want to come or are you too tired?" He dragged out the word "tired" in his high-pitched "girl" voice and Alex growled at him.

"That your stomach?"

"Shut up," she groaned.

"Did you know that a starfish has no brain?"

"Did you know that polar bears are left-handed?" she countered.

"All of them? Think that's where they came up with south paw?"

"You mean from bears that live in the North Pole?" Alex asked

Greg grinned. "Maybe not. But that's very useful information," he said, sarcastically. "I mean, you never know when you might be fighting a polar bear. Now I know I should stay clear of that left paw."

Alex sat up and crossed her legs. "Versus the fact that a starfish has no brain. Now, that's hugely helpful. I keep talking to them and they don't answer." She spread her arms out. "And now I know why."

"Smart ass," he snapped.

Alex jumped to her feet and started sparring at Roback. "What did you call me?"

"You heard me," he said, holding her off with one long arm.

She ducked under his arm and landed a punch to his gut.

"Ugh," he groaned. He doubled over and Alex looped her leg around his and launched him backwards onto the mat.

A few of the people in the gym clapped and Alex leaned over and helped Roback up again.

"Don't mess with her," he said to the room. They laughed again.

Alex wiped her hands on her shorts.

"You heading home?"

She nodded and had started to speak when she felt someone watching her. She turned and spotted a man standing in the far corner of the gym, leaning against a wall with his arms crossed. His face was partially hidden in shadow, but he was clearly looking in her direction. Alex looked away, trying not to make it obvious that she'd seen him. It wasn't so unusual to have a guy stare at her, especially in a gym where she was the only woman.

But she usually recognized them. The gym was dirty and old, not the kind of place that attracted a lot of new people and certainly not the kind of place where someone came to pick up women. And this guy had been around all morning. She'd even caught his eye a few times earlier, but she hadn't seen him do any exercise.

She thought about her attacker. She guessed he was about six one or two, broad shouldered with strong arms and big hands. This guy met that description. She leaned over to stretch and took another look at him. He was still staring.

Greg started to walk away and Alex called him back. "What?"

"Come here," she whispered.

He halted without coming back. "What?"

"Get over here and help me stretch this quad."

Greg ambled back. "Stretch your own damn quad."

She stood up, her back to the guy, and approached Greg. "Don't look now, but there's a guy in the corner."

Greg whipped his head around. "Where?"

Alex grabbed his arm without turning around. "Jesus Christ, you want to scare him away?"

Greg continued to look around the gym. "Scare who away?"

Alex looked back to see that the corner was empty. "Damn," she said, scanning the rest of the gym. He was gone. She saw the door to the men's locker room shut and she ran for it, hearing Greg behind her.

As she reached the door and started to push it open, she heard Greg say, "You can't go in there."

But she did. She pushed the door open and ran in. The room was thick with steam and bodies. She searched the faces for the one she'd seen. A couple of men quickly covered themselves while others whooped and hollered. One snapped a towel at her and another just danced around naked.

Greg grabbed her arm, but she shook herself free. Ignoring the naked man dancing in front of her, she moved around him and looked up and down the rows of lockers. When she didn't find him there, she looked in the shower.

"Christ," one man yelled at the sight of her. "Can't a guy get some privacy?"

She came out of the shower room deflated. Where the hell had he gone so fast?

"You done in here?" Greg asked.

She nodded.

The naked man continued to dance in a small circle around her. When he stopped and gyrated in front of her, she looked down and said, "Can you go ring your little bells somewhere else, please?"

"Nasty," he said, dancing out of her way.

Alex turned and walked out of the locker room and straight for the door.

Greg was on her heel. "You want to tell me what that was all about?"

Alex looked up and down the street, but nothing stuck out. "I thought that was him."

"Him?"

She nodded.

"In the gym?"

She nodded again.

"You think maybe you're getting—"

Alex slapped her hand over his mouth. "Don't say it. Don't say I'm getting soft or paranoid. I'll put your ass on the ground right here. I'm tired, I'm sore, and I think I saw the killer in a fucking cop gym."

"Who you calling a fucking cop?" Greg snapped back with a small smile.

"It's not funny, Roback."

He looked down the street. "I know." They turned toward her car. "Byron's running that print tomorrow. Lou will process the pants as soon as he can. He had something else he had to do first. We'll know a lot more in about twenty-four hours."

She nodded. "I'm going home to take a bath and go to bed."

"You going to be okay?"

"No. Not until this shit is over."

He nodded. "I know. Me, too. I'm going for a run, but I'll beep you if I hear anything from Byron or Lou. Call me if you hear from our man."

"I will." She turned and walked to her car, resisting the urge to look over her shoulder every step. With a quick glance at the backseat, she opened the car and got in. Revving the engine, she put the car into gear and looked out the windshield to see a parking ticket.

"Goddamn it," she cursed.

Yanking on the emergency brake, she opened her door and got out of the car, reaching for the ticket. She snatched it from under the windshield wipers and threw it on the passenger seat. She headed home, too exhausted to think.

As she turned down her street, she wished she were relaxed. Instead, though her muscles ached, she still felt wound up. Maybe the bath would help. She pulled into her driveway and got out of the car, grabbing the parking ticket as she did.

Inside, she dropped her gym stuff on the floor of the laundry room, checked her messages, and sorted through her mail, tossing the junk out. She tore open the remaining mail, all bills, and started to put them on top of the parking ticket when something caught her eye. Dropping the mail, she lifted the parking ticket by its corner and twisted it upside down. On the side where the officer checked a box for the offense and fine, someone had attached a photograph. Looking closely, Alex could tell it was a picture of her car. Exhaling, she studied the street, knowing where it was going to be. And it was. Loeffler's street. A small red date in the corner of the print confirmed it.

Squinting, she could just make out the form of herself in the driver's seat. She stared at the parking ticket form. In neat print, her car's license plate, make, and model had been filled out in the appropriate spots. The violation was parking in a spot reserved for emergency vehicles on Yolo Avenue, and the fine was $250. The time read 3:57 A.M. She studied the officer's name and badge number, but they were both completely illegible. She'd gotten a ticket that night? It was impossible.

The copy that got filed with the station was gone. She looked back at the picture, searching for the red curb. There wouldn't be emergency parking on this street. She closed her eyes. The photo had to be real, but the ticket was almost surely a fake, wasn't it? She blew her breath out. Either way, she was screwed.

If the ticket was real, then it would be no time before the station realized she'd been there. If it wasn't real, then how had the killer gotten a parking ticket form? Unless the killer was a cop. A cop. As the thought echoed in her head, she stood motionless in the middle of her kitchen, slowly looking around. "What the hell happened that night?"

Chapter Thirteen

The room was cold and damp, wet almost.

It reminded her of playing in the morning when the dew collected in the long blades of grass, moist against her skin. She and Brittany and James would roll down the small slope in front of the house. Roll, then run to the top and roll again, until their jeans and T-shirts were wet and covered in grass stains.

Grass had the smell of summer and sun and play, but this place didn't smell like any of those things. It smelled musty like the basement. Only it was colder here—much colder. She shivered and turned her face. There was another smell—spicy, sort of like her dad's smell. She sniffed again. She smelled her daddy.

"What do you think you're doing?" the man said again.

Scared, she looked around. Was that her daddy? It didn't sound like her daddy. Why was he so mad?

"What do you think you're doing?" he screamed.

Confused, she shook her head. Why was he yelling? She couldn't help the shaking. She gritted her teeth, gnashing them against each other. Stop moving, *her mother always scolded in church. But she couldn't stop.*

She heard a loud pop and fell back against the cold floor, knocking her head. Scrambling up, she covered her ears and cried with the others.

Tears streaming down her cheeks, Alex sat upright in bed. She touched her face. She'd been crying. She hadn't cried in years. What was happening?

Red and blue lights shone in strange stripes and flashes across her bedroom as she rubbed at her arms, trying to stop the incessant shaking. The dream was hazy as she tried to pull it back—a man and a gun were all she remembered.

Had she dreamt about Loeffler? She shuddered.

Suddenly awake, she recognized the lights and heard the scream of sirens. The house was on fire! She leapt from bed and descended the stairs in twos.

The pounding on the front door caught her as she reached the bottom of the stairs.

"Bring those men up here. We're going in!" a man's voice commanded.

"Greg," she shouted, running to the door.

"Alex," he screamed back, pounding again. "Are you okay?"

She pulled the door open and Greg rushed in, spinning around the room as though he were expecting someone to jump him. Two patrol officers, Rodney and Schade, rushed past him into her house, their guns drawn. One ran up the stairs, his shoes pounding against the hardwood.

Before she could react, Greg took her by the arms and shook her. "Where is he?"

Alex shook her head, too confused and startled to answer.

"Where's the fucking pervert?" he asked, his teeth clenched in rage.

"What are you talking about?" she finally managed.

Dropping her arms, he crossed to the kitchen, looking around before glancing back at her. His brow was set in a long straight line you could balance a knife on. He ran up three of the steps and looked upstairs and then came back. "Where's the guy? He was here."

Her knees sank beneath her as though the bone had suddenly turned to softened candle wax. "Here?" she choked.

Greg took her by the hand and sat her on the stairs.

The officers reappeared. "Place's unpeopled," Rodney said.

"You had us scared," Schade added.

"I'm fine," Alex said, embarrassed. How close had he been this time?

Greg nodded. "Check outside and get someone over here to dust for prints."

The officers started to walk away.

"And can one of you pick up Gamble? He's handling a missing pet over at Blake and Fulton," Greg added.

Matt Schade chuckled. "That sounds like Gamble's speed."

"You'll handle it?"

"No problem, Roback." The officers left, exchanging soft conversation as they shut the door behind them.

Alex glanced down at her bare legs and imagined the fear and tears on her face, refusing to think about what they would be saying at the station. Her heart had finally slowed, and she took a deep breath. "What just happened here?"

Greg sank to the stair beside her, his thick hair messed, his shirt untucked. "I was about ten blocks from here when I heard your call. I came as fast as I could."

Instinctively, Alex grabbed her throat and looked around. "That's not possible. I didn't call." She opened the closet.

"What are you doing?"

"Looking for my cell phone."

She moved the holster with her gun and pulled the black canvas fanny pack from beneath it. Unzipping the pocket, she sucked in a deep breath and looked inside. No phone. "Crap. That bastard has my cell phone."

"When did you last use it?"

She shrugged. "Maybe a week or so."

•
He shook his head. "You made the call."

"Bullshit, Roback." She pointed upstairs. "I was in bed, asleep." She paused. "For the first time in forty-eight hours," she added. "There is no way I called."

"Worse. It's definite. They played the call on the radio, Alex. I heard it. It was you, saying someone was in your house, trying to kill you."

"What do you mean, it was me?"

"It was your voice."

"You're sure?"

He nodded slowly.

"But I was asleep upstairs."

Greg raised an eyebrow. "Then somehow he put together a tape of your voice, crying for help."

She thought about the calls. He'd been taping them. He'd taped them and used them to call the police. "Oh, God." He was totally nuts.

She stood from the stairs and paced across the hardwood floor, thinking it was the same spot where the killer had attacked her only two nights before. "We need to get that tape. I want to hear it."

"There's no way to get our hands on it now. Schade and Rodney are already treating it like a crime scene. Unless you want to tell them you made the attack up, we're going to need to tell someone that you didn't call. But the lab will be able to tell if the tape was pieced together."

"But if I tell them it was probably a joke . . ."

"Someone in your house? That's not a very funny joke."

"Damn it. I don't want the station pulled into this." Alex glanced over at the parking ticket.

Greg followed her line of sight and went over to the countertop where the ticket still lay. He picked up a pen and pushed it over, inspecting the other side. "What's this?"

As she explained, he shook his head, his expression somber. "If it's a real ticket, then it's probably already been input into the system. Maybe it's better to tell them you were there than to have them figure it out first." His shoulders drooped. "I don't know how much longer you can avoid it."

She thought about James. How could she tell him? It was too much. With his sister in trouble, his own career was at stake. If only she could keep it quiet another day. Maybe then she'd know more.

A knock at the back door interrupted her thoughts. She inhaled deeply, wondering what else could possibly go wrong tonight.

Matt stood in the doorway.

"What's up, Schade?"

He looked past her at Greg. "We found something by the back door."

Alex knew from his expression that it was something very unpleasant. The raw, acrid taste of fear filled her mouth.

"What is it?" Greg asked.

"I think you'd better come look."

Alex shuddered, imagining another dead body, this one on her back porch. They followed Schade through the house and halted at the back door. The garbage had been knocked over outside and the contents were scattered in a three-foot circle. "Damn cats. What did you see, Matt?" she asked as she stepped outside in her bare feet.

Matt looked up at Greg and pointed. Tucked down behind the garbage can was a clear plastic bag. One end had been chewed through and something was falling out of it. In the dim light, though, she couldn't tell what it was. It looked fleshy and pinkish and for a moment she thought it might be raw chicken.

Alex leaned forward, trying to make out the shape. Slowly, recognition dawned, the image connecting in her brain. She gasped, leaping away.

"Oh, God," Greg muttered.

Lying on the ground among Alex's trash was a severed hand. A large gold signet ring decorated one finger.

Just then, she heard another, familiar voice. Alex turned to face James, his red face set in an angry grimace.

"Someone want to tell me what the fuck is going on?"

Chapter Fourteen

James paced the room like a hungry tiger as Alex explained about the caller. Greg sat on the couch, his head down as he pretended to take it all in for the first time. Out of the corner of his eye, James watched Greg, too, as though testing Alex's story. She told him about seeing Loeffler in the bagel store, about his calling her name, and about waking up on the street, the phone calls, the break-in with the mug, her cell phone missing. She had hesitated about telling James about waking up on the street, but she knew it would be smartest to lie as little as possible. As it was, she was going to be lying a lot.

"And he took my watch, I think," she said, the idea coming to her as she spoke. Even headed up by her own brother, Internal Affairs was going to have a field day with the things she'd already done. She didn't want them to have any extra ammunition until she knew who she was up against.

To that end, she left out mention of the earring Greg had found on the floor, the attack, or the blood on her sweatpants. She didn't want to confess that she'd been attacked without reporting it, and she wanted to run the print and know who the attacker was before giving the information to the police. She also wanted to make sure the blood was legit before she did. And she hoped she'd know both things tomorrow.

When she was done, she leaned back and let James have the floor.

"Holy shit," he cursed. "Holy fucking shit." He spun and looked at Greg. "And this is the first you've heard of this?"

Greg narrowed his gaze at James, and for a moment, Alex was worried he would confess. "First," he said, his jaw tight. She could feel the tension between them.

"Jesus Christ," James said. "I can't believe this. Captain of IA and my sister—" He balled his fists as he paced.

Alex crossed her arms. "You worried about your career, James? Or mine?"

"Oh, that's fucking great. I get a call that you've been attacked in your home, rush over here, and you lay all this shit on me—" He halted and pointed his finger at her. "Shit you should've told me a week ago." He pointed to his chest. "And now I'm the bad guy? That's bullshit."

Alex let her breath out. "James, stop pacing. Maybe we can just talk about what we can do next."

"Not we, Alex," he said, motioning between himself and her. "There's no 'we.' You're out of it."

Alex jumped up. "But this is my—"

"Come on, James." Greg cut in.

James ignored Alex and turned on Greg. "Roback, you'd better get the hell out of here if you know what's good for you," he said. "I assume you're not messed up in all this Alex shit." He waved at her as though she were a stray mutt. "This isn't your beat and where's your partner?"

Greg's face reddened as he turned toward James and started to speak.

"He just heard the call on the radio and was worried," Alex said, trying to keep Greg from inserting himself into her problems.

"Fine. Then get."

Greg raised a finger and pressed it almost in James's face. "You're not my fucking boss, James. We used to be friends. Don't turn all that bullshit captain crap on me."

James leaned into him until the men were almost touching. "I'm here doing my job, which is what you should be doing."

"Roback, go," Alex said, pushing them apart. "James is right. You should get back to Gamble."

"Your job," Greg said to James, shaking his head. "She's your sister, you asshole." With that, he turned and stomped away.

"What a jerk," James growled.

"You certainly *can* be," Alex said.

He looked at her. "Me? I'm here saving your ass."

Alex shook her head. "What do you want, James?"

"I need to use your phone."

Alex sank back into the couch. "You know where it is." Leaning back, she closed her eyes and pictured the man at the gym. Where was he now? Somewhere close, watching? A cop. The thought bounced into her head again. She pictured Schade's face when he'd come to tell them about the hand. He couldn't be involved. And Evan Rodney was too sweet, wasn't he?

Just then, James came storming back into the room. "Get dressed. We're going down to the station."

Alex watched his face: Right there at the surface was the fury and fervor with which he always did his job. He'd even gone so far as to call his superiors in the middle of the night. He couldn't risk not responding to a crisis immediately. What if someone were to question his dedication to the force? No, James's loyalty was definitely with his job. She thought about the killer again. Was he a cop? A cop just like James?

Alex waited in her brother's empty office, exhaustion weighing her down like invisible bags of sand. But she couldn't shake free. As though she were caught in some terrible video game, as soon as she had conquered one obstacle, another twice its size fell on her head.

James had called Captain Palowski of the detective division, Captain Lyke of patrol, and Deputy Chief John Doty into the station and they were all meeting in Doty's office. Alex knew none of them would be happy to be called in at this hour of the morning. She squinted at the clock. It was four-fifty. She had waited almost an hour. She could only imagine what was going on behind the closed door.

The door to her brother's office opened and she sat up, pushing her tousled hair off her face and trying to appear awake and alert, neither of which she felt. James held the door open for the deputy chief and gave Alex a look that indicated she had caused him a world of trouble.

Captain Palowski entered the room as he always did, his head lowered and leading in front of his body, his eyes on the ground as though he were eternally searching for clues. His dark curly hair was woven with gray, its long shaggy appearance at odds with the mature color.

Deputy Chief Doty followed, his burly belly first, his face stern. Alex had never seen him look anything but severe, and she wondered how his wife could tell his good days from his bad. Maybe they were all the same.

Lyke came last and gave her a sympathetic look as he passed. She knew from his look that the news they were about to deliver was bad.

James marched into the room like he was about to be given a medal. His head high, his chest out, the aura of the hunt seemed to surround him. He really did love his job.

The men took chairs beside Alex. The room was cold and she had to force herself not to cross her arms and shiver. The last thing she needed was to look defensive. The situation was stacked against her as it was.

"I hope you understand the seriousness of this matter." Deputy Chief Doty spoke first, his mouth set in a line as straight as a knife's edge and twice as grim. "You should have come to your captain immediately after you'd been called to the scene on the street where you woke up.

"Even though we don't want to believe you were involved in the crime, the situation should've been brought to Captain Lyke's attention sooner. You have to realize how it looks." He shook his head. "There's no excuse for not telling us. If the media got wind of that—" He shook his head again and it was beginning to look like he was making himself sick from it.

"They'd crucify us," James said, finishing the deputy chief's thought.

Alex watched Lyke and Palowski glance at him and then at her.

James seemed oblivious to their stares.

"Unfortunately," her captain started, leaning toward her and offering a sympathetic look, "you've left us no choice but to suspend you without pay until we've had a chance to investigate the incident."

Alex let the weight press her shoulders toward the floor. She'd known it was coming. It was, as he said, the only option. Still, she'd hoped somehow there would be something else.

"The hand is crucial evidence from the killer, and we need to know as much about its appearance at your house as we can," Captain Palowski said. He paused. "You know the components to any murder investigation."

She did. Who, what, when, where, and why.

"Whoever killed Loeffler is doing a damn good job making it look like you're involved."

She sucked in a deep breath and nodded.

"To catch this guy, we need to hear every single thing that happens from here on out. If you didn't kill Loeffler, whoever's screwing with you most likely did. And he's a dangerous fuck. Got it?"

She studied his steady gaze, wondering if he really thought she killed him. Palowski kept a straight face, but she hoped he was on her side. "Got it."

Doty broke in again. "You need to come in tomorrow morning and write up, in detail, everything that's happened. You'll work with Internal Affairs." He motioned to James. "Once you've done that, you'll need to leave your badge and gun with me until we've cleared this up." He paused and looked at his hands. "I'm sorry for this."

She nodded. "I'm sorry, too."

"You should go home now," Doty added. "We all should—get some rest."

The men all stood. Despite the tension in her muscles, Alex forced herself to stand.

"I'll call you and keep you apprised of the investigation," Captain Lyke said. "You call if you need anything."

She nodded. They were going to conduct an investigation. She didn't allow herself to consider what they would inevitably find.

Captain Palowski walked by and nodded at her, the closest he would come to offering support. It was the first time she had seen him look anyone in the eye.

She realized she preferred it when he didn't look at her. His eyes were chilling and commanded more attention than she wanted to give.

James marched past without stopping "See you tomorrow morning. Not too late," he added as he headed for the stairs.

"That's an ambitious one, your brother," the deputy chief commented.

She nodded.

The deputy chief walked out, and she heard Captain

Lyke mumble, "Nothing like drawing a little blood from family to really move up the ranks."

Alex gave him a thin smile. It was true. Between James and the killer, Alex was the proverbial sacrificial lamb.

Chapter Fifteen

Alex couldn't sleep. She couldn't even get her eyes to stay closed for more than five minutes. Instead, she spent the remaining hours of the night tossing in her bed, pacing circles around her room, and trying to drum up theories about Loeffler's death. The wife seemed to be an obvious lead. She knew Lombardi would follow that one. He would also follow up on the case files. Alex remembered the file, she'd called up from Palo Alto on the so-called "Sesame Street Murders" and thought it would probably arrive today and get buried in the pile of papers on Lombardi's desk. The Palo Alto Police Department. PAPD. For some reason, it stuck in her head.

By the time she got up at six-thirty, she was worse off than ever. Saying she looked haggard would've been a compliment.

As she entered the station the next morning, her head pounding, she passed a man banging on the desk. "Hello? Is there anybody here? This is supposed to be a fucking police station. Am I supposed to find a pay phone and dial 911?"

From her angle, Alex saw only a thick fist matted with dark hair.

"They let the apes out of the zoo again," Reesa hissed from the front desk. Reesa had been manning the front desk for more than a decade. She was an older woman, plump but firm, with a fierceness that helped her deal with the strange crowd that showed up at the station.

"You need any help with that one?" Alex asked, missing her beat already.

"Nope." Reesa started back for the desk, her thick brow set down over her eyes in a glare. "Hell, knocking these jerks in line's my favorite part of the job."

Mine, too, Alex thought as she headed toward her brother's office to report for work.

James wasn't in his office, but one of the other officers showed her to a vacated office with a small, taupe government-issue metal desk and chair. Except for two chairs, the desk, and a rusted light that dated back to the early seventies, the room was empty.

Alex flipped the light on and searched for a place to hang her coat. No wonder Lombardi had brought his own coat rack. She found a nail on one wall and balanced her coat on it, hoping the weight wouldn't bring down the wall.

On top of the desk sat an old IBM PC, a clipboard with a crime report template, and a note from her brother.

Al—
   The template is on the computer. It'll get you started. Please be as clear as possible. Don't worry about space. Use the additional blank pages at the end of the file if you need them. It'll be important to your case that we have all the information.
   Be back soon.
—J

"Important to your case" kept running through her head. Suddenly she felt like she was on trial for murder. And maybe she wasn't so far from it.

Concentrating on getting the report written, Alex moved question by question, answering with as much detail as she could. She knew the things she'd left out could easily get her fired or worse, but she saw no way around lying. She wanted to clear herself, not crucify herself.

James didn't resurface until just past one, as she finished up. "How's it going?" he asked, leaning against the door frame, one leg crossed over the other.

She straightened the stuff on the desk and put the top back on her pen. "Great."

Unfolding himself, he moved toward her, his gaze skeptical. "Finished?"

"Yep." Standing, she pointed to the computer. "I was just about to get it off the printer. It's also saved under 'Kincaid.' "

"Let's go take a look." James turned and headed out the door. Off to get his report, he looked positively thrilled.

Alex couldn't wait to get out of the station.

They passed the entrance to the detective division and turned into a small room that housed the printers and fax machines. James picked the stack off the printer and nodded.

"I guess I'll be going now," Alex said.

"Sure. I'll call you if I need anything else."

She gave him a thin smile and shook her head. "Thanks. I appreciate the concern, too, James," she added sarcastically.

"What? I'm doing my job."

"I know. You're a real up-and-coming star." Alex turned and started for the door. She'd already turned in her badge and gun, and now she just wanted to go home.

"I know you," came a saucy young voice from behind her.

Alex halted and looked back.

A ratty teenage kid stood in the doorway to the detective division, Lombardi beside him. His dirty blond hair had been buzz-cut except for a few spots that seemed to have been missed completely. These he wore in three-inch braids. His skateboard poised under one arm, he wore shabby black shorts and sneakers in desperate need of replacement. His shirt was even worse, holes exposing his hairless, concave chest.

"Everything okay here?" James asked Lombardi.

Lombardi grunted and started to lead the kid back to the detective division.

The kid wrenched his arm free. "Don't you care that I know her?" With a step forward, he towered above Alex, eyeing her down his nose. "I've seen pictures of you. He had lots of them."

Alex felt like she couldn't breathe, but she wasn't about to be bossed around by a punk. She took a step forward, startling the kid into giving her space. Angry, she jabbed her finger in his face. "Who had pictures of me?"

The kid didn't answer.

Lombardi jerked him around by the arm. "The officer asked you a question."

"Bill," he muttered.

Alex listened carefully to his voice, but it wasn't at all familiar.

James stepped forward until the three of them effectively pushed the kid against the wall. "What did you say?"

The kid cleared his throat. "Bill."

"Bill Loeffler?" Alex asked.

His eyes locked on his shoes, he gave a slight nod.

Lombardi shook him slightly, causing him to jolt. "Speak up."

The kid looked up at him and glared, then pointed to Alex. "Yeah, Bill Loeffler. He had all sorts of pictures of her. His wife found them. No wonder she left him."

His voice definitely wasn't familiar. Her caller had a more threatening voice—deeper, more forceful and definitely more adult. She watched him, realizing he was the kid she and Lombardi had considered might be the killer. But he definitely wasn't the caller.

"They were having an affair," the kid added.

All eyes were on her. "What?"

"An affair?" Lombardi said, his beady eyes searching.

Now furious, she shook her head. "No way. I never even met Loeffler."

James started to speak.

"Okay, I saw him once, but never spoke to him," she clarified.

Lombardi pulled his gaze off Alex and looked at the kid. "Where are these pictures?"

The kid shrugged, shuffling his feet on the floor and making an irritating squeaking sound.

"Did you see the pictures?" Lombardi continued.

With a scoff, the kid looked up. "Yeah, I saw them. I been through all her stuff."

"Whose stuff?" Alex asked.

"Sandy's," he answered, rolling his eyes in annoyance.

"Sandy Loeffler?" James asked.

The kid glanced over their heads at the filing cabinets that housed the mug shots. "Yeah."

"The pictures were in Sandy Loeffler's things?"

His expression hesitant as he looked back at the detective, the kid nodded.

"Then she didn't show you the pictures?" James asked.

The kid suddenly became more interested in his shoe.

James took his shoulder. "You went into Sandy Loeffler's things without her permission. Now, we can forget about that if you help us out with the pictures."

Alex watched her brother, ready to forgive the punk kid in exchange for more incriminating evidence on her. She didn't stop him. She wanted to know what the kid knew almost as badly as James did.

She knew Loeffler. That's what it all came down to. Or he knew her. But she couldn't think of how.

The kid pulled himself from James's grasp, a deep scowl on his face. "I went through her stuff. So what? She moved into my house without my permission. It's not like I took anything." He pointed to Alex. "She's the one you should be asking questions to. He's got stacks of pictures of her—at her house, wearing her cop outfit, running."

Lombardi eyed Alex and then James. "I'm going to need to chase down those photos." With a quick motion to the kid, he added, "Will you get him set up in Room A?"

James nodded. "What's your name, kid?"

"Tim," he muttered.

Lombardi gave Alex a crooked frown and walked away.

Great, Alex thought. *Now Lombardi thinks I had an affair with the murder victim.* She could already see a motive for murder building in their heads. How much longer could this go on?

James started to walk toward the holding room. "Okay, Tim, why don't you come with me? You want something to drink?"

Tim looked at James, a flicker of interest in his eyes. "What you got?"

"Coke? Sound good?"

Tim nodded, trying to look casual.

Alex followed them a step behind. How would she find out more about the pictures if she wasn't here? She tried not to panic. Greg would help where he could. The detectives would talk to other officers about the case, even if they weren't supposed to. It was the nature of being a cop—they needed to talk about the job with other cops.

James led Tim into the interrogation room and told him he'd be right back. He shut the door. "You can't go in there, Alex."

"I just want to ask him a couple questions. Don't I deserve to know how this pervert Loeffler got pictures of me?"

Her brother shook his head. "Not right now you don't. You're in deep shit. If I were you, I'd head out of here immediately. Save someone the effort of putting you behind bars before it's necessary."

"Behind bars? Is that some kind of joke?" Alex felt herself shake with anger. "You're about the shittiest excuse for a brother anyone could ask for."

"Don't turn this around on me," James snapped back, raising his hand in her face.

"Why not? *You* do. It's all about your next promotion, your raise. Hell, if the deputy chief gave you a fucking shovel, you'd bury me yourself."

Furious, Alex turned her back and aimed for the door. James wasn't coming after her. Not his style, especially not when there was work to be done. Damn it all to hell. She needed information and she needed it fast.

"Whoa," Reesa called after her.

Alex turned to see Reesa holding a thick Airborne Express package.

"Want this?"

Alex glanced over her shoulder. "What is it?"

"The file from the PAPD."

Alex halted. "PAPD," she repeated.

"The Palo Alto Police Department."

Alex nodded. "No, I know." She saw the initials in her head and suddenly saw them again on Loeffler's calendar, on his list of places to call. She had requested this file after reading the article from 1971 about the kids in Palo Alto. She frowned. Had Loeffler been looking into this case when he died?

"You want it or should I send it back to Lombardi?"

"No, I want it." Leaning forward, she took the package and pulled it to her chest. "Thank you," she whispered. "I'm going to run to get some lunch. If anyone asks, I'll be back in an hour or so."

"Enjoy it."

Alex wasn't sure if Reesa meant lunch or the file, so she simply nodded and ran down the stairs and out of the station.

In her car, she made a U-turn in the middle of the street and drove ten blocks toward the bay, took a left, and drove another four blocks. Somewhere near the border of Emeryville and Berkeley, she stopped.

It was as safe a place as any. Opening her glove compartment, she pulled out the granola bar that would have to serve as lunch and tore open the Airborne package.

Wiping her sweaty palms on the passenger seat, she flipped through the Sesame Street Murder Case material, searching for something that would make things fall into place, that would give her an idea of why Loeffler was killed.

The report listed the names of the officers involved in the investigation. Lead officer was Peterson, then Kearny and Sansome. None of the names was familiar.

Her eyes skimming on, she searched the names of the eleven children who had been killed after being kidnapped on a class outing. None of those names was familiar either. The warehouse where Walter Androus had murdered the kids was called Richmond. That didn't seem to be the connection. Androus's only family was one sister, Maggie, who lived in West Virginia. Alex scribbled down the name and address of Maggie Androus as a starting place to tracking her down. She wondered where Walter Androus was now.

She glanced up to be sure no one was watching. Apart from the occasional traffic, the street was empty. The granola bar caught her eye and she ripped it open, sticking half in her mouth.

She read on. Maggie hadn't seen her brother in years. She characterized Walter as quiet and shy and not capable of such violence. Alex grunted. The family always said that. *Well, I remember he used to run over dogs for fun, but he wasn't a violent person.*

Frustrated, she exhaled. Maggie had refused to comment on the household she and Walter had grown up in. Alex was sure there was a good reason for that.

Having made notes of the full names of the eleven murdered children and their parents to cross-reference later, with her notes from Loeffler's house, she continued to search the file. At the end of the twenty-page document, she flipped back, glancing up at the clock. Forty minutes had passed and she hadn't found a thing. Nothing seemed to indicate that she was even on the right track. She didn't see any connection to William Loeffler. Why had he even had the newspaper clipping on the murders?

She tried to remember the details from the article. She was sure it had said there were fourteen children. Maybe there were survivors. Loeffler had been about the right age. She searched for a list of the remaining three children and finally found it, buried at the back of the file.

A dog barked and she slammed the file shut and shot upright, looking for the source. The lack of sleep was starting to make her jumpy, which wasn't like her.

An older man walked his pit bull down the street. He waved an apology for the dog.

"Those things should be shot," she said out loud, remembering a recent incident where a pit bull had attacked and almost killed a toddler.

She opened the file again. "Survivors," she whispered to herself, running her finger down the page. She stopped when she got to the first name on the list. *William Douglas Loeffler.* Her pulse beat a quick drum on her ribs. So Loeffler *was* a survivor. She thought about the old class picture he had in his files, the one of the second-grade class with most of the faces crossed out. Now it made sense. Had Loeffler been planning to call the PAPD about this case? Why had he dredged it up again? Maybe Androus was still alive and he killed Loeffler. She flipped through the file until she found the article she'd seen at Loeffler's.

She skimmed the beginning again, making mental notes as she went. The children from Florence Hemingway School had been on a field trip to the Ghiradelli Chocolate Factory. Androus had intercepted the bus by pretending to be a chaperone arriving late. He'd shot and killed all the adults on the bus and then kidnapped the kids and forced them to ingest Valium. Alex found the spot where Loeffler's article had cut off and continued to read:

> *. . . Androus was found shot dead. Three children were still alive, all but one still blindfolded. The survivors' names will not be released, but they have been treated at Sequoia and are said to be in good physical health.*
>
> *The city has made arrangements for counselors to assist the children and their families in overcoming this tragedy.*
>
> *Meanwhile, police are still searching for evidence as to who shot and killed Walter Androus. They have not ruled out the possibility of one very brave child.*

Alex frowned. The killer had been killed—shot dead, maybe by one of the kids. "Shit." Androus couldn't have killed Loeffler if he was already dead. She started to toss the file aside. What a waste. What now? Maybe someone else was involved back then, someone who was back now. An accomplice.

She could talk to the other survivors. The article had mentioned three. She found Loeffler's name again at the top of the list and then scanned down to read the other two aloud. "Marcus Andrew Nader, and—" She gasped. "Oh, my God."

Her hands shaking, she lifted the paper closer to her face and stared at the name, sure her eyesight had to be playing tricks on her. *Alexandra Michael Kincaid.*

Chapter Sixteen

Alex sat in the car for a long time, staring at her own name on the page, certain it would disappear just as shockingly as it had appeared. It didn't. Each time she blinked, the words seemed darker, their image burned into her retinas so that she saw them when her eyes were closed.

How many Alexandra Michaels could there be? If her middle name were anything else—Ann, Jane, Michelle—she would be convinced it was someone else. But Michael? It was her mother's maiden name.

This was ridiculous. It couldn't be her. Her eyes closed, she tried to recall anything about grade school—a teacher, a friend, an outfit, even what she used to eat at lunch. Not a single image popped into her mind. How could she not remember anything? She recalled playing with Brittany and James, but little else.

The photos that had lined the mantel in their home came to mind—James in a plaid oxford with a butterfly collar, the girls in matching striped sweaters. Brittany wore her hair long and feathered, Alex was in short pigtails. Where were all those pictures now?

The one thing she knew for certain was that she'd been born in Palo Alto, at Stanford Medical School. Her mother had moved the family across the bay the summer before Alex started third grade. Alex searched her brain for the reason they had moved. She was sure her mother had taken a new job in

Berkeley, but had that been the only reason? Had they moved because of something so horrible?

If she had been there, she would remember it, wouldn't she? Why couldn't she remember anything? Cursing, she wished her mother were still alive—or her father. Someone who could answer her questions. Would Brittany and James know? But they had been only ten at the time.

Disbelief gnawed at Alex's stomach. How could her mother have kept something like this from her? How could she have died without telling Alex what she had gone through, without leaving her with any hint as to how to handle it?

Fists tight on the steering wheel, she tried to drain her anger. She wished she could cry and scream and let it all out. "I *wasn't* there."

But suddenly her entire body felt numb. Nothing surfaced—no rage, no tears, no well of endless emotion. Only a heavy, dark sense of dread that cloaked her in its cold fear. She looked down at her empty wrist. She needed a new watch. Glancing at the clock on the dash, she saw it was three o'clock. She had been sitting there for almost two hours.

She reached for her cell phone and remembered it was gone. The killer had it. "Don't you remember?" he had asked her. Was he trying to get her to remember the murders from all those years ago? Had Loeffler remembered? He must have.

Marcus Nader was the third survivor. She had to find him. Was it possible Androus had somehow survived and come back? If he were still alive, wouldn't he go after Nader, too? Or was Nader a killer? She wrote herself notes to search for Nader and Androus. She thought about the accomplice angle again and about Maggie Androus. Maybe Alex could find her.

Blinking hard, Alex focused her attention. She couldn't let James or Lombardi find out about this until she knew what was going on. She removed the list of victims and survivors from the report, folding it carefully and sticking it behind the bills in her wallet. Closing the folder, she prayed the page wouldn't be missed until she had figured out what to do about it.

Alex turned the key in the engine. At least now she had a path to follow. She started down the street, trying to digest the information she'd discovered in the past few hours. She had survived a mass murder. And she couldn't remember a damn thing about it.

When she arrived at the station, Reesa caught her as she stepped through the door. Alex jumped slightly, her own mind moving so fast she hadn't paid attention to anything else.

"You okay?"

Alex nodded, not trusting herself to speak. She handed the file back to Reesa.

Before she stepped away, Reesa took her arm and stopped her. "You look like you've seen a ghost."

Alex forced herself to shake her head. "I'm sorry. Just trying to figure this out. Thanks for the loan."

The woman's eyes remained pinned to her face. "So, it helped?"

Alex nodded. "A ton."

Reesa's expression lightened. "Glad to hear it."

Seeking refuge in the office she had used that morning, Alex hurried down the hall in hopes of avoiding speaking to anyone else. She was supposed to have gone home. Logging into the system, she went to search the state for a name. She typed in "Walter Androus" and came up with no current record. She tried "W Androus" and "Walt Androus" and again got no records. She searched just "Androus" and came up with a bunch of listings. Nothing looked quite right, but she printed the list to go through more carefully later.

Next, she tried "Marcus Nader." No current listing. She typed "Nader" and found several. Scanning them, she found a Marc Nader listed in Palo Alto. "Bingo." She printed the list and ran next door to retrieve it off the printer. Back in the office, she folded the pages and tucked them in her bag. Exiting the system, she stood from her chair and then turned toward the door. But James was standing in the center of the frame, blocking her way. She wondered how long he'd been watching her.

"Excuse me," she said, trying to move past him.

"Not so fast.'

Alex tried to push past him again, but he didn't move. She considered knocking him down, but decided against it. "What the hell do you want?"

"Answers."

"Great. Go find some."

James grabbed her left arm. "Answers from you."

"Let go of me," she said, holding in the fury that was coursing through her veins.

"No way. Not until you answer my questions."

Alex spun back and lunged at James, throwing her right fist into his jaw. The sound was a resounding crack and James let go of her and fell back against the wall. "Go on, James. Why don't you go file a little complaint for me assaulting a senior officer?" It was all she could do not to hit him again.

She took another step toward the door, but James stopped her. This time, when she spun around, he was ready for her. He grabbed her right fist and held it back, turning her around and wrapping his arms around her body to hold her down. As he pushed her into a chair, she heard a rattling noise, but before she could react, he'd handcuffed her to the chair.

"You're fucking kidding me. This is police brutality!" She was practically yelling, but no one appeared at the door. Internal Affairs rarely saw this sort of action, so they probably thought the noise was coming from the detective division next door.

James shut the door and sat in the second chair. "What's going on, Alex?"

"You've handcuffed me to a goddamn chair is what's going on."

With an angry scowl, he stood, shoving the chair back into its corner. The chair scraped against the floor and rocked slightly to regain its balance. "You're pissing me off. I mean it. I'm trying to help you, but all you do is screw things up."

"Why don't you just get out of here?"

"Because I can't."

"Oh, right. I forgot, you're the perfect cop. Why not just beat a confession out of me, then? Is that what you want?"

"Don't play that game with me. Do you have anything to say?" he pressed.

She didn't answer.

"Fine, I'll read the goddamn file for myself."

A gasp leapt from her throat without warning. "What file?"

"The one from Palo Alto that you took to lunch with you."

Anger flushed in her cheeks. "Reesa told you?"

He waved his hand at her. "Jesus Christ, I'm your brother. I have the same genes. I don't need anyone to tell me. I know how you think."

"Bullshit," she countered. "You don't know anything about me." She thought back to when she'd walked out of the station. She'd passed Damon Crandle, one of James's IA cronies. "Crandle told you I'd left with the file."

"It doesn't matter, Alex. I'm going to read that file, word for word, page for page. Then, I'm going to have someone in Palo Alto confirm exactly how many pages there were. If there's so much as a corner missing, I promise you, you'll never work on a force in this state again."

His face rigid with fury, he motioned to the cuffs.

"And you can just sit in those until you come clean or until I figure out what was in that file." He paused and raised his finger. "And another thing, don't think I would hesitate a second to get your ass kicked off the force just because we're related."

She turned her back to him, putting her feet up on the desk to wait. "Now there's a news flash. You've all but done it already. So why don't I just help you. I quit. Big relief?"

With a snarl, he swung the chair around.

"Just fucking tell me."

"No."

If he knew, she would become a suspect in Loeffler's murder. She was there the night he was killed; his hand was found at her house. The file would link her to Loeffler, would prove that they had known each other. Motive was just a half turn away. Hell, that kid Tim had probably already provided enough motive for murder. An affair that had gone sour. What a joke.

But she *had* known him, maybe even had met with him on the night he was murdered. What if she had killed him?

She had to know. She wanted to find out on her own, see the evidence of what had happened for herself. And more than anything, she needed to confront the man who had dug this from the depths of her past and thrown it in her face.

"I guess I'll go then."

Alex pulled at the cuff, the metal clinking against the chair. "Seriously, unlock it."

"You tell me what I want to know and I'll think about it."

"You can't leave me here. You'll lose your job. Then we'll both be unemployed. No big deal for me. I don't have a family to support."

Without looking back, he moved to the door and pulled it open. "Watch me."

She gritted her teeth. "James!" The chair scraped against the floor as she leapt to strangle him.

He gave her a fake smile, starting to shut the door behind him. "I'm going to get Lombardi and Captain Palowski, let them know about the file. Must be something really interesting in there."

She shook her head. "You do that."

"Unless you tell me yourself."

Alex felt defeat sink like heavy weights on her shoulders. James had no idea how hurtful he could be. She thought about how he'd react to what had happened to her as a child. Pity maybe. More likely, he'd be embarrassed, the way some parents were embarrassed of children who had been raped or molested. Either it didn't occur to them to try to help the child or they didn't know how.

"You gonna spit it out?"

She nodded slowly.

"I knew you'd come around." He pulled the second chair up, careful not to get too close.

"You going to unlock the cuffs?"

"Not until you've spilled it."

She watched his satisfied grin and wondered how his face would change when he found out. Suddenly, she almost looked forward to telling him.

"So?"

Her wallet in her lap, she opened it with her free hand. "You're not going to believe it."

"Believe me, I've seen it all."

She swallowed hard and quickly told him the basics of the Sesame Street case. Then, she pulled out the folded list and handed it to him. She focused on the desk as he opened the page.

"Hey," he said, giving her a pat on the back. "You did the right thing."

She nodded, trying to keep herself from thinking about what must have happened that day.

After glancing it over quickly, he pointed to the

list of victims. "Am I supposed to recognize one of these names?"

Her lips suddenly dry, she shook her head. "The survivors," she said, though it was barely a whisper when it came out.

"The what?"

She blinked hard, pulling the pages from his grip. Her hand shaking, she laid it against the desk and pointed. "The survivors. The first is a list of the kids who were killed. Then, the three that survived. Read that."

He stood and peered over her.

Her eyes closed, she concentrated on holding back the tears that fought to fall.

"Holy shit."

She flinched as James pulled the list from her grasp. When she opened her eyes, he was pacing a small circle, swinging his arms.

"What the fuck is going on here?"

Swiping at a tear that she hadn't been able to hold off, she shook her head.

"There must be a mistake."

"Or another Alexandra Michael Kincaid?"

James's mouth remained open, his eyes wide. He looked as horrified as she felt.

And yet she wasn't. At that moment, she felt nothing at all. "Will you uncuff me now?"

He raked a hand through his hair, staring at his sister as though he had just discovered she had three weeks to live.

She didn't even let herself think about how he would look at her when he realized she now had a motive to kill someone.

He unlocked the handcuffs and tossed them on the desk. "Jesus."

She rubbed her wrists.

"Maybe it's a coincidence."

It wasn't likely, but she didn't mind grasping at

straws. "What was the name of the grammar school we went to?"

His brow furrowed, he shook his head. "I have no idea."

She exhaled.

"Brittany would remember."

"I do not want Brittany to know about this. She'll want to help and she can't—not yet, not right now." She stared at James. "You've been an asshole about this from the beginning, James. I know it's your job, but I'm your sister and you've been more enemy than ally. But, if you go to Brittany before it's absolutely necessary, I will make it my life's goal to ruin your career. And I won't care if I take mine with it." Hell, hers was already destroyed anyway.

He paused and then nodded.

"Say it."

"I promise."

She watched him for a minute. "You better keep your promise." She lifted the phone and dialed Brittany's work number.

"Dr. Stevens's office," Brittany's receptionist answered, in a high, chirpy voice that Alex could never understand how she maintained for a full eight hours a day.

"Hi, Cassie. It's Alex. I was looking for Brittany. Is she with a patient?"

"Nope, she's right here."

There was a brief pause before Brittany spoke. "What's up?"

Alex stared at her desk. "I'm filling out this stupid form at the station. Do you remember what elementary school we went to?"

"Let me think."

The phone against her ear, Alex squeezed her eyes shut, pressing her hands to her temples, as she prayed that Brittany would tell her they'd actually gone to elementary school in Redwood City or Menlo Park—

anywhere but Palo Alto. She would do anything to be wrong.

The seconds passed like hours as she tried to shake off the sensation that Brittany's words would seal her fate.

James tapped on her shoulder and she waved him off.

"Brittany?"

"Yeah, I know it. It's Florence something. Hold on, I'll get it."

Lead filled Alex's stomach and she was suddenly nauseated. "Florence Hemingway?"

"That's it. Is that all you needed?"

"Yeah, thanks," Alex managed to choke out.

"Okay, I've got to run—I've got a patient. Talk to you later."

Alex dropped the phone in its cradle and turned to the wall, leaning across her knees and throwing up in the metal wastebasket. Wiping her mouth with her sleeve, she held her face in her hands, choking back silent sobs that shook like small earthquakes through her chest.

James turned her chair to face him. Then, kneeling on the floor, he wrapped his arms around her, pulling her close and holding her as he hadn't done since their mother died.

His hold was awkward but she didn't care. Without even knowing it was happening, the sobs shook loose from her chest, tears running down her face as if from a leaky faucet.

"Ah, shit, Alex. You're going to be fine."

"He almost killed me."

James held her head tight to his shoulder and patted her back. "You're okay. We'll get the s.o.b., I know we will."

She pulled herself away. "It's not him, James. He's dead," she whispered. "It's someone else. Someone else is doing this to me."

"I'm not going to let anyone hurt you. I promise. I know I'm not always the best brother, but no one's ever going to hurt you."

His words were calming, and she sucked in a breath, trying not to wonder if irreparable damage hadn't already been done. And who was out there, waiting to finish the job.

Chapter Seventeen

Alex arrived at Judith Richards's house at five past seven. Her legs felt weak, her wrist still sore from the handcuffs James had so hastily slapped on her. But she had forced herself into her best pair of jeans and a striped shirt, then out the door. It was more effort than anyone should have expected after the day she'd had.

At least she was making headway. Or it felt like she was. She had found Marcus Nader easily enough. He lived in Palo Alto, in a home he owned. He'd paid two hundred and sixty-five thousand for it about four years before. He was the only one listed on the deed. Profession was listed as photographer. The answering machine was a man's voice, but not the one of her caller. His message referred to "I" not "we," so she assumed Nader lived alone. Her instincts told her he wasn't Loeffler's killer. She wondered if he was in danger.

"This is Alex Kincaid," she'd said after the long series of beeps. "I think we have something in common and you had better be careful. Call me as soon as possible." Leaving her home number, she hoped he'd call soon. She wondered if the long series of beeps meant that he hadn't checked his messages in a while.

Greg had called to say that Byron had gotten a rush job that he had to do before he could process the print from Alex's house. "He promises to get to it by tomorrow," Greg told her. "Tomorrow" had become an almost frightening word, each passing day bringing a host of unknowns. But she wasn't ready to turn the print over to James. "And the blood?" She'd asked.

"It's human."

She exhaled. "Type?"

"O positive."

"I'm AB."

"I was afraid of that," Greg said.

"Me, too." She paused. "Loeffler's O?"

"Yep."

"Damn." She'd broken the news to him about the murders and being a survivor as best she could. But talking about it made her shaky, and she could hear the raw fear in her own voice as she choked out the words.

"I can be there in three minutes," he'd offered.

"I can't. I have to go see Judith tonight."

"A shrink?"

"A shrink," she repeated, not liking the way it sounded from her own lips.

"It'll probably help," he said, but she could tell he was skeptical. Cops didn't willingly see shrinks. Shrinks were for rich people with dysfunctional families where Mommy didn't express herself to the children like she should. They weren't for people who lived with death like cops did. In some ways, Alex supposed she fit both descriptions. Her mother had certainly left a lot un-discussed.

"Can you run a priors on a couple names for me?" she'd asked Greg, pushing her mother from her mind.

"Sure."

Alex explained about the sister, Maggie Androus, and Marcus Nader and the initials she'd seen written in Loeffler's calendar. "And has there been any word on those pictures?"

"The ones the kid found?"

"Yeah."

"None that I've heard. I know Lombardi interviewed the kid, but I'm not privy to all that detective
shit. I'll see what I can find out."

"Thanks."

"No problem."

There was a long pause and Alex knew Loeffler's
blood was weighing on both of their minds. "The
blood is Loeffler's," she'd said.

"Yeah."

She exhaled and let her head stop. "You're going
to need to turn it in."

"I'm afraid so."

"Do it."

He paused. "I can wait—"

She shook her head. "Do it now. Have Lou send it
in. Tell him to say he got it from me with no
explanation."

"Why don't we—"

"Goddamn it, Roback. Turn it in now. I've held it
back long enough. Now, go." She slammed down the
phone and turned to face the white wall that the killer
had knocked her against like a bag of flour. There, in
the center of the wall, was a tiny splatter of her blood.

Sinking to the floor, she felt deflated. Loeffler's
blood was on her pants. She was about to become a
murder suspect. And she had no way to stop it.

After talking to Greg, she had spent some time
looking back through her notes from Loeffler's calendar: "NT SEC@10 SQ. Call: N, K, DR and PAPD."
Was the N for Nader, the K for Kincaid? Then, who
was DR? How was he related to this?

She still couldn't figure out why Loeffler was killed.
Had he remembered something he shouldn't have?
Was it buried at the back of her mind, too, waiting to
slip free?

Now she sat in front of Judith's house, still going
over the evidence in her mind. The frustration she
felt had become almost like physical pain. There was

nothing more she could do tonight except find out as much as she could about what had happened to her as a child. She hoped Judith could help with that.

The car locked, she headed up the stone path, glancing at Judith's house towering above her. The brick exterior presented itself heavy and solid like a fortress that would protect her. She hesitated, her core rebelling at the very prospect of the comfort it offered.

The need to tell someone else what was happening, someone who might be able to explain it, both repulsed and frightened her. But if she wanted to salvage her job and rebuild her life, she needed to start somewhere. And at this point, somewhere might as well be here. The news of her past still felt disconnected, like it had happened to someone else.

Parts of what she'd read in the report were blurred and dreamlike, as though she had been under medication when she'd read them. She recognized the old mechanism for shielding herself, and she wondered how long it had been in effect, even without her knowledge. There seemed an easy answer to that—at least since she was in the second grade.

She pushed her hair off her face, thinking it was time to cut it short. Looking down at her jeans, she caught sight of a small dollop of dried tomato sauce. She licked her finger and scratched at it without success. "Damn it," she muttered.

Suddenly feeling like a disheveled seventh grader going to her boyfriend's house for the first time to study, she forced herself to stand still and ring the bell.

Judith answered the door, wearing a pair of khakis and a denim button-down shirt. Alex hadn't realized how short she was. In stockinged feet, she couldn't have been taller than five feet.

Judith's face looked as it always had. Her once dark hair was woven with strands of gray, and time had softened the strong jaw and cheekbones. Her dark eyes, too, seemed softer, as though the years hadn't made her older but more at ease. "Come on in. I think I'm burning dinner."

Alex smiled and entered the house. She had to respect anyone who burned dinner. With a last glance at the stain on her pant leg, she followed.

Judith led her through a comfortable-looking den with a large brown leather couch and matching over-stuffed chair. A Native American-style braided rug covered the floor.

Alex eyed the rooms as they passed. Judith appeared to subscribe more to the Alex version of clean-liness than the Brittany one. There were stacks of loose papers on the entry table, and a basket of un-folded clothes waiting to be taken upstairs. Several jackets were strewn here and there, a yellow one tossed on the floor next to a pair of red Doc Marten shoes, much too large to fit Judith. And yet the books on the shelves in the den were neatly lined up by size.

A small oil painting caught Alex's eye. The picture depicted the wraparound porch of an old house. It looked like it belonged by the ocean. Two wicker rocking chairs sat facing outward. The picture seemed to depict loneliness, and Alex felt a shiver run over her skin.

"Do you remember that?"

Alex frowned and shook her head. "Should I?"

She nodded as though she were studying Alex, and probably she was. Alex realized that right now she had to be pretty interesting to someone in Judith's field.

"It was in your house when you were a child," Judith explained. "I'd always admired it, so your mom gave it to me. She'd never really liked it, I guess."

Alex tried to picture it in her house but couldn't. Knowing it had been there made her wonder why her mother hadn't liked it. She had so many unanswered questions for her mother now.

She followed Judith into the kitchen. The atmosphere of the house helped loosen the crick in Alex's neck. And she felt comfortable with Judith.

"Would you like a glass of wine or a beer?"

Alex waved her hand. "Beer sounds great."

Judith pulled out a bottle of Sierra Nevada and handed it to Alex, passing her the bottle opener. She took a swig of her own beer from the bottle and set it back on the counter, turning back to the dinner.

Looking around, Alex searched for something innocuous to talk about. She noticed a chewed pen sitting beside the stove. "Is there a psychological theory about people who chew their pens?"

Judith raised her eyebrow.

Alex pointed. "I chew mine, too. Brittany is always joking that it says something about my personality." She'd never given it much thought before, but suddenly she wondered if the pen chewing was a result of what had happened to her as a child. Ridiculous.

Judith picked up the pen and scrunched her nose in mock disgust. "It's gross, isn't it? I don't know why I do that." She opened the drawer under the counter and dropped it in.

Alex saw that the other pens weren't chewed on. That's what she needed—one pen she was allowed to chew on, sort of like a doggy toy. "Something smells great."

"Roasted chicken," Judith said, taking another swig of beer. "Hope you like garlic."

"Love it."

"The chicken'll take a while so I thought we'd just sit in here while we wait. Unless you'd be more comfortable in the living room?"

Shaking her head, Alex pulled a bar stool up to the tile-covered countertop and sat down, taking a look around the kitchen. Calphalon pans in all sizes hung neatly from a semicircular rack above the stove, and spices sat in a small wooden rack to the right. Alex noticed the spices were alphabetized. The spice rack was painted steel blue and many of the accents in the kitchen were done in the same color.

The floor was light-colored wood except for a small area in front of the sink where an Indian patterned rug lay. The cabinets reached to the ceiling, their glass faces exposing a variety of dishes and stemware. Alex had never made decisions about decorating and couldn't imagine what she would do if she had to start from scratch.

Her mother had left the house to her furnished. While she had moved a lot of her mother's things out and many of her own in, she'd never bothered to change the wallpaper or paint. She pictured her house's salmon exterior. Maybe soon she would have some time to do something about that.

Judith sat up on the counter and gave Alex an appraising glance. "So, how are things going?"

Alex shrugged, looking at her beer. She certainly wasn't going to answer *Great*. She wasn't that good a liar.

"You making any progress on the case?"

Sipping her beer, Alex shook her head. "I'm off the case."

Judith looked startled. "Why?"

"How can I put this?" Alex frowned. "They found the victim's hand in my garbage can."

Judith pursed her lips. "Where did the hand come from?"

Alex smiled at Judith's expression, though she couldn't believe herself for doing it. "Killer cut it off and took it with him."

"Oh, God. Sometimes I can't believe I'm actually in the business of studying these people."

Alex was both surprised and relieved to hear Judith react that way. It made Alex wonder if she would ever get used to the criminals she dealt with. She nodded, thinking of the little girl involved in sex acts on the videotape. She took a drag of the beer, hoping it would somehow wash the sour taste from her mouth.

"I still don't understand why they took you off the case. Did they think you were in danger?"

"Sort of. There are some strange things happening to me."

Judith remained silent, waiting for Alex to continue.

"I've been getting calls from this man—" With a deep breath, she continued, "I don't know who he is, but he knows all sorts of stuff. He's been in my house . . ." He'd done better than that. He'd attacked her. Alex kept that to herself.

Judith covered her mouth in horror. "Jesus, Alex. How did he get in your house? This sounds scary."

She met Judith's gaze. "It is definitely scary."

"Do the police have any leads on who he is?"

Picking at the corner of the beer's green label, Alex shook her head.

Judith narrowed her gaze. "Why is he targeting you?"

Images she had created of that day in the warehouse flashed through her brain and she shook them off. She wondered if any of them were real. "I think I have a pretty good idea."

"Why?"

"Can I ask you something first?"

Judith nodded and sat back. "Of course you can."

Hesitating, Alex glanced at her beer and then back at Judith. "When did you meet my mother?"

The woman furrowed her brow, her finger raised. "I'd just finished my Ph.D. in Abnormal Psych at Stanford and had joined as the director of the Children's Crisis Center. Your mom was working there already. It was . . ." She paused. "Summer of 1971. She'd moved into the house on Pine."

"I live there now."

"Oh, you do? Well, she had all three of you kids in one bedroom until she had the money to add on the extra room. I think she started work about two weeks before me, but by the time I got there, she knew the run of the place. I followed her like a puppy until I learned my way around."

"Do you remember her talking about the reason she left Palo Alto?"

"Well, sure. She said that she had a sister here and with going back to work full time and you three kids, it would be better if she were closer to her."

Alex concentrated on the label, using the beer's moisture to ease the corner of it off the brown bottle. Her aunt had passed away a few years before her mother. There was really no one around to answer her questions. No one but perhaps Judith. "That was the only reason she gave?"

Judith paused. "Your mother was a very private person, Alex, maybe like you that way. Why do you ask?"

"Because I think she had another reason for leaving."

"You mean because of you and the kids who were killed." She nodded. "I'm sure that had a lot to do with it, though it wasn't the reason she gave."

Judith knew.

Alex swallowed. The timer dinged and she exhaled. "Maybe we could wait to discuss it until after dinner."

Judith nodded slowly, studying her. "Sometimes it helps just to get things off your chest. I'm happy to turn the dinner off and we can talk now."

Alex shook her head. "No. I think after dinner would be better."

"Maybe a full stomach will help?"

Alex nodded. A little more time would help.

Chapter Eighteen

Alex finished her beer with the last bite of her dinner and declined Judith's offer for a refill. One beer was enough to release the tension without clouding her thinking. Three beers and she would be on her ass. That might be a solution, but not the one she needed.

They settled in the living room, and Judith set her coffee mug on the table and tucked her small stockinged feet beneath her. Alex suddenly wished she had accepted a cup of coffee. At least then she would have something to stare at. Instead, she glanced at her stubby fingernails.

"You don't have to talk about it, if you're not ready," Judith began.

Alex nodded. "I'm ready. I just don't know where to start."

Judith smiled. "How about the beginning?"

Alex inhaled and tucked her hands in her lap. "Brittany said you and I used to talk about nightmares."

Judith nodded.

"I have to say, I don't remember much about it."

"That's normal. You were very young."

"Not everything about my youth was normal. I was wondering if you remembered the dreams I used to have, if you could tell me about them."

Judith took a sip of her coffee and watched Alex. "You don't remember anything about them?"

She shook her head. "Only waking up with my mom

sitting on the edge of my bed in her flannel night-gown."

Judith set her coffee down and leaned forward. "But nothing about the dreams themselves?"

Alex shook her head, then smiled. "Brittany always asks a lot of questions, too."

"Sorry. Must be a professional hazard. But while I'm at it, can I ask one more?"

Alex nodded.

"James told me about your blacking out and waking up in your car. Have you had any dreams lately?"

"I had one the other night . . ." She tried to think back to it. She awoke sweating; someone had called the police. The flashing red and blue lights on her bedroom walls still shone in her mind.

"Do you remember it?"

Her gaze focused on the wall, she shook her head. "Nothing clearly."

Judith nodded, still watching her.

Alex felt like she was strapped to a lie detector machine. Brittany always told her how much she relied on body language to determine the whole story. Alex was sure that was what Judith was doing now.

"That's okay," Judith said. "Lots of people never remember their dreams. I know I don't. Keep a note-pad by your bed. If you wake up and realize you've been dreaming, try jotting down what you remember."

"You think knowing what I'm dreaming about will help?"

Judith shrugged. "Maybe, maybe not. I think it will be interesting to know if you're dreaming about the same things as you did when you were a kid. We can try a kind of memory exercise if you like."

Alex hesitated then nodded. "Sure."

"In your memory, can you picture talking to me?"

She frowned, unclear.

"If you close your eyes, can you see us sitting in your living room talking?"

She squeezed her eyes closed. "No."

"You're trying too hard, Alex. Relax your brow. Breathe deeply."

Alex sucked in a breath and let it out slowly.

"Now, let's just look at the room. Can you picture it?"

She saw it. "Yeah."

"You walk in from the kitchen, what's the first thing you see?" Judith asked.

Alex opened her eyes. "It's a mess. I'm trying to clean it out."

"Okay, close your eyes."

Doubtful this would work, Alex closed them again.

"Think back to when you were kids. What's the first thing you remember about that house?"

Alex pictured the house, she and Brittany chasing James around the back. "The yard."

"Good. Did you have a favorite place in the yard?"

"The front. Brittany and I used to always roll down the slope of the grass."

"Can you picture yourself rolling down the grass?"

Alex nodded.

"What do you picture? What do you feel and smell?"

"Nothing. I can't see anything."

"Why don't we wait? You don't need to do this all in one night."

Alex didn't open her eyes. "I want to see it. I want to know what happened."

"You will. It just takes time."

Alex blew out her breath. "I don't have time."

"Of course you do. We'll work on it another time."

"Can we try once more?"

"Okay. Keep your eyes closed. Good. Now, tell me what the grass is like. Is it soft? How does it smell?"

"The grass is itchy and smells strong."

"But you like it?"

"We love it."

"What are you doing outside?"

Alex hesitated, trying to picture herself as a child. "Brittany and I would race to the bottom of the hill, get up, run to the top, and race back to the bottom again until we were both too dizzy to stand." As the memories surfaced, the tension in her muscles begin to wash away.

Slowly Judith walked Alex through her memories. They entered the house, through the hall and into the living room. Judith seemed to remember the house perfectly as she helped Alex visualize the rooms then asked her to describe them. Alex told her about the pictures on the wall in the living room and the old floral fabric that covered the couch, surprised how vivid the images were.

With each step, Alex remembered more of the old house, and the feelings of being small again. Most of it seemed sweet, but there was a part of it that surfaced like angry bees, stinging her insides.

"Now, you were telling me about the dream—about the man. He was yelling at you. Do you remember why he was yelling at you?"

Alex nodded. "The gun." The words slipped off her tongue as though they'd been there all along.

"The gun. Who has the gun?"

"I do. I have the gun." Her eyes flew open. "Why do *I* have it?"

Judith frowned. "Because you shot him."

"I shot him?"

"Of course. You don't remember?"

Alex shot up from the couch and spun around in a fury as she tried to find her bearings. "There must be some mistake. I couldn't have killed him."

Judith stood and took Alex's arm, pulling her to the couch. "What don't you remember about it?"

Her head spun like a top. "Nothing."

Judith squeezed her hand. "What do you mean 'nothing'?"

Alex stared into space, picturing the gun in her hand. "Nothing. I don't remember anything."

Judith moved closer. "What about the dream?"

"I don't know. I didn't remember it until just now. I just found out about this today."

Judith's expression was puzzled. "You found out about the dream today?"

Alex pulled her arm away. "No, about the whole thing, the warehouse, the kids, the deaths, Androus, all of it."

Judith's mouth dropped open. "You didn't know—"

Alex swallowed hard. "Not until I read my name on the list of survivors in the case file today."

Stunned, Judith turned. "You didn't remember any of it?"

Alex shook her head, feeling Judith's shock. "No. I still don't."

"What about talking to the police? The therapists?" She motioned between them. "You don't remember that either."

"No, no. None of it. I don't remember anything. And Mom never mentioned it. We never talked about it."

Judith took her hand. "I'm so sorry, Alex. I never imagined you didn't know. I thought she would have told you eventually." She frowned. "This was not the way to find out."

Anger rushed across her. "No, it wasn't. You obviously knew."

Judith stared at her hands. "Not at first. I'd asked your mother what sort of things might've caused your nightmares. Kids have bad dreams all the time. It's not so strange. But when they continued to be the same picture—the man in the warehouse, the dead children, the screams . . ." She hesitated. "Well, I pressed your mother to tell me what had happened. I knew there had to have been something."

"And?"

"For a long time, she denied there was anything. And I thought it could have been something she didn't know about. That happens, too. The child is molested by a friend or, God forbid, a family member."

"How did you find out?"

Judith met her gaze. "It was kind of roundabout, actually. I'd been at Stanford the same time you guys lived in Palo Alto, so, of course, I'd heard about the murders. But I'd never imagined that you could've been there." She tucked a stray hair behind her ear. "One day, I was working on a case and your mother was helping me. The article was part of some research I was helping the D.A. with, involving a man who was charged with molesting and killing a child. Another child had gotten away and could identify the suspect as the killer."

Pausing, she looked straight at Alex. "We searched for similar survivor stories so we could contact D.A.'s offices around the country for information on how they prepared the children for trial, gather some other experts in the field.

"Your mother seemed especially perturbed by this research, which surprised me. She was usually fiery about the abuses of children, but I'd never seen her break down like that."

Judith pointed her finger, memory illuminating her expression. "I remember she said, 'What mother wouldn't be upset by these filthy maggots?' But when she got to the Sesame Street case, she broke down crying and rushed from the office. I found what she'd been reading . . ."

"And you put it together?"

Judith stared at the floor. "More or less. Knowing you guys from Palo Alto and hearing about your dreams."

Fury burning in her head, Alex stared at her hard. The anger spun, gaining heat and electricity until she expected lasers to fire from her eyes. "No one thought to tell me?"

Judith watched Alex carefully. "I still can't believe you haven't known all these years. I'm really sorry." She waved her hand to return to where she'd left off. "I knew your mother didn't want you told then, and I never felt right about it. She was adamant, but I thought she should've handled it differently, and I've always thought I could've done more. It's one of the reasons I was so happy that you wanted to come see me. I thought by now you would know. I hoped I could help somehow, that it wasn't too late."

Alex blinked hard, fighting off angry tears. "And my mother? Why didn't she tell me?"

Judith glanced at the ceiling, momentarily lost in thought. "It was such a different time, Alex. Sexual abuse charges by children against adults were dismissed more often than not. We didn't know nearly as much as we do now. Back then, people thought children got over it, that they'd just forget."

"That was it? She just forgot?"

Judith shook her head. "I don't think she ever forgot. I think she hoped she could take the pain for you. I remember when you were little, you used to tell me how your mother would come to your bed, crying. You didn't cry, but she did. You always thought that was so strange. And I think that's why. She felt the pain. I think she hoped by feeling it herself she could keep it from you."

It was impossible. How could they have done this? How could her mother have thought she could absorb the pain? Alex couldn't even imagine what her mother had been thinking. And now Alex had to deal with it alone. "Didn't you suggest she tell me?"

"I most definitely did. I pushed a little too hard, I think. Your mother and I grew apart within a few months of my finding out. You and I stopped talking." She paused and looked up. "I thought you should

know. I didn't think she had to tell you right then—
you were only in the second or third grade. But I
thought eventually the memories might come back. I
was sure by now you would've remembered it. I never
imagined it would be like this."

The image of her mother at her bedside stuck in
Alex's head. The teases and taunts James and Brittany
had used on her came back as well. They wouldn't
have known the real reason for Alex's terrible fears,
her awful dreams, but their mother had known.
Known but decided Alex shouldn't know. Alex was
furious. "My own mother. Unbelievable."

Judith looked up at her, her eyes apologetic. "She
was your mother. She didn't want to hurt you."

Alex shook her head, incredulous. "I'm not hurt—
I'm pissed. I'm pissed because I don't remember it.
And because now someone's calling me in the middle
of the night, and he knows more about it than I do.
I'm pissed because I woke up on a street corner less
than a block from a murder without any recollection
of how the hell I got there.

"And, I thought, *No big deal,* because I don't know
the dead guy. I think I've seen him once, but I don't
know him."

Abruptly, she started to pace. In the middle of the
room, she spun back to face Judith. "But you know
what?"

Judith didn't answer.

"I did know this guy. He was a survivor." She
scoffed. "Just like me." Angry and upset and scared,
she waved her arms around the room. "Of course,
he's not a survivor anymore, because now he's dead.
And to make matters worse, I just found out I killed
someone when I was six. So what's to say I didn't
knock off this guy, too? Maybe I'm a homicidal ma-
niac. I started young enough," she spit.

She choked and her shoulders sagged. Like a deflated balloon, she sank into the nearest chair and put

her head in her hands. "Oh, God. Did I kill him? I might have. I don't know." She shook her head. "I have no memory of that night either."

Alex looked up and wiped her face.

Judith's gaze remained steady.

Alex didn't give her a chance to speak. "But it's different now. It's different because I know I have a motive—because now I'm one of the statistics. I'm one of those kids who's been abused in the sickest, most disgusting way. I sat in that room with thirteen other children. Only three of us walked out."

Her voice had fallen to a whisper. "I don't remember, but I must have heard them die . . . I must have heard the screams and the panic and the last cries as they begged to go home to Mommy."

A sob choked free. "And why am I still here?" She stood again and stared at Judith. "Because I was at the end of the line?"

Judith stood and took a slow step toward Alex. "You're right. In a lot of ways, you're absolutely right. And anger is okay. Fear is okay. Guilt, anxiety, whatever you feel—it's all perfectly normal. It's going to take time to work through this. You need to give it time."

Alex looked up at her, feeling suddenly tired. "I don't have time. I could've killed this guy."

She paused, thinking. "There are things we can do to help you remember."

Alex winced, her heart pounding. She was afraid of what she might remember. But could she go on not remembering? "What types of things?"

"Hypnosis is one way."

"Can we do it now?" Alex asked.

Judith smiled softly. "You can't rush this sort of thing. It's a very simple procedure, but you need to be completely relaxed. I don't think that's going to happen right now."

"You think it would work?"

"Absolutely. It's really painless."

"When can we do it?"

"Anytime. You can come in this weekend if you really want to."

Nodding, Alex thought about the caller, about his taunting. He wanted her to remember. "I didn't kill Loeffler. I couldn't have." She thought about the blood and brain matter that had splattered around the body. "There would have been more on me. It would have been on my shirt and in my hair."

"Of course you didn't."

"But why was I there? I feel like I'm going crazy."

"It's very normal to feel that way. Sit down, let's talk about it."

Alex felt the familiar buzz on her hip. She pulled her beeper off her waistband and looked at the phone number. It was unfamiliar.

"Why don't you sit—we can talk."

Alex held up the pager. "I need to return this call."

"Can it wait until you're more settled, less upset?" Judith asked.

"No. I need to call now. It might be about the case."

"Of course." Judith went to the kitchen and returned with a cordless phone. "Would you prefer I leave you alone?"

"No. This will just be a minute."

Alex punched in the number and waited while the phone rang. She heard a click as the phone was answered.

"This is Officer Kincaid."

"Officer Kincaid," came the surly voice. "Have you missed me?"

Alex stood and took a few steps away from Judith, turning her back. "What the hell do you think you're doing?"

"I'm watching you, Alex. I was watching you eat. I was watching you sit at her counter. I saw you peel the label off that beer. I drooled when I saw your fingers working. I can't wait until you put those on me."

"The only thing I'm putting on you is handcuffs, you bastard."

He laughed. "Threaten me all you want. You can't escape. I'm here, right outside. No matter where you go, I'm with you. Don't forget it." The line clicked dead.

Judith appeared beside her, but Alex kept her back turned. She needed to pursue the caller first. Find out where he had called from. Nail the bastard.

Alex dialed the police station praying dispatch hadn't heard about her suspension. When the dispatcher answered, she said, "This is Officer Kincaid. I need you to give me the location on a phone number." She read the phone number off her beeper.

After thirty seconds, the dispatcher said, "A pay phone at University and Spruce, in front of Carl's Market."

Thanking the dispatcher, Alex turned to Judith, who was now sitting on the couch, watching her. "Where's Carl's Market?"

"About a block and a half that way." She pointed to her left. "Are you okay?"

Alex let the phone drop to her side. "Fine." She wasn't fine. He had been there—at Judith's. He'd seen her, Goddamn him!

Straightening herself, Alex handed Judith the phone and headed for the door. "I need to go."

"Alex? Please don't leave. Who was that? We should talk."

"I'll be fine. It's just this case. It's crazy. I really need to go."

"I hate to see you leave so upset. Why don't you sit down a few minutes?"

Alex shook her head. She couldn't stay. Nothing was going to help now but finding answers. "I can't."

"Will you call me when you get home, let me know you're all right?"

"I'll try. Thank you for dinner." Before Judith could protest again, Alex let herself out and hurried to her car, giving a careful look around to make sure no one stood waiting for her. Fear was thick in her gut, and she tried to shove it aside, to work through it.

She started her car, locked the doors, and pulled away from the curb. She would have liked to sit in her car and think for a minute, but that would have been dumb. Sitting in a still car was asking to be attacked. So she drove slowly down the street until she found a well-lit gas station. Then, she pulled to the pay phone and got out to check her voice mail.

"It's Greg. Byron called. He's got a hit on the prints. Guy named Alfred Ferguson. I'm trying to pull his records, but your asshole brother is all over me. I'm going to have to wait until it cools down a bit here. I'll see if there's someone else who can pull them. I did get to check Nader. I confirmed the address you gave me and there's no record. Not even parking tickets. Guy's clean as a whistle. Nada on NT SEC or the pictures.

"They're keeping it pretty hush-hush over there. They've been warned that you're involved, so nobody's talking, especially not to me. Brenda's giving it a shot, too. I'll let you know what we find out." Greg blew out a breath of frustration before hanging up, and Alex knew exactly how he felt.

Alfred Ferguson. Was that the man who had been in the gym? She wondered again about how he'd gotten a parking ticket slip. He could have stolen one easily enough. She hoped Greg would be able to track him down. She was anxious to pay Mr. Ferguson a little visit.

She listened to a message from Tom and one from Brittany. Both were invitations to dinner tomorrow night, neither of which she intended to accept. She needed to make a move. She wasn't learning anything in Berkeley. Nader hadn't called her back, but he was her best shot for information. The more Alex thought about Loeffler's notes, the more she thought that N stood for Nader. Loeffler must have called her that night. She was the K. She shook her head. It could have been a coincidence. Cops weren't supposed to place such bad bets, but right now, it was the only play she had. Her next move was to go to Palo Alto, look for Nader. Someone down there had to know something that would help her.

She felt the rise of fear again, fear about where she would turn if this didn't work out. She slammed her fist against the steering wheel. A cop wasn't supposed to be afraid. A cop was supposed to have defenses for these things. Where the hell were her defenses?

She revved the engine and peeled down the street. With the window down, she sped, the wind whipping across her face like the slap of a towel. What the police did now, who they investigated, all of that was out of her control. But she wasn't going to cross the line into prison—or the morgue.

Judith said to call if she needed to talk. Right now, Alex didn't need to talk. She was done talking.

What she needed now was to take control. That meant taking her ass to Palo Alto and figuring out what the hell had happened down there. Until she knew, she wasn't going to call and report in to James or anyone.

She could take care of herself—just as she'd always done up until this started. And she would find out who the hell was behind this.

Just then, she saw the whirl of police lights behind her, and sirens wailed into the night.

Chapter Nineteen

Her gaze snapped to the rearview mirror and she saw the black and white behind her.

Even if Greg had turned over her sweatpants they couldn't have reacted this fast.

She pulled to the side of the road and stopped the car. Letting her head fall against the steering wheel, she was suddenly exhausted, imagining what the talk in the station would be tomorrow. Kincaid arrested for murder in her own beat.

Stepping out of the car, she approached the head-lights of the cop car, squinting at the glare. A heavyset man rose from the driver's seat and took several steps forward.

His shoes clicked against the pavement and she heard the familiar clap as he hit his flashlight into the palm of his hand. The motion was scare tactic normally, a way of warning a difficult suspect not to try anything.

Drunks and drug users were the most common recipients of such treatment. She didn't know why he would use it on her. The man halted behind the head-lights and she squinted, still unable to make out his identity. A chill rippled across her skin. She spun to look behind her. She thought about the parking ticket again. A cop.

Turning back, she shook off the fear that wound down her neck like sweat. Instead, she pumped her hands and tightened her belly. "It's Officer Kincaid," she said, speaking directly into the headlights, both hands at her sides.

Whoever was there should know her name.

"Berkeley PD," she added.

Still no response

Her body was prepared for flight or fight. Alex waited as adrenaline splashed like motor oil through her legs, prepping them for takeoff.

"So it is," came the response.

She didn't think that the voice was the one she'd heard on the phone. But she could've been wrong. She paused, watching the shadow in the darkness. Her muscles twitched with more adrenaline. "Identify yourself."

He didn't respond.

Casting a quick glance over her shoulder, she spotted a yard with a high wall. Judging from the man's size, she would be able to lose him in a chase if she needed to. As long as she moved fast and he didn't get a clean shot at her first. With a deep breath, she decided to give him to three and then she was gone. One. Two.

The headlights went off and Alex's eyes fought to adjust to the darkness as the tap of heels moved closer.

"It's Gamble," the voice said.

A trickle of relief was quickly overpowered by a raging river of fury. She crossed the distance between them and gave him a swift kick in the right shin.

He yelped in response, reaching for his leg. He struggled to touch his shin over his belly and she wondered if his pant seat would tear from the strain. "What the hell was that for?"

She wished she had kicked him harder. As much flesh as he had on his bones, he shouldn't even have felt it. Brittany could've taken a harder kick without whimpering.

"I said why the hell did you kick me?"

"Don't be a jackass, Gamble. I asked you to identify yourself and you didn't. Was that supposed to be some sort of joke?" She still wasn't sure why he'd pulled her over, but she didn't think they would send Gamble to arrest her on his own. No, if she was about to be arrested for murder, James would definitely have been here, she thought cynically.

He let go of his leg and stood up, adjusting his belt beneath his jelly belly. His jaw jutted out so only two of the three chins showed. He scratched his gut with both hands like an ape. "I was about to. You didn't give me enough time."

She gritted her teeth. "I identified myself. You failed to respond. And you're getting off easy with a kick, Officer. If I'd had my gun, there's a good chance I'd have shot you in the kneecap."

Gamble craned his neck, a strange gesture of agitation. She had never seen anyone else do it, but everyone at the station knew it as his mark. Crane Wayne, they called him.

He cleared his throat. "Well, that sort of rash reaction is not at all appropriate," he scolded. "You could get kicked off the force for that."

What a joke. She had probably already been kicked off. Didn't he know what was going on?"

Pointing his stubby finger, he began his lesson. "The proper course of action if someone does not respond is to repeat the request a second time. In chapter fourteen of the manual, it says," he continued, "if you do not receive a response on second request and assume the suspect may be armed, then—"

She exhaled. "Cut the crap, Gamble. Where's Roback?" Maybe Greg had shot himself to get out of being partnered with Gamble. She knew she would have.

"He's out with Pingelli."

She frowned. "Why Pingelli?"

Gamble pushed his shoulder back and craned his neck again. "Guess Pingelli needed some extra help."

That didn't sound right. Pingelli had been on the force almost six years. He had his own partner. "Where's Harmon then?"

"Sick."

Alex frowned. Harry Harmon prided himself on his perfect attendance record. Something about it didn't feel right. What was Gamble up to? "You out here alone?"

Gamble tucked his thumbs beneath his belt and sniffed deep like he had never smelled Berkeley air before. "Yep."

They would never send him out alone unless they were incredibly desperate. And even then, the officer would always be on some sort of restricted duty. "I'm surprised the captain would send you out here on your own so quickly."

"Yep."

Either way, she didn't care. "Great. Glad to hear it's going so well."

"Oh, yeah, great. Busted a guy down at—"

"Right," she interrupted. "Well, I'm heading home. Have a good night."

Waving good-bye, she started for her car, thinking she would have to ask Greg how he got out of that one. Gamble was strange, but seeing him out here alone was even stranger. She was more than happy to leave.

Gamble cleared his throat again.

She thought she heard her name but she didn't stop. She didn't have time for idle chat. It was close to ten-thirty and she needed to get home and get on the road to Palo Alto before it was too late.

"Alex, you can't leave."

She spun back and frowned. "Excuse me?"

Gamble was silent a moment. Then, with a quick thrust of his chin, he continued, "You were speeding."

He spoke in a voice much lower than his usual one. It made him sound like a soap opera star doing a sex scene.

Incredulous, she nailed her hands to her hips. "What?"

"I said, you were speeding." His voice cracked on the last word, but he made a valiant though unsuccessful effort to catch it.

She cracked a smile. "That's a good one."

He shook his head. "No joke."

"You're not serious."

"Absolutely."

She watched him a minute and then strode back toward him, aiming her sights on the other shin.

As though expecting it, Gamble ducked behind the car door. "Not so fast."

Her finger raised, she pointed it between his wide eyes. "I've had a really bad day, okay? Don't fuck with me today. Tomorrow, next week—but not today. Understand?"

The radio cut in. "Two Adam Nineteen, come in. Are you requesting backup?"

Wayne glanced at the console but made no move to answer the call. "I'm sorry, but the law's the law. Can't be doing special favors . . ."

Her jaw muscle tight, she expelled all her energy into pretending his hand was between her teeth. Releasing, she inhaled. "I'm in no mood for you to get high and mighty with me. I'm leaving."

"I don't think so, missy. I'm writing you a ticket. Now, I'm going to need your driver's license."

Alex fought to remain calm. He was recently back on patrol. He was just trying to do his job. It was probably very honest of him. But this was a very bad day. And she wasn't about to get a speeding ticket from a cop in her own department on top of finding out that she had almost been killed at age six and that she was about to become a suspect for murder. Only she couldn't afford more trouble of any kind with the department.

"I think it's great that you're so enthusiastic," she lied. "But I was doing forty-one in a thirty-five, Gamble. And like I said, I've had a really, really long day."

He shook his head. "Don't need to confess the speed to me. I only have you clocked at forty." With his clipboard out, he sat down in his car and began writing.

Riveted to her spot, she watched him, waiting for the joke. It had to be a joke. She was going five miles over the speed limit. It wasn't a ticket she would have written on a normal citizen. But another cop?

The call came again.

He picked up the radio and responded. "Adam Nineteen. I've got an eleven-ninety-four. No backup necessary."

She counted, giving him until ten to smile and tell her he was kidding.

Gamble glanced up and nodded to her car. "As I said, I am going to need your driver's license. I'll wait here if you want to get it. I trust you." Standing from the car, he paused. When he spoke again, his voice was low and raspy. "Unless you want to come here a moment."

She halted, feeling the hairs rise on the back of her neck. "What?"

"We can probably clear this up, just the two of us, if you want."

She took a step forward, seething to the point of shaking. "How do you mean?"

Gamble opened the back door of the squad car and sat down. "You can start by sitting down here." He patted his knees. "I'll show you what to do from there. I promise it won't hurt." He grinned, reaching out to touch her.

Fury exploded through her chest, racing across her arms and legs until it shot out from her fingers and she could no longer hold herself back. Her hands flat on the car door, she shoved it shut full force.

Gamble emitted an agonizing cry that she was sure woke some of the neighbors as the door slammed on his legs.

"I warned you," she said.

Gamble was crying. "Jesus Christ, you're insane. You're fucking insane."

He got that right. Anger still washing around her stomach like battery acid, she started for her car.

"I think you broke my legs," he moaned.

Cursing, she started her car and raced home. She shouldn't have let him get the best of her. And she knew she was going to catch hell from Captain Lyke. And James. Assaulting a police officer—even Crane Wayne—was a serious offense. If she hadn't been kicked off the force by now, she would be after this incident. Even with Gamble's blatant come-on, her aggression would be deemed over the top.

"Forget it." She was going to Palo Alto tonight. There was no more time to waste on all this bullshit—people watching over her shoulder, keeping her off the case, trying to frame her or protect her. She didn't need them.

In her driveway, she stopped the car, yanking the emergency brake so hard she was surprised it didn't come off in her hand. She opened the back door to the house, trying to look past the spot in her trash where Loeffler's hand had been found.

The door locked, she took the stairs by twos and searched for a duffel bag beneath the bed. She scowled at the amount of crap she had managed to stuff under there.

There was an old set of curlers, a digital alarm clock that didn't work, her camping equipment. Where the hell was the duffel? She tore stuff out and flung it across the room. Finally, she spotted it and put it on the bed, then kicked a path through the mess to her dresser.

From it she pulled out three of everything—socks, underwear, T-shirts—and a pair of khakis and loafers for anything she couldn't do in jeans, and tossed it all in the bag. Grabbing her toothbrush from the bathroom, she ignored the rest. Even the crappiest motels had soap and shampoo. She didn't worry that she didn't know where she was staying. She would figure it out. She had a lot to figure out.

At the bottom of the stairs, she opened her coat closet, lifted her holster off the coat rack on the back of the door, and then set it on the couch. She had turned in her badge and gun, so she pulled down the lockbox from the back of the closet and took out her personal weapon—a Smith & Wesson Model 5900 pistol. It was a 9mm, and she like it because it held fifteen rounds. Most 9mms, like her service Glock, only held ten rounds, and it didn't hurt to have a few extra shells loaded in case of an emergency.

She tucked the gun, an extra magazine, and her flashlight in the bag and set her beeper on the table. She didn't want to hear from this guy again until they were face to face. The blinking red light of her machine caught her eye. She pressed Play and listened as she worked. Tom had called twice, worried. She listened through a message from the professor friend of Brenda's husband, wondering if she was busy Saturday night. He had a nice voice, she thought. Pressing Save, she looked over her things.

The pepper spray and Gerber camping knife in her jacket, she pulled a box of extra ammunition down from the closet shelf and put it in her bag. With the bag on her shoulder, the weight of her travel arsenal sank down on the muscles in her back.

She took another quick look around. There was nothing else she needed. Four steps from the door, she halted. Before she left, she needed to tell someone where she would be. A cop never went in alone without notifying someone. It was stupid, dangerous as hell, and an unnecessary risk.

The phone glared at her. Not James, not Brittany. Greg? She shook her head. He would insist on coming and he'd done too much already. Plus, James was already on to him. If Greg knew where she was, James would break him in a second. The receiver tight in her fist, she dialed the only number she could call.

"Hello?" came the sleepy voice.

"Brenda?"

"Alex, is that you? Are you okay?"

"I'm fine."

"I'm sorry about all this shit. I tried to find something out, but it's like a vault over there. All the doors are closed, everything's a damn secret. They're like a bunch of Fibbies," she said, referring to FBI agents.

"Thanks for trying."

"No problem. Jesus, what time is it?"

Alex looked at the clock across the room. It was almost eleven. "Listen, I'm really sorry. It's late. I need a favor." Through the phone, Alex heard Brenda shifting as though sitting up in bed.

"Sure, anything."

Alex glanced at the back door. "I'm going out of town for a few days."

"Where?" Brenda's voice sounded fretful. "Is this about the case, Alex? You sure it's smart to leave?"

With a quick breath, she answered, "I have to go. I'm going to Palo Alto."

"To find out what happened with the dead lawyer?"

"Yeah. It's where it happened. I'm hoping there are some answers down there."

"Did I tell you the one about the tragedy of the bus full of lawyers who drowned?" Brenda said, trying to joke.

"Yeah, yeah. The empty seat. That's an old one. I can't believe you're still telling it."

Brenda was quiet for a minute. "You're sure that's what you need to do?"

"Positive."

"You want someone to come with you?" Brenda's voice deepened, her concern evident in the tone.

Alex couldn't help but break a smile. "No." It would be one thing to lose her job, but she wasn't taking anyone else down with her. "I'll check in with you. I just wanted someone to know where I was. Greg's done too much already."

"He's crazy about you, girl."

Alex smiled self-consciously. "I know."

"I'm having lunch with David tomorrow. I'm hoping to get some stuff from him."

David was a detective who had always had a crush on Brenda and had made it perfectly clear despite her husband. "I appreciate it."

"Is there somewhere I can call you?"

"I don't have my cell phone anymore."

"I heard."

"I'll check messages here."

"You're not telling James?"

"No. And you can't, either."

"You sure you want to do this alone?"

She laughed. "That's a loaded question."

"Damn right it is. I want you to think before you go."

"Thanks, Brenda. I've thought it through—this is my only option."

"If you're sure—"

"I am."

"Anything else?"

Gamble's legs came to mind and she wondered how badly he was actually hurt. "There's one more thing . . ."

"Shoot."

Fingers massaging her temple, she considered what Gamble would tell the captain. "It's a long story, but when the captain starts ranting about Gamble being laid up in the hospital, will you tell him Gamble had it coming?"

"Woman! You shot him?"

Alex broke a sheepish grin. "Of course not. He's probably fine, but there's a chance I broke his leg."

Brenda gasped. "You broke his leg?"

"Okay," she confessed. "Maybe both. He had it coming—bastard came on to me."

"He did not!"

"Did, too."

"And you broke his legs? You go, girl!" Brenda exploded into laughter and her husband groaned in the background. "That is too funny," she whispered. "When?"

"It's a long story. You'll hear all about it tomorrow, I'm sure."

"You can't leave me in suspense."

"Believe me, it'll be worth the wait. I'll call you in a couple days."

"You'd better. You be careful now."

"Thanks, Brenda." Alex hung up the phone and headed out the door.

After a careful detour through the side streets of Oakland and Berkeley, Alex was confident she wasn't being followed. If someone had been behind her, he either would have lost her or been seen. Now, crossing the Bay Bridge, she could just see the Ghiradelli sign, PacBell Park, and the Transamerica Building against the white misty fog as she passed Treasure Island. Living and working in the East Bay, she came to the city less and less often. Looking over at the lights and the water, she remembered why she loved it so much.

The bridge always gave her the sensation of freedom, one she didn't feel as strongly now. She only hoped on her way back from Palo Alto, she would feel it again. Despite the hour, a steady stream of cars still occupied the freeway, and Alex kept a close eye on which exited and which remained around her. It was hard to imagine that someone had followed her, but after the past few days, she knew she had to be extra careful.

Turning up the radio, she felt the click, click, click as her tires crossed over the metal divides on the bridge's surface. The continuing debate in the city was about retrofitting the bridge for earthquake safety.

As she passed through the city and headed down 101 south toward Palo Alto, she hoped she wouldn't have trouble finding a reasonably priced room when she arrived. She didn't have her cellular phone and she wasn't going to stop to call around.

Her bankbook couldn't take too fancy a hotel and the one credit card she kept had a limit of only five hundred dollars. She had never been comfortable with buying things she couldn't pay for.

The desire to sleep tumbled upon her, and she rolled down the window to fight the force of gravity working on her eyelids. She stayed in the far right lane of the five-lane freeway, moving only to pass an occasional turtle-like driver. The speed limit was sixty-five, but even in the slow lane the traffic moved at about seventy-five.

The whole way down, she tried to reason out how a six-year-old could have killed a grown man. The report hadn't disclosed the method of Androus's death. All she knew was that he had died from a gunshot wound. She assumed more detail was missing because it involved a minor and those records would be sealed. But the file had said that the children's hands were bound and they were blindfoldeded. How could she have gotten his gun? Even if the blindfold had fallen off and he had set the gun beside her, how could she have steadied it to shoot him? She couldn't come up with an answer for that one.

It was nearly one o'clock when she arrived in Palo

Alto, exhausted. Her eyelids felt like they now weighed more than her duffel bag. She turned off and found a Red Roof Inn, pulling her car into the closest spot, praying the half-empty parking lot was an indication that they would have a vacancy.

The night auditor looked like a member of the Addams Family, but he checked her into a eighty-dollar room without a problem. Thankful for the prospect of sleep, Alex headed for the stairs after a last glance out at the parking lot. It was silent. Her room was five floors up, but she hated elevators. Suddenly, she caught herself blaming each of her faults and fears on whatever had happened when she was six years old.

She found her room and let herself in. Dropping her bag on the bed, she drew the shades, bolted and chained the door, and checked the bathroom and closet. Satisfied, she took off her jeans and bra, did a rough brush of her teeth, and crawled into bed in her T-shirt and underwear, still wearing her socks.

For once, sleep hit her like a freight train.

Chapter Twenty

White fabric billowed around Alex's head, the face before her a dreamy blur she couldn't focus on. What was happening? She couldn't see the bad man. Where had he gone?

The cool floor was suddenly warmer as something held Alex close, wrapping her in thick white wings. She could smell her daddy again. She breathed in the smell and tried to see him. The blindfold covered all but a corner of her eye and she tried to push it off without using her hand. It was cold and she could feel the outside breeze against her bare arms.

She shivered, moving in tighter as she turned and tried to make out a face. She caught a glimpse, but no image came.

Behind her, the two boys squirmed and whimpered, their blindfolds still fastened across their eyes. Hers had slipped down around her nose and she could just see through the gap between her bangs and the loose blindfold. Moving further from them, Alex saw the gun before she realized what it meant. The gray black of the dull metal contrasted against the white sheet. She stared at the bad man then back at the gun again.

It felt heavy and cold, its tip pointed to the ground.

"You have to shoot him, honey," the voice beside her said. "You have to shoot him or he'll hurt you. Do you want him to do that?"

Alex shook her head, words trapped beneath her fear.

The bad man's eyes stared at her.

Her body shook with a mixture of chill and terror.

"What are you doing?" he screamed.

The gun fought in her hands as she struggled to hold it up. "It's too heavy," she cried.

"You can do it," the voice assured. "Do it for Mommy and Daddy."

Alex tried to look at the angel. "Daddy?" she whispered.

"That's right, baby. Do it for Daddy. Don't worry. I'll be right here until it's all over."

With all her might, she lifted the gun from the ground. Her hands shook as she steadied it. Strong hands helped her, holding the gun out.

"What are you doing?" he screamed again. "Jay, you can't!"

The gun exploded in her hand, knocking her backwards. Her head hit the floor with a thud, and she couldn't move.

It seemed like a long time before she could sit. The boys' crying dragged her up. She rubbed her head and looked at the bad man. He didn't move. He looked asleep, but his eyes were open. People didn't sleep with their eyes open.

Alex looked around. Where was her daddy?

Alex woke with a jolt at six, her stomach in a series of hard knots. The dream skittered by in pieces. Remembering what Judith had said, she found a pad of paper in the drawer. She scribbled "angel" on the top piece and stared at it blankly.

An angel? She closed her eyes to bring the image back in focus, but it was gone. Frustrated, she threw the pad and pen to the floor and got out of bed.

By quarter after, she was showered, dressed, and downstairs. She informed the night auditor that she would be back, paid for another night, and headed down the freeway to University Avenue.

As she pulled off the freeway, she took in the imme-

diate area. The off-ramp divided Palo Alto into east
and west and also split San Mateo and Santa Clara
counties. But more than that, the off-ramp acted as
an invisible Berlin Wall.

East Palo Alto was poor and crime-ridden. Police
often warned West Palo Alto residents about the dan-
gers of the area, but some still paid no heed. A well-
heeled college student was recently beaten to death
by a group of boys just for walking on their streets.

Alex saw the dilapidated buildings and beat-up cars
left abandoned on the streets. Several people stood
on stoops, drinking from bottles hidden in paper bags.
From their disheveled appearances, it was impossible
to tell if they were just getting up or hadn't yet been
to sleep.

The roads were riddled with potholes, many almost
gravel from neglect. Not a single tree struggled
through the black pavement.

Alex turned right and headed west, immediately
struck by the incredible difference. This side was filled
with magnolia trees, their trunks thick, their branches
reaching out to provide shade to the wealthy. A few
even seemed to bow over the houses.

Large Spanish-style homes lined the streets, their
yards carefully pruned. The cars were securely tucked
away in three- and four-car garages. Even the leaves
had been swept up. A bike lane took up part of the
road in each direction so people could enjoy the
beauty on a leisurely Sunday morning ride.

About four miles down University, she began to
see small shops and restaurants. She turned on Bryant
Street and parked next to Restoration Hardware. She
crossed the street to Starbucks, thankful that caffeine
would soon be coursing through her veins. She bought
a plain bagel at the Noah's next door and took a brief
walk to get a sense of the neighborhood.

Stanford students roamed the streets, stopping to
greet classmates or buy coffee before study groups

or games. They looked much the same as Berkeley students—shorts and tennis shoes, sweatshirts for the dewy morning chill, and baseball caps to hide the fact that they probably hadn't showered yet on a Saturday morning.

But unlike Cal, Stanford didn't have the outward personality that came with Berkeley cultures—the punks, hippies, and homeless didn't come to Palo Alto. Or if they did, they hid themselves well.

For a moment, Alex missed the comforts she had always found in Berkeley's diversity. This homogenous neighborhood seemed much too peaceful for something as heinous as Androus's crime—and must have been even more so thirty years ago.

Eyeing the nicely dressed people, she wondered which of them harbored thoughts of murder or rape. People assumed their neighbors were all upstanding, successful businesspeople and concerned citizens. But some of them weren't. As a cop, she knew it better than most.

Caffeine beginning to seep through her system, she drove to the city hall and parked, wondering what, if anything, she might find. The building stood like an immense piece of candy—the white stripes of its beveled columns next to the dark stripes of its deep blue windows. The building sat in the center of a courtyard with grass and black benches that looked freshly painted.

The police station occupied the backside of the courthouse, a smaller, shorter version of city hall, with the same blue reflective windows and modern architecture. She entered through the station's tinted glass doors and found herself in a light yellow room with dark wood furniture and light blue accents that looked more like a doctor's office than any police station she had ever seen.

"Can I help you?" came a voice.

Alex approached a wooden counter and met the

gaze of a young black woman. "I hope so. My name is—"

Just then, a door swung open and a burly man with a mustache marched through. He had thick, wiry eyebrows that seemed to wiggle like caterpillars as he walked. "JB," he squawked.

The nameplate on the desk said Janice Branson, and Alex thought JB was an interesting nickname for a woman. "What is it, Captain?"

He looked like Internal Affairs. It was just a guess, but the deep-set frown, the suit, even the way his eyes seemed to scan over his shoulder made her think IA.

He paused and leaned against the desk, effectively pushing Alex out of his way. She took a step back and let him in. "Just got a message from BPD IA."

Alex sucked in a deep breath and forced herself not to move. Berkeley Police Department Internal Affairs. Damn James.

She must've made some noise, because Caterpillar Brow looked over at her. She forced a small smile.

"Sorry, miss. This'll just take a second. Police business," he added as though she might be impressed.

"Of course," she choked.

"What did Berkeley want?" JB asked, pulling the captain's meandering attention back to the issue at hand.

"They got a cop named Kincaid, AWOL. He's in BFT and they think he might show up here. Alex Kincaid. If he does, they want to be informed ASAP. You let me know first and I'll handle it from there. Is that PC?"

BFT? PC? Alex had always been annoyed when people assumed hers was a man's name. For the first time, she was relieved.

JB nodded. "Perfectly clear," she responded.

The captain gave a small salute and ambled out as he had come in.

JB turned back to Alex. "Sorry about that."

Alex shrugged, trying to play it cool. "Can I ask what BFT is?" She couldn't help herself.

JB smiled. "Big fucking trouble." She waved at the door the captain had come through. "Everything's an acronym with that guy. Calls me JB. Name is Janice Branson, but he doesn't care." She shook her head. "Considered it EUT." She pronounced the acronym "yout."

"Yout?" Alex asked.

"EUT. Efficient use of time."

"Got it."

Janice shook her head. "Now what can I help you with?"

Alex flushed and stuttered, "I think I'm in the wrong place. I've got a parking ticket that I wanted to talk to someone about."

"I'm afraid that's next door and they're not in on the weekend. They open Monday at eight."

Alex smiled. "No problem. I'll come back." She turned to walk away, trying to figure out what to do next. She couldn't ask about the Sesame Street murders now. Maybe it would be public record. "Is there a public library in the vicinity?"

Janice pointed to her left. "Next building over."

"Great." Alex hurried out of the building and around the corner before pausing for a breath. If she had given her name three seconds earlier, it would have been over. Without access to the case, she was SOL. Shit out of luck. That could have been her motto lately.

She found a coffee house and ordered a large black coffee. Taking it to a table, she sat down and pulled her notebook from her bag. She had made a list of people to try to contact from the case: lead detective (alive?), other detectives, first cop on the scene, evidence processing (still in archive? results?), Nader. His name had two stars beside it. At least she could still try to reach Nader. She'd do that before hitting the library.

Finishing her coffee, she stood and walked to the register. "Do you know where Ramona Street is?" she asked the woman working.

She shrugged. "No idea."

"I can tell you."

Alex turned to see a young man seated at a table with a Palm Pilot and a laptop hooked up to his cell phone.

"Where is it?"

The man typed something and hit enter. "Just one second."

Alex watched over his shoulder as a map came onto the screen. "We're here." He pointed to a small red circle on the screen. "And Ramona is here. You need to take University out and head southwest. You'll run into Ramona in about six or seven blocks. Sorry I can't print this out."

Alex shook her head. "That's okay. I'll find it."

"What's the address on Ramona? I can tell you exactly."

"That helps a lot," she said without answering his question. "Thanks again."

Alex turned and left before he could ask anything else. She found her car and followed the directions to Ramona. When she found the street, she read the sign and turned left toward 216.

The house was about a block and a half down on the right side. It was a small taupe ranch-style house. The yard was hedge-lined, the lawn carefully kept.

Alex stepped out of her car and headed to the front door. Three steps led to a porch about two square feet. She rang the doorbell and waited.

A curtain moved at the house next door and Alex glanced over. No face appeared behind the burgundy drape, but a nosy neighbor was often a cop's best friend. If Alex needed any information, she knew where to start.

Her attention back on Nader's house, Alex found herself curious to find out how this third survivor had turned out. Loeffler appeared from what she'd seen to have made a name for himself as a successful prosecutor, but he had harbored plenty of secrets.

Down on the curb again, she looked at the windows on the front side of the house. Nothing stirred. As she circled the property, she stopped and put her face to the windows to look inside, careful not to touch anything.

The rooms were masculine in style—sparse in furniture, and painted in dark, bold colors: forest green in the living room, brown and burgundy in the kitchen. The living room held only a huge dark blue leather couch, a chair and ottoman, and the biggest TV she had ever seen. Definitely a bachelor pad. But besides that, everything inside looked normal, like he'd just gone out. Not like when she'd found Loeffler sprawled in the hallway.

She circled the house and knocked on the back door, but still no one answered. She peered into the garage and saw a car parked inside. It was black and looked like an Acura.

She stood back from the garage. Maybe he was on vacation. She hadn't seen mail piled up by either door and no newspapers, but maybe he'd had them held. That would also explain why his answering machine had beeped so many times before her message. She considered going to ask the neighbor, but she wasn't ready to explain who she was yet. She circled the other side and found one room with the shades drawn so she couldn't see in, which she assumed was his bedroom. There was also a very sparsely furnished dining room. In one corner was a tall wine rack filled with bottles. They were almost all red.

Around the front of the house again, she searched

for a mailbox but saw that he had a slot that went in the front door. Leaning down, she pushed it open using the corner of her shirt and saw a pile of mail on the floor. Nader *was* on vacation. That was the last of her leads.

Defeated, she went back to her car and drove toward the freeway. She couldn't go back to Berkeley. There was nothing but trouble waiting for her there.

She drove without purpose for twenty minutes before she decided to stop by the public library and see what she could dredge up on the case. It was something she could have done in Berkeley, but she was here, so she might as well try it. Plus, maybe the local papers had better coverage of the crime.

She found a meter and dropped in enough quarters for two hours before getting out and jogging to the main entrance. Her head ached with each step and she rubbed it with the heel of her hand as she walked in the door.

The Palo Alto public library reflected the police station's modernity. Unlike Berkeley's library, housed in an older stucco building, Palo Alto's was huge and modern, with cathedral ceilings and high windows tinted greenish-blue. Skylights lit the entryway and most of the rooms as she walked in.

Leaving her awe at the information desk, Alex headed straight to the reference section and found an unoccupied computer. Her notes beside her, she typed in "Sesame Street Murders" on Lexis-Nexis to see what came up.

There were seventeen articles listed and Alex scrolled through them for one that might give her additional information. "Interview with a killer's sister," one read. It was from a Stanford publication, written by a Dr. J. D. Daniels. Alex clicked on the document and the computer made a series of grinding clicks and burps until it filled the screen.

Alex had leaned forward to read the article when she heard a familiar voice behind her.

"I thought I might find you here."

Alex spun around to look into a familiar set of brown eyes.

Chapter Twenty-one

"What the hell are you doing here?"

Greg smiled. "Shh. This is the library."

"How did you find me?"

"Followed you from Nader's house."

She crossed her arms and looked around. "How did you find me there?"

He pulled up a chair and sat down. "I knew you'd go there. I called you last night and you weren't home. Made me nervous. I called Brenda."

"She told you?"

"Didn't have to. As soon as she told me to mind my own business, I knew exactly where you were. I drove down at five this morning and waited about a block from Nader's."

"And why didn't you say anything there?" Alex asked, frowning.

"You looked intent in your search and I didn't want to get shot."

She pointed at the door. "You need to go back."

"Not a chance."

She shook her head and turned away from him. "You're working today."

He moved in closer. "Called in sick."

She pushed his chair back and spoke in a harsher tone. "Roback, this is serious. You need to stay the hell away from me. I'm going to be arrested for murder."

"I know. That's why I called you last night."

Alex felt like she was about to be knocked in the gut. She clenched her stomach muscles and awaited the punch.

"They've got the watch. Someone I.D.'d it as yours. I guess James doesn't remember that you told him about it and he's through the f-ing roof. That and the blood—" He gripped the arm of her chair and she leaned forward, waiting for him to finish his sentence even though she knew exactly what he was going to say. "There's a warrant," he finished.

Alex pulled her hands to her stomach, effectively knocking the wind out of herself. But the news had already done it. She really was going to be arrested.

"They've already called down here."

She nodded. "I know."

"How?"

She explained about overhearing the IA captain speaking to the receptionist. "I'm screwed."

Greg didn't say anything.

"This is exactly what the killer wanted. He fucking planned it." She exhaled. "What else is going on up there?"

"They've subpoenaed phone records—yours and Loeffler's. He called you that night."

She opened her mouth to talk and found she couldn't speak.

"Loeffler, I mean," he said.

"What night?"

"The night he was killed. At about eleven-thirty. You spoke for six minutes."

She shook her head. "I couldn't have. I don't remember." She wiped her hands on her pants, feeling herself sweat.

"It's going to be all right, Alex."

She waved her hand. "Don't. Don't bother." She blew her breath out and nodded. "Tell me what else. What else is going on?"

"They've also been surveying Ferguson's house. As

of last night, he hadn't showed up. They were going
to go in with a warrant this morning. I called up there
but no one could tell me what happened."

"What about the murder weapon? It couldn't have
been my gun." Even as she said it, she wasn't sure.

"It wasn't. County ballistics tested it yesterday. It
was a Glock, like a service issue, but not yours." He
raised an eyebrow. "Guess whose they're testing
next."

"Yours."

He nodded.

"They think I could've taken yours."

"You got it."

She let her head fall into her hands for a moment
and then pulled herself up. She couldn't be weak.
After a deep breath, she looked at Greg. "What
now?"

He glanced at the computer screen. "What's that?"

"An article by some doctor—looks like an interview
with Androus's sister."

Alex began skimming the article, but her mind was
on the gun. It couldn't have been Greg's. Intellectu-
ally, she knew that, but she couldn't help but feel a
little tremor of fear at the possibility.

The subject had been interviewed at her home in
Upshur, West Virginia, on November 1, 1972, as part
of the Stanford University Department of Psychology's study of criminal psychology.

Alex skipped the rest of the introduction. Nothing
stood out, so she scrolled down to an excerpt from
the full interview.

DR. DANIELS: *Can you tell us something about your
brother, Ms. Androus?*
MAGGIE ANDROUS: *I don't know much. I left home
when I was sixteen. He was only thirteen. He left
two years later.*
DD: *Why did you leave home?*

MA: *Don't see how that's relevant.*
DD: *I understand the questions may be difficult. But we need to ask them to help us understand why your brother did what he did.*
MA: *Oh, I know why he did it. Our father was screwed up. Worked the coal mines down here— drank too much.*
DD: *Did your father hit you?*
MA: *On a good night.*

The doctor notes that Stanford research has shown a history of familial abuse is a prominent theme in homicides. Androus's family environment fits this pattern.

Alex skimmed over the rest of the discussion on family abuse and kept reading. She thought about Maggie Androus's words, flat and unemotional on the page, imagining her voice when the words had been spoken. Had they been angry and upset and spiteful?

A cop was trained to sense the emotion below the surface. Alex wished she could have heard the tape.

She had started to scroll down again when Greg grabbed her hand. "Slow down. I'm reading." Alex waited until he nodded and moved further down the page.

DD: *Did your father sexually abuse you?*
MA: *(No answer.)*
DD: *Did your father force you and your brother to perform sexual acts with him?*
MA: *(No answer.)*
DD: *How about with each other?*
MA: *(No answer.)*
DD: *I know this is difficult, but the information you're providing is going to be pivotal to helping us understand what happened to Walter.*
MA: *Yes, he did. All of us.*
DD: *All of you? Can you be more specific?*

MA: *Me, Walter, and Ben.*
DD: *Ben?*
MA: *My brother.*

Alex halted, puzzled. Androus had only one sister as far as she knew. Where had the brother come from? The next sentence grabbed her attention and she continued.

"Whoa, slow down. Who's the brother?"

"Shh. I'm trying to find out," Alex said, reading on.

DD: *Ms. Androus, we don't have a record of Walter having a brother. Where is he now?*
MA: *Dead.*
DD: *When did he die?*
MA: *Six years ago. In New York. He was eighteen.*
DD: *How did he die?*
MA: *Killed himself.*
DD: *How?*
MA: *Jesus Christ, have some respect. Does it really matter how he killed himself? He isn't going to help your little project. He's dead.*
DD: *I apologize, Ms. Androus. Maggie. May I call you Maggie?*
MA: *(Nod.)*
DD: *Maggie. I know this is difficult, but it will help us. Understanding how Ben was feeling, how you're feeling, too, will help us with how Walter felt, what led him to do what he did.*
MA: *Fine. He shot himself—with a .22—our father's .22. I never even knew he had taken it, but I guess he did. Walter confirmed it was Daddy's gun.*
DD: *Was Ben older or younger than you and Walter?*
MA: *He was Walter's twin.*

"His twin? Holy shit," Greg said, voicing Alex's own reaction.

"B.A.," Alex said.

"What?"

"There was a picture in Loeffler's things—a guy with red hair. On the back were the initials B.A." Alex had read theories on twin behavior in her psych classes. Plus, she'd seen James and Brittany anticipate each other's thoughts and feelings in more intense ways than most siblings. She couldn't believe Ben was still alive and had decided to come finish what his brother had started. It was too Hollywood to be real. But why was his picture in Loeffler's file? If it was his picture? And where was Maggie now?

"Ben Androus," Greg said.

She looked at him and raised her eyebrows.

"Ben Androus is Alfred Ferguson?"

"It's possible, I guess." She thought about the man in the gym. He hadn't had red hair, but that would be easy enough to change. And she hadn't gotten a good look at his face. He'd seemed younger than she would have imagined Androus would be. Androus would have to be almost fifty-five by now. But it was possible. "Did you see his picture?"

"I couldn't get in. James—" He stopped and shook his head.

"I know."

She could see him getting angry and he motioned to the screen. "Keep reading."

DD: Who found Ben?
MA: Walter. Walter found him. He hadn't heard from him in a few days. They were very close, Walter and Ben. Ben was living in New York, Walter was in L.A. So he bused out to see him. Then he called me. Ben had been dead awhile, I guess.
DD: How about your mother?
MA: She was a drunk, too. I felt sorry for her. She drank to get away from him.
DD: From your father?

MA: Right.

DD: Did you have any correspondence with your brothers after you left home?

MA: Walter would drop me a note once in a while.

DD: Did you keep his notes?

MA: No. For a while, we kept in good contact. After Ben died, it stopped. Then, about four years ago, we started to write again. But Walter's notes were strange. I barely read them sometimes. He wasn't right—if you know what I mean.

Alex cringed. Obviously he wasn't right. She read on.

DD: What gave you that idea?

MA: He was seeing a doctor and stuff.

DD: Do you remember anything that he told you about the doctor?

MA: Hardly anything. He used to write tons about going to a school out there.

DD: What school? You mean as a student?

MA: Don't remember the name, but he wasn't no student.

DD: How was he going to school?

MA: As a patient.

"Write that down—he was a patient somewhere," Greg directed.

Alex nodded and wrote.

DD: Maggie, could you elaborate? What sort of patient was Walter?

MA: I don't remember much now. Said he was going to some special center—being evaluated.

DD: As in mentally evaluated?

MA: I always assumed that's what he meant.

DD: Do you remember anything else about his correspondence?

MA: *He used to say weird things.*

DD: *What sort of things?*

MA: *Like the power of the mind. He used to say he had to capture the power of the mind. That's what life was all about.*

DD: *Anything else?*

MA: *He used to write about a friend named Jay.*

DD: *Jay? Do you know who that was?*

MA: *I think it was his doctor.*

DD: *Can you tell me what specifically made you think that?*

MA: *Oh, I think he told me that in one of his letters. Otherwise, I wouldn't have thought it. He used to talk a lot about Jay—Jay this, Jay that, how great Jay was. Always struck me as off.*

DD: *Why's that?*

MA: *Our father's name was Jay.*

Chapter Twenty-two

Alex scrolled down and looked for more interview, but the rest was commentary. She skimmed a bit of it, discussion about Walter's attempt to replace a father figure with a shrink of the same name.

"Fucking weird."

Alex nodded. She typed in NT SEC and scrolled through the hits: Windows NT, the website for the Securities and Exchange Commission, articles about the SEC. Nothing seemed to fit.

"You saw that in his calendar?"

She nodded and continued to search.

"It's probably shorthand for something," Greg said, watching over her shoulder.

Alex blew her breath out in a frustrated stream. "We need someone who has access to the case. Someone who knows if Ben Androus was checked into, if he's really dead. Also, Maggie's whereabouts and who Walter's friends were. Who could have helped him? Maybe we can find his shrink and ask him." She exhaled. "And I want to confirm who was the shooter." She paused.

"Confirm that it was you, you mean."

"Right. Confirm that I shot him." She shook her head. "What a week."

Greg put a hand on her shoulder. "I'd say."

"The Internet isn't going to help with this. We need insider info. And most of the guys who worked this case are going to be retired if not dead."

"I agree. But even if we find someone, remember it was a long time ago. If it was obvious back then, the police down here would've answered these questions. It's not going to get clearer after thirty years."

She sighed. "What do you suggest then?"

"I think we need to find someone in the police station."

Alex slumped into her chair. "And how do you suggest we do that?"

"I have an idea."

"I hope it's a good one."

Greg put his hand on hers. "I think it is."

Alex felt a strange tension, but she didn't pull her hand away. She needed Greg like she'd never needed anyone. Later, when this was all over, she could figure out how she felt, how he felt. There wasn't time for it now.

"I've got a connection down here." He paused. "It's not a great one, but it's okay. It's my mother's cousin's kid. She's a detective."

"A kid detective?"

"She's about forty, I guess. I haven't seen her since we were kids. But her dad was a detective here, too. Maybe she knows something about the case."

"She's a cop, Roback. She's not going to talk to me."

He caught her gaze and held it. "Not if she knows who you are, she's not."

"I hate to lie to a cop."

"You want to get arrested?"

Alex thought a moment. "I can lie."

"I knew you could." He stood from his chair and put his hand out to pull her up. "Come on. We're meeting her at my great-aunt's diner."

"You have a great-aunt with a diner?"

Greg pulled her out of her chair. "There's a lot you don't know about me."

Alex followed him back through Palo Alto and

down a narrow street called Hamilton. He parked across from a brightly lit diner. A small sign hung over the door, suspended by two large hooks: "Cardinal Café." Inside, clusters of red chairs sat around white tables. A trim older woman worked the counter.

Greg waved to her and she frowned.

"Is that little Gregory Roback?"

Alex smiled.

"Hi, Mina." He turned back to Alex. "My great-aunt."

After the two of them had caught up, Greg introduced Alex as a journalist friend and Mina directed them to a back booth. "Chris is on her way. She was at the station this morning."

Alex watched Greg nod, knowing he was thinking the same thing that she was. Greg's second cousin, Chris Anderson, would already have heard the warning about Alex Kincaid.

They sat down and Alex shifted uncomfortably in the chair.

"You're nervous."

She shook her head. "I just want to talk to her and get out of here."

"You think James is going to show up with a task force to pull you out of Mina's diner?"

She raised an eyebrow. "It is James."

"Point taken."

A woman with short blond hair and no resemblance to Greg walked in the front door and stopped at the counter. The badge clipped to the waist of her slacks identified her as Chris. Alex waited for her to turn toward them.

When she did, Alex watched her gaze. She waved to Greg and headed over. She had no visible reaction to Alex. That was exactly what Alex had hoped. Chris pulled out a chair across from Alex.

"Long time," she said to Greg.

"I know. Sorry about that. This is Jamie," he said, pointing to Alex. "Jamie, my cousin Chris."

Alex nodded. "Nice to meet you."

"Likewise." Chris turned to Greg. "What brings you down here?"

"Jamie is writing a story on an old case you guys had—Sesame Street murders."

Chris raised an eyebrow and leaned across the table. "You're wasting your time then."

Alex crossed her arms and sat back. "Why's that?"

Chris didn't look at her. Instead, she focused on Greg. "Because I know she's not a reporter and I know her name is Alex Kincaid." She glanced at Alex. "Your picture's all over this town. You want to tell me what the hell you're doing here and why you've wrapped my cousin into your mess?"

Mina came over and handed out menus. "You guys know what you want?"

Alex had completely lost her appetite. She continued to hold Chris's gaze until Chris broke it and shook her head. "Not quite yet."

Mina walked away and Greg stood up. "We should go."

"No, she's right. You shouldn't be involved in this, Greg. It's my deal." She looked back at Chris. "You might not believe it, but that's what I've been telling him all along."

"She didn't do anything, Chris. She's being framed." Greg walked to Alex's chair and waited for her to stand. "And she's just found out what happened to her as a kid."

"What?" Chris asked, shrugging. "I'm supposed to feel pity? There's a warrant out for her arrest."

Alex leaned forward. "I don't want anyone's pity. I came here looking for answers about an old case. You wouldn't know anything about it, anyway—too young. But I went to work a week ago as a cop, like any other cop." She glanced over her shoulder to make sure no one else was listening.

"And since then, my life's been a goddamn circus. Yesterday, I found out I was almost killed when I was six years old. And then I learned that I supposedly killed the son of a bitch. I shot him." She shook her head and lowered her voice. "The more I read about the case, the less it adds up. I can't believe a six-year-old with her hands bound and a blindfold on would have the wherewithal to hold a forty-five still enough to shoot it fifteen feet and hit a moving target. So I want to know what really happened that day." Alex exhaled and slapped her hands on the table. "I think I deserve some answers." She stood up and headed for the door.

"I know the case," Chris said before she was out of earshot.

Alex stopped and turned back.

"It was my dad's. His last case—he retired after that one." She shook her head. "Case always really pissed him off."

Alex didn't move.

"Sit down and I'll tell you what I know. Then you've got to get the hell out of here."

Alex sat back down.

"And you've never even heard of me."

She nodded.

Chris turned to Greg. "And you'll stay clear until the dust settles. Because you aren't going to be any help behind bars."

Greg didn't answer.

"Promise."

He nodded. "I'll lay low."

Mina came back by and Chris smiled at her and said, "Three cheeseburgers, three Cokes."

It was the first time Alex had seen Chris smile. She was actually an attractive woman, but one who was clearly very serious about her job. Alex respected that and she gave Chris her full attention.

"They tested your hands back then and confirmed the presence of gunpowder residue. Like you, a lot of people found it hard to believe you could have shot the gun by yourself. My father, especially. I was eight at the time and bigger than you were. He even tested his theory on me by tying my hands and having me hold his gun up and try to shoot it. He never tried it with bullets. My mother would've had his head. But he never thought you could have pulled the trigger on your own."

"What was the evidence that she did?" Greg asked.

Chris answered without taking her eyes off of Alex. "Besides the gunpowder, she confessed to it."

The burgers arrived and they paused long enough for a bite.

Chris swallowed and wiped her mouth. "Good, huh?"

"Great," Greg agreed through a full mouth.

Alex picked at her food, trying to remember confessing to murder when she was six. "Were there other problems with the crime scene?"

Chris nodded. "There was another set of footprints."

Greg stopped eating and sat forward.

"So Androus had an accomplice?" Alex asked.

Chris shook her head and swallowed her bite. "Kid prints."

"I don't understand."

"There was a set of kid prints walking away from the warehouse."

"Could they have been there earlier?" Alex asked.

Chris shrugged. "They didn't think so, but as you know, evidence processing wasn't all that great back then. According to the detectives, the prints were on top of the ones that led to the warehouse."

"Another child who got away?"

"No. You were all accounted for. There were only fourteen kids on the bus. Eleven of them were dead and then you and the two other survivors."

Alex tried to figure this new piece of evidence. "Is it possible one of the kids made a run for it and Androus caught up with him?"

"Not according to the detectives who processed the scene. The prints went into the warehouse and then out to the street, in that order. Kid never came back again."

"Maybe a neighborhood kid who heard the ruckus and came to look?" Alex suggested.

"That's the theory, but they tried to find the kid and never could."

Alex thought about Alfred Ferguson. She looked up at Greg.

"Ferguson?" he asked, reading her mind.

She nodded.

"Who's Ferguson?" Chris asked.

Greg explained about the break-in to Alex's house and the print she'd lifted from her arm, as well as about the surveillance at Ferguson's house. He patted his pocket. "I've got someone calling me on my cell as soon as they hear."

Alex wished the damn thing would ring.

Chris wiped her mouth and pulled a pen from a pocket. On a clean napkin, she wrote Alfred's name. "I can search the name and find out if he went to school down here. Maybe he's our witness."

"Nader lives down here, too," Alex said.

"Who's Nader?"

"Sorry. He's another of the survivors. Marcus Nader. Lives over on Ramona."

"Close to the station."

Alex nodded. "I went by, but it looks like he's on vacation or something."

"I'm not sure he could add much. Just don't be disappointed if he doesn't remember anything.

She nodded. It was solid advice. Still, she needed to pursue every angle.

"I don't mean to be negative. The case is officially closed, but the detectives who were around still talk about it. And we still get the occasional call on the case. Mostly crazies, though. There was a guy just a few months ago who'd killed his wife; he called a few times, swearing to have some information he'd trade for some help with an appeal." She shook her head. "That's just the nature of the game for convicts. You know what they're like, always looking at old cases, for a way to cut a deal. Everyone wants the get-out-of-jail-free card."

Greg nodded.

"What's his name?" Alex asked.

Chris frowned. "Whose?"

"The guy who killed his wife."

"Taylor. Somebody Taylor. We checked him out. He didn't even live here back then. Didn't mean to get your hopes up."

"No. You didn't," Alex lied.

"Is there anything else you can tell us?" Greg asked.

Chris shook her head. "Nothing else comes to mind."

Alex wasn't ready to give up yet. She was still hoping that something might spark a memory. "Can you tell me more about the crime? The layout, how he maneuvered the kids?"

Chris began to sketch on a napkin. She drew a large rectangle with an X at one end.

Alex took another bite of her burger and leaned forward to study Chris's crude drawing.

"This was the door," she pointed to the X. "The way the police figured, all the kids were drugged, moving slowly, when they arrived. Androus had them all sit here." She marked Xs along the far end of the warehouse. "He turned them with their backs to the door and made them sit cross-legged. Their hands were bound, and the Valium kept them pretty quiet."

"Plus, he had a gun and he told them that he would hurt them if they disobeyed," Alex interjected, pulling stuff from her memory of the file.

"Exactly. One of the kids, a little boy, made a run for it early on and Androus shot him. Kid died instantly."

"A warning to the others," Greg added.

Chris sipped her Coke. "Right. Then he pulled his body back for the others to see."

Alex swallowed. She was unfamiliar with this part of the story, and knowing she had been there, that it could have been her running, didn't help. "How did they determine that's what happened?"

"Bloodstains from what looked like the boy's body dragged across the floor. All speculation. No one ever did get a chance to ask many questions of the survivors. Their parents—your parents," she corrected, "plus the attorneys, the counselors—no one wanted them put through any more than they'd already seen. You can imagine." Chris shook her head. "Sorry. Of course you can."

Alex shook her head. "Don't apologize."

She shifted her head in a slight nod and continued. "It looked like he showed the dead body to the others, warning them not to mess with him. That body was the only one shot and it was separated from the rest of the pile, so we speculated that he offed that kid right at the beginning."

Alex glanced back at her drawing, the small Xs that indicated the children sitting in a semicircle along the warehouse's far wall.

"Is it possible that the kid who was shot was the one who walked back out of the warehouse?" Greg asked.

"No. Like I said, those prints never came back in. It looked like he was dragged back."

Alex thought about it. They would have known if Androus had chased the kid out of the warehouse. "And Androus's footprints never went back out?"

"Right."

"And there was no other evidence of an accomplice?" Alex asked.

"None. The warehouse was surrounded by a gravel lot—no footprints other than Androus's and the kids', no other car, nothing. And Androus was known to be a loner. He taught piano to local kids, lived alone, no one ever saw him with anyone. He paid his bills, spent a lot of time in the library. That was about it."

"We read an interview with his sister, Maggie. I guess he had a twin brother who killed himself."

Chris shrugged. "I don't know anything about a brother. The police contacted the family to try to gain insight. I didn't hear that anything ever came of it."

"What about a shrink?" Greg asked. "The interview mentioned that Androus had been seeing a psychiatrist."

Chris nodded slowly. "I remember reading something about that. I think we got the basic response from the doctor—shock, dismay, disappointment, but nothing very enlightening. The doctors tend to keep whatever they know to themselves—all that doctor/patient privilege crap. I'm sure the doctor knew that Androus was a sick fuck, but I don't think we got a confession on that."

Alex thought about Androus's crime. "Androus taught piano, right? Mostly to young kids. According to your files, none of them had any complaints, though."

Chris nodded.

"What are you thinking?" Greg asked.

"It's strange, don't you think? He had opportunity and means all the time, but didn't use them? He waited until he had fourteen at once."

"It is weird," Chris agreed. "Maybe he was worried he'd be caught, since they were his students and they'd be easy to track back to him. Doesn't stop aunts, uncles, cousins, and parents, but it has to be considered."

"Or he'd always fantasized about offing a whole bunch of kids at once and finally gathered the courage to try it," Greg suggested.

Alex nodded. "True. His lessons were all private— only one kid at a time. Maybe that didn't make him hot enough."

Chris shrugged. "At one point, I searched unsolved cases to see if there might've been others that we hadn't linked to him. I got three that fit, but none in California and only one in the last fifty years in this country."

Alex wished she'd had access to the station. There was so much more she could do from in there. But she was an outsider now. "What sort of pattern did you look for?"

"Multiple victims. Strangulation. Androus used his bare hands. Appeared to have gotten off on at least a couple of them—hard to say which ones, but he had a real mess in the front of his jeans, if you know what I mean."

Chris halted as she realized what she'd said, and Alex could feel her and Greg watching. She forced herself to nod. "What else?"

Chris nodded apologetically but didn't address the awkwardness. "He was organized—brought a gun, which much to his dismay was used against him. But he also had a knife."

"Used it to cut the rope tying their hands together."

Chris nodded. "And sliced a few of them."

Alex paused, her jaw sagging. "I don't remember that."

Chris and Greg glanced at each other and back at Alex.

"It's in the file," Chris explained. "Actually, he branded each of them—each of—" She stopped.

Alex crossed her arms against her chest. "Branded them, how?"

"With the knife—a small X carved into the inner thigh."

Alex stared.

Greg didn't take his eyes off her, and she refused to meet his gaze. "Survivors, too?" he asked.

Chris looked down at her plate. "All of them."

"Goddamn it," Alex muttered, pushing her plate away. She held herself from reaching beneath the table and touching the inside of her leg as though it were a foreign object. She didn't have a mark there. She would have noticed it. Maybe she wasn't a survivor. Relief flooded her. There had been some mistake.

Chris put her burger down and laid a hand on Alex's shoulder. "You okay?"

Alex nodded. She stood from the table. "I need to use the rest room."

Greg stood and Chris took his hand and yanked him back down. "She can go alone."

He flushed. "I know. I was just trying—" He waved his hand through the air and sank back down. "Oh, to hell with it."

Alex turned and concentrated on the bathroom door across the room. She focused so hard she almost expected it to disappear.

The doorknob was cool in her hand and she pushed inside. She looked around the white room, carefully supplied with toilet paper, paper towels, and a ceramic soap dispenser. There was no window. Suddenly, she yearned for fresh air. Fighting off panic, Alex sucked in a deep breath and exhaled slowly.

The door locked, she turned on the water and splashed the cool stream on her face. She wiped her hands and tossed the towel in the basket.

With her jaw set, she unfastened her belt and pulled down her pants.

Chapter Twenty-three

Alex buttoned her pants and kicked the wastebasket, letting out a low growl. "Goddamn you, Androus."

When she got back to the table, Chris and Greg were talking, their heads almost touching.

Greg noticed her first and sat up. Chris's gaze followed.

"You okay?" he asked.

She nodded, but they all knew it was a lie. She wasn't okay. She'd been branded and all sense of okay was long gone. She was angry and she was scared, no closer to the truth than she had been a week ago. The walls felt like they were coming in. She needed to move and clear her head. She pulled money from her pocket.

Chris put her hand out. "Lunch is on Grandma."

Alex forced a smile. "Thank you."

Chris nodded.

Alex looked at Greg. "I want to go to the scene, to the warehouse. I need to see it."

He started to speak, but she interrupted. "I need to go alone."

"The warehouse is gone. They tore it down a few months after the—" Chris paused. "A few months later."

Alex didn't care. She still wanted to see the location. It had been thirty years. She wasn't expecting to find anything, but maybe the scene would help her remember. "A doctor I talked to about my memory thought it might help to try to picture it. Maybe going there will help."

Greg stood up. "Richards?"

She nodded.

Chris drew a map on a napkin. "Here's how you get there from here." She stood and handed the napkin to Alex.

"Thank you. And I appreciate all you've done," Alex added.

"You're welcome. Greg was telling me about the brother—I'm going to go back and see what I can find out about him. I'll call Greg if I learn anything."

"I'm going to check back in with the station," Greg said. "Where should I meet you?"

She shook her head. "You shouldn't. Go back up before someone finds you down here. I'll call you tonight."

"Call me on my cell phone."

She agreed. Thanking Chris again, Alex left the diner and entered the sunlight, squinting. It seemed hard to imagine that life was proceeding as normal for some people while she was trapped in a live nightmare.

She got in her car and revved the engine, pulling the visor down against the bright sky. As she followed the map Chris had made, she thought about the subtle cross on her inner thigh. It should have been spotted years ago. By her doctor or a boyfriend if not herself. Men had touched that tender skin. Fingers had run across that very spot. Why hadn't someone noticed it? Damn them all. And damn him—damn him for touching her, for scarring her.

She slammed the car into first gear and sped across the border between East and West Palo Alto.

East Palo Alto spread out before the car like the ruins of a war-torn city. Alex turned down Donahue and stared at the vacant lot where Chris had drawn the X on the napkin. A weary chain-link fence surrounded the gravel surface, bent and broken from people climbing over and under for access. A group of children squatted in one corner, their attention focused on something Alex couldn't see. Alex honked her horn and one of the kids looked up, the curious look on his face quickly replaced by fear. Within moments, the children gathered whatever they'd been concentrating on, hopped the fence, and sprinted down a side street.

Drugs, Alex thought. The children had looked grammar school age, despite their weathered faces and the trendy oversized pants that barely hung on their shapeless frames. It didn't surprise her. She saw the same things in Berkeley. On another day, she would have chased them down, tried to talk some sense into them, tried to save them from the fate of their parents and older siblings. Tried to do something. But not today.

Now she simply stared at the lot, paralyzed by the knowledge of what had happened there and trying to remember something about it. Hadn't she had a dream about a warehouse? But her memory was as empty as the lot.

Alex opened the car door and got out. The faint smell of rotting garbage invaded her senses. She took two deep breaths until it filled her nose and she no longer noticed it. Trick of the trade. No matter how bad it smells, inhale deeply and the nose will quickly shut out the scent.

There wasn't much to see now. The nearby streets were quiet, the people at work earning meager wages or still sleeping from the long night before. Treeless lawns looked brown and abandoned, only a rare spot of green breaking the silent bleakness.

Alex ducked under a jagged edge of torn fence. Raw iron scraped across her back, making her wince. She didn't stop. Instead, she walked to the middle of the empty space, trying to picture the warehouse in her mind. Crushed stone crackled under her feet, dust spraying across her shoes.

No images surfaced. There's nothing here, she thought. After nearly thirty years, it would have been completely different. But she sensed something.

Halting in the middle of the lot, she scanned the area, and spotted someone standing in the shade of a car parked on the street across from her. Not wanting to scare him away, she turned her back again. Someone was watching her. Her pulse sped and she put her head down, checking for others in her peripheral vision. She could only see the one person.

Alex knew it was probably just a curious kid, but her gut was warning her to be cautious. These days, nothing was what it seemed.

From the corner of her eye, Alex looked at him again and spied a camera lens in front of his face. Someone was taking pictures of her. Was it the same person who had taken pictures for Loeffler? She couldn't let him get away. Her adrenaline rushing like whitewater, Alex counted to three, turned, and sprinted toward the cameraman.

He jumped and tore down the street. The slim, awkward figure reminded Alex of a teenager. Big clunky shoes she'd seen on kids backed the theory. But the camera had been large and expensive—the kind with a zoom lens and automatic focus. A kid from this area wasn't likely to own one of those. Had he followed her? If not, why run?

Alex hurried after him, her shoes slapping against the cracked pavement.

He emerged on the next street, a good fifty yards ahead, and Alex pushed herself to keep up. She would keel over before she'd let the one chance to get some answers escape.

He wouldn't get far with the camera and the backpack he was carrying. And Alex bet the kid would risk getting caught not to lose something worth so much money.

The camera knocked awkwardly against the kid's side, slowing his pace. Alex closed some of the distance as she found a rhythm in her running. She knew she'd outlast him. He was bumbling along, not used to running, his legs gangly beneath him.

As soon as Alex felt confident she'd catch him, a cramp pierced her side. With her fingers digging into the pain, she pushed on. It wasn't like her to cramp, but she knew the burger wasn't helping.

The kid crossed a patch of grass and ducked between two of the dilapidated duplexes on the block.

She watched him head toward the short back chain fence that separated a yard from the house behind it.

A gutted brown couch sat in the middle of the crispy brown grass, a strip of green shag carpet rolled out before it and empty forties scattered about. A regular outdoor entertainment center. All it needed was some popcorn and a Raiders game on TV.

The kid reached the far side, but Alex was gaining on him. Equipment and all, he struggled to lift himself over the fence. As he looked back, fear registered in his eyes. His face registered in her mind.

Adrenaline edged her on. She knew this kid. He was the same kid she'd met in the police station, the one who said he had found pictures of her in Loeffler's stuff. The son of the man Sandy Loeffler was living with now.

"Hold up," she screamed, racing faster. "I just want to talk to you." It was a standard police fib. What she really wanted to do was shake the truth from his scrawny bones. But he wasn't likely to stop for that.

The kid stumbled and fell on the far side of the fence, the camera landing a foot from his sprawled figure. A thin yellow coat, tied around his waist, tripped him as he tried to untangle himself. He moved quickly, gathering his limbs and pulling himself to his feet.

But she was faster. From the top of the short fence, she dropped herself onto his back, pushing them both to the ground.

He let out a low "Oomph."

His right arm pulled behind his back, she pinned him down. "Long way from home, aren't we, Tim?"

"I don't know what you're talking about," he moaned.

She tightened her grip. "You don't?"

"No."

"Next you're going to say you've never seen me before."

"I—I haven't."

Grabbing his shoulders, she rolled him over, pressing him into the ground. "Listen, kid. You want to end up spending the rest of high school in jail? 'Cause I can make that happen. Miss a lot of good parties, maybe a few girls. But you'll certainly get a nice selection of men. Of course, you won't do the choosing. Nope. They'll probably like you, though." She paused, letting it sink in. "Right now, you've got a choice."

With a moan, he closed his eyes.

She shook his shoulders until he opened his eyes again. "I suggest you pay careful attention. This is the best deal you're going to get. You want to hear it?"

He gave a stiff nod.

"You tell me what the hell you're doing here and everything you know, and I won't write you up for resisting arrest." It wasn't exactly a fair trade since she didn't have a reason to arrest him. Plus, she was suspended, so she didn't even have the right to detain him. At this point, she didn't much care. "What do you say?"

"I didn't do anything," he protested.

On her feet again, she pulled him up. "Okay, let's go to the station then."

"No," he cried, and she had a feeling he was familiar with juvenile hall. It didn't sound like it had been a positive experience and she was thankful for the small favor.

The kid slumped back to the ground and rested his face in his hands. From her angle, his lanky figure was all elbows and knees, and she wondered how old he really was.

"Want to talk about it?"

"What choice do I have?" he said in a voice close to tears.

"Good point."

His bag tight to his chest, he snarled in her direction.

"How about you start with the camera?"

He gave her an angry stare. "It was a gift."

"From who?"

His gaze found the ground. "I don't know," he mumbled.

"Excuse me?"

He looked back at her and spoke softly. "I don't know."

"When did you get it?"

"Yesterday."

Talking to this teenager was like pulling teeth. Now she knew why parents complained so much. "How?"

"In the mail."

"At your house?"

He nodded.

She gritted her teeth. "I'd really prefer if you just told me how the hell you ended up following me and taking pictures."

His shoulders hunched.

A group of kids had piled back onto the empty lot and were playing soccer with a deflated basketball.

Alex looked back at Tim.

"Yesterday morning," he said. "I got the package before school."

"Who brought it? Any return address?"

He scowled. "I thought you wanted *me* to tell the story."

She crossed her arms. "I'm listening."

"I don't know who sent it. My dad just called me into the kitchen and said there was a package for me."

"What was in it?"

His scowl deepened.

Rolling her eyes, she motioned for him to continue.

"It was a box—a camera box. It's not my birthday or anything. Plus, I never got anything this nice. I opened the box and there was an envelope inside. And a note."

"You have it?"

His expression was blank.

"The note. Do you have it?"

He nodded and pulled his backpack onto his lap. Shuffling through it, he put his hand on something and looked up at her.

"Oh, no. Hand it over."

Slowly, he pulled the envelope out. "It's mine."

She snatched the envelope from his grasp and opened it, whistling. "Wow, you're rich!" A stack of perfectly pressed fifty-dollar bills was accompanied by a note. The note open, she read the typed instructions.

Be at the corner of Broadway and Broadway Terrace at nine a.m. with a pen and paper. Answer the phone on the right after the second ring. If you want to keep the money, you gotta earn it.

"The money's mine," he interjected.

She looked up. "Bullshit. It's police property."

"You bitch." He jumped to his feet, and Alex took a step forward. The kid was easily six inches taller than she was, but she could knock him on his ass in four seconds flat if he touched her.

"Stay here. I'll be right back."

"Hey, that's my money," he called after her.

"It won't be unless you stay put and shut up."

The kids on the lot had turned their attention to her and Tim. Maybe they'd seen the money, but she didn't like the way they were starting to drift toward her.

The money tucked into her waist, Alex pulled her gun out of the back of her pants and opened her wallet to her cop I.D. Since she didn't have her badge, it was the best she could do. Holding one in each hand over her head, she crossed to where the kids were standing. "Police business," she said in a firm tone.

Then, waving at them, she said, "Move along."

The largest of the group turned to face her and puffed his chest out like an angry bird.

Alex waved the gun in his direction. "I said, move along."

The kid crossed his arms in an Italian version of *fuck off* and turned his back, strutting across the lot. The others followed like a series of ducklings, each of them mimicking his gesture as they turned their backs.

"Nice."

Alex returned to where Tim was standing, comforted by the softening sound of gravel crunching beneath the feet of the kids as they stormed off.

Tim stretched his hand out toward the envelope.

She shook her head.

He looked angry and stomped his foot. She prepared for a strike.

Instead, he put his hands in his pockets, tucked his chin to his chest, and looked up at her. "Please."

Alex laughed at his attempt. "That work with anyone?"

"Bitch."

"Yeah, yeah. Sticks and stones. You going to give me the rest of the story or what?"

He pointed to the envelope. "You going to let me keep that?"

She shrugged, seeing the fierce desire in his face.

"Depends on how good the story is. And no making stuff up."

His eyes widened, and he showed a smile, a wide gap between his two front teeth. "Really?"

It was the first time she had seen him smile and she was beginning to think she might just let him keep the money. After all, she'd probably be in jail within a few days. And if he got it from the killer, she didn't care if it was returned. As long as he played along, that is. "Spill it."

"Okay. Uh—"

"You were telling me about the note. You followed the instructions?"

"For a cool half-G?" He spread his arms and crossed them high over his chest. "I'm not stupid."

"What about school?"

"Whatever. You know anyone who wouldn't cut school for a day for a half-grand and a camera like that?"

"Good point. So I take it someone called you."

"Yeah, this guy called and told me to get a pen and take notes." He looked up, his brow furrowed. "It was weird, like he was watching me, too, 'cause after I said 'Okay,' I waited, and like a second later, he told me I needed to take paper out and write or the whole deal would be off."

"What did he have you write?"

"Directions to here, that I was supposed to follow you and take pictures, find out where you went, who you talked to. Told me you were his woman."

"His woman?" Thoughts raged inside her head like angry bees. Why would he take the time and money to send a kid down here? Surely, he had to know she would spot him. "Why would he send you?"

The kid shrugged. "I asked him the same thing. Why pay me to take pictures if you're his woman? Why not take them himself?"

"What did he say?"

"He laughed and said he couldn't 'cause he was working on a really big surprise for you."

Alex didn't even want to consider what the surprise might be. But to buy a kid a brand-new camera just to take some pictures didn't make sense. "He just left you this camera?"

The kid nodded. "The camera was in the box with everything else."

She stared at the camera. It was brand new. Someone had paid a lot of money just to get a few pictures of her. She thought about the pictures that Loeffler had. "Did you take the other pictures of me? The ones you said you found in Sandy's stuff?"

He shook his head. "No. I told you at the station I didn't take those."

"You know who did?"

"Bill did."

"Bill Loeffler? You're sure?" she asked.

The kid nodded. "His wife, Sandy, told my dad he admitted he did. He said it was for an old case, but she didn't believe him."

Why had Loeffler taken pictures of her? Because he knew she was a survivor? Why not just come to talk to her? "And you swear Bill took them?"

He nodded.

What the hell was going on? Alex looked back at the camera the kid had.

Maybe she could track where the camera had been purchased. She motioned to Tim's bag. "Where's the camera box?"

He shrugged. "I threw it away."

"Where?"

"Same place as my notes."

She shook her head. "What notes?"

"On the phone, he said to write everything down and study it on the way here and then to throw the paper away at the gas station across from the Holiday Inn."

"He told you to do that?"

Tim nodded. "And he said he'd check to make sure I did it. If I didn't, I couldn't keep the money."

"But you *have* the money."

"He said he could get it back and get me in a lot of trouble with the police."

His reference to the police made Alex think about the killer again. What contact did he have with the police? Why risk them knowing? "And you have no idea who this guy is?"

"No. I got no idea."

Grabbing the kid by the shirtsleeve, she tugged. "Let's go."

"Where are we going?" His voice was shaky.

"To this garbage can. Give me your keys." She didn't want him going anywhere.

He stared at her, wide-eyed.

She motioned them over. "If you behave, I'll give them back and I'll let you keep the money."

He narrowed his gaze. "You promise?"

"If you behave."

Nodding his head, he dumped a heavy set of keys in her hand.

She drove and the kid directed. He led her to a Union 76 station, and pointed to a garbage can over by two pay phones and an air and water station.

Alex jumped from the car and pulled the top off the can. Cigarette butts, a half-full Coke can, a Mc-Donald's bag, and some candy wrappers. With a deep breath, she began to move things around, searching for the camera box.

Tim came over and looked in the can. "It's not there. I put it right on top."

"Where the hell would it be?"

He shrugged.

"He told you exactly where to put it?"

Tim nodded.

"Maybe he planned to come back for it," she said to herself.

Her head up, she scanned the area. Was he watching her right now? She spun back to the kid and instinctively he leaned away from her.

"What were you supposed to do with the film after that?"

"After what?"

She rolled her hand in agitation. "After you took the pictures of me."

"Oh. Uh—drop it off at a post office here in town."

"You have a return envelope?"

He shook his head. "A box."

"A box? What type of box?"

"Like the ones at the post office."

"A post office box?"

"Yeah."

Hot adrenaline seared her stomach. "Here?"

"Right on University."

"What's the box number?"

He smiled. "Twenty-seven forty-two."

"Then where's it written?"

Pointing to the garbage can, he shook his head.

Her jaw clenched, she nodded. "Right. You memorized it. Let's go to this post office."

His expression hesitant, he scrunched his nose. "I think I should tell you something else first."

She looked around. "What?"

Tim tilted his head. "There was something else he told me to do."

She closed her eyes. "What?" she repeated.

"He told me where you were staying, your room number and stuff."

Her jaw dropped. "Where I was staying?"

"And he told me to find a way in and put something in your room."

"What?"

He unzipped his pack and pulled out a film canister.

Her fingers shaking, she snatched it from him. The canister reminded her immediately of Nader, a photographer. She should have thought about him earlier, when she saw the expensive camera. "Oh God," she whispered, dreading what might be there. She opened it and looked inside.

Tim leaned over her. "It's some piece of paper soaked with something that stinks. And there's a note."

The scent hit her, and she stepped back.

"Didn't seem like much of a surprise to me either."

It smelled like film developing chemicals.

Her head buzzing, she reached in and pulled out a curled strip of paper with another message.

Follow your nose to the next one.

"No," she whispered, knowing she wouldn't need her nose. She knew exactly where the next one was.

Chapter Twenty-four

Alex read the note again. "The next one," she said aloud.

"Yeah, I didn't get what he meant by that part," Tim said. "Next what?"

She looked at his face, a sprinkle of blond stubble on his chin and at his sideburns.

"What does it mean?"

Alex shook her head. She stared at the note and the canister. It had to be Nader. "Damn." She ran back to the car.

"Where we going?"

She didn't answer him.

"We going to see that vocab guy?"

Alex looked at him. "What?"

"I can't remember the guy's name, but it was one of our vocabulary words last year." He shrugged awkwardly. "But I don't remember which one."

She puzzled, then shook her head. He must have meant Nader.

"You know, we get like ten every week and we have to spell them and use them in a sentence and then at the end of the week we—"

"I know what vocab words are," she snapped.

"Oh, yeah, sure. You were young, too."

She scowled.

His face turned beet red. "What I meant was—"

"Do you mean Nader—Marcus Nader?" she asked before he could insult her again.

He looked relieved. "You know him?"

"Not exactly, but I know where he lives. How do you know him?"

"His name and address were in my notes. The man told me I might have to show you to his house."

She got into the car and started the engine. As soon as Tim was in, she put it in gear and started for Nader's house. *Don't let it be too late,* she thought. She should have sensed something was wrong when she'd gone there earlier.

She parked in front of the little taupe ranch house and jerked on her emergency brake, pulling the keys from the ignition and pocketing them. She caught Tim's eye watching her and shook her head. "Don't try anything."

When they were both out of the car, she locked the doors and headed up Nader's walkway. She mounted the three stairs to the front porch, hearing the clod of heavy shoes behind. When she halted, Tim nearly ran into her. Turning back, she stared at him.

"You want me to wait here?"

Without speaking, she nodded.

He took a couple small steps backward and stuck his hands in his shorts pockets, his shoulders hunched over. "Sure."

"Thanks." With Tim safely on the curb, Alex stiffened her shoulders and walked back to the porch. She dreaded what she would find in this house. Someone had murdered Loeffler and then sent her here. She prayed she was wrong.

"Uh, Alex, you going to ring the doorbell?" Tim asked.

Alex stared down at the doorbell. "Of course I am," she muttered, using the sleeve of her shirt to push down hard on the button. "Go back to the car."

Inside she heard the loud buzz but no other motion.

After a minute, she buzzed again.

Still no answer. Shrugging, she stepped back. What now? She had to get inside.

Down on the curb again, she looked at the windows on the front side of the house. Nothing stirred. As she circled the property, she stopped and put her face to the windows to look inside, careful not to touch anything. It looked exactly as it had when she'd been there before.

Alex opened the screen on the back door and, covering her hand with her shirt, tested the doorknob. It was locked. As she started to turn away, the dog door caught her eye. A quick glance over her shoulder confirmed the coast was clear. Not that she had expected anyone, but she was quickly learning to check.

Scanning the house next door and seeing nothing, Alex decided at least to take a look. Down on her knees, she opened the dog flap with her elbow and peered into the kitchen. Everything appeared normal there, too. Before she dropped the flap, a cold breeze from inside fluttered across her cheeks. She was reminded instantly of the chill of the morgue.

As the flap slapped against the plastic rim on the door, Alex froze. Her nostrils flared, the hairs in her nose singed from the smell. She pulled back.

It was the smell of developing chemicals, same as in the canister Tim had. The killer *had* been here.

She turned slowly, looking at the small, carefully kept yard. Alex moved to the front of the house, searching for a way in. The knob tight in her shirt-covered fist, she rattled the main door, the frame shaking beneath her anger.

"You trying to break in?"

She spun around and met Tim's gaze. "Go back and wait by the car."

He shrugged and turned his back, scuffing his red shoes against the ground. " 'Cause if you're trying to get in there, I could maybe help you."

She looked down the street in both directions. How

soon before the Palo Alto police turned up? Someone had to be missing Nader. She needed to get inside and process the scene for clues before someone else arrived, but she didn't want to break a window and leave evidence that she had been there.

Tim hung back a few yards, refusing to go to the car. "I mean, first thing is, you probably don't want to do it from the front door."

Her brow tight, she focused on him again.

He smiled a little proud smile. "Can't believe you don't know this and you're a cop."

Alex moved around the side of the house again, thinking about how to get inside without attracting attention or leaving a trail. If she was going in there, she needed to do it quickly.

As he walked by, he patted her back. "Don't be down. I'll show you."

"I don't need help. You need to go back to the car," she said, pointing again.

"I can do it in ten seconds. It's an easy one. I tried it earlier this morning."

Alex stared. "You broke in here earlier?"

His jaw slack, he looked back. "Well, only to test it—you know, see if I could. I didn't actually go inside or nothing. I only came here to make sure I could find the place."

She shook her head in disbelief. "Open it. Fast. But don't touch anything with your bare hands. And then you've *got* to wait by the car."

Tim covered his hand with his shirtsleeve. In less than three seconds, he picked the lock and pushed the door open.

Alex looked inside and drew her gun before entering. From the first step into the house, she picked up the chemical scent. Goose bumps lined her arms like tiny soldiers. The house was freezing, the smell bitter in the cold air.

With purposeful caution, she moved through the

kitchen, her nose leading the way. Both hands on her gun, she hunted for the source of the smell.

The shuffle of feet fell in behind her and she halted, looking back.

Tim shrugged, his expression innocent. He glanced around. "It's like a refrigerator in here."

"You need to wait outside," she said.

"You wouldn't be in here if it weren't for me."

"If you want to keep the money, you'll wait outside." His keys and the money were tucked down under the seat in her car. At least the car was locked.

"I'm supposed to just wait?"

"Yes. And let me know if anyone shows up."

He grinned. "You mean, like keep watch?"

"Exactly."

He nodded and hurried outside.

The squeak of her shoes against the linoleum was the only sound she heard, but she stopped at the edge of the kitchen and listened carefully. A cup of clear liquid sat in a plain gray coffee mug on the kitchen table. She bent down and sniffed—chemicals. It occurred to her that they might be there to cover another smell.

Adrenaline scorched its way across her chest. At the academy, they had discussed this feeling, how it made people react, the benefits as well as the disadvantages of "the rush."

Adrenaline produced much the same high as cocaine or heroin. And it didn't cost a dime. Some people were willing to risk everything for it. Cops, their lives. Criminals, their freedom.

The search for the rush was probably the single common ground between criminals and cops. It was one thing both would agree they loved.

She paused, letting the rush stream into her veins. The sound of a clock ticking came from one side of the house, a steady drip from the other. She turned toward the clock. Her shoes fell silent on the carpet.

Pressing her back to the wall, she moved heel-toe across the carpet, her gun in front of her every step. Something creaked beneath her and she wheeled around, checking her back. It was clear. When the adrenaline settled slightly, she continued.

The familiar heat pooled in her stomach, propelling her on, giving her courage. Behind the smell of chemicals, another scent drifted across her senses, more subtle and a bit like metal. It smelled like death and it filled her with dread.

The odor intensified with each step. Her back pressed against the cool white Sheetrock wall, she paused for a breath. The thermostat caught her eye. It had been set at fifty. She knew what the cold did. It preserved a dead body. As she inhaled, the metallic scent grew increasingly bitter. Iron. It was blood. She pressed on, easing down the hall.

She reached a closed door and hesitated beside it, listening for any noise. Then, with a full breath, she grabbed the knob, cool even through her T-shirt, and pushed the door open. The door resisted as though something were holding it back. Straightening her shoulders, she pointed the gun to the door.

Counting to three, she prepared to enter. One. Two. Three. She kicked the door open, feeling the hinges loosen beneath her sole. A new musky smell assaulted her as she entered the room.

On the far bureau, at least two dozen sticks of incense had burned to their ends. As she took another step into the room, something caught her eye.

Her gun ready, she spun and pointed it at the face. The body was propped against the wall behind the door. Blanching, she stepped back, knocking against the bed and falling back. "Oh, God. Oh, God." She stood and turned her back, rushing into the bathroom and vomiting. "Jesus, no."

More than anything, she wanted to sink onto the bathroom floor. Instead, she wiped her mouth with the sleeve of her jacket and forced herself back into the hall. Her breath shallow, she crept through the rest of the house. Her feet spread, her gun out, she swept each area in a wide arc, checking carefully for suspects before moving on. When she was sure the house was empty, she returned to the body and stepped into the bathroom.

There, she splashed cold water on her face, checked that the bathroom was undisturbed, before facing the room. She wiped her hands on her pants. Process the scene. No prints, no evidence. Just work it like any other.

Forcing herself back into the bedroom, she stared at the body. His hands folded before him, he looked peaceful. He wore only a T-shirt and shorts and from the look of his hair, he'd been sleeping when he was awakened. Only the red splatter pattern behind his head and the empty stare in his eyes gave him away. She looked at the wound. He'd been shot in the neck, just like Loeffler. She had found the next one and it was too late.

If Nader was second, then she was third. Why hadn't he killed her when he'd had the chance? He could easily have shot her in her home as he did the other two. Why was she any different? Was it because she couldn't remember?

It felt like he was taunting her. The calls, the evidence planted at the scene and at her house, the break-in—it was all some sort of manipulation. She thought about the killer—he was arrogant. Arrogant, obsessed with controlling her, detached. She tried to fit the personality factors into a face and knew it was impossible. Even if she met him, she might not know him. Deceit was part of the game.

And she had no idea what the final play was. Was the plan to make it look like she was the killer? That she'd savagely killed Loeffler, cut off his hand and thrown it in her own trash? And then come down here to kill Nader before taking her own life?

There had to be more than just wanting to clean up what had happened all those years ago, something that triggered all of this happening now. There was something he wanted her to do before he killed her, or something he wanted her to know. It all had to do with that day in the warehouse. Was her punishment different from Loeffler's and Nader's because she may have shot Androus? Or maybe she was singled out because she'd seen something they hadn't. But she didn't remember it.

He wanted her to remember. It was the only thing she could come up with. It seemed risky—too risky to gamble her memory on his freedom. But he'd already proven he was willing to take risks.

She looked back at Nader. When had he died? With the temperature so low, it was hard to guess by looking at the body. He could have been here for several days. She assumed the incense would burn only twenty-four hours or so. She thought about the message she'd left Nader and wondered if he'd heard it.

Leaving the bedroom momentarily, she found the answering machine in the kitchen. The light wasn't blinking. Opening the top with her knuckle, she looked inside. The tape was gone. Someone had been here since she'd called. They had the tape with her call—more evidence against her.

She looked around and then headed back into the bedroom. She knew the police could be here anytime. He'd probably called them himself. She should leave, but she needed to search everything first.

As quickly as possible, she looked over Nader's bedroom. The walls of the room were covered by framed eight-by-tens of scenery. She saw a photo of Joshua trees in a pink sunset that looked like it had been taken in the African tundra. Rows of lush, green rice fields, from Bali or someplace close by, filled another. Only one picture showed him, standing with a group of local Indians in a jungle somewhere. He was certainly talented.

Forcing herself to move on, she picked up a stick of the incense and examined it. No name, no brand. The wastebasket held no packaging either. Using the incense, she poked the trash. A beer bottle, some mail, a couple tissues. No wrapping.

Tucking her gun away, she moved around the room, looking at it as though through Lombardi's eyes. He would come to this scene. It would be ruled part of the Loeffler case and she knew he would visit. What would he find that she had missed?

She pulled off the thin fleece jacket she was wearing and put one hand in each of the arms in lieu of a pair of gloves. Moving around the room, she opened the drawers and poked through the contents, careful not to touch anything with her bare hands. The bedside table held a copy of Paolo Coelho's *The Alchemist*, a small flashlight, earplugs, a row of four lubricated condoms, and a tube of Chapstick.

She moved to his dresser drawers and went through them one at a time, beginning at the top. White briefs in the top left drawer, socks on the right. The socks were matched and folded in half, stacked by color, darks on the left, lights on the right. She moved the stacks and searched beneath them. There was nothing.

The second drawer was T-shirts, then shorts and long-sleeved shirts and pants as she moved her way down. The bottom drawer was wide and especially deep and held workout clothes—Nike shorts, T-shirts, fleeces, and three pairs of biking pants. The clothes weren't stacked like the other drawers. It looked like he used this drawer the most. Leaning down, she pulled the jacket off her hands and lifted the clothes from the drawer onto her lap, searching for something out of place.

At the bottom of the drawer in the middle, she saw

a white envelope. Putting her hand back into her jacket sleeve, she picked up the envelope and opened it. She pulled out a white receipt. At the top, it read "N.T. Security P.I. Services." It was a bill for a two-month period the prior fall. The address was in Menlo Park. She remembered Loeffler's calendar. Meet NT SEC. Loeffler's calendar had also had something about SQ. What did that mean?

Had both Loeffler and Nader worked with the same P.I.? She refused to believe it could be a coincidence. Maybe they had been in communication about what had happened all those years ago. Then why hadn't they called Alex? She was a cop. Didn't that make her the perfect person to contact? Or maybe they were trying to make contact, and that was why Loeffler had pictures of her, why she had ended up at Loeffler's that night.

Returning the clothes to the drawer, she tucked the receipt in her pocket and turned toward the door. As she did, her toe caught a lamp and it came tumbling off the dresser. Before she could think, Alex caught it in her bare hand. "Damn it."

Using her jacket, she wiped her prints off the lamp and returned it to the spot on the dresser. Then, moving quickly, she looked through Nader's closet, under his bed, through the small second bathroom he used for photo developing, and finally tackled the desk in his office.

She had turned to leave when she spotted Nader's checkbook open on top of his filing cabinet. The dates read July and she wondered what someone was doing looking back at those months. PG&E, Pacific Bell, TCI cable, Acura of Palo Alto, USAA insurance, cash withdrawals. Nothing seemed unusual.

Using the tail of her shirt, she turned the page and scanned the entries. The third read "N.T. Security, 700.00." She flipped back several pages to January and found another payment to N.T. Security, this one for over a thousand.

From what she could tell, Nader had paid N.T. Security almost every month from September of 1998 until November of 1999. The amounts ranged from under two hundred to nearly two thousand. She needed to find this P.I.

With the toe of her shoe, she nudged the door open and started to step out.

But she wasn't alone.

Chapter Twenty-five

Greg stood with his arms crossed and a brow cocked and aimed at Alex. At least it wasn't a gun. "We've got to stop meeting this way."

"You scared me."

"You know you shouldn't be here."

Alex pushed by him. "I didn't have a choice."

Greg walked past and started to push the bedroom door open.

"He's dead, Roback. Shot in the neck, just like Loeffler."

Greg went in anyway. He stared for almost a minute and came back. "He's still got both hands."

She nodded. "And feet."

"Guess we won't need to go through your trash then," he said. The words might have been funny in very different circumstances. Things were too serious now to joke much, and becoming more serious all the time.

"We should get out of here," he said when she didn't respond.

She turned and headed to the back of the house, thinking she'd have liked to do something for Loeffler and Nader. Finding their killer seemed like the best she could offer. Images of the two of them in death flashed into her head. "Why the neck? Why shoot them there?"

"Breath," Greg said. "Food. Speech."

"Speech?" Alex grabbed onto the idea. "Maybe he

shot them in the neck because they'd spoken? Because I can't remember, I can't speak."

"Maybe that's why he slammed your head into the floor, as a way of telling you to remember."

"Remember or else?" Alex opened the back door and squinted at the sun.

"Something like that."

"I've got some information from the station."

Alex turned around and looked at Greg. "What?"

He looked over his shoulder. "We should get out of here first."

Alex started for the street. "Where's Tim?"

"Who?"

She looked around. "The kid. Tim."

"There wasn't anyone here when I got here."

She frowned and approached her car. "How'd he get his keys? I locked the door." As she got closer, she saw that the small triangular window on the passenger side had been broken. "Goddamn it." The inside passenger seat was littered with tiny pebbles of glass and a fist-sized rock sat beside her left front tire. She popped the trunk and saw that her purse was still there. At least he hadn't gotten that. The envelope of money and his keys were gone, but that was it. "The little prick."

"Who the hell are you talking about?"

Alex told Greg about Tim's appearance, the camera, and the clue that led her to Nader. "Ah, screw it." She reached her hand out. "Give me your phone." She wanted to go to N.T. Security next. She hoped they could tell her what Loeffler and Nader had learned.

Pulling the receipt from her pocket, she opened it up. The receipt had a stamp with a phone number. She dialed the number and waited while it rang. "Come on." She heard three high-pitched beeps and a message that said the number had been disconnected.

She dialed information. "Menlo Park for N.T. Secu-

rity P.I. Services," she said, thinking the name was
a mouthful.

"No listing," the operator announced.

"I assume that isn't evidence from the scene of a
crime," Greg said, pointing over her shoulder at the
receipt.

She shushed him and spoke into the phone. Maybe
they moved. "How about Palo Alto?"

"I'm afraid not."

Alex clenched a fist. "Can we try San Francisco,
Oakland, or Berkeley, please?" She loved the fact that
AT&T now had nationwide information at one number. She didn't care that Greg would probably pay
heavily for the convenience.

"No listing in any of those cities."

"Can we try San José?"

The woman exhaled. "No problem," she said even
though she didn't mean it.

Alex waited.

"Nothing in the 408 area code. I also tried the 510,
the 415, the 925, and the 650. Those are all the codes
in your area. Is there anywhere else you'd like me
to try?"

"No. Thanks." Alex turned the phone off and
handed it back to Greg.

"Who were you calling?" He put his hand up. "Before you get into it, let's get out of here and go somewhere we can talk."

She nodded and walked around to the driver's side.
"I know just the place, follow me," she said, getting
into the car.

Greg following in his car, she drove the fifteen minutes to the abandoned lot and parked. It seemed like
as good a place as any. The killer had the information
about her hotel, so she hated to go back there. She'd
have to worry about getting her stuff and moving later.

And she didn't think anyone would expect her to
come back here.

"Nice." Greg opened the passenger side door of her car and swept the glass onto the floor before sitting down. "You staying in the neighborhood?"

Ignoring the comment, she explained about the bill from N.T. Security Private Investigator Services and the note she'd seen in Loeffler's calendar.

"But there's no listing?"

She shook her head. "Maybe they're out of business."

"Or out of state, or changed names, or added someone, or any number of things."

"If we had access, we could check the licensing bureau. If it's a real P.I. service, they'll have a license."

Greg's face sobered and he didn't answer immediately. "I'll try to get Chris to do it," he said.

"It's that bad at the station?"

He looked at her and shifted down in the seat. "It's pretty bad."

"Do you have anything?"

"I've got a lot. You can thank Brenda for most of it." He pulled out a couple of folded sheets of paper. "Ballistics came back on my gun."

"And?"

"No match."

Alex exhaled.

Greg slapped her shoulder playfully. "You knew there wouldn't be. Don't look so surprised, you make me nervous."

"I knew it wouldn't match, but the way this guy's working, I wouldn't be surprised if he could pull a rabbit out of your hat."

"He may still yet."

Alex stared at him. "What?"

"They've confiscated Brenda's."

Leaning back in the seat, she shook her head. "What do you bet James volunteered his gun for the pile, too?" she said, steaming.

"It's shitty, but they won't find anything."

"It's still shitty."

Greg was quiet for a moment. Then he said, "Did you know cat urine glows under a black light?" He paused again. "I hate cats."

Alex couldn't bring herself to joke right then. "What else—on the case?"

He unfolded the papers in his lap. "Alfred Ferguson was up at Quentin for six years. First offense but VC stuff," he said. "Not a real bright one, our Mr. Ferguson."

Something immediately felt off. She expected Ferguson to be smarter than the average killer. Who else could have set her up this way? "What do you mean not real bright? What kind of violent crime did he commit?"

"Got drunk during a bowling game, went home, got a gun, came back, and shot a guy he said was screwing his girlfriend, then went home and got into bed. Police picked him up an hour later, tucked into bed wearing his pajamas."

"Not exactly an Einstein."

"That's not the worst of it."

Alex looked out onto the lot. "Dumber than that?"

"Much. He was released on the manslaughter charges four years ago. Starts frequenting a convenience store near where he lives. Worker is a woman Ferguson dates on and off. Everyone in the store knows him. Owner always complains because he has these big boots and he tracks mud in and out all the time. One day when his girlfriend isn't working, Ferguson shows up in a ski mask with an assault rifle and robs the place."

"Let me guess, he tracks the mud in," Alex said.

"Yep. Owner knows him instantly. Even says something to him about the mud."

A pit hardened in Alex's gut. This wasn't her man.

"And Ferguson doesn't stop. He still robs them— even ties the owner up when he gives him trouble.

Calls him by name as he's dong it." Greg folded the papers until he had made a small cube and then began to unfold them.

Alex rubbed her face. "It doesn't make sense. Whoever's putting this together isn't stupid. Ferguson isn't right. Did you find a picture of him?"

He pulled a photo out of his pocket and handed it to her.

She stared at the mug shot. Ferguson was thick-necked and meaty. He had a birthmark like a red splash of paint across his upper lip. He had a wide chin that she thought she recognized. But he definitely wasn't the same man as in the photo labeled B.A. she'd seen at Loeffler's.

"Is it the guy from the gym?" he asked.

"I think so." She handed the picture back. "It's still not right, though. Our guy is smart. It can't be Ferguson. Not alone."

"Maybe he's learning from experience."

She shook her head. "What's he been doing since he got out?"

"Working construction in Oakland—project at Fortieth and Broadway. According to the foreman, though, he's only there every third day or so."

"And he still has a job?"

Greg shrugged. "I guess labor's hard to come by. They take it when they can get it."

"No way. It's someone else. He didn't leave a single print at Loeffler's house. Somehow he got me there, took pictures of me in my car, splattered my pants with blood, broke into my house, and planted the mug . . ."

"You know the attack was him."

She nodded. "Okay, so the attack was him. But he's not doing this on his own. I don't buy it. Too many variables. I mean, he got Tim involved, bought the camera." She shook her head again. "And why Tim? What's the connection—that he knew Loeffler?" She tapped her foot and tried to reason it out. "It's not Ferguson. He's more sophisticated, whoever he is. Ferguson doesn't have the resources. He couldn't have afforded that camera on a few days' work at a construction site."

"Hey, construction pays pretty well."

She grabbed his arm. "Listen to me. It's not Ferguson. That camera cost a grand. Plus, he wouldn't have given the kid half a grand to go with it. Someone else is involved. Someone from back then. It has to be."

"Who?"

"That's what I don't know. What's the connection between Ferguson and our guy?" She tried to run down the possibilities. "Where did Ferguson grow up? Down here?"

He shook his head. "Modesto."

Modesto was in the central valley, too far from Palo Alto to be the link. "Damn. What about cellmates or buddies in prison?"

"The most recent cellmate is still in. I couldn't check the previous go-around. I don't know about buddies. I can try to find out."

"Shit. I need answers on this stuff. We need access to the station," she said angrily.

"I'm doing the best I can, Kincaid."

"I know," she said in a softer voice. "I'm sorry. I appreciate what you've done. I'm just frustrated."

He nodded.

Alex sucked her lungs full of air and let it out in a long, low hiss. "Let's think of the positives. What else do we have? Anything on Androus's brother or sister?"

He shook his head. "I did get a hold of a picture of Walter Androus, though." He pulled another picture out of his breast pocket and handed it to her.

"What else've you got in that pocket?" she asked, looking at the face of Walter Androus.

"That's it, I'm afraid."

Androus wasn't at all what she'd expected. Unlike Alfred Ferguson, who looked like the thug he was, Androus actually looked like an intellect. He wore small, round rimless glasses and had a straight, thin nose, which had never been broken that she could see. He was thin with red hair. "He's definitely related to the guy in the picture I saw at Loeffler's. No doubt about it, that must have been a photo of Ben."

Greg motioned to the picture of Androus. "You think he's involved?"

She raised an eyebrow. "Walter or Ben?"

"Ben."

"Involved? As in, not dead?"

He shrugged.

"I don't know. Maggie admitted she never saw him dead. Walter was the one who went to New York and called her. What if he isn't dead?"

"But why?" Greg countered. "And why would no one ever have seen them together in Palo Alto?"

She thought about how much alike they looked, but not close enough to be mistaken for each other. Not by people who saw them often enough, anyway.

"Let's check into the circumstances of the death. Do we know what year it was?"

"The interview said 1972 and she said he'd died six years before, so 1966 or 1967. Maybe '65. Can you get to New York records?" she asked, knowing people would be watching his every move.

He shrugged. "I can get someone to call it in if I have to." She could tell from his voice that he was frustrated. "You find anything at his house besides the receipt?"

"The receipt and the body. That was about it."

"What are you going to do now?"

"I need to track down this P.I." She thought about what Tim had told her. "And I need to switch hotels. Our friend is giving out my current room number."

"Where are you staying?"

"I was at the Red Roof Inn. I don't know where I'll go next." She tucked her hair behind her ears and hated the feeling that it, like everything, was getting out of control. "Something better break. If it doesn't, there's nowhere to go."

"It will. Something has to." He sat up in the seat. "I'll get in touch with New York and find out what happened to Ben Androus. Chris was going to see if she could take another look at Androus's file. I was going to meet her at her house at four. Will you come?"

She shook her head. "I don't think I should."

"Where will you be?"

She shook her head.

"I'm not leaving until you tell me, Kincaid. We both know you'd be dumb not to have someone watch your backside. And you're not dumb."

"You should go. James hears you're down here and he'll have your ass."

"I'll cover my own ass, thank you very much."

Greg opened the glove compartment and pulled out a pen and a folded napkin. He wrote something on it and handed it to her. It was an address and phone number. "We're going to talk about the case. Chris isn't going to let us down. Somehow, I'm betting you'll be there."

She smiled. "I'll try."

Out of the car, Greg leaned over and peered back inside. "You can catch this guy, but it's stupid to do it alone. Stupid and dangerous. Meet me at Chris's. We'll form a game plan then." When she didn't answer, he backed away. "Four o'clock. Don't make me wait."

Alex drove away, deciding her partner knew her as well as anyone. And at least he was thinking clearly. She was dumb to believe she could handle this guy alone. He'd done nothing but handle *her* so far.

She went straight back to the library and got on the

Internet. She searched for N.T. Security and got a bunch of hits. Some were ones she'd already seen, but most were new, so she looked through them until she'd reached the last. Not a single reference to a private investigator. Refusing to give up, she tried variations of the name until she'd run out of options. Where the hell had N.T. gone?

She remembered the reference to SQ and plugged that into the Internet. Nothing useful.

Gathering her things, she relinquished the computer to an agitated-looking high school student and headed out the door. She had considered not showing up at Chris's, but the hope that either she or Greg had come up with something was all she had left. Revving the engine, she glanced at the clock on her dash. She had about forty minutes before Greg was meeting Chris.

Before she pulled from the curb, she hesitated. The logical thing to do was to change hotels, but something made her pause. What was the killer going to do with the knowledge of where she was staying? It didn't seem likely that he would kill her. He'd had multiple chances to do that already. If she stayed in the same hotel, maybe he'd approach her again, which would give her a chance to catch him. If she was ready for him, she just might be able to do it. If she moved, she'd risk losing him. She couldn't lose him.

She thought about Alfred. Was he going to be the messenger again? The more she thought about his history, the more she was convinced this wasn't Alfred's game. He was someone else's pawn. Maybe he was getting paid or maybe he was being blackmailed, but someone else was calling the shots.

Alex pulled away from the curb and drove slowly around Palo Alto rather than going to her hotel room. She had paid for another night. She was staying. Let him come get her. She'd be waiting.

As she drove, she kept a close eye on the rearview mirror. It was cop habit, but it had never felt more real than now, especially since he knew where she was staying. He must have followed her, but she hadn't noticed him on the drive down, and that fact made her uncomfortable. She was trained to notice things. She didn't know how she could have missed him, unless he was trained to keep from being noticed.

She had to be careful. Her own attentiveness and some fast answers were the only things that could save her. She wasn't used to depending on luck, but she could sure use some now.

She drove down Chris's street and pulled to the curb a block from her house. Suddenly, everyone's motivation for helping had to be considered. Greg would be there, she reminded herself. And she needed whatever information they had gathered.

She put the car in gear and had started down the street when she spotted a figure walking along the sidewalk toward her. The walk, slightly bowlegged, reminded her of James. Braking, she stared. It couldn't be James.

The growing darkness shielded his face. She scanned the street in the direction he had come. Squinting, she caught sight of a car parked on the street. A black Toyota like her brother's. And beside it stood a man in a trench coat who looked just like Lombardi. Jesus, it *was* Lombardi.

They were here to pick her up. Had Chris called them? Or had they somehow discovered Greg was her cousin and guessed that she would know where Alex was? Either way, Alex wasn't sticking around to find out.

Her heart pounding, she watched Lombardi turn up toward one of the houses. A woman came out the door and looked down the street. Alex recognized the blond hair, the even gestures. Chris.

Alex shrank down in her seat. Her stomach sank

like a lead weight. James was there, come to arrest her himself.

The two disappeared from view and Alex exhaled, giving them time to get inside before she left. On five she would move. "One. Two. Three. Four."

She eased on the gas. She'd gotten halfway off the curb when she saw James come running down the front steps. Chris was only two steps behind him, waving at her frantically.

Chapter Twenty-six

Alex threw her Honda into reverse and maneuvered backwards to give herself room to turn the car around. She sped back, then shifted into first gear and peeled off.

The sound of fists pounding on the trunk made her jump. Her foot slipped off the clutch, and the car stalled.

She cursed, her hands shaking as she fumbled with the keys.

James was at the window. "Alex!"

She ignored him, glancing down at the inside of the door. The passenger door was locked. With a quick breath, she turned back to the keys.

James jerked at the door, trying to open it. "Alex. Stop. You have to listen to me. You're in trouble."

"No shit, Sherlock," she mumbled, locking her own door with her elbow as she fumbled to restart the car. The engine sputtered twice and rolled over.

"Alex. Listen to me. I'm your brother. Let me help you."

Anger streamed down her spine like hot oil at the thought. James's help was the last thing she needed now. He'd help her all the way to San Quentin. Something tickled her brain, but James pounded on the window again and she lost it.

"You're making it worse. You should come in while you can."

She shuddered as she hit the gas. James ran after

her as she pulled down the street. From the corner of her eye, she could see him grow smaller in the rear-view mirror, Lombardi behind him.

A lump of thick emotion caught in her throat. She welcomed tears, knowing they would bring some much-needed catharsis. But she also knew they wouldn't come.

She needed a plan. And she didn't have one. The only thing she could think to do was to go back to the hotel and hope he came to her.

She sped toward the freeway, one eye on the rear-view mirror. At any moment, she expected a line of police cars to appear and surround her. The traffic light started to turn and she raced through it.

As she reached the middle of the intersection, she spotted a black Toyota coming at her from the side. Her heart roared like an engine in the red and she pumped the gas pedal, missing the car by inches as the screeching sound of tires filled the air.

Her car fishtailed and she quickly straightened the wheel. Without pausing to look back, she sped on.

Less than a block later, the black car had caught up and was now right behind her. She squinted at the license—3APC461. She slammed her hand against the steering wheel and pushed the pedal to the floor. It was James. His license had always stuck in her mind because he was born in April of 1961. Lombardi was in the passenger seat.

Racing another light, Alex pulled onto the freeway and changed lanes. James stayed right behind.

She watched him in the mirror, trying to predict his next move. There had to be a way to escape. She scanned the traffic, but there was no sign of other cops. Still, James wasn't stupid. He knew where to get backup if he needed it.

His hand emerged from the driver's window.

Her heart hammered in her chest, and adrenaline sparked every nerve. He was going to shoot at her.

Her hands reacted without her brain, swerving her car and ducking into traffic. Tires screeched behind her. The blare of horns followed.

She glanced back, relieved and amazed that she hadn't caused an accident. "Calm down, Alex." With a deep breath, she glanced back again. James was still in the far right lane, two cars back. His hand was back in the car, but something unrecognizable on the top of his car caught her eye.

She blinked as a red light flashed and swirled. "Shit." He had his police light on.

Cars yielded to him and he pulled into the lane behind her. She sped out again, dodging traffic and passing the exit for her hotel. She didn't dare pull off the freeway. Experience had taught her that it was much more difficult to pursue a suspect on the freeway than in town. She glanced at her gas indicator and wondered how far a third of a tank would get her. Petaluma at least, maybe farther. If only he was on empty. Not James, though. He would be prepared from every angle.

He was right behind her now, his headlights flashing to motion her to the side. She concentrated on the road. She wasn't pulling over. She kept her speed consistent and continued on.

From the next lane, a horn blasted and Alex started. As she looked at the car beside her, her shoulders sagged. It was over.

A highway patrolman in a marked car motioned her over, his expression an angry grimace.

She returned her attention to the road, hoping he'd go away, but he honked again. Glancing back at him, she could tell it wouldn't be long before he called in backup.

He shook a fist at her. She could see his lips form the words, "Pull the hell over."

"Fuck." Slowing, she pulled the car to the shoulder. She was dead, going to jail, and her own brother was sending her there. Her eyes suddenly heavy, she blinked back an onslaught of emotions. When had this happened to her? When had she fallen apart?

In the rearview mirror, she could see James speaking to the patrolman. Lombardi stood behind them, listening.

Alex shook her head. They were probably arguing over who got to claim credit for her arrest.

The patrolman lifted his hands in surrender and headed back to his car, shaking his head. His shoulders hunched, he seemed unhappy with whatever James had told him.

But instead of approaching her, James waited, his eye on the other officer.

Alex considered darting into traffic again, but she knew it was worthless. With the police light, James would be back on her tail in a matter of seconds.

As the officer pulled back into the stream of traffic, his eye caught hers. He slowed and scowled at her, studying her face as though he might be required to help a police artist draw it later.

A knock on the window made her jump.

"We need to talk," James insisted, peering into the car.

Leaving the keys in the ignition, she released her seat belt and stepped out, following her brother back to where Lombardi waited. Arms crossed over his chest, Lombardi leaned against the front bumper.

Cars were beginning to use their headlights as the day faded to dark. Alex used to be a night person, thriving when others were sleeping. These days she hated the nights most.

Lombardi approached her. "You know you almost got us all killed," he said, patting his lucky coat as though it were the reason he was still breathing.

"You never should've left Berkeley," James chastised.

"I should've just sat around, waiting for you to come and arrest me?"

"You've only made matters worse by coming down here."

"At least I've been searching for answers."

"And gathering witnesses," Lombardi added.

"What does that mean?"

"The kid came forward, Alex."

She shifted forward. "What kid?"

"Tim," James said. "He says he saw you kill Nader. Gave us a tape with you threatening him."

The words were more potent than a physical punch to the gut. "That little asshole. The killer is paying him—"

"Zip it," Lombardi snapped. "We know something's wrong with his story."

"What?"

Lombardi raised an eyebrow. "He said he saw you off Nader this morning, but the M.E. says he's been dead at least three days."

Three days meant he was dead before Alex called. "Tim's lying. I didn't kill him."

"He's definitely lying about something," Lombardi agreed.

Alex ignored the implication that he might not be lying about the murder. "You guys have to talk to him. He was hired by the killer to come down. The killer—Ferguson or whoever Ferguson's working for— gave him five hundred in cash and a brand-new camera."

Lombardi nodded. "I'll tell the detective down here."

Alex looked shocked. "What do you mean? You're not working this case?"

"Why would I? It's not my jurisdiction."

"What about the fact that Nader's death is related to Loeffler's?"

Lombardi shook his head. "We don't have any proof of that yet."

"We were all survivors of the same mass murderer

thirty years ago. Now, they're both dead, shot in the
neck, and I'm being framed." Alex spun around on
the edge of the freeway, feeling every bit out of control. "How much more damn evidence do you need?"

"Right now, we need to get you up to Berkeley,"
James said, interrupting. "If more evidence comes up
here, Lombardi will head back down."

Glancing at the ground, she tried to think of a way
out. She needed time. "James, I can't go to jail."

He reached out to her. "You won't, or not for long.
I'll talk to the captain. We'll work together. But we
need to go up there before things get worse."

She shook her head. "I mean, I can't go now. I have
to do this."

His expression hardened. "No. It's over. No more
running. Anything you do will only make things worse.
I have to bring you in. I told the deputy chief I would.
Alex, I'm not even sure I can help you anymore. It's
gone that far."

"You didn't do anything to help me to start with."

"Oh, Jesus," Lombardi said, rubbing his head.

Watching James's face, she knew the look. She had
seen it in a hundred different forms on his face, a
thousand different times: *Don't screw with the job.* The
next step would mean stepping over the line. It wasn't
about her anymore. It was about him, about his job.
He was always a cop first.

He wasn't going to change his mind. He was taking
her in. "You understand how it looks, don't you?
Even if you weren't involved, Alex—" He shook his
head. His eyes clouded with doubt. "Even if you're
not, it doesn't look good . . . You were there that
night. You have to face the consequences."

Lombardi was watching her, shaking his head. He
believed it, too.

Straightening her back, she prepared to fight. She
wasn't going to jail. Once she was behind bars, there

was no chance she'd catch the son of a bitch who put her there.

As she shifted, she felt the cool handle of her gun against her stomach. Stiffening slightly, she caught herself and nodded slowly. "Okay."

James gave her a slow once-over then gestured to his car. "My car?"

Alex nodded, heading to the car. Holding her breath at what was to come, she got in behind him.

Lombardi sat in the passenger seat and turned sideways to watch Alex. His eyes darted under the dark fur of his brow like tiny rodents under brush.

James watched her in the rearview mirror.

Without blinking, she stared back.

Finally, he looked at the road and started to turn the key.

In one fell swoop, Alex pulled the gun from her belt and held it to Lombardi's head. "Hands in the air." She should have been appalled at her own behavior, but suddenly she felt the part. She was a renegade, a fugitive. Solving this mess herself was the only chance she had left.

"Holy shit," Lombardi said, raising his hands. "A fucking psycho woman. This was a dumb idea, Kincaid. I told you she wouldn't come easy. You didn't listen. Got to come down here like a fucking hero instead of letting the locals bring her up for us." He shook his head. "Christ, I'm going to get offed by a chick."

"Shut up," Alex snapped. She blinked fast, horrified at what this had come to. She'd had no choice—no choice, she repeated to herself. It didn't help.

James didn't move.

Alex pointed the gun at him. "Hands up."

He lifted his hands slowly, though he didn't look the least bit scared. "Alex, don't be ridiculous. You could never shoot anyone."

"That's what I thought. But I was wrong."

His eyes widened, and Lombardi let out a low moan.

Alex swallowed the self-disgust like bile in her throat.

James's gaze grew distant, appraising. The cop had taken over. She had driven away whatever little piece of brother had been there.

"What are you talking about, Alex?"

She would give him what he wanted. "I shot Androus."

James frowned. "Androus has been dead for thirty years."

Alex gave him a twisted smile and nodded, playing the part. "I know. I shot him."

"What are you talking about?"

"That I'm probably the youngest murderer alive. According to the police theories, I killed Androus. In 1971, after he had killed eleven children, I took his gun and shot him."

"That's outrageous," James refuted.

"It's worse than that, James—it's true. Ask Chris, ask Roback."

"A kid killer. You're nuts." Lombardi groaned. "Both of you are fucking nuts."

"Who told you that? Chris?" James asked.

"Judith told me, but if that's not good enough, it's in Chris's file. Get yourself a copy, why don't you?" She cupped her left hand by his. "Now, give me the keys."

He glanced at her in the rearview mirror and then pulled the keys from the ignition and handed them to her.

"Weapons," she demanded. "One at a time."

Lombardi brought his out first, handing it to her muzzle to the ground. She took the magazine and unloaded the shells into her hand. "Gun, James."

James gave her his gun and she emptied it, too.

She nodded. "And your cell phone."

He motioned to the glove compartment. "It's in there."

Alex turned the gun back toward Lombardi. "Get it. Nice and slow."

The detective opened the glove compartment and handed Alex the cellular phone.

"Radio," Alex said.

James pulled out the handset on the radio, and with a quick jerk, she yanked it free. She opened the car door and started to get out.

"You may not believe this, either of you, but as far as I know, I haven't done anything wrong. And I'm going to prove it to you." She slammed the door and headed for her car.

Halfway there, she turned around and pointed the gun.

Lombardi ducked but James didn't move, his stare piercing her.

Alex pulled the magazine from the gun and held it out for him to see. "Empty," she yelled. She stared at James and shook her head. "I'm sorry, James. I really am."

Alex darted through traffic to her hotel. She parked in the loading zone and rushed to her room, her pulse frantic. In a mad rush, she packed up her things and left, refusing to allow herself to think about what she'd just done to her brother and a man she'd once hoped to work for.

She needed to dump her car and find herself another hotel. She had wanted to stay at the Red Roof Inn, but now she couldn't risk that James would break Greg and find out where she was. Even a new hotel room wasn't a guarantee that they wouldn't find her.

Back on the road, she kept a constant eye on the rearview mirror as she headed to the San Francisco airport. She found a space in long-term parking and entered the departure area. After taking out money at an ATM machine on the departures deck, she went downstairs to arrivals. At the hotel information desk, she found a listing for the Hyatt and called for reservations under the name Carmen Hayes. She picked a more upscale hotel than she normally would have, knowing that James would look for her at the cheaper places first.

If the police were searching for her, they would know she'd have to get rid of her car. And cabs would be the first place they'd look. She changed clothes in the bathroom, pulled her hair into a bun, and put a baseball cap over it.

Then, hurrying back outside, she went to wait for the Hyatt shuttle, doing her best not to fidget. When it arrived, she took a seat in the back of the crowded van. Her luggage in her lap, she pretended to sleep like an exhausted grad student.

The room she had been checked into was on the eleventh floor. She would have liked to have a room on a lower floor, but she had not wanted to draw attention. As she rode up in the elevator, she focused on her duffel bag, her hands clenched, her knuckles white.

She'd paid for two nights, knowing the following day was Sunday and would bring her no good news. Without Greg to count on, she was on her own, without a single lead. She had nothing to work with but what was in her head.

She considered ordering room service but didn't want to risk anyone seeing her. Instead, she opened the mini-bar and pulled out a small tin of twelve-dollar peanuts.

As she lay back in bed, hungry and tired, she considered what a mess she had created. She would be lucky if she didn't spend the rest of her life in jail.

Breaking and entering, assault, assault with a deadly weapon, assault and battery of a police officer, kidnapping, reckless endangerment, burglary, robbery, resisting arrest, involving a minor in a criminal act—and she was sure there were others she hadn't thought of yet.

Desperate for an outlet for her energy and not willing to risk venturing out, Alex worked out on the hotel-room floor. She did reps of twenty-five push-ups, fifty sit-ups, one hundred leg lifts on each side, then her tae bo moves—roundhouse, front and back kicks, and punching an imaginary speed bag—until she was dripping with sweat and could feel her muscles like pounding fists beneath her skin.

With her energy burned off, she lay down on the bed. As she let her heavy eyelids fall closed, she felt strong and solid. She could beat him. Now all she had to do was find him.

Chapter Twenty-seven

The officers stood above her, dark uniforms making them look like a pack of monsters waiting to descend. Their voices echoed in her head, a cacophony she couldn't block out, tones she couldn't separate. Images whirled in her brain like water down a faucet, and she felt dizzy and nauseated.

She pulled her knees to her chest and held herself tight, rocking slowly on the chair. As the men moved and spoke around her, their badges caught the light, creating tiny blasts of white in the darkness.

One of them leaned over her again, faceless, nameless. Why were there so many?

"Okay, Alexandra, tell us one more time. How did you get the gun?"

She pictured the long blond hair that had tickled her skin. "Don't be afraid, honey," the voice had said, a melodic murmur to a frightened child's ears.

"Alexandra?" the officer asked.

"An angel," she repeated and rolled her eyes. Why didn't they understand?

As she glanced up, he gave her a smile and she shivered. He backed away and she caught fragments of the conversation that followed.

"She's confused," one said.

She pulled her knees tighter, tucking her chin to her chest.

"A fucking angel?" another asked, his voice angry.

She rocked harder, humming to herself.

"... a lot ... stress," a softer voice said.

"Maybe someone ... angel."

"Impossible," the angry one spoke again.

She covered her ears, humming louder.

Another knelt next to her. His touch was like the angel's, so light it was almost imaginary. "Alex? People call you Alex, right? Not Alexandra."

She looked at him, watched his eyes as he spoke. It was the man with the soft voice. She nodded.

"I know this is hard, but we're grown-up people. We're not as good as kids at understanding things. Can you help me?"

She stopped rocking and nodded.

"Thanks, Alex. Now, can you describe the angel for us?"

"It was an angel," she insisted.

He nodded. "I believe you. Is there any way we could talk to this angel?"

She frowned. "Don't you know? You can't talk to angels. They come down to help and then they leave."

He thought a minute like little kids did when they didn't understand something. "Where do they go?"

"Fucking waste of time," the angry man said in the background.

The quiet one looked back and stared at him like her mother stared at her when she'd been bad. Alex stared at the angry man, too.

He leaned over and spoke again. "Sorry, Alex. Now, where do the angels go?"

"They go back to heaven—like my dad."

The man hesitated and then moved closer.

Alex scooted against the bars of the chair. She didn't want anyone near her ever again.

The man moved back immediately. "Was this angel your daddy?"

Alex thought a moment and smiled. Her daddy. "My daddy," she repeated.

"Was it your daddy?"

Her daddy was the only angel she knew. She nodded. She'd finally met her daddy. Boy, where James and Brittany going to be jealous.

"What does your daddy look like? Like the angel?"

She shook her head. "He looks like my dad. I have a picture on the table by my bed. I can show it to you if you want."

"And this angel that you saw looked like your dad?"

"No. The angel looked like an angel," she said, tired of explaining. "With long blond hair and wings."

"Wings?"

She nodded.

The man stood up and she could hear them whispering.

Alex closed her eyes and rocked again, her knees warm and strong against her. She was cold and she wished the angel were there now. The angel would tell them. She had to pull the trigger. She had to or she and Billy and Marcus would have died.

Over her shoulder, she could see another officer talking to the boys. The officer motioned to her and the boys shook their heads. She looked back at the floor. They hadn't seen the angel. They had been blindfolded. Plus, the angel had picked her to talk to, not them. The boys didn't hear. They weren't close enough.

She closed her eyes and tried to picture the angel's face, but she'd never seen it. The angel seemed smaller now, like a cupid in comparison to the big police. She wished she could see the angel's face. Then, she could tell them what it was like.

The voices raised again, the mean cop yelling at the others. She rocked and covered her ears.

"What the fuck. She's crazy."

"Stop," she whispered, rocking harder.

There were more murmurs. She couldn't hear them. She raised her voice. "Stop. Stop." She yelled. "Stop!"

A hand touched her arm and she jumped.

Alex bolted up, her face damp with sweat. Her hand shook as she flipped the light on. She blinked hard and looked around. The room was empty. The bright green numbers on the clock read four-thirty. She'd hardly been asleep five hours.

Flashes of a dream came back to her, and a face appeared in her mind like an image through a camera's lens. She tried to focus on it, to clear the blurring. Something clicked, and like a shutter closing, the image was gone.

Propping the pillows behind her back, she focused on the fleeting image of an angel. What did it mean? Nothing but the word "angel" remained in her memory.

Deep in the recesses of her mind, it was all there. She thought about Judith. Maybe she would hypnotize Alex into remembering everything. She stared at the phone and shook her head. Surely James had contacted Judith by now. James would have thought of everything. She was truly on her own.

Tim came to mind and she wondered if the caller had contacted him again. Did he know where she was staying now? Was the kid on his way here with another roll of film?

Frustrated, she lay back down, feeling more tired now than she ever had from insomnia. She imagined herself taking a bath in her lion's-foot tub and wondered how long it would be until she would again, if ever.

Before she went back to Berkeley and guaranteed her own arrest, she had to ask all the questions she could come up with here. A part of her knew it was dumb to leave the hotel room today. She would sit tight and wait to make sure the dust had settled with James, but she didn't have the time to waste. The answers weren't going to come to her there.

At least she knew where she was going. There was only one person she could think of who she prayed would be able to help.

Alex showered and tucked her hair under her cap and dressed in jeans and a sweatshirt. Out the window, she spotted a Kentucky Fried Chicken. Her stomach protested at the thought of another hour without food, but she ignored the temptation and reached for the phone book. She found a number and dialed.

"Yellow Cab," the voice answered with all the briskness of a New Yorker.

"I need a cab at Kentucky Fried Chicken on Willow Pass Road."

"Across from the Veterans Hospital?"

Alex looked around and spotted the thick gray building. "Yes."

"Got it."

"How long will that be?" she interjected as he started to hang up.

"Five to ten minutes."

The click informed her the conversation was over. "Charming," she mumbled. Tucking some cash and her police I.D. in her pocket, Alex set the "Do Not Disturb" sign on the door and left.

The stairwell was silent except for the clatter of ancient water pipes working overtime. She jogged down the stairs, not allowing herself to stop until she'd reached the bottom. There, she took thirty seconds to slow her pulse and then headed out into the lobby.

It was quiet. She had expected it would be. Judging from the people she had ridden from the airport with, the Hyatt's business seemed to come primarily from conventions and conferences. Generally, there were very few weekend patrons in such hotels before Sunday evenings. No one even glanced at her as she made her way through the lobby, her dark glasses pushed close to her face.

She jogged toward the KFC. The cab pulled to the curb as Alex arrived and she hopped in.

"Noah's Bagels on University," she said.

A gray-haired black man sat in the front seat, casting a quick glance at her. "Picked up at Kentucky Fried to go get a bagel, eh?"

She gave him a quick smile. "My car broke down about three blocks up."

He looked in the mirror again and then dismissed it, though she didn't think he believed her. Thankfully, the address she had given him was three blocks from where she was actually going. Even if he told someone, it would take them a while to find her. That was the best she could hope for now—a little extra time.

When he stopped at Noah's, she paid him and paused, taking a moment to scan the area carefully for signs of local police or James before getting out. She entered Noah's, bought three plain bagels, a small container of plain cream cheese, a cranberry juice, and a large coffee, and then left again. She found a bench on the side of the block, away from traffic, and ate one bagel with cream cheese and drank the coffee.

When she was done, she circled the block and watched her back before heading to Nader's. Cutting down a side street, she walked the three blocks until she could see his house. Even from the end of the block, the yellow crime scene tape was brightly visible, swaying like a flag of surrender in the morning wind.

Except for the crime scene tape, though, Nader's house looked the same as it had the first time she arrived. No one appeared to be keeping watch, but she didn't dare chance it.

Instead of heading down Ramona, Alex walked to the next block and counted houses until she was at the one directly behind Nader's. The streets were clear. After surveying her surroundings, she cut between the houses to Nader's. A quick glance confirmed nothing was happening at his house. She pushed off the momentary urge she felt to go back inside and search for other clues.

Turning, she approached his neighbor's door and

knocked. She prayed the woman she had seen in the window yesterday would be home.

The sound of a bolt latch came from the inside. The slide of metal against metal and the clink of a chain followed.

"Hello?" Alex called when the door didn't open.

"Who is it?" a shaky, shrill voice called.

Alex realized the woman had not unlocked the door but locked it. "It's Alexandra Michaels."

"Who?"

"I'm a detective, ma'am," she lied. "Here to ask you a few more questions about your neighbor." She was certain the police had already questioned her.

The door remained closed. "I've already answered all your questions. What else do you need to know?"

"I apologize, ma'am. I know this is an inconvenience. Do you have just another quick minute?"

"No such thing as a quick minute," she snapped.

Alex continued to press. "It's very important. I wouldn't be bothering you otherwise."

"The officer that was here told me the police would call if they had more questions."

"Yes, that's usually the case. I came back by to take some track prints on Mr. Nader's car." She was getting pretty decent at the lies. "I just thought of a few other things I'd like to ask."

"Oh, good Lord."

"I promise it won't take more than a few minutes."

Silence followed. Alex strained to listen for motion. Was the woman leaving? Going to the phone?

At the click of the bolt releasing, Alex exhaled.

A thin woman with wisps of blue-gray hair and high cheekbones opened the door, wearing a housedress with small blue and pink flowers over a pair of light blue polyester pants and white slippers. She furrowed a wiry brow and stared.

Alex made no move to get closer, and the woman made no move to let her inside.

The exposure to the street made fear twist in Alex's gut, but she held her composure.

"You were here that day—with the boy."

She nodded. "The boy brought me here."

The woman scowled and mumbled something Alex couldn't hear. Her eyes appraised each inch of Alex as though the woman had X-ray vision that would warn her if Alex was good or evil. At any moment, the alarms might sound in her head. The door shut again, and metal squeaked as the chain was released. The door then opened slightly wider. "You can come in," the woman said, "but make it fast."

"Yes, ma'am." Alex surveyed the room carefully as she stepped inside.

The woman made a beeline for the closest chair in the small den and sat.

Something cracked as she did, but Alex wasn't sure if it was the woman or the chair. They appeared to be about the same age.

"What could you possibly ask me that they didn't already ask?"

It was a good question. And since Alex didn't know what had already been asked, she avoided it. "I was wondering if you know about a security company your neighbor might have hired."

For a split second, the woman's eyes darted across the tabletops. They snapped back to Alex's as she shook her head. "I didn't talk much to him. He wasn't around much. I think he worked a ways from here. And weird hours."

As the woman answered, Alex took inventory of the tables. A plastic container surrounded by different sized jars of medication seemed to be the only thing out. Alex read the name "Louisa Carter" from the closest one.

"So I wouldn't know who he had working for him," she added.

Alex looked back at the woman, who was watching

her suspiciously. "You seem to keep a good eye out the window. I noticed when I was here the other day. May I ask why?"

The woman's eyes narrowed. "I'm an old lady. I don't have any children, my husband's dead, my friends are all in Florida or dead. There's not much to do, Officer. Is there something wrong with watching out the window?"

Alex smiled her biggest smile. "Absolutely not. In fact, it's a huge help to the police. I only wish we had more people like you to keep a lookout for us."

The woman straightened and smiled, proud. The narrow, suspicious glare transformed into a soft cheery gaze.

Alex was laying it on thick, but it seemed to be working. "I think it's a wonderful service that you do for us."

The woman sighed. "Well, I don't know about all that. I guess it was just plain luck more than anything else." She was blushing.

"Oh, no," Alex argued, knowing a flattered witness would spill a lot more than an angry one. "It takes a very keen sense of duty to keep that sort of watch."

"Well, after my friend Anna Mae witnessed her neighbor's house burglarized not even a mile from here, I started to pay close attention."

Alex nodded, ready to pop the question she'd come to ask. "Did you notice anyone going to Mr. Nader's house several days ago?"

"Only the kid."

Alex nodded. "But that was yesterday."

Mrs. Carter pointed a finger. "I saw him yesterday, too. But he was here before that."

Alex frowned. "He was here before yesterday?"

Mrs. Carter folded her hands together and closed her eyes.

Alex watched her, praying she didn't stop breathing or something. "Mrs. Carter?"

Her eyes sprang open and Alex sat back in the chair. "He was here late in the evening—three nights ago. I saw him cross the yard between the two houses, just like you did yesterday."

"Did he go inside?"

She frowned. "I'm not sure."

Alex shook her head. Why hadn't James or Lombardi mentioned that small fact? And why would Tim tell her he'd broken into the house earlier that morning without confessing that he'd been there before that? He had told her he'd just come down to Palo Alto that morning. Had he been there earlier and gone back up and come down again? It didn't make sense. "Did you tell the other police this?"

Louisa cupped her hand over her mouth. "You know, I don't think I did. It didn't even occur to me until you asked. They asked if I'd seen anyone suspicious around Nader's house, but the kid hadn't seemed suspicious." She paused and her gaze fluttered around the room as she shook her head. "Isn't that funny? He was wearing a baseball cap and he just looked like a regular kid. I never thought to mention him. He looked more scraggly yesterday without the hat on."

Alex frowned. She hadn't seen Tim in a hat, but maybe it had been in his bag. "Do you remember what the hat said?"

The woman shook her head. "It was red, I think." She waved her hand. "It was a whole mishmash of an outfit, to be honest. Big clunky shoes. They were red, too. And that yellow jacket, no missing that either. That's how I remembered him from the other night." She frowned. "I'm glad you came back. I never would have thought to tell the police about the boy and now you can tell them."

"You're sure it was the same kid?"

"My night vision's not good anymore," Louisa Carter confessed. "To be honest, he looked more like a kid that night. Smaller or younger." She waved her hand as though she couldn't find the perfect word to describe what she meant. "That's why I didn't think to mention it to the police."

Alex still couldn't imagine that Tim had come to kill Nader. Her gut told her he wasn't capable of murder, and her gut was usually right on. What was going on? "But you're sure it was the same kid?"

"Yes, siree. I'm sure."

Alex was frustrated and dissatisfied with the answers she'd gotten, but she couldn't think of anything else to ask to clarify. "You've been so helpful, Mrs. Carter. You should be very proud. Anything you might remember would be so much help to us."

The woman didn't look at Alex. "Honest, I—I don't know." She paused and her lips formed a meek smile. "The brain goes first in my family."

Something about Mrs. Carter's nervousness made Alex think she was holding back. But why? Did she suspect Alex wasn't who she said she was? Or was there something about Nader she just didn't want to share? She shrugged it off. She'd have to ask Greg to tell Chris about Tim's presence at the house the other night. The real police would want to talk to Mrs. Carter again. As much as Alex would have liked to follow up on it herself, she knew she wouldn't be able to get near Tim now.

"Well, as I said, it certainly was a huge help that you were watching." Alex started to turn for the door and then turned back. She pulled out a piece of paper with her home phone number and gave it to Mrs. Carter. "If you think of anything else, please call me."

Mrs. Carter squinted at the paper. "Where's the 510 area code?"

"It's a new one down south," she lied, hoping Mrs. Carter wouldn't check it. New area codes were springing up like weeds in California. "It shouldn't cost more than a local call." Not much more anyway. Certainly not compared to life imprisonment.

Mrs. Carter folded the paper and nodded. "I hope you catch him. I'm not sleeping well these days."

Alex nodded. Neither was she.

Chapter Twenty-eight

Alex checked her home answering machine again before she turned off the light. It was after midnight. If anyone was going to call, surely they would have done it by now. She had expected—no, hoped—that Mrs. Carter would have called with more information about Nader. The way she'd scanned the room at the mention of Nader's name made Alex think she had been hiding something.

Alex had also hoped to hear from Greg with some miraculous discovery—like the identity of the killer. Or news about Ben Androus. Word of the story behind Walter Androus's brother and confirmation of his death might have cleared some of the seemingly impenetrable haze. Alex was sure James was watching Greg like a hawk. There was little else that would keep him from calling. She hoped he still had a job.

Nothing short of a miracle would help her unravel this mess before it exploded in her face. She couldn't stay in any one place for too long. Tomorrow, she'd probably need to look for yet another hiding place. Exhaling, she kneaded her temples to ease the deafening pain that resonated through her skull. Even a message from Brenda, a word of concern or possibly encouragement, would have made her feel better, less alone.

The light off, Alex sank into the bed and pulled the covers to her chin. The cool metallic feel against her thigh reassured her of the proximity of her gun.

*   *   *

Shivering, she rocked against the cold ground. It was so cold. When had she lost her coat? She had it this morning. Her mother always held it out as she walked out the door. The green parka with a bright yellow stripe flashed into her head.

"I don't need it," she'd argue.

"You get in here," her mother would reprimand, pushing her arms into the coat sleeves with a scolding click of her tongue. "And you wear that coat when you go outside," she'd add. "You'll catch your death of cold one of these days for ignoring your mother. Do you hear me?"

Alex would nod solemnly as her mother zipped the front of her jacket, kissed her on the head, and then herded her toward the door.

"Now, remember to do exactly what the chaperones tell you on the field trip. Don't go wandering off," she'd said this morning.

Alex had pondered the notion of a chocolate factory—elves watching over thousands of brown cows, collecting the chocolate as it came out.

"You think we'll get to taste the chocolate, Mom?"

"I'm sure you will, Alexandra. But don't go eating too much and upsetting your stomach. I'm making yellow chicken tonight."

The mild curry chicken dish was her favorite. The rich spicy flavor cleared her senses. She loved the steamy soup. A spoon clenched in her fist, she would dig down and hunt the broth for the pieces of tender chicken soaked in juice.

"Remember, do whatever the chaperones tell you," her mother called after her.

"But the chaperones aren't here now, Mommy," she whispered to herself, rocking harder. "I would have listened, I promise. But they're gone. Where did they go?"

The yellow bus had been full of kids. The chaperones

sat among them, talking to each other over the excited squealing. Alex had been sitting directly behind Jimmy's mom, Mrs. Cooney.

As she walked by, Mrs. Cooney had told her how grown-up she looked. Alex sat behind her and watched her talk. Mrs. Cooney was beautiful, like a woman on television. Her long cinnamon-colored hair spilled over her shoulders like thick maple syrup. And she smelled sweet like a whole garden of flowers. Alex leaned forward and pressed her nose into Mrs. Cooney's hair, taking in the wonderful smell.

But then something happened. Remembering, Alex rocked harder. Terrible sounds pierced her ears, like the ones that sometimes came from Mom's old car, only one hundred times louder. Alex covered her ears. The kids were screaming. Everyone was screaming. She couldn't look—she didn't want to look. Someone shook her, and she opened her eyes. It was the man—he handed her a cup. He looked like he was going skiing, a thick mask covering his face. But she didn't think it was that cold outside. She huddled deeper into her jacket, glad her mother had made her bring it.

The man shoved the cup toward her "Drink this," he demanded.

Sealing her lips as tightly as she could, Alex shook her head.

The man hit her. It felt like James's softball smashing into her head. Running her hands over the place where the man had struck her, she could feel a warm sticky spot. The man grabbed her hand and held it to her face. "Blood," he yelled. "Your blood." He shoved the drink back in her face. "Now, drink."

Tears ran down her face as he pushed the cup to her lips and forced her jaw open. She had expected a terrible flavor, like the dirt James had once made her eat. Instead, it tasted like punch.

Confused, Alex looked around. Mrs. Cooney wasn't moving. Neither was Mr. Choy, Charlie's dad. None of the grown-ups were moving. Then, as suddenly as it stopped, the bus started to move again.

Her eyelids felt heavy the way they did when her mother sometimes let her listen to the radio show on Saturday night. It was a special treat to be able to stay up past eight-thirty, and Alex always struggled to stay awake, squirming next to Brittany and James to keep her eyes open. That was how she felt now.

But her mother would pull Alex into her lap on those nights, and she would wake up in her own bed without any recollection of the end of the story. Sunday morning after breakfast, her mother would send James and Brittany out to play, and with a cup of coffee and Alex in her lap, she would recount the end of the story for her.

She wanted to be in her mother's lap now, safe and warm. Where was she? Why was this man doing this? Her knees pulled to her chest as a shield against the terrible man and the cold, Alex tried to remember the end of the last story. Blindfolded now and groggy, Alex heard the man talking to himself. No one answered him.

She blocked her ears against him, squeezing her eyes shut and thinking about her mom.

Alex rocked harder, the solid feel of the ground reminding her of where she was. Tears fell faster. She wanted to believe what her mother had told her about people who did bad things. She wanted to think that this man was just very sick and needed to go to a doctor. But as the second and then the third child screamed out, their pleas for help going unanswered, she couldn't help but think that he was crazy.

The long blade of his knife scraped against the cement, a low, resounding grate like metal on a dirty chalkboard. The noise came in three short clicks and a long scrape. Click, click, click . . . scrape. Click, click, click, scrape.

She rolled away from the sound. Palming the surface,

she searched for a clue to her fate. Her fingers found something solid and metal. With the object tight to her chest, she peered through the gap in her blindfold. A gun. The realization came to her as though she'd been holding guns forever. The feeling was as familiar as the satin edge of the blanket she had slept with for seven years or the honey smell of her mother's favorite soap.

Hoisting the gun, she pointed it to where she thought the man was. Make a sound, she thought. Let me hear you. Another series of creaks sounded from the distance.

"Dr. Jay," he screamed. "You can't!"

She shifted her aim slightly and found her way to the trigger. Pop. Pop.

Alex shot upright in bed, sweating like at the end of a run. Her hands were jettisoned before her, her gun tight in her grip. Staring down at her hands, she felt as though they belonged to someone else. It was a shock to find herself clutching the gun with her finger pressed on the trigger.

Unmoving, she stared at the far wall, scanning for bullet holes. There were no bullets, she remembered. She hadn't loaded the gun. The gun fell from her grasp, and she moved up the bed away from it, shivering from the sudden cold of realization. She could easily have killed someone in her sleep. Maybe she already had.

The safety refastened, she tucked the gun on the floor out of her reach and stared at the clock. It was two-thirty. She crept back into bed and pulled the covers over her, trying to remember the dream she'd been having.

Her eyes closed, she took a deep breath and let her shoulders sink into the bed. Like a warm breeze, sleep coated her, pulling her under its spell. Without the energy or desire to fight it, she surrendered.

Click, click, click, scrape, the heater churned out warmth.

Alex flipped sides and cupped the pillow to her chest.

Click, click, click, scrape, it went again.

She opened her eyes.

She sat up and exhaled, throwing the covers off. Across the room, she found the switch to turn the heat off and frowned. The heat was already off.

Click, click, click, scrape.

Spinning around the room, Alex grabbed her gun off the floor and pointed it in the dark. With a snap, she released the empty magazine from her gun and slid a full one into place.

Moving against the wall, she crept toward the door.

Click, click, click, scrape, the sound repeated.

Someone was trying to get into her room. Almost excited about the prospect of seeing him face-to-face, Alex took a deep breath and inched toward the door on the balls of her feet. A shoe caught her path and she tripped over it, hitting the wall with a low but audible thud. "Shit," she mouthed, not allowing herself to speak.

Her balance restored, she moved to the door, looked quickly through the peephole, and then pulled back. Nothing. She waited, listening for two minutes, until her ankles stiffened beneath her. Looking again, she still saw nothing.

She unlocked the door slowly and waited again before pulling it open and peering into the corridor. The hall was silent and empty. "Damn it." She shut the door, bolted it, and secured the safety bar. She hadn't imagined that. Maybe it was the ice machine.

A couple of quick flashes outside shone through a small crack in the curtains, catching her attention. Intrigued, Alex walked to the window and sat in one corner. Moving her hands at a turtle's pace, she lifted one edge of the curtain and surveyed the parking lot below her. At first glance, it appeared empty. The cars were parked in perfect rows, motionless, anonymous in the blackness.

Alex scanned the cars one at a time, sensing some-one hiding in the darkness. As she scanned the area, another flash caught her eye and she trained her vision toward its origin. Sitting patiently, she waited, feeling her stomach tighten like an angry fist. It reminded her of her one experience on a police stakeout. Sitting, poised to move, she fought to maintain her focus.

A far grouping of cars sat bunched together, and it proved difficult to focus on the entire area at once. Someone was out there, though. She sensed it. She only hoped he would make a mistake and give away his location.

A camera flash was the only household item that generated a low yellow light like the one she had seen. Tim's brand-new camera flickered through her brain, and Alex wondered who else the caller might have sent after her.

Unblinking, she crouched on her knees beside the window, awaiting another sign of motion from outside. Ten minutes later, none had come. Restless, Alex paced the room for a few minutes. She felt like a sitting duck. What had Nader been doing when the killer came for him? Sitting in his bed, reading? Maybe sleeping? Maybe pacing his bedroom like she was doing now.

If someone was out there, watching her, she was going to find out who. She pulled on her jeans and tennis shoes and zipped her coat against the cool air she felt through the window. Her gun loaded and tucked into her waistband, she headed for the door. In the dark, Alex checked the hall through the peep-hole, then cracked the door and slid out of her room.

With a brisk stride, she walked down the hall and jogged down the eleven flights of stairs, the burn of adrenaline in her lungs as welcome as the drag on a cigarette used to be. To avoid being seen, she skirted the lobby and took a side corridor instead. Out the back door, Alex walked to the far end of the parking lot and began slowly to circle the hotel, moving in from the perimeter toward the area she'd been watching from her room.

Following police raid techniques she had practiced at the academy, Alex moved only five to seven feet before stopping and checking for any changes that might indicate she had made herself known. Within five minutes, nearly bursting with impatience, she saw the front parking lot come into view.

It was quiet, the steady hum of trucks on the freeway in the distance the only sound. Alex stood opposite the cars she had been watching earlier. She scanned the license plates, searching for one that looked familiar. Maybe it was James or Greg out here, tracking her down. But none matched Berkeley undercover police plates, some of which she knew by heart, all of which she thought she would recognize.

As she prepared to move again, a noise from behind halted her. Turning as slowly as she could, Alex watched as someone in a dark, hooded sweatshirt and sweatpants walked within three feet of the spot where she crouched.

The figure carried a plain gym bag over one shoulder. Alex studied the stranger, realizing by the thin limbs and somewhat gangly walk that it had to be a young adult, maybe sixteen or seventeen. Perhaps it was an employee coming to work or leaving. The kid was shorter and smaller in stature than Tim and seemed even younger. But like Tim, this figure shared the same lazy, loafing stroll.

A suspicious chill raked its way across the hairs on her neck, forcing her to wait in hiding until the kid had passed her.

Never lifting his head, he pulled open the door of a dark American-looking sedan and climbed in. Turning back, Alex tried to judge where he had come from, but the street behind her was silent. A walk this late at night? Or had he been out here taking pictures? She tried to dispel her misgivings.

The headlights flipped on and Alex rose slightly to see the license plate as the car left. The car lurched back and then halted before starting forward again. Just like a new driver, she thought. From this angle, she couldn't see the plate. Crouching again, she waited for him to leave. He turned out of the parking lot and onto the road behind the hotel, heading for the freeway. She watched him until he was out of sight.

Frustrated, she had started to stand when she heard the sound of another engine. It came from behind the hotel, where the kid had just come from. Alex stayed low. It was too late for so much activity, and the presence of another car confirmed something was up. Squatting, she pulled her gun from her waistband and waited for the car to get close.

Following the path the kid had taken, the car started around the row of cars toward the exit, and then suddenly it turned back, accelerating. Alex blinked, adrenaline washing against her stomach.

The car was speeding right at her.

Chapter Twenty-nine

Heat and energy pumped through Alex's body like blood at the end of a race. She raised her gun, but the headlights shined in her face, making it impossible to take aim. She shielded her eyes from the blinding brightness. Like a stunned deer, she didn't move until the screech of tires and the howl of the engine made it clear the driver was not going to stop.

Alex lunged left, running full force through the bushes of the hotel boundary, down the incline, over the curb, and onto the main street. The path yielded only a few moments of safety. Within seconds, the car swung out of the parking lot and gained on her from behind. Alex raced back up the incline she'd just descended.

Through the bushes, she returned to the hotel parking lot. She spun around, looking for a safe haven, but the hotel was the only thing in sight. She shook her head. It would take too long to get there.

In the middle of the street, the car stopped dead. Alex inhaled and followed its progress with her weapon. She had started to aim at a tire when the car whirled one hundred and eighty degrees and started back. She lowered her gun and waited. She wanted to take the best shot she could. If he was coming back, she'd wait.

The hotel doors beckoned her, but Alex didn't move. He wasn't getting away. In the meantime, she could use the hotel boundary's small row of ivy bushes and trees for cover. The comforting feel of her gun in her palm reminded her she could protect herself if she had to.

She needed to get a license plate, something. The car could be stolen, but this guy had to make a mistake sometime. The car screeched up the driveway and into the parking lot, the engine revved high. Alex waited on her toes, ready to run. She trained her gun on the front left tire. "Come on, you son of a bitch."

If the driver wanted to hit her, he would have to jump the curb. That would mean crashing through the bushes and trees and totaling the car. She was betting he wouldn't do it, but she was ready to run if he did. She focused on the bumper, waiting for even the slightest angle to give away the plate number.

The car approached at full speed. Alex aimed the gun and shot twice, putting out one headlight but missing the tire.

The car continued toward her. Without time to shoot again, she dove left, landing hard on her shoulder just as the car hit the curb. She groaned, the wind knocked from her, and rolled herself onto her back and farther from the car.

Brush and branches snapped under the tires as the car barreled down the incline. There was a moment of silence before the metal scraped and crunched and it landed on the street below.

From the corner of her eye, Alex watched the car, but she couldn't move. Her left arm felt numb and she realized something was wrong. Her gun, which had been tight in her hand, was gone. She felt her heart in her belly, the splash of panic. Where the hell was it? Using her right hand, she groped the ground around her but didn't feel it.

At the screeching sound of tires heading away, Alex exhaled. "Damn it." She'd lost him. Her head back, she felt the soft brush cool against her neck. In a minute, she promised herself she would get up. She just needed to slow the dull humming in her head.

She rubbed her head, but instead of relief a slow dread began to seep into her gut. She raised her head. The hum wasn't her—it was coming from outside.

The engine wasn't moving farther away as she had expected. Instead, it drummed louder, vibrating through her toes and then crawling up her body. She choked on her breath as she forced herself upright, pain blazing a hot path down her side. The car was coming back!

"Get up," she yelled to herself, rolling onto her right side to avoid the pain in her left. She struggled to her knees as her eyes caught the one remaining headlight coming back up the hotel driveway.

Alex staggered to her feet. The pain sped up and down her left arm and shoulder, making motion excruciating. She couldn't make it to the hotel.

The car was still forty yards away as she prepared to dive again. The loss of one headlight made the bumper slightly more visible in the dark. Squinting, Alex focused on the advancing license plate. California. She just needed a few of the letters—first or last or middle. It didn't matter. "Come on," she hissed, her fists tight.

The car raged forward, closing the distance to fifteen yards or less. Alex remained still, struggling to read the plate. Too close, her internal alarms screamed. The car was within feet of her now, the driver a dark huddle behind the wheel.

Her pulse catapulted, and she leapt from the car's path, seeking refuge between two small trees as the car hit the curb again. In the flash as the car whizzed past, Alex caught the letters 2XP on the plate. Behind her, the car hit the street with a louder crunch than the first time.

Ready to end the game of dodge ball with the car, Alex dropped to her knees to hunt in the dark for her gun. Her left arm coddled against her, she counted. If she didn't find it in five, she'd have to run for it. One. Her hands hit dirt, caking her nails as she dug for the gun. Two. Three. "Come on." Four. As she moved to stand, a brief glimmer caught her eye, and she spotted the gun and grabbed it.

Exhaling, she pushed herself off the tree with her right hand and steadied herself. She held the gun in her right fist, trying not to shake. She could hear the engine growing closer. A clanking rattle made it sound like the car was about to stop mid-route, but it continued toward her. She aimed the gun at the front right tire and pulled the trigger. She saw the spark of the bullet on the metal of the fender. The kick of the gun knocked her backwards and, on uneven ground, she fought to keep her balance. She raised her gun and fired again. She heard the tire blow, and the car swerved to the right before straightening and coming again. Though moving more slowly, the car was still coming fast enough to hurt her.

She raised her gun to fire at the other tire as the car got within twenty feet. She aimed, fired, and heard the shot, but nothing happened.

He closed the distance. Fifteen feet. Twelve. He was too close. She raised the gun and aimed. Her finger was on the trigger when she heard a loud pop from behind. Something whizzed by her ear. Gunfire.

Dropping, she rolled across the ivy. She cursed as she rolled over her injured left arm, the pain like a fire inside the joint. The car slowed to a stop and Alex panted, waiting for the next move. Tears lined her eyes and she blinked them back. The pain in her shoulder was unbearable. She tried not to breathe, listening. There was something in the distance that sounded like shoes on the sidewalk. But then, suddenly, it was silent.

The car had stopped fewer than seven feet from where she lay. Slowly, she rose from her belly, using the tree for protection. She looked in both directions and saw nothing. The driver of the car must have run for it. She peered into the darkness behind her in search of the shooter. But it was all shadows and she couldn't make out a figure. There was nothing behind her but empty streets. She didn't know how anyone could have come up behind her without her knowing. The only real protection in any direction was the thin boundary of brush and ivy and a few scattered trees where Alex was sitting. It extended to her left and her right, but she saw no one in either direction.

Focusing back on the car, she pulled herself up and began to creep slowly around the front of it. The engine was still running. And the one headlight made it difficult to see inside. She crouched against the fender, her gun out before her, and kept a close eye on her back.

The driver was gone. She came around the driver's side and rose inch by inch until she could see over the hood of the car. The first thing she saw was the web of broken glass around a single hole. A bullet hole. She sprang to her feet and pulled open the car door, using the edge of her shirt.

Alfred Ferguson was exactly how he had looked in his photos. Only now he had a large red circle that smeared across the center of his forehead.

His eyes were open and he looked about to say something. Something he would never get a chance to say. Alex moved in a slow circle, her gun raised, searching for the shooter. She hadn't shot Ferguson. She'd been aiming at the tire. Someone else had shot him. But why? Had he said too much, done too much? Was he too much of a risk? She thought about the kid in the hooded jacket who'd driven off only minutes before Ferguson had started at her. There had to be a connection. Had she been wrong—was that Tim?

She looked back at the bullet hole in the window. Most cops didn't shoot that well. She moved around the car, keeping her back to it until she was on the passenger side. If someone was out there, they would've made their move already. She had to assume she was alone.

She pulled on the passenger door, but it was locked. Damn it. Moving back around, she opened Ferguson's door and leaned across his body in search of something that would yield the identity of the shooter. The motion made her wince in pain. The console was clean. An empty coffee cup from 7-Eleven was wedged between the seat and the emergency brake. Some loose change littered the passenger seat and floors. Careful not to touch any surface that would hold a print, she felt his front pockets for something there. The muscle in his legs still felt strong and alive, and the sensation of touching it made her shiver.

But she didn't stop. She could feel loose change in his front right pocket, but his left appeared empty. She reached behind him and pulled his wallet from his rear pocket. Using her shirt to hold it, she flipped it open and looked inside. It was a cheap, fake leather in a grayish black. Inside, he had one credit/ATM card for Wells Fargo Bank and about six hundred dollars in cash, mostly fifties like Tim had. There were two business cards—a parole officer and an Oakland auto repair shop called Montali Repair with no specific person's name. She also found two folded Post-its with handwritten phone numbers and a folded sheet of yellow lined paper. She pocketed the Post-its and the folded page, and committed the auto repair shop's name to memory.

Leaning across Ferguson, she felt the bulk of his gut against her arm as she shut the engine off. She took the keys and unlocked the trunk. It contained jumper cables, a Club, and a couple of stained rags. One was a large white towel that had been ripped in half. The part she could read said, "ford" in red capital letters. "Stanford," she figured the whole thing had once read. She lifted the towel and looked beneath it.

There were a few miscellaneous tools and a pair of running shoes, and that was it. She turned the running shoes over and looked at the bottoms. There was a thin layer of reddish-brown dust that was consistent with what she'd seen at the warehouse lot in East Palo Alto. Besides that, the sole was clean.

She unlocked the passenger door and jumped back at the sight of Ferguson's now raised hand. Pressing the heel of her hand to her chest, she told herself to breathe. It had to be some sort of postmortem twitch. He wasn't alive. Forcing herself to look back at him, she noticed a long blue thread caught in his watch. She looked down at her jacket and knew it had come from her. She yanked it free and tucked it into her pocket.

In the distance she could hear the low wail of sirens the way she sometimes heard the neighbor's baby crying at night. Moving quickly, she closed the passenger door, returned to Ferguson's side, and put the keys back in the ignition. Ignoring the pain, she ran back to the side door of the hotel. It was weird that she hadn't found a gun on Ferguson. Maybe it was under the seat.

Using the keycard for her room, she opened the side door and stepped into the stairway on the first level. Just as she made it back to her room, the phone began to ring.

Chapter Thirty

"Alex? Where have you been?" Greg asked. "It's the middle of the night."

She frowned. "How did you find me?"

"Carmen Hayes. She was the woman whose husband used to beat her up."

Alex was too tired to think. "So what?"

"So that was the name you registered under. James called about fifteen local hotels and had registries faxed to him. We looked through the names. When I saw it, I knew it had to be you. You always had a soft spot for Carmen Hayes."

She'd known Greg would recognize the name. Wasn't that why she'd chosen it? But somehow he seemed to be everywhere lately and it made her jittery. She shook her head. Greg was her friend, her partner. She was tired and in pain and not thinking clearly. She cupped her left arm to her body and tried to ignore the ache. "Where's James?"

"I left him with Chris. I headed back up to Berkeley. I'm supposed to be at work in the morning, but I wanted to check in with you first. You didn't answer me. Where have you been?"

Police cars filled the parking lot and Alex could tell that Greg had heard the sirens.

"What happened there?"

"Someone shot Alfred Ferguson."

"Someone?"

"It wasn't me."

"You need to get out of there."

She carefully looked out the window to see what was happening. "It's too late now. The police are all over the place. I'll wait until the morning and try to sneak out early."

"You want to catch me up on what's going on?"

Reluctantly, Alex told Greg everything, from the sound at her door to the bullet that killed Ferguson. When she was done, she took the Post-its out of her pocket and dropped them on the bed. She read Greg the phone numbers, then opened the folded page and scanned it. It appeared to be notes from a phone conversation. Alex read them out loud.

" 'Don't involve kid. Take care Kinkhead.' "

"He was taking notes. Someone was telling him what to do and he was taking notes."

"Yeah, looks like it. My name's spelled wrong."

"You think the kid he's referring to is Tim?" Greg asked.

"That's exactly what I think. I told you—Ferguson's not in charge. He wasn't in charge," she corrected herself. "Someone else is. This guy manipulated Ferguson the way he's manipulating me."

"Who?"

"That's what we need to find out." She kept reading. " 'Follow. Don't act. Remember power of the mind.' "

"Power of the mind," Greg repeated.

Where had she heard that before? "Power of the mind," she whispered and then it clicked. "The interview—Maggie Androus said Walter used to say the same thing."

"You're right. I'll be damned. What now?"

"I've got to find the link between Alfred Ferguson and Walter Androus."

"Who are you thinking—the brother or sister?"

She clenched her fist. "They seem like the only solution. Who else would dig all this up? Unless there was an accomplice at the time."

"But there weren't any other prints," Greg argued.

"Except the other kids'," Alex corrected.

"You think he had a kid accomplice?"

She moved her sore shoulder in slow circles. "I don't know. Maybe someone saw it as a kid and became obsessed." It sounded ridiculous. She was the only survivor left. "Somehow, though, our guy met up with Ferguson."

"I've already got a call in to find out more about who was in prison with Ferguson. See if there was someone he hung with, maybe someone from down here who could be linked to it from back then."

She thought about the person she'd seen walking toward the car in the lot earlier. "See if there's anyone small—built like a teenager."

"Like a midget?"

"No. He seemed lanky."

"But you were squatting, right?"

"Yes, but he wasn't built like an adult." She sighed. "Maybe I'm wrong. I don't know."

"I'll see what I can find out."

"It's going to be a bitch to get anything out of them right now."

"Hey, I'm used to bitches."

She smiled. "Thanks, asshole. Check out the plate number, too. Not that I think it'll tell us anything."

"Will do." He paused. "I should get going. You going to be okay?"

She told him she would. What choice did she have?

"Be careful tonight. Whoever was out there knows you're still around."

"I'll be okay. He's not coming back tonight, not with all these cops."

She prayed she was right.

After a restless night, Alex woke at five-fifteen, her left arm stiff and throbbing. She fingered her shoulder, relieved to find it didn't feel dislocated or broken. A thick scratch across her cheek was tender, and she could feel the cuts and bruises on her hands, chin, arms, and legs. None of them was anything major, but she had pulled or perhaps even torn a muscle in her shoulder that might have sent her to a doctor under better circumstances.

But today left no time for healing. After taking four Advil, Alex drew a hot bath and soaked for ten minutes, hoping the water would lessen the pain and stiffness. If it did, the change wasn't noticeable.

Dressing presented the next challenge, and she cursed and gritted her teeth as she worked her way back into her clothes. She made a makeshift sling with a T-shirt and tucked it into her duffel bag to put on later. First she had to get past whatever police were still downstairs taking statements. She combed her hair straight, carefully letting the one side fall over the scratch on her left cheek. She watched herself in the mirror and shook her head. If a cop saw the scratch, she was in trouble.

It was still red enough to give away the fact that it was recent, and the night desk clerk would know it hadn't been there when she checked in. The small contusions along her chin and on her hands would also be plenty of evidence for someone trained to notice those things. She hadn't brought makeup, so she had nothing to cover them with. She just hoped no one looked too closely at her.

Because the hotel was in San Jose, she was gambling that it would take the police a little time to connect Ferguson's murder with Nader's in Palo Alto. But she knew that wasn't much to bet on.

Her bags packed, Alex called a cab to meet her at the Veterans Hospital. Once she was safely out of the hotel, she planned to call the numbers from Ferguson's wallet and then spend the day in the main branch of the San Jose library, looking up New York obits. Greg had told her Ben Androus was listed, but she wanted to read the notice herself and see if she could learn anything more.

Pausing before she left, she decided to check her messages. It was only six in the morning, but maybe Greg had gotten some news. Or Brenda. She blew her breath out and punched in her password.

"You have one message," the electronic voice informed her.

Seated on the edge of the bed, she prepared herself for the familiar echoing voice of the killer. But the one she heard couldn't have been more different.

"Officer, this is Louisa—Louisa Carter," the elderly woman began.

Alex gasped, pressing the receiver closer to her ear, determined not to miss so much as a sigh.

"It's late," the frail voice continued. "I hope I didn't wake you up." The woman paused and drew a deep, raspy breath. "I don't sleep well anymore. Up and down all night. I guess that's what happens when you get old. It's a terrible waste, really."

Her voice shook just slightly and Alex wondered if she might have been drinking when she called.

The voice paused and Alex held her breath, praying Mrs. Carter didn't hang up before explaining why she was calling.

"I'll be at home tomorrow if you want to call me. Perhaps you could stop by for a few minutes and I'll give this to you. You have my number."

Give her what? Alex had started to hang up the phone when the woman added, "I'm going to try to go back to sleep, so if you wouldn't mind waiting until after eight to call." The message clicked and Alex hung up the receiver.

She shook her head, trying to decide if a detour to Palo Alto was worth the risk. Louisa Carter probably had some picture of Nader or something she thought might be of relevance to the police. Ninety-nine times out of a hundred a trip like that was a waste.

Alex threw her bag over her good shoulder and entered the hall, careful to make sure the "Do Not Disturb" sign was still on the door. She took the stairs to the ground floor and walked back like she was heading to the hotel's gym. Passing a few business travelers arriving on a Monday morning, Alex didn't see any cops. She walked in wide strides with her head down and hoped no one bothered her. She entered the gym and then into the pool area. She saw a door on the far side and started for it.

"Ma'am," someone called as she approached the door.

Alex ignored them and reached for the door.

"You can't leave through that door, ma'am."

Alex turned back to see a hotel employee shaking his finger at her. He frowned and pointed to the banner across the door that warned opening the door would trigger alarms.

Jesus, what was she thinking?

"You can go back through the gym and down the corridor to your left. There's an exit halfway down and one at the end. Are you parked in the back?"

"Yes, exactly," she lied.

"Take the exit at the end of the hall, then."

She nodded and followed his instructions, feeling the weight of stares as she left the pool. One woman made a tsk-tsk sound as she walked by.

Alex made it to the exit without further incident and was relieved when she reached the main street. Keeping an eye over her shoulder, she crossed the street toward the Veterans Hospital, where a cab was already waiting in front. She got inside and said, "Airport."

After the incident last night, she assumed someone was on her tail at every moment. She planned to cab to the airport, travel as far as the gates on foot, and then exit on the arrivals level and take another cab back to Palo Alto.

Alex trained a watchful eye on the traffic around her as the cabdriver headed toward the airport. There had been no sign of the car she'd seen leave the hotel parking lot just before Ferguson attacked her, but she had known there wouldn't be. Even if the driver of that car were the one who killed Ferguson, he would have ditched last night's car for a new one.

She arrived at the airport and sprang from the cab, rushing hastily through the glass doors and toward the departure gates, hoping to look natural among the bustle of hurried travelers. She slipped into a bathroom before reaching the metal detectors, and pulled on a baseball cap and removed her jacket before exiting.

At a bank of small pay phones Alex dialed the first number from the Post-it. A woman's voice sounded on a recording. "You've reached Candy Treat," she cooed, and Alex guessed she was a prostitute. The second number was also answered by a machine, but there was no voice, only a beep. She'd have to call again. She bought a muffin and coffee, and watched the people until it was quarter to eight.

Then, moving as calmly as she could, Alex walked down the escalators toward baggage claim and out the front doors.

Across from the rows of cars awaiting passengers, she stopped at the taxi stand and jumped into the first cab.

She arrived at the block past Nader's at eight-twenty, feeling confident that she hadn't been followed. Someone could be watching Nader's house, waiting for her. Still, Alex had no choice but to risk it.

As she hurried toward Mrs. Carter's house, she hoped the woman hadn't chosen this morning to go out for a leisurely stroll. With a thorough survey of the area, Alex moved among the houses to Louisa's door, where she gave one last glance over her shoulder. She forced herself to stop worrying and rapped quickly on the door.

"Who is it?" the woman called as Alex celebrated the fact that Mrs. Carter was home.

"Alex—" Pausing, Alex strained to recall what name she'd given yesterday. "You left a message on my machine," she added quickly.

Without another word, the woman opened the door, peered out, and with a careful look around, waved Alex in.

Sitting in the same chair as yesterday, Louisa began to fiddle with a pile of papers on the table in front of her. She wore red pants and a striped shirt, her hair more styled than yesterday though it was flat on her left side, possibly where she'd slept on it. Her lips showed the faint outline of lip liner. She appeared to have gotten dressed up for something, but Alex couldn't imagine it was for her.

She had been concerned Louisa might notice her arm, but the woman was much too preoccupied even to look up. "Do you want to tell me why you called?" Alex asked, wondering if this wasn't James's idea of a setup. Counting slowly to ten, she rocked on her toes, preparing for flight, refusing to admit even to herself that she wouldn't get far with her injured arm.

"There is one more thing I haven't told the police," Louisa whispered as though it were a deep, dark confession. "Not purposefully, of course," she added in a tentative voice, still without looking up.

She wrung her hands together and spoke up. "Well, not at first. I'd forgotten about it at first. It had been so long ago. But then when you came around and mentioned N.T. Security, it jogged something in my brain."

Alex raised an eyebrow. Maybe this wasn't just a wild good chase.

"About four months ago, I went out to get my mail, just like I always do. I go out after the truck leaves, wave to Stan—" She glanced at the door. "Stan's our mail delivery man. And I brought the mail into the living room to open. I keep my letter opener there, you see," she explained, as though it were pertinent to whatever she was about to say.

She looked down at her hands, which made motions as though she were knitting a sweater with no needles and no yarn.

"It's force of habit, I guess. I take the whole stack in my lap, turn them facedown, and tear them all open, always have. Used to make my husband, Harold, so angry." She glanced up but refused to meet Alex's gaze.

"He was a postal worker, you see, for nearly thirty years. He always warned me that someday I was going to open someone else's mail by mistake. That was a federal offense, he always told me. I used to laugh him off. 'Oh, Hal. Cool off,' I would say. Harold had a tendency to be very uptight about the mail. Pride in his job, some might say. It never bothered me much, but I never gave it much thought, either."

Something creaked, and Alex started.

Louisa met her glance for the first time then quickly looked away. "Hot water heater in the basement. Does that every half hour or so."

Alex nodded slowly. "You were saying . . . "

"I opened a letter that was addressed to Mr. Nader." She stared at Alex, looking like she was ready to cry. "I didn't know. By the time I realized it wasn't for me, I'd read almost the whole thing."

Alex stepped forward. "So what did you do?"

Mrs. Carter smoothed her long, bony fingers over the bottom edge of her red-and-white striped button-down. "I didn't know what to do. Harold's warnings came rushing back to me." Her hands shook as she waved one through the air. "I couldn't call the police. I thought I would be arrested. I didn't think Mr. Nader would ever miss the letter. How could one letter matter? But now. After you mentioned it . . ." She dropped her head and shook it.

Alex frowned. "Do you have the letter?"

Nodding slowly, Mrs. Carter pulled a folded piece of paper from the pile, and hesitated momentarily before handing it to her. "I just didn't know," she whispered, collapsing into quiet sobs.

"I'm sure it's okay," Alex said, taking the paper with her good arm and patting Mrs. Carter quickly on the back before turning to spread it open on the coffee table.

Dated about four months ago, the letter was handwritten in light ink, and Alex brought it closer, squinting to make out the words.

Dear Marcus,

I'm sure you have heard the news about what has happened to me. The last three months have been hell. I want you to know I am innocent, though I know the evidence against me seems overwhelming. Feels that way too.

As far as your case, I felt like I was just getting somewhere—well, closer to somewhere anyway. I tracked down a Dr. Hennigan from Stanford. He's still in the area and I think he might be able to help. He might know who Androus saw as a therapist back then. I think that might be the next place to go. I've left a message on his voicemail, but I never heard back. Then all this happened, so I haven't been able to follow up. I suggest you pursue the issue, with or without my help. I know a few people in the area I can suggest.

I would be happy to share what I have learned, but under the circumstances, I will understand if I don't hear from you. And I will certainly repay the balance of your account as soon as I get things here straightened out.

I am preparing for the appeal as we speak. There has been a terrible mistake and I am still trying to figure out who would do this to Lucy.

Sincerely,
Nat Taylor
N.T. Security

Dr. Hennigan? Lucy? Who the hell were they? Her heart drumming, Alex blinked and read the closing line again. Nat Taylor. She'd found the P.I. Catching her breath, she looked up at Mrs. Carter. "This man, do you know him?"

The woman looked puzzled.

Alex held the letter up. "The man who wrote the letter."

Mrs. Carter closed her eyes and shook her head. Opening them again, she pointed to the letter. "Oh, no. I never finished it."

Her mouth fell open. "What do you mean—never finished what?" Alex asked.

"The letter. Halfway through it, I realized it wasn't for me. I stopped reading and searched for the envelope. When I found it and saw Mr. Nader's name and address, I put the letter back inside.

"I never read another word, I swear." Her eyes wide, her right hand lifted, palm out, Mrs. Carter looked like she was swearing in court as a witness.

Alex glanced at the note again. "But you never took it to him?"

"Oh no. I just couldn't." She pressed her hand flat to her chest, her expression grieving. "I wanted to, but I couldn't. It was so obvious that I'd opened it. It was terrible, I know. But, understand, please—I was a widow, an old lady. I didn't want to go to jail."

Alex shook her head, fighting a smile. "You wouldn't go to jail for this."

The woman stared, incredulous. "It's a felony," she whispered, like it was a curse word spoken in church.

Alex nodded. "Mail fraud is a felony. This wasn't mail fraud, Mrs. Carter. You made an honest mistake."

She shook her head, refusing to allow herself to be acquitted. "You can't tell anyone. Please. Harold told me all about what they do to people who violate the mail laws."

"Mail laws?"

The woman nodded vigorously, as though shaking the terrible demon out of her soul as she did so. "Oh, yes. The tiny cells, the public humiliation . . . I'm too old. I couldn't stand it."

Alex approached the woman. "Mrs. Carter, you didn't do anything wrong."

Her fingers wrapped tight around Alex's hand, the woman implored, "Please. Promise you won't tell a soul."

Alex nodded. "I swear." She paused, meeting the woman's gaze. "But I need your help."

She nodded. "Anything."

"I need to borrow your phone book and your phone to call Nat Taylor. Would that be all right?"

The woman frowned and glanced at the note. "Nat Taylor? That's who wrote that note?"

Alex exhaled. "You know him?"

"Oh, yes. But you won't be able to reach Nat Taylor now."

Dread sank into Alex's limbs. "Why not?"

"He's in jail. Killed his wife. Ran her over with his car. They lived less than a mile from here. It's very sad. He's serving time at San Quentin now."

Alex looked back at the note. It all fit together. See NT SEC @ SQ. San Quentin. Chris had said a man named Taylor had called in with information on the

Sesame Street case, but because he was in jail for
killing his wife, no one had taken him seriously. He
must know something. She spun around to Mrs. Carter, who still looked mortified at what she'd done.
"Can I use your phone?"

"Well, of course. It's right—"

Following her gaze, Alex snatched up the phone
and dialed information.

"What city please?"

"San Quentin. I need the prison's main number."

"One moment please." The electronic voice rattled
the number off as Alex scrambled for a pen. Her hand
shaking, she dialed the number and tapped her foot
impatiently as she waited for an answer.

"San Quentin," a voice barked.

"Yes, I need to find out about visitors' hours."

"Inmate's name?"

"Taylor. Nat Taylor."

After a pause, the voice replied, "Mr. Taylor is allowed visitors on Mondays from eight-thirty to ten-
thirty A.M."

Alex stared down at her watch. "That's—"

"Right now," the operator finished.

"Do I need an appointment?"

"Nope. Just arrive before ten-fifteen and they'll
bring him out."

It would take her at least an hour and fifteen minutes to get there. "I have to go, Mrs. Carter. Thank
you for calling me. You've been a wonderful help."

The woman stood and held out a hand. "You promise you won't tell anyone about this?"

"I promise." Alex grabbed her hand and squeezed.
"Don't worry. It'll be our secret."

Before Mrs. Carter could answer, Alex was out the
door. She took two steps and halted, staring at the
street. Her car was at the airport. She didn't have a
car! "Shit!"

Nader's car caught her eye, and she took two quick

breaths. "No," she said out loud, shaking the idea from her head and trying to replace it with rational thought. Stealing a dead man's car was a bad idea.

Back on Mrs. Carter's doorstep, she knocked.

"Hello?"

"It's Alex again."

The door creaked open and the woman's face poked out only enough to take a quick look around and then set her gaze on Alex. "What is it?"

"It's my car."

The woman stared out on the street. "Where is it?"

Alex nodded. "That's the problem. It's at the airport," she answered.

"What's it doing at—"

"It's a long story, but I was wondering if you could call me a cab."

"Oh," she said, shaking her head. "A cab will take forever. I've waited some days over an hour. I use the local dial-a-ride to get to the store and such."

"Mrs. Carter, this is a police emergency. I need to get to San Quentin in the next hour. I need a car."

"You swear you won't tell anyone about what I did, right?"

"Of course, Mrs. Carter. I'll never tell. I promise. Now, I need—"

"You can take my car," she offered, then added, "if it will start."

Alex shook her head. That wasn't a good idea either, "That's very kind, but I don't think—"

"Nonsense. You're a police officer and you've helped me quite a bit today. My conscience hasn't felt this clear in months." She disappeared and then returned a moment later, dangling a set of keys out the screen door. "I insist. It's parked right there."

Alex tried to shake her head again, but instead her hand moved out to take the keys. She needed to get to Nat Taylor. She'd apologize later, buy her a new car, do community service, whatever. "I promise I'll bring it back today."

"No hurry. I can't drive, anyway. Lost my license on my last test." She tapped the corner of her right eye. "It's the eyes. The car's only here for when my sister flies in from St. Louis. She won't be here till Thanksgiving. Bring it back today or tomorrow."

Alex cupped the keys, tossing them slowly in her hand as she considered the offer. She shouldn't take the car. What if something happened to it? She didn't even know Mrs. Carter. *You shouldn't take the car,* she could hear James telling her. Tricking an old lady out of her car was surely fraud; impersonating a local police officer . . . She was breaking all sorts of laws—ones she hadn't even broken before now.

"Go on now, or you'll be late."

Alex clasped the keys. "I'll fill up the tank."

"That would be very sweet of you." She started to turn and looked back. "Still our secret, right?"

"Absolutely."

Mrs. Carter grinned and shuffled back into the house, looking like Alex had just told her she was winning the lottery.

"Damn," Alex said, running toward the car. "Please let it start," she said to the sky as she ran around the older model light blue Lincoln Town Car. "And no accident," she added, in case anyone was listening.

With only her right arm to work with, she struggled to get into the car with her duffel bag, smashing her left shoulder into the doorjamb as the door closed on her. Pain jolted across her muscles and she bit back a moan.

She pulled the seat belt across her body, locked the doors, then turned the key in the ignition. The engine made a rattle-like cough then roared to life.

She was in business. This was it. Come on, Nat.

The traffic toward San Francisco started out light, and Alex kept her speed at sixty-five, the limit. Within thirty minutes, at just past nine-twenty, she was half-way there. Feeling good, she stepped up the speed to seventy.

Rounding the corner near 3Com Park, though, the traffic quickly grew congested. It was early and many commuters were still trying to make their way into the city. "Come on," she whispered, moving to the left lane.

Within two miles, traffic had practically stopped. Minutes ticked by like hours, and Alex stared at the dash clock, fretting over the wasted time. She wasn't going to make it to the prison before visiting hours ended. Closing her eyes, she drew deep breaths and tried to stay calm. At quarter to ten, she couldn't stand to waste another moment.

As traffic crawled forward, Alex edged to the right and exited the freeway. She was still in South San Francisco and the prison was north of the city, a good twenty miles away. In good traffic conditions, by freeway, it was a thirty-minute drive.

Surprisingly, Mrs. Carter had a car phone. Something her sister probably had insisted on. Alex reached for it, turned it on, and dialed Greg's cell phone. She got no answer, so she tried his extension at the station, hoping he might happen by his desk.

"It's me. I've found something." She thought about who might be able to listen to Greg's voicemail. "I'm going to see N.T. from N.T. Security. And I'm checking out some Stanford doctor named Hennigan. I'll call with more ASAP."

Off the freeway at Potrero, she sped through the city. The Mission district was quiet and easily passable. The dark heaps on the street looked like trash waiting to be taken out instead of humans trying to keep warm on the cold, damp cement. She hit a nearly red light and ran it, feeling her skin go cold as she shot through. She had to make it there. She couldn't wait a week. She couldn't get a subpoena to speak to the prisoner outside visiting hours. She needed to know who this Hennigan was now.

Ticking off the seconds by beating her thumb against the steering wheel, Alex turned up Van Ness, cursing at the electric-generated Muni buses as they cut in front of her to make their appointed stops. The clock on the dashboard said 9:55. She had twenty minutes. Dread poured into her belly and she shut it out. Stay positive. She would make it. She had to.

Across the Golden Gate Bridge, she headed for the off-ramp to San Quentin. Over the hill, she could see the prison resting along a winding road set up from the water. It was ten after ten. She was just going to make it!

As she started to merge right to exit, the excitement drained from her limbs. An orange road sign read, "Off-ramp closed—detour ahead."

"No!" she screamed, pumping the gas and heading for the next exit.

By the time she reached the prison gates, it was ten twenty-two. She had missed the cutoff. Ready to try for a miracle, she drove through the gates and ran into the building.

"Can I help you?"

"I need to see an inmate."

"Visiting hours are over."

Alex nodded, trying to catch her breath. "I know. This is an emergency."

The guard shook his head. "No exceptions."

Alex swallowed hard, still panting. "I'm a Berkeley detective, working homicide. This inmate may be able to identify a killer." It was mostly true.

He shrugged. "You can try. Alice runs the visiting hours like a Nazi. I don't think you're going to get past her, but go ahead. You need to remove any metal items and put them through the belt. Any weapons have to stay here. Then, go down a level and take a right."

"Thanks." Looking down, Alex realized she hadn't brought anything but the keys with her. Tossing them in a dish, she moved through the metal detector and was waved on. Mrs. Carter's keys back in her pocket, she took the stairs by twos and sped into a large room.

To her left, two guards watched over a long row of two-sided cubbies, separated down the center by a thick, bulletproof glass: criminals on one side, visitors on the other.

Alex spun around in search of Alice. A tall, heavy-set black woman sat behind a low counter, staring at a stack of paper.

"Excuse me," Alex began.

The woman didn't move.

"I'm Detective Kincaid," she lied. If the woman wouldn't even look up, Alex figured it didn't much matter if she lied or told the truth. "I need to see Nat Taylor."

With a quick glance, the woman shook her head and looked back at her paperwork.

"I'm a homicide detective. I need—"

"Don't care who you are," the woman interrupted. "Visiting hours are over."

"Mr. Taylor may be able to identify a murderer. His interview is crucial to this case."

The woman still didn't look up. "You have paperwork from a judge stating you should be allowed to see Mr. Taylor outside of visiting hours?" She enunciated the word "judge" by saying it two octaves higher than the rest of the sentence.

Alex exhaled, frustrated. "There hasn't been time."

"You can get a judge's note or Mr. Taylor will always be here next Monday."

Alex felt her pockets for her I.D. She didn't even have it on her. "Listen, I won't be longer than a few minutes. This is very urgent. There is a killer on the loose."

"No exceptions."

Her fist clenched, Alex jerked her left arm in anger and then choked on the pain the motion brought. "Please."

The woman looked up and gave her a small smile, then quickly dismissed her. "No."

Anger rose in her throat like vomit, and Alex had to hold herself in place. She had come too far. She'd lied to an old woman, practically stolen her automobile, hidden from her own family for two days, nearly been run over by a car, fired bullets, and raced forty miles. She was not going to be discouraged by a bureaucratic bully of a guard.

Leaning over the counter, Alex had started to speak when the woman stood up. "Visiting hours are over in five," the woman yelled down the corridor and turned to walk away.

Murmurs filled the room as people rushed to end conversations before time was up. Alex stared at the guards and then tried to locate the woman, but she had simply vanished.

"You're going to have to leave now," one of the guards said.

Alex looked at him.

Frosty gray eyes met hers.

"Please."

He shook his head and turned his back.

Alex stared around in disbelief. She couldn't possibly wait until next Monday—that was another week.

She didn't have a week.

A week from now, she would be dead.

Chapter Thirty-one

The muscles in Alex's arm and shoulder tightened, wrenched closer to snapping with each step. On the way in, she'd caught her ankle and it pounded with the dull ache of a sprain. Weak and weary, she hobbled toward the stairs.

"Excuse me," Alex imagined she heard someone say as she inched along.

"Excuse me," the voice repeated more loudly.

Alex stopped and looked back, cupping her arm and cringing at the thought of yet another assault on her efforts. The woman before her couldn't possibly work for the prison. In a long pinafore dress with a white turtleneck beneath it, she was petite, almost fragile.

It looked like a maternity dress, but this woman was too thin to be pregnant. Her hair was pulled back in a loose bun and she wore no makeup. Except for the missing small white hat, she appeared Amish.

"My name is Edna."

Alex frowned. "That's nice," she said, starting to turn away.

"I think you want to talk to my brother?"

Alex spun back. "Your brother?"

She nodded meekly. "Nathan."

"Nat Taylor?"

"Yes."

Alex scanned the rows, searching. "Where?"

"He's at the very end. Come on." The woman

turned and hurried away, Alex right on her tail. At the
final cube, a man sat waiting behind the thick glass.

"Sit down quickly," she said. "When Alice comes
back, she'll kick us all out."

Alex sat in the chair, facing Nat Taylor. He wasn't
much larger than his sister and didn't look like he
could hurt a fly. Alex wondered if that was why he
had chosen his car as weapon of choice to kill his wife.
He sat upright, his small hands crossed on the table.
He was clean-cut, with a neatly kept reddish-brown
beard and small oval glasses with wire frames. His
face was unexceptional except for a patrician nose.
The overall look was academic. It was difficult to picture Mr. Taylor as a private investigator, let alone a
killer. But Walter Androus had been the same way—
the small glasses, intellectual-looking. In fact, Walter
and Nat were more alike than she cared to think
about.

Nat leaned forward and picked up a phone receiver.

"Here you go," Edna said, handing Alex the phone
on their side. Then, kneeling beside Alex like she was
preparing to pray, Edna waited.

Alex brought the receiver to her ear, glancing down
at Edna before looking through the thick glass at Nat.

"She's okay," Nat said, referring to his sister. "Only
member of my family who didn't desert me after Lucy
was killed." He shook his head with the expression of
someone whose life had been turned upside down so
fast he hadn't had a chance to even soak it all in.

Alex only nodded.

"I didn't hear what happened, but Edna said you
were looking to talk to me."

"I was." She watched the open anticipation in his
expression and glanced down, knowing her news was
not what Mr. Taylor was hoping to hear. "I'm actually
here about Marcus Nader."

Nat nodded, showing a few small, square teeth in a
weak smile.

Alex met his gaze again and shook her head. "He's dead."

Nat's mouth dropped open and from the corner of her eye, Alex saw Edna make the sign of the cross. The woman choked back a sob as her brother asked, "How?"

"Someone broke into his house and shot him."

"Why?"

Alex shrugged, knowing she had a lot of explaining to do and no time to do it.

"Two minutes," a guard bellowed from the far end of the room.

Nat flinched.

"I promise to tell Edna everything you'll want to know so she can tell you. But I only have two minutes. I need you to try to answer some questions for me."

Nat nodded.

"Nader's neighbor intercepted a letter from you to Marcus where you told him you had information on his case. You were working for him?"

Alex knew Nat must have wondered why a neighbor had intercepted his letter, but he just nodded without interrupting.

"About what happened back in 1971—"

He nodded again.

"As quickly as possible, can you tell me what you learned?"

Without blinking, Nat started in. "I had done some work for Marcus Nader a while back. Then, all this happened and I hadn't heard from him until a guy named William Loeffler contacted me about a month ago. He was working with Nader. I never actually spoke to him, but we exchanged a couple of letters. Have you talked to him?"

Alex squeezed her eyes closed and shook her head. "He's dead, too."

Nat looked over his shoulder quickly and turned back. "Jesus Christ."

"I need to know what you found out. Whatever it is, I think that's why they're dead. I need you to tell me what you told them."

Nat nodded slowly, the fear shining in his eyes. At that moment, Alex knew for certain that he had not killed anyone. She pushed the thought aside and focused on his words.

"I told them about Walter Androus's family. His brother—"

"Ben," Alex supplied.

"Right. I thought Ben might be alive."

"And?"

"Dead. Died just like they said."

Alex nodded, searching for the piece that fit. "You also mentioned a Hennigan."

"Blake Hennigan—he was the head of the research at Stanford."

"Did you find him?"

Nat nodded. "He keeps an office at Stanford and is only there one day a week. I left a message on his line there but never heard back." He motioned around. "But I told Loeffler to try to talk to him."

"What did you think Loeffler would find?"

"Androus was part of a psychiatric research project at Stanford. I think Hennigan headed it up."

It didn't seem like much to go on. "You think Hennigan had to do with the murders?"

Nat shrugged and straightened his glasses. "I doubt it. I hoped he could tell me more about Androus—his friends, his habits."

A guard touched Nat on the shoulder and waved him off the phone.

Alex exhaled, sinking back against the seat. The police would have covered all that three decades ago. It felt like a dead end.

"Time's up," the guard on her side bellowed.

"Do you know the name Alfred Ferguson?" Alex

asked, casting a glance at the guard coming toward her.

Nat shook his head. "Never."

There had to be something she was missing. This couldn't be it. What did Nat know that had gotten Loeffler and Nader killed? "Was there anything else you told Loeffler or Nader that you can think of?"

Nat frowned and shook his head. "I gave Loeffler a contact in New York records and Hennigan's name. That was it."

"Time's up," the guard on her side repeated, now closer.

Alex felt defeated. She had come hoping for some incredible revelation. But she had nothing.

Nat's voice dropped as he continued, "If you find anything, I'd appreciate you letting me know. The more I think about it, the more the timing of the whole thing bothers me. I talk to New York records and call this guy Hennigan and two days later, I'm behind bars for killing my wife."

"You think someone killed her to frame you?"

He shrugged, knowing he didn't have enough to convince a cop.

"Where were you when she was killed?"

"In the shower. They found the keys in the ignition, my wallet and cigarettes on the car seat, and me upstairs, just coming out of the bathroom. My eighty-year-old, half-blind neighbor testified that she saw me run Lucy over, get out of the car, and go inside. The theory is that I ran my wife over with the car, in our own driveway, wiped the steering wheel clean, and went inside, but left my wallet and keys behind. Does that make any sense?"

Alex didn't comment on his innocence. She knew better. "I'll let you know what I can find out."

Alex could see the guard approaching again. The cubicles beside her were emptying and people were milling about, the noise level increasing.

The guard tapped Nat's shoulder again, this time with more force.

Nat stood and turned back. "There is one more thing."

"What?"

"There was a J. D. Daniels at Stanford back then, too. I gave his name to Loeffler as well. In case he couldn't reach Hennigan."

She remembered the name. "He did an interview with Androus's sister, Maggie, a year or two after the murders."

Nat shrugged. "I never saw it."

"Let's go," came a voice behind Alex.

The guard pulled the phone from Nat's hand and hung it up.

Nat's expression met Alex's, apologetic and helpless.

The guard took him by the shoulder of his orange suit and began pulling him toward the door.

"You pushing your luck, girl," a female voice echoed from behind.

Alex turned to see Alice staring down at her. "Right."

Edna stood and smoothed her skirt, ignoring Alice's glare. "I hope what he said will help."

Frowning, Alex turned toward the door. It didn't seem like she'd gotten anything at all. She could follow up on the New York records and call Hennigan and Daniels, but there had to be something else she was missing.

"Can you tell me what happened to Marcus Nader?" Edna asked.

Without stopping, Alex spoke over her shoulder. "Give me your number and I'll call you as soon as I can."

"I know Nathan will want to know what happened. He really enjoyed working for Marcus. Terrible thing Marcus went through as a child, really."

Alex cringed at her own memories, or lack of them. "You knew him?"

"I referred him to my brother."

"But why? Why did he need a private investigator?"

"He said he'd seen the police file, that he had questions about it."

"What sort of questions?"

She shrugged. "He didn't talk about it much. I learned a little more from Nat."

"You have to tell me," Alex urged.

She glanced back at the jail and Alex knew she was debating if Nat would want her to tell.

"It could help Nat," Alex said.

Edna's eyes flashed large and she bit her lower lip. "He said he was having a dream about a voice, another person. He'd talked to someone on the phone and then he'd started to have dreams. He just wanted Nat to look into it, find out if there was any information that was missing."

"Who had he spoken to?"

She shook her head. "I honestly don't know."

Alex nodded, defeated. She wished she'd gotten to Nader before the killer had. She was missing something. It was there somewhere. "How did you know him?"

"We were in school together."

"What was he like?"

"Despite what had happened, he always seemed so strong and independent," Edna continued. "I thought it was incredible how well he was doing."

Alex slowed her pace as she listened to the description of the third survivor.

"He's a wonderful photographer," Edna said, as though it made him a saint. "Was a wonderful photographer," she corrected herself.

Alex glanced over to catch the starry gaze in Edna's eyes, silent tears falling as she spoke.

"But he was more than that. His work was so good. He was an artist really. Oh, he did weddings and parties to get by, and did pretty well, I think. But his real passion was nature. You should have seen his house. He had the most amazing pictures. I always told him he should work for *National Geographic*. He was that good."

Alex nodded, agreeing. They left the prison in silence. She assumed they were both thinking about Marcus Nader, but for very different reasons.

At her car, Edna pulled out a slip of paper and a pen and wrote her phone number down. Handing it to Alex, she said, "Please do call."

Alex saw the loss reflected in her eyes as she nodded. "I will."

Without knowing quite where to go, Alex headed into town and stopped at a Chevron station. Rather than run up Mrs. Carter's cell phone bill, she went to a pay phone and dialed information. When the operator answered, Alex requested the number for Stanford, hoping she would be able to reach Blake Hennigan. She wished she had thought to call Stanford while she was down in Palo Alto. She reached the main number for the university and was put through to the psychology department. The whole process seemed to take an hour.

"Psych department," a young-sounding woman answered.

"I need to speak with Blake Hennigan."

"Dr. Hennigan isn't here."

"Can you tell me how to reach him?"

"He doesn't have a set schedule, so he's kind of hard to reach. Can I ask what you were looking for?"

"My name is Alex Kincaid and I'm with the Berkeley Police Department. I'm trying to get some information on a participant in your research study in 1971. His name was Walter Androus."

She hesitated before saying, "I'm afraid I don't have access to those records. The files are kept here, but only Dr. Hennigan and one other researcher, Alan Mersch, have access."

"Is Mr. Mersch available?"

"I'm afraid Dr. Mersch isn't in today."

"How about Dr. Daniels?"

"Dr. Daniels left before my time."

"Is there a home number where I could reach him?"

"Who?"

Alex exhaled. "Hennigan, Mersch, Daniels. Any of them. I need to speak to someone now."

"Actually, Dr. Mersch is at a conference in London until the end of the month. I think Dr. Hennigan may be there as well. I don't have any information on Dr. Daniels."

Alex forced a deep breath. "Can you give me the names of any of the other researchers who participated in the study?"

"I don't have access to that, either."

"Is there someone in the department who *would* have access to that?" Alex asked impatiently.

"Uh, I don't think so."

"Can you find out for sure?"

"Uh—"

"I'll hold," Alex snapped.

Several minutes later, the woman returned. "We can only release those with a subpoena." Someone spoke in the background. "Signed by a judge," she added.

Alex frowned. "You need a subpoena?"

"Uh, yes, that's right."

Alex sighed loud enough to be heard. "Fine. I'll have one sent," she said, wondering how that would be possible. "But I suggest you get started on finding someone who can help us, wherever they are. This isn't going to wait until they get back."

"Uh—okay."

She asked to be transferred to Blake Hennigan's voicemail and left him a message with her home number. She did the same for Mersch, noticing that both doctors had young women on their recordings. She just wanted to ask them about Androus's involvement in a study there. Surely after all these years they would talk to her—if she could just reach one of them. Now she had no idea what to do next. She'd exhausted all of the possibilities.

Back in the car, Alex gripped the steering wheel and stared out the windshield. Without enlisting the help of someone at the station, she wasn't going to be able to get anywhere.

Gathering her courage, she got back out of the car and returned to the phone booth. A woman in tight black jeans and a red sweater at least two sizes too small was approaching the phone, too, holding a cigarette off one hip.

Alex snatched up the phone first and quickly turned her back.

"Excuse me. I was going to use that."

"You're going to have to wait in line," Alex answered without looking back.

"You cut in front of Della," came a voice that sounded like a lumberjack's.

Alex hooked the phone under her chin and turned around.

Della looped the cigarette hand on her hip and tucked the other under the arm of the man standing beside her. He was hardly a man—at easily two hundred and fifty pounds, he looked more wildebeest. Thick hair spilled over his cheeks and down onto his chest. A sleeveless undershirt covered only a small portion of his furry physique.

"I said, you cut in front of my Della."

Alex smiled. "I got to the phone first, that's for sure. Guess her heels slowed her down." Normally,

Alex would have started her phone call, preparing for an attack, even with her back turned. But with her injured shoulder, she wasn't so sure she'd be ready for him. She still had use of her right hand, which was her stronger arm, but he was awfully large.

The lumberjack took a step forward, detaching himself from Della, who sat back on her heels and smoked, examining her nine inch fingernails and tapping her foot as though reminding her boyfriend how urgent the phone call was. Maybe she needed to get in to see her manicurist.

The lumberjack stopped less than six inches from Alex, his hand in a fist. Alex spotted familiar prison tattoos across his fingers. "You gonna move?" he barked.

She shook her head, putting the phone back to her ear now that he was close enough to watch.

He chortled, leaning back enough to free his undershirt from the belt of his pants and give her a view of about eight inches of hairy flesh.

Grimacing, she dialed the police station and waited for the AT&T operator to ask for her calling card number.

"I don't like it when people ignore me, especially chicks."

"I'll bet," she muttered. She felt his breath on her cheek and she spun toward him, moving her face to his. "Back off."

He didn't move an inch. After a several-second delay, of either shock or the working of a very slow mind, he laughed again, this time harder.

"You gonna take that, Ray?" Della called from behind.

"Fuck off, Della," Ray hollered back.

Alex punched the numbers for her calling card and hoped someone at the station would answer before Ray decided to get physical.

"Listen, bitch. If you have any brains in that ratty

ass head of yours, you'll move away from the god-damned phone."

"Berkeley Police Department," came Reesa's voice on the line.

Thank God. Alex turned to stare at Ray as she spoke. "Reesa, it's Officer Kincaid. I need to speak with Roback."

"Alex! Thank God. Everyone's been so worried."

"Roback, please," Alex repeated.

"Sorry, hon, he's not here. He's still out on patrol. Your brother wants to talk to you, though."

"Not yet, Reesa. I'll call back in an hour, I swear," she lied. "Will you put me through to Roback's voicemail?"

"Okay, but don't you dare tell your brother I talked to you without putting him on. He'll have my head."

"Cross my heart and hope—" She halted.

Reesa laughed, seeming not to notice that Alex's tongue had gotten twisted in her mouth. "Here you go."

Tucking the phone under her chin, she motioned to Ray. "If you have any brains in *your* ratty ass head, buddy, I suggest you take your ass to another fucking phone before I have you thrown back in the state pen."

Eyes wide, Ray put his hands up and backed off. "No need to get hasty, Officer. I'm sure there's an-other phone around here somewhere."

"Right."

The phone clicked, and she heard Greg's voice. At the end of the beep, she left a message. "Roback, it's me. I didn't find anything from Taylor. Only that he thinks Androus was involved with some psychiatric research program at Stanford before the murders. He gave me a couple names: Hennigan and Daniels. They're doctors down there. When I called, they mentioned an-other guy—somebody Mersch. Stanford wouldn't give me any information without a subpoena."

She shook her head. "I don't know how else to find out about it. Unless you know someone who was down there in the early seventies. Maybe Chris knows someone." She halted and slapped the Plexiglas of the phone booth. "Oh, wait. I know who." She started to put the phone down and then brought it back to her ear. "I'll call you in an hour. I'm going to go talk to someone who was there." She replaced the phone on the receiver and jogged back to the car.

Shivers of anticipation spread across her shoulders as she revved the engine and pulled out of the lot.

"I'm closing in on you, asshole," she whispered. "And when I get you, you're going to fry."

Chapter Thirty-two

Back in Berkeley, Alex pulled to the curb in front of the converted house where Judith Richards kept her small private practice. The office was on a quiet, mostly residential portion of Ashby, three blocks west of the hospital. She was less than a dozen blocks from the station and she was more than a little nervous about being spotted. A charming stucco ranch-style house, it was a perfect choice for a children's psychiatrist.

In what once was the house's foyer, the receptionist sat behind a light wooden desk in a waiting room decorated in a style similar to that of Judith's home. The receptionist was a petite middle-aged woman with striking blond hair cropped short and carefully coiffed. Dressed in a black blazer and large Jackie O tortoise-shell glasses, she looked like she belonged in a New York ad agency.

Two couches and half a dozen chairs filled the rest of the area, with toys and magazines in large wicker baskets. The room smelled like chocolate chip cookies, and Alex felt her stomach growl.

The receptionist looked up from her computer screen. "May I help you?"

"I hope so," she said. "My name is Alex Kincaid. I'm a family friend of Judith's. Is she available?"

The woman stood and moved around the desk. "Oh, yes, Judith mentioned you. I'm Sally."

Alex shook her extended hand.

Sally glanced briefly at Alex's left arm tucked pro-
tectively to her chest but didn't comment. With a
quick glance over her shoulder, she said, "Actually,
Judith's down in the playroom with a patient."

Alex followed her gaze down three stairs to a set
of heavy-looking closed doors. "It's awfully quiet,"
she said, dropping her voice.

"Soundproofed," Sally explained, laughing softly.

"Soundproofed?"

She nodded. "Kids make a lot of noise. Without the
soundproofing, we couldn't really have a waiting
room. If a kid was in there crying or screaming, you
could hear it a block down."

"I can come back," Alex offered, the image in her
mind of a screaming child behind the closed doors.

"Oh, no." Sally led Alex toward the back of the
house. "Come wait in her office. This patient is particularly sensitive to strangers, so I think it will be easier
if you're back here."

"I probably should have called first."

Sally patted her shoulder and shook her head.
"Really, it's no problem. This is Judith's last patient
for the day."

"It's only noon."

Sally nodded. "Judith keeps Mondays open for what
she calls 'weekend disasters.' If something happened
over the weekend and a parent feels their child really
should be seen as soon as possible, they can get in to
see her on Monday. Usually they're really busy days,
but today's been absolutely dead."

In the hallway, Sally stopped to pick something off
the floor and straighten a picture, and Alex noticed
the thick beige carpet lining the hall. It was immacu-
late. She couldn't imagine how on earth Judith managed to keep it clean with kids tracking in and out all
the time. Alex could hardly keep her own hardwood
floors clean. And Judith's house had been so casual.

Alex wasn't sure what to make of the difference between Judith's home and office.

Sally opened a heavy wooden door off the right side
of the hall and motioned Alex inside. "Here we go."

Alex entered Judith's office and looked around.
Nothing about the place was familiar, but, of course,
it wouldn't be. Judith hadn't had a private practice
back when Alex had met her. And they had always
talked at Alex's house.

The decor was subdued here, too, with cream-
colored walls and rugs. White bookshelves stood
against the far wall, lined with framed photos and
thick medical textbooks. Children's artwork hung
along the wall nearest to the door, splashing bits of
color against the walls. But unlike in Judith's house,
everything here was perfectly placed.

"I can't believe the children don't make a mess in
here."

Sally laughed. "Oh they do, but Judith is incredibly
meticulous about things—sometimes too meticulous, I
think." She stooped over to straighten the fringe on
the rug. "Make yourself at home."

Alex watched her move the rug and shook her head.
Judith hadn't seemed that meticulous to her.

"Really, take a look around," Sally urged.

Alex took a few steps toward the back of the room,
where two overstuffed cream chairs and two couches
sat in circle formation as though prepared for an afternoon tea party. The couches, though, were drastically
different from one another. One was floral and ruffled,
with what seemed like two dozen small lacy pillows.
The other was burgundy leather with four dark pillows, their designs depicting old Air Force fighter
planes.

The receptionist laughed. "Everyone makes that
face when they see those couches."

Alex glanced back. "They're just so different."

Sally moved past her and straightened a pile of papers on the desk. "Judith says it's sort of a way to get a kid to take the first step. Ask them to pick a couch and they are usually immediately drawn to one or the other. Judith says she can learn from their choice."

"Interesting," Alex said. She spotted a large pair of Doc Marten shoes. They seemed too large to be children's. She turned back to the receptionist. "Should I have taken my shoes off?"

The woman furrowed her brow.

Alex motioned to the shoes. "I thought maybe those were a patient's shoes."

"Oh, no. Those are Judith's."

Alex bent down and picked the left shoe up. She remembered seeing similar shoes at Judith's house. "They're huge. Her feet can't be this big."

Sally laughed. "She uses them as a patient prop. 'Getting into someone else's shoes'—only literally. Most of the kids can put their feet in those without taking their shoes off."

Alex flipped the shoe over and read the bottom— size ten men's.

"Judith does it, too," the woman continued, straightening as she moved around.

Alex frowned. "Does what?"

"Wears her shoes inside those."

Alex put the Doc Marten shoe up to her own. It wasn't *that* much bigger. "Really? What kind of shoe?"

"I can only do it with sandals on. But for Judith, I don't think it matters. She wears a size three shoe."

Alex tried to picture her feet but couldn't. "Wow, tiny."

"She has to buy most of her shoes in the kids' section. I guess it makes them cheaper."

Sally clicked her tongue twice and motioned to the room. "Well, I've got some work to finish up before I leave. It's so quiet, I'm going to take a half day. Do you want something to drink?"

Alex shook her head. "I'm fine, thanks."

"Make yourself comfortable, then. Judith should be in soon."

"Thanks again." The receptionist closed the door and Alex set the shoe down. Size three shoe. She reminded herself to look at Judith's feet when she arrived.

Alex looked back at the couches. She was too wired to sit. She walked along the wall and inspected the drawings. Though she knew little about child psychology, none of the pictures seemed disturbing. The colors were bright, the faces smiling.

Alex remembered Brittany telling her about how art was a way for children to represent their experiences and emotions. She wondered if she'd ever drawn about Androus or the warehouse. Would she be cleaning out the attic one day and find a box of crayon drawings filled with images of children dead and dying?

Shivering at the thought, Alex had started to turn away when writing on one of the drawings caught her eye. As her eyes grazed the words, her heart faltered and her arms went limp.

Blinking hard, she took a step forward, as though perhaps the distance had caused an optical illusion. But the words were still there, exactly the same: "For Dr. J. Love, Sammy."

In a flash, she heard the echo of a man screaming, "Dr. Jay, you can't!" But she couldn't hold on to the voice, couldn't place what it meant. Her ears started to ring and she looked slowly from picture to picture, searching. None of the other drawings were addressed to Judith. With a mental shake, she turned away.

Alex was shocked to see Judith called by her first initial. Maggie Androus had reported that her brother's psychologist had the same name as their father: "Jay," not "Dr. J." But the police stenographer wouldn't have known the difference.

It was a coincidence. *You don't believe in coincidences.* A sense of dread weighed her down. She moved across the room. She went back to the size ten shoes.

Mrs. Carter claimed to have seen Tim walk into Nader's house two nights before she and Tim were there. She had been unable to make out his face. Instead, she had recognized him by his shoes. "Bright red, they were," she had told Alex. "And that yellow jacket, no missing that either." Alex stood and looked quickly around the room. There was no sign of a yellow coat. But she'd seen one at Judith's house, hadn't she? Along with a pair of red shoes.

What about the kid she'd seen in the parking lot? Lanky with a goofy walk but smaller than Tim. Could that have been Judith? She shook her head. She was overreacting. A couple of words on a page and a pair of shoes didn't make a killer.

She looked around at the pristine room. There was something else. Moving quickly, she turned to the desk and began to pull the drawers open. Her heart pounding, she fingered through the files, unsure what she was looking for.

Her hands were moving too quickly for her judgment to kick in. She needed to get out of Judith's office. The slow pulsing pain in her arm spread down her back and up her neck. She needed to leave.

But her hands wouldn't let go. She closed the file drawer and opened the drawers on the other side of the desk. Everything looked normal.

Then, tucked on a small shelf behind Judith's desk, she saw it—a framed photo of Judith and her father from 1968. Leaning forward, Alex picked up the frame and squinted at the Stanford Diploma held tight in Judith's grasp. The name embossed across it was Judith Diane Daniels. J. D. Daniels. She scanned the walls, but the diploma wasn't there.

As she set the frame back on the shelf, Alex heard the smallest click.

Hot adrenaline poured into her stomach as she straightened her back and turned toward the door.

"So you do remember," came a voice Alex now recognized from her nightmares.

Chapter Thirty-three

Alex looked up and forced a smile as her heart trampled a path over her other organs and into her throat. "Remember what?" She practically choked on the words and decided to try to keep talking. "I love this picture of you and your father." She paused and glanced at the surface of the desk. "Actually, I was looking for a piece of paper. I wanted to leave you a note."

Judith nodded without smiling and crossed the room. "No worry. I'm here now. How have you been?"

Alex moved to the couch, trying to look casual but refusing to turn her back. "I'm sure you've heard about the nightmare at the station."

Judith picked a small wooden box off her desk and brought it over, sitting opposite Alex. "I haven't."

Alex watched Judith's eyes, devoid of reaction or emotion. "It's been hectic," she lied.

"Looks like you've hurt your arm."

Alex nodded, knowing she needed to make a move before the receptionist had time to leave, if she hadn't already. With a deep breath, she launched into her story, praying it would work. "I came by because James located a doctor at Stanford named Blake Hennigan who performed a research study back in the late sixties. Do you know him?"

Judith didn't respond.

Alex forced herself to continue. "Walter Androus

participated in that study and we were hoping to get some information. Hennigan is in London, but I figured you might know of some other doctors who participated in the study."

Judith shrugged. "I'm afraid I can't help."

Alex rose from the couch. "Well, we thought it was worth a try. I told James you would be too young to know them, but he insisted we check it out. Maybe we can have dinner again."

"I enjoyed that," she said without feeling.

"Okay, well, I'll call you later in the week."

Judith didn't move from her chair as Alex walked as calmly as possible toward the door. Her pulse drummed a steely rhythm in her ears, making every step feel like a mile. Closing her eyes, she put her hand on the knob and turned.

The door didn't open.

"It's locked."

Alex turned back. "I didn't realize. How do we unlock it?"

Judith smiled for the first time. "We don't, Alex."

"We don't?" she breathed.

Judith shook her head. "I'm afraid not."

Alex turned and tried the door again, wrestling with the knob and then pounding on the door. She felt her waistband for her gun. It wasn't there. She had left it in her car.

"Don't touch it," Judith snapped. "Turn around slowly."

Alex did as she was instructed.

The small box Judith had been holding was now open on the table, a nine-millimeter in her hand pointed at Alex.

Alex took a breath. "Judith, James and Greg know I'm here. They'll be here any minute."

Judith shook her head. "It won't matter. By then, it won't matter."

Reason slipped from Alex's grasp like sand. Turning

back, she kicked the door hard without making the slightest dent. Like a caged animal, she searched the room. There were no windows. She hadn't noticed it earlier. How could there be no windows?

Judith approached her slowly, and Alex prepared to strike. She would wait until Judith looked away and knock the gun from her hands, if only she could distract her. She forced breath into her lungs. "It was you. All this time. We trusted you. I was beginning to think it was Ben Androus, finishing his brother's work."

Judith shook her head. "He's been dead for years. His sister, too."

"You killed Loeffler and Nader."

Judith laughed loudly. "Loeffler deserved it. He was into kiddy porn and all sorts of stuff. Can you believe they let scum like that into the justice system?"

"The porn was probably a result of what happened to him as a child," Alex snapped back.

"Really?" Judith leaned toward her, interested. "And what sort of kinky stuff are you into as a result?"

Alex refused to be provoked. Judith would not kill her without a fight. Keep stalling. "I was there—that night at Loeffler's?"

She nodded. "Loeffler called you. I waited until you had arrived. You showed up at the door and I had the needle in your arm before you had taken three steps. I'd intended to kill you, too, but when Loeffler told me you didn't remember anything, I was so curious.

"I wanted to see if I could make you remember. What a fascinating experiment to see what it would take. Of course, I had no way of knowing you wouldn't remember being at Loeffler's. I had to be sure."

"How? How could you be sure?" Alex realized the combination of Restoril and whatever Judith had drugged her with had probably blocked her memories.

"It was a gamble, I admit. But I had an alibi for that night. So I walked you to your car, watched you spend the night there, even snapped a photo for evidence just in case. I left before you were dressed and went to the station. I met you coming down the stairs that next morning. Don't you remember?"

Alex looked at Judith. "No."

"I was coming out of the station when you were coming in. I dropped some files. You looked right at me and didn't even blink." She smiled and spread her arms like a magician at the end of a trick. "I knew then that it had worked. You had no idea you had just seen me."

"You bet that I wouldn't remember, but what if I had?"

She shrugged. "Like I said, I had an airtight alibi for the night before. I spoke at a benefit for children and spent the rest of the evening milling around a party with more than a hundred people.

"Plus, there was all sorts of evidence that you killed Loeffler. Even a chewed up pen I was ready to plant if need be. And I treated you after the trauma you suffered as a child. It's natural for you to have aggression toward me. Blaming me for the murder you committed would be a perfect example of that." She hiked the gun up a bit higher.

"You planted the earring."

"The earring, the blood on your pants, his hand, the watch." She smiled. "It was all me."

Alex shook her head, watching the gun in her peripheral vision. "Why not kill me when you had the chance? The other night when you shot Alfred. Why not me?"

Judith beamed. "I was still waiting for you to remember. Imagine it. You were the only one to see me that day in the warehouse. And yet, you had no memory of any of it."

"You were at the warehouse."

"Oh, yes. And you saw me. You were the only one." She paused. "Of course, I never thought you would remember me, specifically. I was wearing a wig and was very made-up. But, the fact that you didn't remember any of it—" She shook her head. "It was too exciting a study to pass up."

"A study?"

Judith just smiled.

She was a study. All of this had been some sort of sick experiment. She thought about Stanford, about Androus's history. She noticed the gun had dropped slowly. *Keep talking.* "You knew Androus through the research study?"

"He was my patient." Judith's chest rose like that of a proud mother. "When Walter started coming to me in late 1970, he was concerned because he had grotesque fantasies about the children he taught."

"But how did that involve you in his crimes?"

"I involved myself. It was all about controlling him. What he thought, what he did."

Alex's jaw dropped. "You suggested he kidnap and kill children?"

Judith returned a tight smile. "You wouldn't understand. It's much too sophisticated for someone with no education on the subject."

Alex pressed her teeth hard against her tongue. "Please. I'm interested."

Judith didn't break eye contact as she continued. "We worked together for several months to try to rid him of the images he had of killing the children, but he was unable to stop them. I thought perhaps there was a way of purging the fantasies." She narrowed her eyes. "You must understand, there was very little known about mind control at the time. Charlie Manson had just been sentenced. Everyone wanted to understand his power. It was an incredible time for this sort of study.

"And I was conducting groundbreaking research.

People die all the time, Alex—women, children." She waved her arms nonchalantly. "In wars, for the benefit of the whole. That's what this was. I was trying to understand the true nature of people's susceptibility to brainwashing. My work will provide insight into people like Androus. To that end, I helped him live out his fantasy."

Alex watched the woman's delusion emerge. "But you couldn't think you could control him."

"I did. That was the incredible thing. I learned so much more than I ever thought I would. Androus, Ferguson—" She smiled. "You. I controlled you all. I had you run, jump, and swing to my every whim. The mind is truly fascinating. You can convince someone to do something like kill or maim with the simple tool of words."

"You're talking about hypnosis."

"No. It's just the power of suggestion. The power of the mind."

"That's bullshit. You chose people who were predisposed to violence. You can't assume that would work with a normal person."

Judith raised an eyebrow. "But it worked with you, didn't it?"

"I never killed anyone, did I? You did it."

"Of course, but how close did you get? Stealing, breaking and entering, lying . . . the list goes on." She paused and took a few steps. "And how many times did you doubt yourself? You thought you might be a killer, you told me so yourself."

Alex shook her head.

Judith swept an arm across her room. "I've written volumes on the research I've done, and it all started with Androus. I was there, directing really. I even suggested the marks on the inner thigh. Have you ever seen yours, Alex?"

Alex willed herself not to flinch, but she felt a tremor deep inside.

"I told him serial killers needed a signature," Judith continued. "I think he could've chosen something more clever than an X but that was his entire problem. I saw it in his eyes once he'd gotten started on you kids. He wasn't especially bright and he wasn't going to stop. He would've come for me eventually. I had no choice but to shoot him."

"But I remember pulling the trigger."

"You did. I wanted you to have the gunpowder on your hands. But he was already dead."

"But how did you get away without leaving evidence—" Alex halted as she registered Chris's theory about the extra footprints. She pointed to Judith's feet—children's size. "Your shoes."

Judith smiled. "They're tiny. No one's ever paid much attention, but it came in very handy that day. The police all assumed the extra prints were a child's."

Alex flinched. It all made sense. She forced herself to speak. "Why risk letting any of us live?"

Judith's mouth formed a straight line. "Originally, I had intended to take care of you all that day, but I became curious about how you would all recover. The Palo Alto School District was more than happy to offer information to those of us at Stanford on the progress Nader and Loeffler were having with the school therapists. So, I knew I was safe with them. I assumed you were seeing a private therapist, but I figured even if you remembered something, you'd be the only one. It would be everyone's word against yours.

"When I met your mother and realized you didn't remember, I befriended her so I could watch you. I knew she'd never tell you. After a few years, I was confident you'd never remember on your own."

"How did Loeffler find out?" Alex asked.

"Unfortunately, a private investigator Nader was working with gave him my name. Nader had started

to remember hearing another voice. He contacted
Loeffler to talk about it. They talked to a retired cop
who was convinced no kid could have pulled that trigger. They put their heads together and came up with
a theory that there had to be someone else. Somehow,
the Stanford research came up and so did my name."

She motioned to the photo on the shelf. "My
maiden name. Loeffler had called me to ask some
questions. I'm afraid I answered a few too candidly.
He put it together." She shook her head. "I suppose
I gave myself away. Unlike you, the others remembered the incident, so a few extra tidbits and Loeffler
started to insinuate that I'd been involved. He called
you to his house that night and I knew he was going
to tell you. I had no choice but to take care of him.
Then, it was only a matter of time before Nader figured it out, too."

The gun dipped and Alex shifted toward the edge
of the couch.

"I wondered if his death might make you remember, how close to the edge of your memory the truth
was. I couldn't resist the urge to find out. I've been
feeding you clues, watching to see how you'd react to
the news of your damaged childhood."

"So you framed Nat Taylor," Alex said.

Judith gave a nonchalant nod. "To get him out of
the way."

"And Alfred?"

She shrugged. "Another patient."

Alex remembered Brittany's comment about Judith's
patients. "Those two patients you had who shot each
other—you rigged that, too? Another experiment?"

Judith just smiled.

"And you used Alfred to track me?"

"You're not as dumb as I would have thought. Too
bad you didn't figure it out a little sooner. I had it all
covered, though, Alex. You couldn't win. Like I said,

if you tried to tell anyone, you'd simply look crazy in light of the evidence implicating you in the murders."

Alex felt her blood cool. "What about Tim?"

"Alfred's idea. Very dumb."

"How did Alfred get linked to Tim?"

She shook her head. "My fault, I'm afraid. Tim's a patient of mine as well. He and Alfred have met a few times here in the office. When I heard from the deputy chief that Loeffler had taken some pictures of you, I told Alfred it was a good idea. I bought him the camera and told him to go to Palo Alto. Alfred decided he didn't want to follow you around with a camera, so he gave it to the kid to do. He was lazy." She sounded angry. "But at least he paid Tim off to say you killed Nader. That was a nice touch. Too bad the kid has to be next."

"What about the tape of me someone called into the police on my cell phone?" Alex pressed, buying time as much as anything else.

She waved her hand. "He taped the conversations, but I put the tape together. He liked making the calls, but he wasn't very smart—almost got caught the night he broke in to steal your cell phone."

"And the parking ticket?"

"Me, me. I got it from the station. Had to do it myself. Just snagged it and filled it out." She sighed and shook her head. "Alfred was my least successful attempt. I don't want to talk about him anymore." She motioned Alex up. "Let's go."

"Someone's going to make the link that Alfred was your patient. Questions are going to be asked."

"But you killed Alfred, too, Alex. Your fingerprints are in the car."

"It wasn't my weapon," Alex countered.

Judith shrugged. "How hard is it for a cop to get a weapon? It won't keep them from convicting, I don't think."

Alex couldn't even form a sentence.

"No more questions, then? I guess it's time for business." Judith brought her left arm around Alex's back. The motion was slow and deliberate. Alex never could have imagined what was coming.

The buzz at her neck sounded like an electric razor, but the shock that followed shot through her like a fiery bullet. Every muscle in her body contracted in a wave of excruciating heat.

Alex dropped to the ground, landing directly on her left shoulder. A scream sprang from her lips as she felt her ligament tear from the bone.

"Go ahead and scream, Alex. There's no one here to hear you. And, of course, this room is completely soundproof."

Alex fought to gain control of herself, to move her hand or leg. But it was as though her brain had been wrenched away from her body. She couldn't so much as lift a finger.

"It'll wear off," Judith said. "It did on Loeffler and Nader. But it's very convenient, really. Gives me a chance to prepare for the final touches."

Alex winced as tears began to stream down her face.

"Enough of that." Judith pushed Alex's hair back from her face, wiping her tears. "You should be able to watch this. I've always enjoyed watching, myself. Androus was quite good at what he did. A very interesting psychological profile, a fantastic study. Much more rewarding than Alfred. I was doing a great thing. I wish you could know that your life wasn't wasted."

Panic rushing through her blood, Alex tested her finger. It wouldn't move. Her teeth clenched, she tried again unsuccessfully.

Judith laughed as she walked to the bookcase. "There's no use fighting it."

Alex watched as Judith pulled a heavy-looking burgundy textbook from the shelf. She opened the textbook, and Alex saw that the center had been hollowed out. Judith pulled out several small vials and a syringe.

Gasping, Alex struggled again.

Tearing the syringe from its plastic wrap, Judith lifted it and one of the vials so Alex could watch. Slowly, Judith drew the liquid into the needle. With the syringe full, she turned it upright and tapped its side.

Her panic was strung so tight, Alex almost missed the motion she felt in her shoe. Her toes. She was moving again. She only had one chance.

Judith started to turn toward her as Alex focused her energy on this last effort.

After using a few seconds to gather her strength, Alex lifted her leg and kicked Judith with all the force she could muster. The woman fell backwards and Alex reached for the stun gun.

Judith got to it first. Turning it toward Alex, she caught the side of Alex's hand with the electrode. Alex screamed and fell back, cupping her hand to her chest.

Tears flowed down her face like water from a faucet. Why hadn't she told someone where she was going? Fight, she told herself. *Fight.* But she couldn't. The pain overwhelmed even the most basic instinct for survival.

She felt the prick of the needle in her shoulder before she saw Judith's hand holding the syringe. Alex pulled her knees to her chest, fighting to maintain her dimming will to live.

"It's too bad you up and ran off, Alex. Someone from the force might've missed you otherwise."

Alex shook her head, trying to block out Judith's words. But they sank through, and Alex knew she was right.

"Now no one will know any better. You'll be missing a few more days. Then you'll show up dead somewhere. They'll realize the guilt of the murders finally got to you. All very neat with a bow on top."

A thick, drunken buzz began to settle over Alex. She shook her head to fight it.

Judith patted her head. "Don't worry. You won't lose consciousness. I'll be right here until it's all over."

Chapter Thirty-four

Alex caught glimpses of Judith as she moved around the room, but her eyelids were like bricks, dragging her eyes closed. Each time she opened them, it felt as though she'd been sleeping, and yet she had no idea at what speed time was passing.

The next time she woke, Judith was slapping her face. "I might've given you a bit too much," she admitted. "You're not as big as I'm used to."

Judith pulled Alex into a sitting position. "We're going to the basement," she explained as though she were helping Alex instead of trying to kill her. "You're going to need to stand."

Alex shook her head and fell back.

Judith put the stun gun in her face. "Every time you don't do what I say, I'm going to give you a little jolt."

Clamping her eyes closed, Alex ignored her.

"Fine," Judith said, her tone smug. "You'll learn."

The cool touch of metal made Alex flinch. The stabbing shock that followed made her vomit.

Judith clucked her tongue disapprovingly as she rolled Alex to her side. "Doesn't look like your last meal was very big."

Alex rocked, holding her stomach and fighting the pain.

"Open your eyes," Judith demanded, tilting Alex's head toward her left shoulder.

Alex opened her eyes and saw redness on her arm, where the flesh felt burnt. But the pain had dulled, as though her limit for it was a circuit that had just been blown.

"Now, sit up."

Too weak to fight, Alex sat up.

Judith pulled Alex toward her and then led her toward an open hatch under the rug where the floral couch had been.

Down the hatch, Alex could see a short wooden ladder. Below it was a crawl space. A mound of dirt was surrounded by a square cement area not larger than twenty feet by twenty feet.

"Let's go," Judith commanded.

Alex fought for her footing as Judith shoved her toward the hole. In the back of her mind, she heard heavy thumping like footsteps overhead.

Judith pushed harder. "Not a word."

Alex sensed anxiety in Judith's voice and felt a breath of hope. Halting, Alex turned toward the door. "In here!" she screamed with every bit of strength she had left.

Judith pulled the stun gun out and connected the current to Alex's injured shoulder.

Groaning, Alex collapsed. But the pain wasn't what she had expected. She had shifted slightly before Judith reached her. Instead of the electrifying shock, Alex felt only a brief jolt.

Heavy pounding shook the door. "Police, open up!"

Alex saw the stun gun drop to Judith's side as she turned to the door. Fighting the sharp pain in her shoulder, Alex pushed Judith backwards.

Judith fell off balance but caught herself. The stun gun dropped to the floor, but Judith had the real gun pointed at Alex.

With Alex's arm injured, Judith seemed especially strong. She grabbed Judith's wrist, struggling to point the gun into the air. A shot went off.

Judith twisted toward her, connecting her knee to Alex's stomach.

Doubling over, Alex held her stomach and counted to three. Then, in a last burst of strength, she drove her right shoulder into Judith, shoving her backwards.

Judith let out a shriek as she tumbled, knocking against her desk and rolling onto the floor. The gun dropped from her hand.

Grabbing for the gun, Alex felt numb, her limbs heavy, her senses dull.

Judith scrambled back up and was at her desk as Alex tried to lift the gun.

Alex's vision was blurred, as though she were looking at everything through water. As the image cleared, she found Judith lunging at her, a letter opener tight in her fist.

At the edge of the crawl space, Alex steadied herself from falling. Judith was coming fast. Unable to focus, Alex pointed the gun and pulled the trigger twice, hearing the pop, pop. But Judith was already in midair and her dead weight fell forward, knocking Alex backwards. Alex tumbled into the crawl space, slamming her head at the bottom. She tried to make a sound, any sound, but couldn't.

Eyelids heavy, Alex closed her eyes, as the sharp pounding in her head grew to a dulling pain.

Chapter Thirty-five

The angel's long white dress floated in front of Alex's face. "You need to do it," the angel said, handing her the gun. "If you don't, the bad man will hurt these boys and it will be your fault. Do you want that to happen?"

Alex shook her head.

The angel wrapped Alex's small hands around the gun and pointed it at the bad man. He wasn't moving. But the angel insisted she had to shoot him. He would come back, she said. With the angel's help, Alex pulled the trigger.

"Good girl," the angel said.

Alex caught a glimpse of the angel's face and recognized Judith Richards as she lunged forward with a letter opener. Alex pointed the gun again and pulled the trigger all by herself.

Alex opened her eyes, blinking hard at the harsh overhead light. She tried to move but her arms and legs were bound. As she struggled against the restraints, pain knocked her back.

"It's okay, Alex. It's okay."

Alex stared at the face, the familiar face. But instead of terror, she felt calm.

"It's me. It's your partner."

She choked back a sob as Greg touched her face. Turning his attention to her restraints, he loosened them. "You were thrashing so much, they had to tie you down. You pulled out stitches in your shoulder three times."

His words spun around her head along with a million questions, tangling her thoughts. "Judith," she finally whispered.

Greg pulled his chair up to her bed and held her hand. "Judith's dead. You shot her."

She frowned, looking around the room. "Where's James?"

"He's on his way. He's been here the whole time— Brittany, too. They went to talk to the doctor. They'll be right back."

"How did you—"

"Shh. Don't talk. You need your rest."

She squeezed his hand. "Tell me."

"After you called, I checked up on that Hennigan guy. Turns out he was good friends with Judith's ex-husband who had also worked with her at Stanford. It didn't take us long to track down Hennigan. He hadn't even left for London yet. He had a lot of interesting things to say about her. Seems the main reason she and her hubby split up was because he thought she was mentally unstable. Then I found her name on Alfred Ferguson's parole sheet."

She nodded.

"Turns out she even offered to help Androus coordinate the kidnapping so long as he allowed her to watch."

"How . . . how do you know that?"

"She's got a series of journals kept in hollowed-out psychiatry textbooks. Everything's recorded there. We're just starting to go through them. Androus wasn't her only victim."

Alex cringed at the idea of Androus as a victim. "Alfred, too. And those patients who shot each other in her office—she helped one of them."

Greg nodded. "And she did the same thing in 1986 with another patient here in town. The whole thing got botched, though, and the kid and his supposed killer were found dead in the back of his van. The kid had been shot in the head and the killer in the mouth. His shooting was deemed suicide back then, but it turns out she killed both of them."

"She did this four times?"

"That we know of."

"I still don't remember that night at Loeffler's. She said I was there."

"I know. Brittany said you may never remember."

She tried to accept that she might never fully understand what had happened. At Loeffler's, or at the warehouse.

"From what we can piece together so far, we think you drove over to Loeffler's, drugged and half-asleep from the Restoril. Judith had already killed Loeffler by the time you arrived. Before you were even in the door, she injected you with something. We're checking out her medicine cabinet to find out exactly what. But whatever it was, combined with the Restoril you were already taking, it knocked you out. Maybe she figured she could pin the whole thing on you."

"No, she planned to kill me." Alex sat up in bed, stiff, like she'd been beat up by a gang. "But when she realized I couldn't remember anything, she decided to play with me. She was taunting me to remember."

Greg gave a light shrug. "She was one sick pup."

Alex swallowed. "I killed her?"

He nodded slowly. "She managed to get the gun and take a shot at Lombardi, though. Just missed him. You should hear Lombardi talk about his lucky coat now. You'd think it's Superman's cape."

Everything around Alex felt fuzzy and distant, and she couldn't shake it. "Lombardi?"

"We were all there—James, Lombardi, and me."

Alex exhaled, tears running down her face. She tried to stop them but couldn't. There were too many to hold back, and they'd been too long in coming.

"It's all over," Greg said. "Most of the charges

against you have been dropped." He grinned. "James is still working on getting the rest dismissed."

"James?"

Greg laughed. "Deputy Chief Doty put him on it full-time."

"You're kidding."

He shook his head. "Told him he ought to better prioritize family and maybe this would get him on the right track."

"How many charges are left?"

"I think it's down to twelve."

"Twelve?"

"Breaking and entering, impersonating a police detective, resisting arrest, automobile fraud. There are a few more."

She put her head in her hands. "Oh, Jesus."

"Ah, it'll be good for him. But Doty insists you apologize to Gamble yourself."

"Oh, no. I'd forgotten all about him. Is he okay?"

"He's back on desk duty."

"I really hurt him, huh?"

"Nah. He just decided patrol was too dangerous." Greg winked.

Alex laughed.

Then, she heard the familiar sounds of Brittany and James arguing in the hall and it made her smile. She thought about James and his damn job. But he was still her brother. She'd have to work on forgiving him. He and Brittany were all she had left, and family was too important.

She thought about Nat Taylor losing his wife and then being tried for her murder. "What about Nat—"

"James is having that case reexamined, too."

She looked up and sniffled. "How did you know about Nat?"

"You mumbled about him all the way here in the ambulance. Brenda was by, too. Said you'd better rest up. Something about a baseball player."

Alex smiled. But even the knowledge that some of Judith's wrongs could be righted didn't stop the tears.

"Did you know two-thirds of the world's eggplant is grown in New Jersey?"

She wiped her face. "Winston Churchill was born in a ladies' room during a dance."

Greg frowned. "Ick." He paused and added, "A tiger has striped skin not just striped fur."

"Cats' urine glows in the dark under a black light."

"Hey, *I* told *you* that one."

"I know. And I still hate cats," Alex said.

"Me, too."

Alex tasted the tears as they fell down her face.

Greg put his head against hers. "It's okay to cry," he whispered. "Shit, any of us would after what you went through. It'll make you feel better."

She smiled and wiped her face. "They're not tears, Roback," she growled.

"Oh, yeah. What are they?"

She paused and said, "My contacts are acting up."

Greg laughed. "Okay." He stood and kissed her cheek, staring down at her as though he was amazed she was alive.

She blinked hard and stared back. "I mean it—they're not tears."

"Right—contacts." He smiled in a way she had never seen before and touched her cheek. "And I promise not to tell anyone that you have perfect vision."

"Better not," she warned and closed her eyes again, the touch of his fingers warm on her skin. Maybe she would have to rethink her no dating cops rule.

ONYX

Tom Savage

"A thriller with heart...no one is safe."
—Lorenzo Carcaterra, author of *Sleepers*

VALENTINE

Now A Major Motion Picture

Jillian Talbot has it all: a beautiful home in New York's Greenwich Village, a string of bestselling suspense novels, a handsome and adoring lover.

She has something else, too. A silent stalker. A secret admirer who sends her pink, heart-shaped messages—with an unmistakable warning in blood-red letters.

A killer has invaded her privileged sanctuary. He will imprison her in a nightmare more real than the fiction she creates. And, as the price mounts ever higher for a crime that Jill had once committed but only her nemesis can remember, he will meet her at last at the hour of his triumph.

Her judgment day.

❑ 0-451-40978-7 / $7.50